For
LOVE
and
COUNTRY

A novel by Bo Svenson

First Edition: November 2015
10 9 8 7 6 5 4 3 2 1

ISBN: 978-0-692-57922-0

Bo Svenson
MagicQuest Entertainment

info@magicquestentertainment.com

www.bosvenson.com
www.forloveandcountrythenovel.com

On IMDb: imdb.com/name/nm0004149

On Facebook: facebook.com/For-Love-And-Country-The-Novel-1520350954924286/

On Twitter: twitter.com/FLACthenovel

Cover Design: Cliff Hauser, hauser-advertising.com; Bo Svenson

Book cover photo: Val Verse, Andy Andersson, Daniel Ljung

Acknowledgments

Having a wonderful family and having had a wonder-filled life—a childhood in Sweden, six years in the U.S. Marines, nearly fifty years in Hollywood; having been everywhere, including Antarctica; having had face-to-face talks with good people like Bill Clinton and Mohammed Ali, as well as with the worst like Pablo Escobar and Slobodan Milosevic—I have come to lament that not everyone gets to be fully valued in life as the persons they know themselves to be and would like others to appreciate; that many don't get to have someone who loves them and children who look like them.

So I don't do well at funerals—I can't help but feel that the deceased would have treasured the flowers and the kind words much more if received in life…

What makes it all the more strange is that this novel *was* sparked by a funeral, my father's, at which I learned of the existence of the Finnish-Russian Winter War—and even then strictly by happenstance from his former comrades-at-arms.

My father had been wounded before I was born while fighting as a volunteer on the Finnish side during the Winter War—but he never spoke of it to me…

I wondered why and set off for Finland after the funeral; I came to return to Finland many times in the ensuing years.

While in Finland, I received support of many, including:

General Aimo Pajunen, a true friend who in life quietly straddled the line of being a professional military man and great philosopher;

Pertti Lampi, a most wonderful man and poet whose heart truly beats for all that is Karelia and Finland;

Åke Lindman, an honorable man who told me: "We Finns are difficult, we just are this way—we are also careful, we hold up our pants with suspenders as well as belts;

Esko and Kirsti Muhonen, who understood that I wasn't prying but learning the ways of Finns and Finland;

Ambassador Max Jakobson, whose ethnicity and grasp of international politics caused the Soviet Union to veto his nomination as Secretary General of the United Nations;

Antti Toivanen, Hanna Hemilä, Mikael Planting, Toje Planting, Thomas Romantschuk, Minister Stig Hästö, Prime Minister Johannes Virolainen, Minister Jaakko Iloniemi, Valtioneuvos Riita Uosukainen, Presidents Ahtisaari and Halonen; and

Others who gave me support and assistance—they know who they are and how much I value what they did for me.

In addition to published sources, I obtained information not made public before, including documents from the personal archives of Josef Stalin.

Lastly, but certainly not least, my writing wouldn't be what it is had it not been for Val Verse, a most wonderful and capable editor.

Bo Svenson
Pacific Palisades
November 28, 2015

Prologue

Today. At a truck stop outside Oklahoma City, a large oil painting hangs over the pass-through to the kitchen.

Oddly out of place amongst the jumble of patriotic paraphernalia and poorly executed posters of John Wayne and Willie Nelson, the painting depicts a young couple facing each other; his face is in shadow and hers is kissed by a setting sun. She has a view of the ocean that lies endless and placid behind him.

Manny, the truck stop's owner, doesn't know where the painting came from or who painted it—it is not signed and was there when he bought the place—but Manny *does* know that the artist must have been deeply in love with the girl in the painting: her beautiful, strongly intelligent face is shaped so lovingly that not a brushstroke can be seen and her light blonde hair glows like a halo.

Thousands of travelers have noticed the painting. Manny has been told that it was painted in the late '30s, that it is art of the highest degree and worth a lot of money.

The pony-tailed Toronto art dealer on his way to Florida for the winter standing spellbound by the painting has asked for the manager. Manny reluctantly leaves his busy and understaffed kitchen where the orders are piling up and his people are in need of constant supervision. Wiping his hands on a towel, he scrutinizes the painting's umpteenth admirer, knowing full well what is coming.

"Hey, man, you the manager?"

"Sort of."

I

"I wanna buy that painting."

"It's not for sale."

"Everything is for sale, man."

"Not that painting."

"Why not?"

"I like it."

"But it shouldn't be hanging in a truck stop, man!"

"Why not?"

"It's… it's too good! Who besides you sees it here?"

"Lots of people."

The art dealer's gaze is still locked on the painting as he sighs:

"Okay, tell you what, I'll give you five thousand for it."

"Thanks, but it's not for sale."

"Okay, I'll give you ten thousand, but that's my final offer!"

Oh, gee... ten grand! That would pay for a new gas stove and then some...

Looking up at the couple in the painting, Manny once again marveled over the effect it has had on those who notice it—how their faces soften at the painting draws them deep inside themselves.

He has seen men walk in and take a seat at his counter, silently sliding in as the Nobodies they were on the road, order their coffee and sit there perhaps reflecting on their lives, their days of glory, sometimes even revealing those dreams gone by to whomever will listen.

He doesn't know exactly what they see in the painting, but he believes men see themselves in the young man so obscurely depicted and that they recall the girl of their dreams in the young woman with light golden hair.

II

He has watched them rekindle dreams they had when they were young and life was theirs for the taking but then slipped away for this or that reason.

As they look up at the painting, a kinder truth seems to engulf them, holding them captive—somehow making them feel important again

He has seen them sit emotionally naked and vulnerable at the counter, staring at the painting, remembering when their needs were met with hugs and loving glances instead of the angry gestures and hostile glares they encounter on The Road.

He has seen in their eyes that they no longer feel all to be lost, that once again they can actually *feel* something— and that makes them proud somehow and even *more* emotional. Their eyes become soft and wistful and he can almost hear them think words that so many take silently to their grave: ... *that girl sure looks a lot like Betty when we was young... before things fell apart... I shouldn't have said what I said... done what I done... but that was then an' this is now... can't see him in that there painting... could be anyone except for the way she looks at him... must have been someone special why else the painting... I should get on The Road, got a long way to go... maybe I'll just sit here a while longer and think... why we do what we do... is there a meaning to... if we could just go back...*

They unbutton shirts that are stretched to the point of tearing over bellies bulging from eggs and bacon, biscuits and chicken, top sirloin with mashed potatoes and gravy; sip the last of their coffee, look up once more at the couple frozen in time forever, pay their tabs and leave the counter, now more ready for The Road, brimming with emotion and some kind of hope for a Better Tomorrow.

III

They head for the restroom and do what they have to, splash some water on their faces and look at themselves in the mirror; their shoulders become firmer, their backs straighter, their eyes brighter—as if they are thinking: *Life isn't so bad after all...*

Manny has seen them lift their baseball caps with the visors bent and molded to their liking, check that there is still some hair atop their head, tug at their drawers and move their privates to a more comfortable and out of the way place, put the caps back on their heads, give their image in the mirror another glance or two, and then head for the parking lot and their rigs, nodding to the ladies of the evening and their buddies from The Road—all while seemingly feeling a bit better about themselves.

He has seen them hesitate before climbing up into their rigs, seen them clomp the ground beneath the soles of their boots as if to remind the Earth that they are still alive and well; seen them glance at their competitors' rigs and puff up their chests like roosters as if right then and there they truly feel they *are* somebody and not the anonymous beings they are on The Road.

They climb up into their rigs, slip into the familiar surroundings they have come to both love and hate, turn the ignition and feel the shudder as the diesel ignites in all cylinders, the engine smoothes out and they are all once again ready for The Road.

Manny imagines he can hear what follows—
    Okay, here I go...

But the first gear doesn't want to.
    Something must be bent in the shift-linkage...I'll just push a little harder...ah, there it goes...

IV

The rig eases forward.

Hey, make room there, buddy! Move over! Somebody coming through!

The eighteen-wheeled behemoths ease away from his truck stop and onto the highway and soon fade out of sight.

Manny knows they'll be back—there's certain comfort in that—and turns to the art dealer standing there with cash in hand.

"No, man, the painting isn't for sale—not for all the money in the world."

. . .

Chapter One

1918. The Great War in Europe was winding down; the world was full of hope for a Better Tomorrow. The leaders of the warring nations were talking over fine wine and food about an Armistice, while the men in the trenches were still killing each other by the thousands.

On all fronts, carpenters idled and worried: coffins and crosses had exhausted their supplies of wood. Soon the carpenters too would be sent to the trenches.

An author sat in a pub in London and wrote what would become a popular song that ended with the words "…*and never war no more.*"

Nice and a bit expansive perhaps, but the author, who earlier that day had received an advance from his publisher, felt drunkenly magnanimous. Though the words felt good on his tongue and in his soul, the inspiration for his unrealistic promise didn't come to him from any noble sentiment or divine intervention—it was fueled by an extraordinary amount of dark ale.

On that same day, a group of Bolsheviks murdered Czar Nicholas II and his family.

Not nice—murder never is, no matter how it is justified.

The man who provided Nicholas II's *coup de grâce* was named Naumovich Habarov. A thin man with rotting teeth, Naumovich had but a few years earlier been a devout Czarist and had named his own son Nicholas after the Czar. However, when the boy developed a hideous

1

reddish-brown skin tumor that covered half his face, Naumovich, a locomotive mechanic by trade and a mystic by diversion, interpreted his son's affliction as a prophesy and joined the Bolsheviks.

As he and his comrades herded the Romanoff family into the cellar for the execution, Naumovich noted in the torchlight how perfect the Czar's children's features were.

Moments later—fueled by self-righteous vengeance—Naumovich helped end the Romanoff dynasty.

While the Czar and his family were being murdered and interred in the soil they had lived so high above, as their cries of protest and fear faded into whimpers and then nothingness, a thousand kilometers to the west in the northern part of Finland's province called Karelia, the cry of a newborn boy could be heard from inside a simple farmhouse at the edge of the spruce-filled wilderness.

. . .

His beginning was modest. His cry was heard by only three people: his mother, his five-year-old sister, and his father who poured himself a glass of vodka from a bottle that he kept in a cupboard and brought out only for special occasions.

While reverently holding the cracked vodka glass with fingers gnarled from too many years of carving wooden Orthodox crosses for cemeteries in which he, an outsider of indeterminate religion, would never be allowed to be buried, the father looked at his son and his frail and prematurely white-haired wife.

The sun moved ever so slightly. A ray of light filtered in through a dusty windowpane and lit on the newborn boy who stopped crying when his mother placed him to her breast.

In the distance a loon called out.

The father, hearing the loon's call, thought it celebrated the event. He smiled as he watched his son gurgle contentedly, emptied the glass in one gulp and let out an audible sigh; the liquor had rushed through his empty stomach and warmed him—even though it wasn't very good vodka.

Running his fingers pensively through his unkempt, nearly pitch-black hair, the father leaned back on the one-legged milking chair that he no longer needed in the barn after he was forced to sell the goat. He stretched his long back and groaned. His muscles ached and it felt good to stretch. He was tall, nearly two meters, had a wiry body, and had been sitting slumped forward on the chair since his wife had gone into labor the night before.

As he stretched his lanky frame he felt the muscles in his back relax—but he could also feel the fibers in his worn-out linen shirt begin to tear. He quickly leaned forward again and placed his arms on his legs that were hot under the heavy trousers his wife had made from a discarded army blanket.

The father studied his son and saw that he looked healthy. A bit ruddy perhaps, but he remembered that so had the girl and she had turned out fine, with pretty features and flaxen hair. His son had bright blue eyes like his mother and sister, not dark brown like his. For a moment he felt disappointed and that bewildered him—he didn't know that it is normal for man to want children in his own image.

The boy gurgled again. The mother moved him away from her breast.

Although the father had not eaten for a day or two—he couldn't well have gone fishing while his wife was in labor—he felt good, pleased that the child and his wife were well and that for several days there had not been any volleys of shots in the distance.

Perhaps would there not be much to worry about for a while.

The father, a simple and peace-loving man, didn't closely follow worldly events. They didn't have a radio—and even if they did, the Karjalainen farm didn't have electricity to power one. They were quite far from the village, a good hour's walk from the closest neighbor, and the only newspapers they ever saw were old ones wrapped around the occasional piece of bartered meat.

From the talkative Finnish Border Guard who stopped by now and then and greeted them with a hearty "*Hyvä päivä!*" ("Good day!") even when the weather was foul, the father had learned that Finland had not been directly involved in The Great War or with the Russian Revolution which had somewhat spilled over into Finland. In fact, Finland's independence had been recently granted largely because The Great War had weakened the Soviet Union— a nation already preoccupied with domestic concerns.

When the talkative border guard had stopped by the previous day with his usual "Good day!" greeting, the father, who was anxious about his wife's painful labor and the pending birth, had snapped:

"What's so good about it?"

The talkative border guard was taken aback by the father's curt response, but he had nevertheless replied courteously in the customary rural vernacular:

"One would think any day he finds himself above a hole in the ground to be a good day. One would also think that the thousand or so Reds who were shot on the ice outside Helsinki Harbor last week and now wait for the ice to break so they can be carried to the open sea for their anonymous burial might be envious of one who can stand here and talk about this and that."

When the father had tacitly nodded that he agreed, the border guard had continued to unburden his soul.

"One welcomes that he is of the same mind," said the border guard in the formal, traditional Finnish vernacular. From inside his tunic he had then pulled a carefully folded newspaper that he held up almost reverently. "The times are changing. The paper says there seems to be no more Reds, that Finland's Civil War has come to an end, and that Russian White refugees already in Finland might get dispensation to stay. Has he seen any come by in the past few days?"

The father shook his head. "Not a one." He looked off toward the nearby border. "Perhaps have those with enough strength already done so…"

To which the border guard had somberly added: "And others were perhaps stopped by hunger or bullets…"

A moment had passed while in their minds' eye they pictured the horrors of the refugees' plight.

The father then sighed: "One wonders about the human race…"

"One does indeed…" And with that the border guard walked off to resume protecting the border.

. . .

Relieved by the news that an end to hostilities was in sight, and feeling renewed hope for the future, the father now studied his son,

…Hope…

He rose from his chair.

"Let him be called Toivo."

Toivo meant Hope in Finnish, the only language he knew. He sometimes wondered what his real family name was and from where his father had hailed. His father had been a pragmatic man who understood the importance of fitting in where you live.

Upon his arrival in Finland he had assumed the family name Karjalainen because it suggested that the family hailed from Karelia, the huge area that encompassed the province in eastern Finland in which they had settled, as well as much of northwestern USSR, where it was Soviet Karelia.

As Finland's border with Soviet Karelia was just a short walk away, the father thought it odd that Karelians —who ostensibly were one people—were separated by a line drawn on a map by men who had never set foot there.

"Hope is a good name for your son."

The mother's voice was faint, but firm. She was well aware that there were far too few events in his life over which the father had control—no matter how hard he worked, or how many hours he put in. The father couldn't control the weather and what it did to the potatoes and barley on which they and their livestock were dependent.

Naming his children should at least be his to determine.

. . .

From the boy's birth onward, the blond and blue-eyed Karjalainen siblings would share a box-bed in the kitchen and sleep atop straw in each other's arms. As they grew up they became inseparable; there wasn't a day when they wouldn't play together, be it in the forest, in the nearby lake, or in the fields of wildflowers.

The two had become one.

. . .

Although the siblings were as one, they were also uniquely different. She liked to poke in the soil and grow things, he liked to ponder the world and find meaning in what he saw: how they got where they were, why they were where they were, and where they went when they were no longer there. He asked his father the most curious questions that the father couldn't readily answer.

"Does grass hurt when I walk on it?"

"No, son. It doesn't."

"How do you know?"

"Well, I don't really know. But I don't think so."

"What about the trees? Can they see me?"

"I don't think so."

"Why not? I can see them."

The siblings thrived on the remote plot of land their father's father had bought on the outskirts of the parish in the sparsely populated county district. When he had arrived from a distant land as a widower with a small boy and only a sack of silver for baggage, he had not been allowed to buy land close to the village at the center of the parish because he didn't hail from there. He was, well, different.

When he built he had been careful to do so in the style of the parish. The main dwelling was a low-rafted log building roofed with wooden tiles. Rag rugs led into the vast living room that had a stone stove in one corner, beds in another, and a trestle in the third. There were wooden utensils on the table and saws, axes and carving tools hung on the walls.

The barn was built of sturdy timber. Two of the walls were homemade stucco; two were sided with planks of fir. The sties, stalls and stable were all in one large room. The animals had been sold off over the years; the only remaining animal was an otter the father had trained for fishing.

The outhouse stood under a weeping birch and was comfortable in summer—but excruciatingly cold in winter when the temperature often dipped to 40, sometimes 50, below zero. The obligatory turf-roofed, wood-burning sauna stood only a few steps from the lake.

While the small Karjalainen farm had remained much the same over the years, the village at the center of the parish had grown and prospered, adding several stores and businesses. The buildings were always freshly painted—whether the owners could really afford to or not.

The villagers felt they were stable and important and treated the Karjalainen family with reserved courtesy, not because they were poor—but because they were peasants lacking local history and therefore local status.

They were Nobodies.

The boy felt the looks and heard the snickers that were meant to degrade them. Over time he watched his tall and erect father sag, his proud and kind mother shrivel, and his pretty and cheerful sister go silent. He felt it was unfair and silently vowed that one day he would become a Somebody.

Once the father's trained otter caught a pike so large that he took it to sell at the village market. The boy got to ride on his father's pushcart with the pike and the otter. He was very proud—no one else in the whole county district had an otter trained to catch fish. The boy basked in the looks of amazement and the whispers of respect. He proudly stood by his father's side.

It was a day he would remember.

When the otter died soon thereafter of natural causes—or so his father said, the boy stopped going into the village. He decided that his world would be his sister, their parents, and their peaceful life on their small farm at his world's edge.

. . .

The quiet was once shattered by a railroad worker who could no longer endure the pain in his lower back and groin. After having coffee with his elderly mother in the

8

village, the weary worker took the first road and walked as far as his cancer-ridden body allowed.

He came upon a meadow with gently swaying birches; he failed to notice the nearby Karjalainen farm because his attention was on the huge granite boulder at the center of the meadow.

Shaped by a sub-glacial river during the Ice Age, the boulder looked like a giant stuffed chair with a smooth dip that was warm and dry and well suited his aching backside as he gratefully eased down into it.

He didn't notice the birch leaves that rippled in the summer breeze like waves in a foaming ocean, or the brilliantly blue sky with billowing clouds, or the red-breasted finch that serenaded him as he placed the stick of dynamite in his mouth and lit the fuse.

The boy was in the workshop watching his father carve a filigreed doorframe for the local postmistress when he heard an explosion and strange matter began to rain down nearby.

The father badly needed money and was so intent on finishing his work that he hardly looked up when the curious boy walked off to investigate the cause of the noise he had heard.

As the boy entered the birch-filled meadow he saw strange wet bits in the trees and on the ground, but it wasn't until he walked around the huge boulder he knew so well that he found the headless man peacefully resting against the blood and tissue-stained rock.

The boy turned and ran. On and on he ran—he thought his heart would burst, but he didn't dare slow down to look behind him. He ran and ran until he found his sister helping their mother wash clothes at the lake. Heaving for breath, he collapsed in his sister's arms. When finally he could speak he made her look behind him and promise that no one was coming to get him.

For days thereafter he wouldn't look behind him. No matter how his family pleaded, he wouldn't talk about what he had seen. It took the father weeks before he detected the corpse by its smell.

Occasionally a visitor or a villager stopped by. One Sunday, Esa Muhonen, a gaunt and tempestuous drunk, came. Esa brought a few liters of whitewash for their barn; it was a gift, he said.

The real reason for his visit was that he all too pleased to say goodbye to everyone in the parish. He had married into money, given up farming and was now emigrating with his wife and their infant daughter to America—to some place called Chicago.

The boy watched as his father offered Esa a vodka. He didn't like the way Esa smelled, but he nevertheless waved goodbye to him when he left—his mother had taught him good manners.

Little did the boy know at that moment that Esa would change his life.

. . .

Chapter Two

The most frequent visitor to the small farm was the buyer of the father's elaborately carved, filigreed wooden grave markers. One day when the buyer arrived, he was coughing more than usual, so the siblings helped him load his wagon. A few days later both of them took gravely ill.

The anguished parents knelt in vain by their children's bed as their condition worsened. Fearing the worst, the mother rushed off to the get the parish pastor—there was no doctor within many miles.

When the aged, white-haired pastor arrived, he didn't know what to do: the family had never attended any of his sermons and only the Karjalainen children had been born in the parish. Plus, the parents were dark-haired and rumored to be from some far away place...
They could be the Anti-Christ, or worse yet, descendants of those who killed Christ, Our Lord and Savior...

Erring on the side of caution, the pastor decided to keep his hat on.

Through a feverish haze, the boy saw the black-clad pastor peer down at him and his sister, whose labored breathing the boy could no longer hear. The boy had never known her to sleep so still. He held his own breath when the pastor held up a small, glistening mirror.

The old man breathed solemnly on the mirror, wiped it clean with his sleeve, and then held it close to his sister's lips.

It did not fog up; she had no breath. His sister was no longer that; she was now an angel in Heaven.

The old pastor absentmindedly laid the mirror on the pillow next to the girl's body, said a short prayer and turned to the parents, shaking his head as if to show them that he lamented their loss and pain.

A ray of late afternoon sunlight peeked through the window, lit on the mirror and bounced onto the ceiling.

The boy stared at the mirror that had stolen his sister's breath and placed it onto the ceiling.

He was so mesmerized by the relationship between the mirror and what he saw on the ceiling that he failed to notice the pastor close his sister's eyes and his mother weep.

. . .

His sister was buried at the forest's edge not far from the farmhouse. The pastor read from the Bible with professional, solemn indifference. The father stoically tapped into place an especially elaborate grave marker that he had carved with trembling hands and stained with his very private tears.

The pastor finished reading and cleared his throat—that was as much as he was prepared to do for free.

The mother reached into her blouse and withdrew a coin that she gave to him.

The pastor flipped through the pages of his bible until he came to Verse One, Chapter One of the Creation—his favorite passage in the Bible, which he then hurriedly read aloud.

In the beginning God created heaven and earth...

The mother, weeping loudly, placed wildflowers atop the grave and flicked away pebbles from the mound of dark, moist soil.

The boy didn't want his sister to become an angel in Heaven; he wanted her with him in their world.

So he fled the event that caused him so much pain, climbing up into a tall pine where he clung to its top.

High in the sky, a noisy flock of migrating geese flew by. The boy pretended he was one of them and watched them intently. Numb with grief, he didn't hear his parents' pleas to come down from the tree.

He remained there until long after nightfall.

. . .

At the small, one-class-fits-all country district school, the other children avoided him. They all knew that his sister had died and they now treated him as if he were a carrier of disease—some even moved their desks away from him.

The teacher pretended not to notice.

To combat his loneliness the boy began to draw pictures in his schoolbooks of his sister as an angel—for which he was reprimanded by the teacher, ridiculed by his classmates, and then sent home.

On one long walk home, he stopped and scratched her outline in the snow with a stick. He also drew a halo over her head.

A few days later he drew her image with a piece of charcoal on the barn wall his father had whitewashed with the lime given him by Esa Muhonen. His parents didn't scold him, perhaps because the boy seemed happier when he was drawing.

The parents didn't talk about their troubled son. The father had never been much for words on any subject and couldn't bring himself to speak of their anguish. The mother took out one of her few remaining heirlooms from the linen chest—the others had long ago been traded for food and other necessities—and walked to the village where she traded it for some artist brushes and paints.

The father made his son a painter's canvas from a faded piece of linen and discarded slats of wood.

The parents watched as their son—at first hesitantly, then with greater certainty—painted his sister as a blond angel on a white winged horse.

She looked just as serene as the angel in the pastor's bible.

. . .

The father made more canvases. The mother got him more paint.

The boy painted and painted—and he painted well. He cherished the freedom he found at the canvas—the freedom to create his own reality.

The freedom and tranquility his canvasses afforded him at home were often dashed his classmates' disdain for him at school: he didn't mind that he often went hungry, or that his clothes were the most patched, or that he had to wear his father's worn-out, over-sized shoes, but he *did* mind the snickers.

They called him the Pauper—but inside him he had a wealth of emotion.

He was eleven.

. . .

Chapter Three

One cold February morning Toivo helped his parents load a push-sleigh with woodcarvings they were going to sell at the village's Winter Fair. His parents had dressed in their best clothes; the black wool made them look oddly important against the stark white landscape.

His father had stacked the woodcarvings higher than usual on the sleigh's little platform. The load was heavy; the boy had to push with all his might to help his parents get the sleigh moving.

He waved to them just before they disappeared around a bend in the road, but he wasn't sure they saw him as they seemed so small.

He felt a lump in his throat but didn't know why; his insides vibrated with an ominous hum.

He wasn't able to paint that day. He was restless, yet his mind was listless. He walked from room to room, oddly compelled to pick up things especially dear to him: his sister's limp clothes, folded on a chest, not yet put away—that would be too final; the family photo taken at a fair a few years earlier, processed too quickly, rapidly fading; his father's razor, a magical device that turned his chin from rough and disagreeable to smooth and pleasant; his mother's woolen head scarf that was rough to the touch but gave off the delicate scent of her gentle soul.

The boy's heart pounded. The dreadful hum spread from the core of his being and deadened his senses—all except the unpleasant, frightening, whirring sensation that nauseated him. His soul trembled then withered as he looked out the window and saw that the falling snow had obliterated the tracks made by his parents' sleigh.

His mind skittered. The snow kept falling—then he saw the old pastor approaching and quickly hid under his bed.

The pastor knocked on the door.

The boy closed his eyes and held his breath.

The pastor knocked again; still no response. He tried the door, found it unlocked and opened it. He cleared his throat several times and tried to call out the boy's name, but the words wouldn't come out. A few weeks earlier he had woken up with a severe headache, was no longer able to talk very well, and had lost the use of one of his arms. Although his speech was impaired, his hearing was fine— and he could faintly hear someone whimper.

He found the boy cowering under his bed and motioned for him to come out, but the boy grabbed hold of the bed's leg farthest from the pastor. Finding his voice, the pastor spoke firmly: "Boy, you need to come with me."

"I don't want to."

"You have to."

Something in the pastor's tone made the boy come out from under the bed. He stared at the pastor who, unnerved by the boy's gaze, fiddled with his coat lapel with his good hand and looked away: "Get dressed and come with me."

The boy obeyed as if in a dream, donning his coat and otter fur cap. His heart pounded like never before; the ominous hum now permeated his whole being; his breath became labored and shallow.

Outside it was deadly cold.

As they walked away from the small farm, the snow fell heavily—reducing visibility to barely a few meters.

The boy felt as if they were trapped in a tunnel.

They walked in silence; the only sound was the crackling of the fresh snow as their boots crushed it against the frozen road.

The boy knew something dreadful had happened, but—numb with fear—he didn't want to know what it was. He glanced up at the unshaven old man next to him, but the old pastor stared straight ahead, lost in his own morbid thoughts.

The snow stopped.

They arrived at a frozen lake. The country district's lorry was parked on the road at a point where it had fallen into disrepair.

The boy's heart pounded wildly. He felt faint. In stark shades of white and black he saw the sleigh tracks veer off in the direction of a hole in the ice—next to which his father lay in his best clothes with a stiff arm pointing to the bleak sky. Men with grappling poles were still pulling his mother's wet, rigid body from the dark water.

An anguished moan escaped him. The old pastor put his arm around his shoulder, searched for words, but didn't find any. The boy felt nauseated, then suddenly had to urinate. When the old pastor inexplicably felt compelled to join the boy in his sorrow and voided next to him, the boy turned his back to him while he continued to empty his bladder.

They rode in silence on the bed of the lorry with the uncovered corpses next to them. His parents' clothing had frozen into solid shrouds; the bodies rolled back and forth as the driver negotiated the winding, bumpy road.

To avoid looking at his mother and father, the boy tried counting falling snowflakes but the effort made him feel lightheaded; instead, he counted the whiskers on the pastor's face.

After a while, uncomfortable with the boy's stare, the pastor knocked on the driver's window. The driver stopped and the pastor climbed down from the lorry's bed and into the heated cab.

Alone now, the boy sat the rest of the way alone with his back against the cab and his parents' bodies right in front of him. He tried not to look at them, but when he closed his eyes he was overcome with motion sickness and felt nauseated; when he tried to look away, his face was pelted with sharp, icy snow.

He pulled his coat tighter around him and looked at the last members of his family as they rolled back and forth.

His father's troubled eyes had relaxed in death; now and then his outstretched arm would point right at his son —as if the boy had caused their deaths. His mother lay on her back with her eyes open; the boy thought she was looking up into the sky—and that, at long last, she was smiling.

. . .

His parents were buried next to his sister. The country district had allocated very little money for the funeral. The pine coffins had been quickly and crudely made—so much so the boy could see his parents through the cracks between the boards.

Two district workers unloaded the coffins from the lorry and placed them in the graves that they had sworn loudly over while digging—as the ground had been solidly frozen; they then had a few impatient swallows from their well-worn pocket flasks as the old pastor silently mouthed something they couldn't hear over the coffins.

Toivo was surprised how little it took to fill in the graves, how soon it was all over—and how quickly he was utterly alone in this world.

. . .

That evening, as sleep eluded him in the bed he had shared with his sister an eternity ago, he heard eerie sounds that seemed to come from the walls. He quickly dressed and ran off into the night.

The next morning a villager found Toivo curled up with a calf in his barn. He took the boy back to the Karjalainen farm, and then reported the matter to the district council.

The council held an emergency meeting during which it was decided that the boy would become a ward of the parish and that he would live at the church with the old pastor.

Toivo spent another sleepless night alone; he was relieved when the lorry driver arrived the next morning and told him to pack a few things because he was no longer allowed to live there by himself.

He got to sit in the cab this time, but he couldn't resist a look through the window at the lorry's bed; he thought he could see dampness where he last had seen his parents.

He was overcome with emotion when the lorry pulled away from his home, but remembered that his name meant Hope and concentrated his thoughts on a Better Tomorrow—and to learn all he could at school.

He was twelve.

. . .

Chapter Four

He was a talented student and relished learning, but, as fate would have it, it was at school that he would learn just how lonely he was.

He liked his school: the wooden, ocher-colored building with green trim; the large, warm rooms; the sturdy, well-made tables and chairs; and the blackboard that squeaked when just the right amount of pressure was applied with the chalk; and he liked his classmates, but they didn't like him—he was an Outsider.

Although the country district encompassed a large area, it was close knit and everyone was in at least a distant way related to everyone else—and there *he* was, the sole survivor of a family that lacked the local roots needed for community acceptance.

He wondered where he really belonged, whether *anyone* truly belonged anywhere at all. At school they had learned about Darwin and Evolution—that all of them had monkeys for forefathers. Yet his classmates claimed they were better than him, which didn't ring true for him since Darwin said they were all related and none of their distant ancestors originally stemmed from their community—or for that matter, even from Finland.

In class one morning he mustered the courage to speak up: "Is it not Life that ties us together, not the ground we walk on or where we were born?"

Cold silence fell as the teacher and his classmates stared at him. She continued with her prepared, set-in-stone lesson plan as though he had never spoken, while his classmates ridiculed him with ugly grimaces.

21

It would be a long time before he would again speak up in school.

The matter of his immediate ancestry and his family's origin weighed on him. He knew that his mother's relatives had died long ago in an explosion at a munitions factory in a faraway place. But he knew nothing at all of what had happened to his father's father who, when his son had begun to tower over him, had packed a few personal belongings and walked away from the farm he had built—leaving it to his son who had become a man.

Shortly thereafter a migrant family with teenage children sought shelter on the isolated Karjalainen farm during a blizzard. The son, who was to become Toivo's father, had shyly but eagerly set his eyes on the migrant family's oldest daughter—and she him.

The migrant mother had noticed her daughter's interest in the young man. She had also noticed the large copper pot with a matching ladle on the Karjalainen stove —it was exactly what she had yearned for.

The young woman remained—the rest of her family departed with the copper pot and ladle.

The boy knew that his parents' bond had begun as necessity. He never saw any physical contact between them, and he couldn't remember them ever having laughed like he and his sister often did, but there was no doubt of the depth of his parent's relationship: his mother had told him that she and his father belonged together; that they were each other's *basherte*.

. . .

Each morning at the parish church he would have porridge with the pastor, who would mumble grace then fall silent, even though he had partially regained his speech.

It was when Toivo would walk or ski to the district school that he would be most sharply reminded of what he no longer had; the hugs at the door, the waves from a window, the smiles of love and encouragement.

He was cheerful and friendly and even funny at school, but the others didn't notice. They were preoccupied with classmates who were not only friends but also neighbors; friendships that could continue after the final bell; friendships with which he couldn't compete. None of his classmates would ever consider coming by the church— the house of God was too foreboding.

Shunned as he was—with no one to play with, no one to touch, no one to feel with, and no one to wonder about this or that with—he came to miss his family terribly, becoming withdrawn and despondent.

In an ill-conceived attempt to soothe the boy, the old pastor brought him to the altar where there stood a tall, painted wooden statue of Christ. As the pastor talked about Christ's benevolence and omnipotence, the boy studied the features of God's son, adorned with a beard and a crown of thorns; the man who knew everything, who could create miracles, who could do anything— including coming back from the dead.

Strange thoughts and deeply disturbing feelings were triggered in the boy. He took a step closer to see better, saw the wormholes in the statue, the peeling paint, and became utterly bewildered.

How can this be the Son of God who took my sister and my parents from me?

He spit at the statue.

The pastor made him scrub the entire church floor seven times. When he was done, the boy asked: "If God loves me, why is he not nice to me?"

The pastor whacked him with a cane.

The boy understood then that God didn't love him and he vowed to not set a foot in a church unless forced to.

The pastor fretted. His own anger had greatly unsettled him. He told the boy that nothing good would ever come from him, that he was a bad boy.

"I know that someday I will read about you—and it will not be anything good," the pastor said as he slammed his door shut.

The boy would often visit the graves of his family where his childhood too lay buried; he had become an adult long before he was ready.

He tried not to cry when he placed wildflowers or pine branches on the mounds.

. . .

He became adept at suppressing his feelings—except when he saw migrating geese or swans in their ever-changing formations high in the sky.

He found something magical about flight, not the mechanical flapping of wings, but the act itself that allowed the birds to flee anywhere they wanted to go.

. . .

He didn't speak much at school. He stayed within himself, became expert at avoiding reality, at daydreaming—and at channeling his feelings through a paintbrush onto canvas.

24

The pastor would sometimes show the boy's paintings to parishioners. They were impressive works of art, albeit unsettling with their motif of Death: his sister's, his parents'—even his own.

. . .

The boy's room at the village church was small, Spartan, and cold—to both the eye and the touch. The walls were stucco, the floor granite. On one wall was a cross, which he would cover with his threadbare jacket. He had one blanket and his bed was a box of straw. The straw was changed when the church caretaker, a local farmer, was in a good mood—which wasn't very often.

Although his life at the church had few comforts, he did have an almost unlimited supply of candles. He treasured the light the candles provided; some nights he had dozens of them burning. At night, in the flickering light that cast diffusely dancing shadows on the walls, he would let his mind wander freely while he painted or read to quench his voracious thirst for knowledge.

It was also during the night that he began to realize he was becoming a man—his hormones were in full bloom.

He was thirteen.

. . .

Chapter Five

One day when the old pastor had ordered him to clean the Inner Sanctum, he found a book about America. Written by an expatriate Finn harboring bitterness toward his homeland and extolling an inflated view of his adopted land, the book was filled with photos and text that glowed with promises of the Good Life in America. The people were smiling and seemed to be enjoying themselves to the fullest. Everyone appeared to be Somebody; no one seemed the least mean-spirited, or petty-minded.

He didn't know about editors; he didn't know that books are published for many reasons, some altruistic, others not, and that this particular book had been published with help of the U.S. Government.

Nor did he have a clear sense of where he belonged. He was young, knew not yet who he was, saw in the photographs what he wanted to see—and became obsessed with the Dream of America and its life without strife.

He had found his Better Tomorrow.

From that day, he read all he could about the Land of Plenty. The village bookshop became like home. He read voraciously. For someone who wanted to learn, there was no better place than the bookshop. Surprisingly well stocked, it was managed by a spinster who had been a librarian in England. She took an instant liking to the wonder-filled boy and secretly taught him English.

Energized by his daydreams of this Better Tomorrow, Toivo beleaguered the old pastor with questions and requests for help with emigration to America.

The pastor remembered Esa Muhonen, the parish drunk who had emigrated to America some years before. He looked through the church register and found to his relief that Esa had provided an address in America.

He sat down to write Esa a letter, but wasn't sure of what to write and called for the boy.

"What would you like me to say?"

"That I would like to come to America."

The old pastor mulled over the letter some more, grumbled to himself while scribbling with his pen and paper for what Toivo thought was an eternity, and then read the letter aloud:

"We hope this letter finds you in good health. Since you left our church has a new coat of whitewash. Nine children were born, two to Hanna Laurila, one died the next day. Antti Virkki, Pekka Virta, Jorma Salmi, and Aaro Pajari also died. And the Karjalainen boy became a ward of the parish. He would like to come to America and wants to know if you can help him with that."

He gave Toivo a piercing look. "Does that suit you?"

"It would if you wouldn't refer to me as the Karjalainen boy. My name is Toivo. You called everyone else in the letter by name."

"So you want me to rewrite the letter?"

"Perhaps you can add a sentence at the end with my given name? And perhaps—from now on—you can call me Toivo and not just boy?"

The old pastor complied—even though it had been easier to just call him "boy."

. . .

It was during this time that Toivo received his first kiss. Her name was Tessa. The same age as he, she had dark hair and dark eyes that sparkled with energy. She also had an independent mind developed while she was in America —only recently having returned to Finland with her mother and sisters after her father was imprisoned for having sexually abused her.

Completely self-centered, cunning and manipulative to the highest degree, Tessa was physically well developed for her age. Her hormones were in full bloom, filling her with lustful ideas—and she was an eager and quick learner.

Tessa had surveyed all the candidates for courtship at the district school. Other than Toivo, there were only a few: Timo, dark-haired and handsome, but not very smart; Jussi, Timo's best friend, grossly overweight and aggressively jovial; and Reijo, taller than Toivo and just as attractive, but in a harder, more masculine way.

The symbol of Reijo's dominance was the fingerpull: a test of strength in which two combatants interlocked middle fingers, then twisted and turned their hands until one of them gave in or had his finger broken.

Tessa knew that Reijo had set his eye on her and that he had told the others she was his, but she had set her eye on the melancholy Toivo. He was the most lovable of the lot, and her already well-developed womanhood sensed that he was also the one most capable of a passion that matched hers.

However, Reijo's hormones, too, were in full bloom. He was gripped by a primitive urge to procreate and knew instinctively that any competition for Tessa would come from Toivo, for whom he had a grudging fondness and regarded as a fellow artist.

Reijo was an accomplished violinist—albeit strictly in a technical sense: he lacked 'the touch' which one either has or hasn't, and which one cannot acquire from sheer effort.

In short, Reijo liked music but had no music within him.

Like other male animals, Reijo was intent on protecting his turf. Thus after he caught Tessa kissing Toivo during a recess, he took Toivo behind the school.

"What's wrong with you, boy? I told you to stay away from Tessa! She's *my* girl!"

"I don't think she knows that. Maybe you should tell her. And don't call me *boy*. My name is Toivo."

"Is it? Well, here's something for Toivo's eye," Reijo said and punched Toivo as hard as he could.

It wouldn't be the last black eye Reijo gave Toivo.

But Reijo wasn't altogether primitive: he had seen a few moving pictures and also knew from some women's magazines he had read on the sly that brawn wasn't always the answer. When he was certain none of the others were around he would bring Tessa flowers and play the violin for her, but his efforts were in vain: Tessa knew exactly who she wanted. She had watched through the keyhole in the door when the local boys were given their physical for the Home Guard, had seen them nude, and thought that Toivo looked, well, the manliest.

Toivo thought serving in the Home Guard would help him make friends; he worked hard at being a good soldier—and he was.

But, again, his quest for acceptance failed.

When the others saw that he was the best soldier among them—that he never fell asleep when he had guard duty, was the best shot and the best skier as a result of the many years he had skied to school in the worst of conditions, never complained when they had to go on forced marches, and could move more quietly than any of them at night in the forest—they were intimidated and froze him out.

His quest for acceptance failed.

Being shunned by his peers caused Toivo great pain; the gnawing ache of loneliness and rejection that pierced his stomach would only subside when he painted—or when Tessa brushed up against him at school or winked at him without Reijo noticing.

One night Tessa could no longer endure the madness of her sexual fantasies; no matter what she did to herself, her vision of Toivo and his manhood overwhelmed her. She left the bed she shared with her two sisters and quietly slipped out from her home.

It was a beautiful spring night, filled with the sounds of a vibrant nature awakened from a winter that had lasted too long. Tessa broke off a few branches from a white lilac and rubbed her body with the flowers. As she did, she touched herself and thought she was going to faint.

She hurried to the parish church, found Toivo's window open—she knew where he slept, she had rehearsed this moment many a time—and climbed in. She woke him and wouldn't be refused; she told him they would only touch each other and leave it at that.

It was a night that Toivo would never forget—nor would the pastor for that matter; nearly a dozen times he heard strange sounds from Toivo's room.
Each time he thought that Toivo must be in his death throes, found his door locked, and knocked on it.

From behind the closed door, Toivo reassured him that he was fine, but the old pastor sensed there was more to the night than he was told and was annoyed when Toivo wouldn't unlock the door.

Through the open window above Toivo's door, the pastor caught the scent of lilac and what he—a life-long bachelor —thought was a strong scent of fresh apples.

Tired and confused, he didn't want to make a fuss; he surrendered and went back to his own room.

Although Toivo and Tessa had not fully consummated their amorous relationship, Tessa told everyone that they had—and Toivo got another black eye from Reijo.

Such was Toivo's first encounter with manhood——

He was fourteen.

. . .

Chapter Six

In the year that followed, the old pastor became increasingly bad-tempered with everyone, especially with Toivo, and wildly irrational in his sermons. He often bristled with fire and brimstone and threatened the parishioners with eternal damnation for their slightest transgression.

The parishioners retaliated by staying away and withholding the customary offerings of money and donations of food to the church. Often Toivo and the old pastor went hungry—for which he blamed Toivo.

Toivo retaliated by pulling pranks on the increasingly more openly hateful pastor. One time, after the pastor ordered him for the sixth time that day to remake the pastor's wood-framed bed, Toivo placed termites in it.

The old pastor took it as a telltale sign from above that his days on Earth were numbered when his bed of more than fifty years disintegrated into dust.

Toivo's relationship with Tessa was just as unsatisfying. As much as he needed the comfort and warmth he sought from Tessa, he felt alone while with her: His connection to her was only physical; he found her to be soulless and manipulating, completely devoid of humor—especially when he remembered how he and his sister had laughed at the simplest things.

He found the laughter he yearned for among the country district's old people whom he visited and helped. They were, for the most part, at peace with where they were in life, could laugh at themselves and life's oddities, and had much to offer from their wealth of life's lessons—hard earned as well as self-taught.

One of the old-timers, a former tree-faller in his nineties whose eyes were failing and for whom now and then Toivo would read the old pastor's discarded newspapers, shook his head and sighed after Toivo had read an article about a disgraced politician who had failed to keep a dishonest act secret: "There they are in their fancy suits, shirts and ties, deciding all manner of things for us common folk, yet they don't know that while the truth may hurt for a while, lies can slay."

Toivo would come to live his life by what he learned from the old tree-faller during that mosquito-infested summer evening spent by a still lake on his land.

. . .

Around the time of the summer equinox, a traveling photographer arrived in a dusty and road-worn dark blue Volvo that he parked behind the country district's small post office.

Penniless and exhausted from many hours of driving to escape the wrath and ire from customers he had cheated after his most recent stint in jail, he was certain that he was once again just a step ahead of the law.

Grudgingly resigned to his fate, he leaned the driver's seat all the way back, placed his head on his folded jacket and was about to doze off when he heard the plump postmistress lock up for the day.

Quickly sizing her up, he exited the Volvo armed with the fancy Hasselblad camera he had talked a gullible camera salesman in Helsinki into letting him take from the store so he could try some outdoor pictures—an outing from which he had not returned.

Aiming the camera in her direction, he exclaimed with well-feigned enthusiasm:

"Madame, please don't move! You look like Greta Garbo in that light. Fantastic! You must let me capture your beauty in a photo!"

She blushed and swelled with pride; after having been neglected for many years by her husband who had recently left her and their son for another woman. Hungry for validation, she was the photographer's for the taking—and take her he did.

The following day, after a night of debauchery and a hearty breakfast, the photographer was strolling through the village, sizing it up, when Tessa passed him by on a bicycle with her skirt rolled up over her thighs.

"Wait!" He held up his arm as if hailing a taxi. "Hold up!"

Tessa gave him a look as if he was a leper and kept pedaling.

"I am a photographer," he yelled. "I want to take your picture for a magazine!"

Tessa stopped pedaling.

The photographer knew he had another sucker on the hook—a young and pretty one for a change.

. . .

Over the next few days, the photographer had Tessa pose for him in her favorite meadow—a lovely clearing strewn with round boulders left by the retreating Ice Age and lined by gracious, hanging birch—all the while manipulating her with compliments.

Gradually he broke down her distrust as only a heartless, ruthless, master of deception can, and then only with a willing subject—which Tessa was.

The photographer soon had Tessa believing that her face would grace the covers of the nation's top magazines— and that only he could put her there; all she had to do was help him out a little.

He was experienced at seducing women—and cunning. He took his time with her.

She was his after a few days: there wasn't anything he didn't ask of Tessa and nothing she wouldn't oblige him.

All the while, however, he spent the nights with the love-starved and grateful postmistress who gladly cooked for him, washed his clothes and mailed his small parcels with photos to oddly-named publishing companies in Denmark —photos which, unbeknownst to her, were of Tessa in various stages of undress and naughty poses.

This went on for several weeks during which the postmistress increasingly felt neglected, a feeling to which she was allergic after the many years of her dysfunctional marriage. She grew increasingly suspicious that all wasn't as advertised by her formerly ardent suitor.

. . .

By now emotionally detached from Tessa, both Toivo and Reijo knew what Tessa was up to. They had seen the photographer's Volvo parked with fogged up windows in the meadow they both knew from experience was Tessa's favorite place in which to surrender to passion.

Toivo took to spending much time at his farm in the wheat field that was now filled with wildflowers.

He would lie on his back for hours on end, watching clouds appear, sometimes from out of nowhere, and then go by; noticing how they would evolve from one shape to another, at times dispersing into the nothingness from which they had been formed—much like the life-force of living beings, he thought.

He would let his imagination soar, sometimes transferring what he had seen in the sky, or had imagined to be there, to paintings filled with diffuse and unrecognizable shapes.

He thought his paintings resembled him and his jumbled emotions. He wondered who he really was and if there was a reason for his existence, fueling his conviction that he didn't belong on the farm where he was born—or for that matter anywhere near the village he couldn't even find on a map.

As he lay there amongst the wildflowers and watched the clouds go by he wondered if Life was real, if *he* was real, perhaps he was even dead, and, if so, did it really matter?

With uncontrollable sadness often engulfing him, he knew that he had to find something that would give him *real* hope for a Better Tomorrow, releasing him from within his own soul and sphere into the Life that surely must be out there somewhere; if not, he would surely implode into his own being and in so doing desecrate the purpose, if any, of why he had been placed on this earth.

America…

He would daydream of the land of opportunity at the end of the world where he would become all that he was supposed to be.

America was the magic potion that would make him whole, where he would find solace and happiness, his purpose for existing; the cure-all for all that ailed him.

. . .

Now and then girls would secretly seek Toivo out. Tessa, who was known to be a tempestuous and formidable foe, had let potential competition for him know that he was off limits and that she would severely punish those who failed to heed her edict. And Reijo circled the girls like a canine alpha male, now and then allowing Jussi and Timo his rejects, unaware that Timo helped himself without his permission and had more than his hands full.

Hormones being more powerful than fear of pain, rhyme or reason, propelled girls curious about heeding the call of womanhood to Toivo; interrupting his solitude on his farm, sometimes for relatively innocent talks about this or that, at other times for less thinly veiled flirtation, but most often to have their lustful dreams fulfilled.

. . .

The warm spring became a wet and cold summer. Rain fell steadily for several weeks during which Tessa and the photographer spent most of their time together in his Volvo, obscured by its windows fogged from the heat of their bodies entwined in the now flattened passenger seat, broken from a use for which it had not been designed.

One evening as darkness was creeping up on them and he was momentarily spent—with his remaining libido fading in anticipation of yet another dreaded interrogation by the postmistress—the photographer untangled himself from Tessa.

Buttoning his shirt and pants as he found his way back into the driver's seat, he announced that he had been offered a contract with National Geographic, and that his first assignment would be in Arizona where it never rains, the sky is always blue and the evenings always warm.

"Why don't you come with me to Arizona?" he said, gently touching her face with the tips of his fingers. "You could be my assistant. Would you like that?"

"Oh, yes," she replied breathlessly and placed her hand inside his upper thigh.

Moments thereafter he dropped her off some distance from where she lived with her mother and younger sister.

The following day when they met, his face was set in stone.

"What's wrong," she asked.

"Nothing," he replied and looked off into the distance.

"I can see that there's something wrong. What is it?"

"Nothing you can help me with."

"How do you know," she asked, worried and frustrated. "Tell me. Let me help you. Tell me what it is."

He hesitated, and then sighed: "The contract with National Geographic requires that I have a better camera, a Leica. And I have to send them proof that I have one, which I don't."

"Buy one then," she said, suddenly feeling nauseous and threatened, her vision of basking in the sun where it never rains fading.

"I don't have the money. The time I have spent here with you has been precious, but they haven't yet paid me for your pictures."

"How much does a camera like that cost," she asked, desperate to get away from the cold and rain.

He told her.

"That's a lot of money..." Tessa felt sick to her stomach—then she remembered her mother's savings hidden in a hole in the wall behind the kitchen cupboard.

"I'll get the money," she said, and then added: "But then I want to be your equal business partner. Do you agree to that?"

He did.

The following morning she brought him the money and then watched as he drove off to Helsinki to buy the camera, noting for safety's sake the license plate number of his car—although he had said that he would be back in a day or two.

An hour or so later, not far away, the photographer pulled over to the side of the road. Counting Tessa's mother's money, he laughed, stepped out on the road, stretched with great satisfaction, looked up at the sky and smiled— then replaced the Volvo's license plate that he had stolen off a Citroen with one he had stolen off a DKW.

. . .

After waiting a week for his return, Tessa looked up the county constable, gave him the license plate number, and wasn't much surprised when told a few days later that it belonged to a black Citroen, not a dark blue Volvo.

What *did* surprise Tessa was learning a few months later that she was pregnant. Being an unwed mother was *not* on her agenda. She told Toivo and Reijo of her condition; but when neither was willing to marry her, she decided to resolve her dilemma her own way.

Toivo found her in her favorite meadow, unconscious and bleeding profusely, astride the round boulder she had strained to lift while in a wide stance.

He carried her to the county doctor who said that while she would live she would never be with child again.

They were fifteen.

. . .

Chapter Seven

Soon after Toivo's sixteenth birthday a letter arrived from Esa Muhonen, Finntown, Chicago, U.S.A. Enclosed was a sponsorship document signed by Esa and stamped by U.S. Immigration. Toivo was cleared to live in America; he was overwhelmed—*now* he could become Somebody!

Although the matter of the lack of money for his passage wasn't yet resolved, the old pastor took the news of Toivo's potential departure with a deep sigh of relief— as did Reijo.

Tessa, however, got drunker than she had ever been, walked naked into the mansion of the richest bachelor in the district, Lt. Pennanen, the local Home Guard Commander, crept into his bed, professing her love for him, then literally raped him.

It was the ride of his life: although she wasn't much of a person, she was a force to be reckoned with as a sexual being.

In the middle of his night of nights, he proposed. Far from surprised by the question, she walked through the house that she once before had visited while delivering a parcel for her mother, re-inspected the fine furniture and silver— and accepted his proposal.

The next morning, when she saw her pudgy, balding husband-to-be in daylight, Tessa has second thoughts. She told Pennanen she needed to get something, threw on some of his clothes and fled his mansion.

She looked everywhere for Toivo and finally found him on his farm in his wheat field, daydreaming about America. She threw herself on him and sought refuge from the reality she had created.

Toivo was of little help; he was lost in daydreams and preoccupied with his dilemma of how to find money for his journey.

Within moments Pennanen approached in his yellow Renault automobile, feeling better than ever—his loin was empty, he was proud of his manhood; many times that morning he had relived the previous night and had reveled in his performance.

A cow grazing in the roadside ditch suddenly bolted out in front of his car. Pennanen slammed his foot on the brake. The Renault skidded to a stop barely a meter from the beast, which calmly chewed her cud and looked with beautiful but dumb eyes at the whirring thing.

Pennanen wasn't a man who readily tolerated having his progress impeded, but he was feeling magnanimous and decided to wait for the cow to move. She turned her rear to the automobile, firmly planting herself across the road.

Pennanen rolled his eyes up at the blue sky, sighed, cracked his knuckles, wiped his face with his hand—and smelled Tessa. He was immediately overcome with the sense memory of last night's debauchery; every sound, every smell. Aroused, he forgot the cow and began to plan the wedding: he would order his Home Guard Unit to attend; he would wear his finest uniform—no, better yet, he would have a parade uniform sewn by Field Marshall Mannerheim's tailor in Helsinki.

The thought of a new uniform and the wedding made him happy. He allowed himself a smile and another look at the sky—it was a fine morning, cow or no cow. He thought that he would like to learn how to fly—

42

... a pilot... now, that's something to be... with goggles and a helmet... and a white silk scarf around my neck... we'll rule the sky... perhaps the world... my plane and me ...

He was startled out of his daydream by the cow emptying her bladder in his direction. He backed up the car—as he did, he caught sight of Tessa in Toivo's arms.

Bitterly disappointed and filled with pain, he reversed direction and sped straight at the cow that suddenly personified all that was wrong with his life—it was the kind of moment that invited serendipity, but the cow moved aside and Pennanen wouldn't add to Finland's road statistics that year.

Tessa heard a car speed away, spinning tires spitting dirt, lifted her head from Toivo's shoulder and recognized the yellow Renault.

Knowing that the man she really wanted was intent on going to America, and that she was about to lose the man in whom she had invested the uniqueness of her libido, Tessa quickly untangled herself from Toivo.

She dashed across the field and onto the road, finally catching up with the car while she pleaded for Pennanen to listen to reason. He forced her to briefly run after him, and then slowly put on the brakes and brought the Renault to a stop. Yet he pointedly kept the motor running—although she might rule the night, he would rule the day.

Tessa was impressively persuasive. After she had told him about Toivo's imminent emigration to America, Tessa and Pennanen, cut from similar cloth, quickly came to terms: with Toivo's childhood home as security, Pennanen would loan him the money for the journey to America—and Tessa pledged to become Pennanen's wife.

Toivo readily accepted the loan and gave little thought to how he would repay it; after all, he wasn't coming back— ever.

43

Reijo was devastated when he learned of Tessa's decision to marry Pennanen. He jumped on his bicycle, looked everywhere for Toivo, whom he had thought was his principal rival, and after searching the whole village he found him on the Karjalainen farm at his family's graves, in the midst of telling them he was leaving for America.

"...be leaving soon and don't think I'll be back—"

A dry twig cracked under Reijo's foot when he stepped off his bicycle. The discordant sound jarred Toivo who wasn't pleased to have had the sanctity of his talk interrupted by an unexpected visitor, especially not Reijo.

An awkward silence followed. Reijo then cleared his throat. "So you are really leaving then?"

"Yes."

Another awkward moment followed. Again Reijo broke the silence.

"Why?"

"I don't feel I belong here."

"And you're not coming back?"

"There's nothing here that I want." Toivo said.

He noticed the red ants crawling out from their nest and onto Reijo, who shifted his weight from foot to foot; Reijo knew that something was biting him, but he had more important things on his mind.

"Do you know about Tessa and Lieutenant Pennanen?" Reijo asked with the pain of a rejected suitor.

"Yes, she told me."

"So what do you think?" Reijo wanted to know, still feigning ignorance of the ants that were now nibbling on his back and chest.

"That's Tessa for you." Toivo knew Tessa better than anyone.

"That's all you have to say?! How could she pick him over either of us? It can't have been his looks!" The ants were really bothering Reijo.

"Tessa must have seen something special in him."
That was as much as Toivo wanted to say about Tessa and
Pennanen. He was mesmerized by the drama unfolding in
front of him.

The ants were now crawling all over Reijo, including
his head—yet he still feigned a stoic disregard of what
had to have been quite a painful experience.

"It's a nice day," he said. "I think I'll go for a swim."

"You're welcome to swim in my lake," Toivo said,
feeling sorry for his former rival.

"Thank you. I might just do that. And I might just see
you in America some day." Reijo was peeling off his
clothes and heading for the lake long before he had
finished the sentence.

. . .

Toivo traded his parents' belongings for two masonite
suitcases into which he packed his artist's paraphernalia
and some clothes; what he couldn't pack he gave to the
parish's poor.

All others, Reijo included, avoided him those last few
days. It was as if he had disowned them when he
embraced what Fate had held out to him.

A misty rain fell the day he walked away from his
birthplace where he had felt so much pain. Helsinki, the
capital, was more than five hundred kilometers to the
south, and the steamer bound for America was due to
leave in a less than ten days.

He made it with only hours to spare.

As the steamer left Helsinki's harbor and his fellow
passengers stood in the stern looking back at what they

were leaving, Toivo stood in the bow looking ahead at the beckoning sea and what might be beyond.

Unlike the others he didn't look back; he was thrilled to leave all that belonged to his childhood behind him. He was convinced that what lay ahead, America, was the land of opportunity where he could become Somebody—he just knew it.

He was sixteen.

. . .

Chapter Eight

Crossing the Atlantic was a terrible experience; worse than death said the ship's cook who had worked as an undertaker during a cholera epidemic. Toivo vowed he would never again set foot on the deck of a vessel of any sort. The Finnish steamer pitched and rolled for eighteen days. Many times Toivo feared he was turning himself inside out while clinging to the leeward railing. One of the men in his cabin, a big, strong Finnish-born New York high-rise welder in his forties, kept whimpering for his mother.

Toivo's birthday came and went while they were crossing the Sargasso Sea.

. .

Days later, when they were all standing exhausted on deck in calmer waters off the coast of New York and the steamer's captain told the crew and passengers that it had been the worst crossing of his thirty years at sea, Toivo asked in jest if they would get money back for all the meals they had missed.

It was early morning when the steamer pulled into New York harbor. Toivo stood at the railing of the ship and looked up with awe at the Statue of Liberty; his heart pounded and he raised his arms in jubilation.

The ship passed so close that he could see the inscription on the plaque at the statue's feet: *"Give me your tired, your poor, your huddled masses yearning to breathe free..."*

He looked up the words in his English-Finnish dictionary to be certain of their meaning: he knew they were written just for him—his whole being resonated with their meaning.

He had arrived in the Promised Land—now he could become Somebody!

It was 1935.

He was seventeen.

. . .

Chapter Nine

The first Americans he met were U.S. Immigration officials. He thought they were rude and unkind, talking so quickly that he couldn't understand them. He wanted to ask them about the train to Chicago, but the S/S Mauritania had just docked with three thousand immigrants who were lined up in long queues behind him; before he knew it he was ousted into the rain and cold.

As the drizzling rain beaded on his face, he realized he had lost one of his two bags. It had been grabbed from him by someone, a child he thought, while he was standing in one of the many queues inside—but he was gloriously happy nevertheless. He was in America at last and would soon be Somebody.

Toivo stood on a sidewalk in Lower Manhattan gazing enraptured at the tall buildings and the faces of the people streaming by; these were Americans, and now so too was he. He saw only what he wanted to see—and all that he saw was good.

He clutched his one remaining bag tightly in his hand as he whirled around and around, jubilant and grateful—his future was here.

His euphoria soon deflated. He lost his other bag on the train to Chicago while he slept; fortunately, his wallet with his remaining forty-three cents, his passport, other official papers, and the slip of paper with the address where he was going were safe in the pocket he had sewn inside his pants during the Atlantic crossing.

He now stood outside Chicago's Union Station, exhausted from traveling and overwhelmed by the din and hustle and bustle. Night had fallen. He felt dizzy and slumped down on the curb to gather his thoughts. He had not been sitting long before he was rudely tapped on the shoulder. He looked up at the Chicago policeman's unfriendly face and received a harder tap from the nightstick that stung!

Getting to his feet, he started to speak, got another thwack from the nightstick—and that one *really* hurt! The message was clear: the sidewalk was the policeman's domain, not a place for strangers to loiter. Toivo scurried off with both a hurt shoulder and injured feelings.

. . .

He came upon a restaurant. His mouth watered from the smells; he had not eaten since he disembarked from the Finnish steamer three days earlier. None of the waiters understood his English; none could read his English-Finnish dictionary. He didn't understand their language, nor did he know they were Greek.

But despite his hunger and exhaustion, the restaurant's central, large painting caught his eye. The illustration of a young blonde woman on a white, winged horse reminded him of how he had depicted his dead sister in one of his earliest paintings; grief overwhelmed him.

Moved by the tears flooding the young man's eyes, the waiters sat him down at a table and fetched him some food.

The restaurant catered to artists; the tablecloths were butcher paper, there were pencils and charcoal in a cup at each table, and patrons were encouraged to draw.

Toivo picked up a piece of charcoal and sketched the four horsemen of the Apocalypse; he didn't know why he chose them—perhaps because he was so hungry and the horsemen appeared like skeletons in his mind's eye.

The waiters—who knew and appreciated art, and sold the best sketches to *Lutz Illustrations*—admired Toivo's sketch; one of them replaced his tablecloth with a fresh one, another placed a feast in front of him for which he was charged thirty cents. He paid the bill; studied the thirteen cents remaining in his wallet, the waiters' friendly faces, and placed the last of his money in the cracked saucer on the table—he knew the importance of receiving appreciation from one's fellow man.

As he stood up to leave, Toivo once again stopped to study the painting of the young woman on the horse. He didn't know that blonde women were a fixture in Greek mythology; he simply thought she looked so very much like his sister and tears again filled his eyes.

The waiter who collected the thirteen cents assumed that once more the young man had been moved by Greek culture. He remembered that a week earlier a local artist had given his supplies to the restaurant to pay for the sizable tab he had run up. Later that same evening, the artist had gassed himself. The waiter asked Toivo in broken English if he would like some paint brushes and other things; Toivo gratefully accepted.

With Mediterranean grandiosity, the waiter brought out the dead artist's oils, brushes, canvasses, and easel. Toivo was elated; he became even more so after the waiters insisted he drink several tall glasses of *retsina* wine. He set up the easel and a canvas and drank the rest of the bottle while he painted.

It was a wonderful painting; shades of white, gray, and black depicted the whitewashed restaurant; dashes of warm earth tones conferred the *gestalt* of the waiters; and in the background fluttered stanchions adorned with blue and white pennants. Although Toivo and the waiters couldn't understand each other's words, they did understand what they felt for each other was a kinship of sorts and Toivo gave them the painting. They embraced him and urged him to return. He thanked them and walked off into the night with the dead artist's supplies.

By the time he located the tenement where Esa Muhonen lived, the high from the wine was leaving him. His head hurt. He was exhausted and soaked to the bone. He entered the tenement hallway, water puddling around his feet as he looked at the door on which was a wooden plaque with the inscription 'Esa and Mirja Muhonen'. Someone had made an attempt to scratch out the 'and Mirja' and had added a cross.

Toivo started to knock, but hesitated; he knew the hour was late and considered leaving, but then something caused him to look around. He noticed that long ago the hallway had been painted a warm welcoming yellow that was now peeling off in large flakes. He liked that the doors had been painted green, the moldings stained dark brown, and that the floor was well-worn natural oak. Feeling reassured, he took a deep breath and knocked on the door.

From inside he heard a great deal of grumbling, the door was flung open and there stood Esa—looking much like the devil with unkempt hair and glaring, ice-blue eyes tinged with red. He was drunk—dead drunk; behind him appeared a beautiful blonde girl of Toivo's age.

As the young people's eyes met, time stood still; they stopped breathing and were drawn into each other's beings; their souls melded, they were no longer separate entities—they were One.

Even as drunk as he was, Esa caught the look in Toivo's eyes; he whirled to look at his daughter, saw the look in hers—then promptly slammed the door in Toivo's face.

Stunned and bewildered, Toivo slumped against the wall, holding his breath and feeling his heart pound like it never had, not even during the ghastly ocean crossing.

The door softly cracked open—and there she was again, with a blanket and a pillow that she gently tossed to him.

Their eyes again met and time again stood still—or was it racing? He didn't know; but he knew he wanted to feel like this forever.

From far off Esa harshly ordered his daughter back inside. She leaned a little closer to Toivo without entering the hallway.

"My name is Kerttu," she said softly.

"Toivo," he stammered. "My name is Toivo."

Her eyes never left his as she mouthed his name silently to herself. As she slowly closed the door, they both understood that even a closed door no longer mattered—that from now on there would be no barriers between them.

He could see her bare toes under the door where she paused for a moment before turning off the light for the evening.

The clock in the nearby Roman diocese began to strike eleven but Toivo was too tired to note the hour, too emotionally bewildered, too anxious to think, too wet and cold to be physically comfortable. Yet his mind raced and his emotions soared; he was in America, he was in love, and he didn't have any belongings or clothes or money or a place to stay—

... Will I see her again... how will I eat... where will I paint... how can I ever become Somebody...

He slumped to the floor. He could taste the garlic from his dinner and dimly wished he had a toothbrush as he pulled the coarse woolen blanket around him. His world spun as he placed his head on the pillow; he smelled her scent and was soon blissfully asleep.

. . .

At the same moment in a hospital bed in New York City, another young man was painfully awake. He had realized something about himself that he didn't want to accept and had jumped from a third-story window, breaking his back in two places. His family was wealthy; he would live, but he would never again walk without crutches.

...

Chapter Ten

When Toivo awoke, he could hear the nasal drone of what he couldn't know was a stern papal dictum being delivered by a priest in the acoustically blessed Roman diocese several blocks away. He didn't recognize the language and at first couldn't even remember where he was. The blanket was over his head. His hip and shoulder ached. The clock at the diocese began to strike; he counted six strikes, realized that he was waking up, then he remembered her—his heart began to pound. He thought he heard a cough, became anxious, sensed that someone was watching him.

Peering out from under the coarse blanket—and saw a thin old man seated on a chair eyeing him intently. The artist's paraphernalia he had been given at the restaurant was placed neatly against the wall, yet he didn't remember doing so.

"I see that you paint, but do you *paint paint*? My building could use a *schmerer*," said the thin old man pointing to the flaking walls. "If you can scrape paint and paint, you can eat," he said. "I know you have no money."

"How you know?" Toivo felt his voice crack.

"How I know? What? A *schmekel* I am? Rich people sleeping dripping wet in my halls? A Rockefeller you are not. So, money or no money, which is it?"

"No money."

"Aha, I knew it," the thin old man said and smacked his hand hard against the wall.

Toivo thought he surely must have hurt himself.

"Didn't that…" He got no further.

55

"Of course it did! But pain means nothing to banks, and my building is up for re-evaluation", the thin old man blurted out. "So, do you paint paint? Do we have a deal?"

Toivo hesitated.

The old man folded his arms, studied Toivo, and concluded he might be a Finn; the accent gave him away. He had been a landlord in Finntown for many years and could readily spot them. They were unique: their language was unlike any other, as was their culture; most had attractive faces and intelligent eyes; their personalities were reserved, cautious; some were downright joyless, and they were honest to a fault—and often politically charged.

"Are you Red or White?" he asked, suddenly suspicious.

"Black," Toivo replied. He liked all colors but was well aware of the danger of becoming partial to any particular one; he had heard that Whites in Finland had killed Reds on the ice outside Helsinki, that the corpses had lain there until spring thaw when they had melted into the sea; and that Reds in Russia had killed thousands, if not hundreds of thousands, of Whites. He had also been troubled when he read that brown men in India had killed scores of yellow men, and vice versa—no, as much as he liked all colors, he didn't like to label anyone with them.

The old man had not expected an intelligent or erudite answer. A former university professor in Poland, he had found his way to America eleven years earlier when anti-Semitism had begun to become official policy and his wife, Sayde, had suddenly died—she always had been anxious about her ethnicity and sometimes her anxiety affected him.

"What's your name?" he asked, without really knowing why.

"Karjalainen," Toivo replied, without really knowing why he chose to give his family name.

"Ka... That's a name?" He leaned toward Toivo and tested the water. "What do you think of the name Biederman, Mr. K.? Ben Biederman. Do you have any problem with that name, Mr. K.?"

Toivo shook his head. Although he didn't understand the significance of the question, he sensed it had something to do with religion or politics, topics which he shunned; the former for personal reasons, the latter because whenever he had overheard a discussion about politics he disliked the participants' tone of voice and the fact that no one could ever agree.

"Names are more than names, Mr. K., much, much more," Biederman said, probing for what he didn't know.

There was much Biederman already knew; it was his vast knowledge that had allowed him to endure adversity in Poland, then to prosper in America. He instinctively knew that the young man in front of him was a humanist, and could perhaps be like the son he never had—but he also knew that his need for someone to talk to, to discuss things with, was rushing him away from the control he had to maintain and how careful he had to be.

"I like equality and sameness, Mr. K., there is a certain comfort in that, so I want you to call me Mr. B."

Biederman turned around, fiddled with something in his coat pocket, then faced Toivo and handed him a dollar bill.

"An advance," said he who usually had little faith in humanity. "The walls are thin and I know what I know. I know you have met Miss Muhonen. I know you will be here every day like an alley cat so you might as well work while you are here. You begin work at seven and end at six, and the pay is ten cents an hour. Don't look at me like

I am God. I know I will get my money's worth out of you."

He got up from his chair. "Come, Mr. K., I will show you your room. It has good northern light, just right for a *schmerer* like you."

He picked up his chair and walked off with it down the hallway.

Toivo grabbed the blanket, pillow and his art supplies and followed his newfound benefactor.

As they left, someone quietly closed the Muhonen door.

. . .

Chapter Eleven

Early September 1939: Four years had passed since Toivo's arrival in America and his fateful meeting with Kerttu in Chicago's Finntown—a jumble of shops, restaurants, homes and tenements inhabited principally by Finnish immigrants. Although few Americans were paying attention to the press accounts of Japan's incursion into Manchuria or to its strong interest in the Hawaiian Islands following the American-induced economic blockade of the Land of the Rising Sun, some were closely following the developments in Europe.

England and France had declared war on Germany. Earlier, Hitler had taken Czechoslovakia and Austria, had split Poland with Stalin, and had contrived the Ribbentrop agreement—the non-aggression pact with the Soviet Union that Stalin signed strictly to buy time to get ready for war, hoping that the war he knew was coming would be fought by others and pass him by.

Few Americans knew, or cared, that Stalin had become increasingly more irrational and paranoid; that he had executed 80% of the Red Army's generals and 50% of the Red Army officer corps out of fear that the Soviet Union's elite was against him—and that he had virtually annexed Estonia, Lithuania, and Latvia.

But the inhabitants of Finntown knew that, and more: they were angry still about a resolution passed by the League of Nations in which the Western Powers had accepted Stalin's claim that the Soviet Union was entitled to Finland.

Finns were also rightfully concerned by rumors that Stalin had unofficially disavowed the non-aggression treaty he had signed with Finland in 1932. For nearly a year, Stalin had been demanding through secret emissaries that Finland move its border north and away from Leningrad —as well as provide the Soviet Union with a large military outpost on Finnish soil near Helsinki. In political terms, it was the equivalent of Finland giving up its sovereignty.

Finland had a population of less than 4 million—and of all the European countries had the longest border with the Soviet Union and its population of 180 million. The tiny country had enjoyed independence from Russia for merely two decades; prior to that, had for centuries been part of the Swedish Empire.

For those twenty years, the Finns had thrived on their newfound freedom; they were well aware at what cost it had been achieved—and that the Soviet Union would be a formidable opponent.

It was a time for soul-searching—and Finntown was often the destination for pilgrimages by concerned Finns of all ages from the greater Chicago area. They would meet on Sundays at the Lutheran church; it was an opportunity for many to speak their native language, meet friends and relatives, hear the Word, and receive the latest information about the state of affairs in Finland.

There was always a guest speaker: a high-ranking Finnish politician, military officer, or Government employee; a scholar; an author—once there was even a soprano who sang Jean Sibelius's *Finlandia*.

Afterward, everyone would be inflamed with national fervor, which unfortunate immigrants from Russia and the Ukraine would learn about in the days that followed. The Finns had developed a sense of cultural superiority toward anyone from the Soviet Union and an almost fanatical loathing of communism.

Toivo wasn't interested in the European developments. He preferred to remain lost in the world he and Kerttu had created in his studio on the top floor of the tenement owned by Mr. Biederman—with whom he had a strong friendship, but with whom he also constantly fought over money, a commodity that Toivo never had enough of.

Toivo thrived in his pursuit of his American Dream in which he would become a Somebody. In reality, he continued to be a Nobody at the galleries in Chicago; his giant paintings were not selling. While clearly painted by a great artist many years ahead of his time, the paintings were too thought provoking with their motifs of Death and depictions of fascinating but disturbing images from Toivo's childhood.

There was little room for the suffering of an unknown artist on the walls of contemporary collectors, who for just a few dollars more could have a copy of a really famous sufferer like Van Gogh.

Although the walls and floors were covered with his gloomy paintings, the rest of the studio was light and airy with delicate bouquets of flowers. It had a womb-like feeling; he had given Kerttu free rein to do what she wanted with it—short of covering up his work, which she liked but wished was happier. The flowers came gratis from their Italian florist friend Rosa diVecchia—who took great pride in selling only the best and discarded what wasn't perfectly fresh.

But by far, the room's centerpiece was a glistening American flag-themed mirror ball that Toivo and Kerttu had hung from the ceiling. They had fallen in love with the mirror ball after seeing it a second-hand store window and had bought it even though they couldn't afford it. It nourished their dreams of their Better Tomorrow, an American Dream in sparkling Red, White, and Blue.

In the evenings, dreading Kerttu's departure from their bed and her return to the apartment that she shared with her father—in 1939 it wasn't only unacceptable but *illegal* for unmarried people to live together—they would lie in each other's arms, safe and content, and dreamily watch the glistening mirror ball that turned in the ceiling above them and sent thousands of fragments of light dancing around the room; thus they had a star-filled universe of their own—and their love was at its center.

The mirror ball was more than romantic reminder of all that America has to offer: it also provided Kerttu with the dazzle of the light and excitement she yearned for and needed—she was a talented dancer with dreams of dancing on Broadway; for Toivo, the fragments of light refracted by the revolving mirror ball reminded him of the pastor's mirror on the pillow as it captured the soul of his sister and sent it dancing in the sky. Only now she wasn't alone—his parents were with her.

Toivo and Kerttu more than thrived in each other's company—being apart was outright painful for them. She knew that he was the One and only man for her; he knew that there would never be another woman for him and that without her he would flounder.

Although he was deeply in love with Kerttu and knew all that he needed to know about her and the two of them, he shunned any talk of marriage; he still was a Nobody and couldn't provide for her. While she didn't agree with him, she accepted that those were his feelings and would, at least for the time being, remain in her father's apartment on the floor below Toivo.

Toivo had the better and brighter apartment, a fact that Esa had added to his long list of grievances against his daughter's suitor, to which Toivo rightly, but unwisely, had responded that Esa neither needed nor wanted the light that Toivo required to paint.

"All *you* need is a closet. You like the anonymity of darkness," Toivo had said to Esa, who was unemployed and not bothering to look for work. Instead, he whiled away his days and nights with the alcohol he bought out of Kerttu's meager salary from grinding meat and gristle in a butcher shop. The Romanian who owned it wanted her body as well as her soul, but feared her ire and skill at filleting and thought it prudent to satisfy himself with merely her presence.

. . .

Toivo brooded that Esa didn't like him or his relationship with Kerttu, and Toivo didn't handle the rejection well; he would often play practical jokes on Esa. At first he short-sheeted him, he had himself been short-sheeted during his passage to America; he remembered well his feelings of confusion and frustration when he couldn't get his feet completely into his bed—and thought Esa well deserved that experience. The practical jokes took a more serious turn when Esa insisted on being a bad sport. Most recently Esa had arrived home drunk, jerked his door open—and had it fall on him; Toivo had removed the hinge-pins.

Esa had been both startled and enraged.

Toivo's open and engaging personality grated on the introverted Esa; thus, when he learned a short while after Toivo's arrival that his daughter and the painter had become lovers, he secretly wrote a letter of complaint to the old pastor in Finland.

In the ensuing correspondence Esa learned that there was another young man in the parish who wanted to come to America, a young man from a well-to-do family willing to put up significant money for their son to start a business in Chicago.

The young man was Reijo, Toivo's nemesis during their time with Tessa. Esa received a letter from Reijo and a photograph of him in a Home Guard uniform; he liked what he saw and read, and convinced U.S. Immigration to let him sponsor yet another Finnish émigré to America.

Reijo arrived in Chicago a year after Toivo. Esa helped the young man buy a music store on Finntown's 'main' street, where the rents were far too high for a business like his; however, nothing was too good for Esa who wanted to show off the young man he intended to have as son-in-law—but he had not reckoned with his daughter.

When her father introduced Kerttu to Reijo, she quickly understood what was expected of her. She promptly locked herself in the studio with Toivo—and purposefully broke off the key in the lock so that a locksmith would have to be called.

It was Sunday and Kerttu knew she would have nearly 24 uninterrupted hours with the man of her choice. Throughout that evening and night she let the tenement know in no uncertain terms how determined she was to remain Toivo's woman and what a dynamic lover he was.

In his own bed, unable to sleep, Mr. Biederman had contemplated putting on some clothes to reason with the young lovers, but had relented, remembering with fondness his own passionate youth.

Mr. Biederman, who knew everything there was to know about his tenants, had never liked Esa—the *schmuck* who was now vainly banging on Toivo's door, loud enough to overshadow Kerttu's joyous rapture and disturb the other tenants.

Esa left Mr. Biederman with no choice but to reluctantly get dressed and climb the stairs to the floor above, his creaking knees protesting every step.

Esa stopped banging on Toivo's door when he noticed his landlord.

"Uh, I, uh—" Esa didn't get any further. Mr. Biederman stopped him with an admonishing finger.

"Mr. Muhonen," Mr. Biederman began, somewhat softly, "are you thinking of moving?"

"No. Why?" Esa wanted to know, clutching a bottle of illegal cheap rye.

"You are disturbing the peace banging on an innocent door." Mr. Biederman paused; the stairs had taken their toll. "My door; a door I paid for with hard-earned money." He added, and then continued with an edge to his voice. "There are people living here who actually work and need their sleep."

"But that's my daughter in there. Can you hear her?" Esa asked and cringed when he heard an extra loud moan from the other side of the door.

"Who can't?" Mr. Biederman said. "You standing here banging on my door is not going to stop her. Besides, your voice is more of a nuisance that your daughter's. Let her have whatever she is negotiating for or leave the youngsters alone."

The moaning stopped.

"I can't do that," Esa said, "I want her to do what I say."

The moaning resumed, louder yet.

Biederman sighed. "You have even less upstairs that I gave you credit for. You ruling her will not happen in this life or the next. It's three o'clock in the morning. If you don't leave right now, I will get the cops and have you evicted. Good night, Mr. Muhonen."

Esa glowered at Biederman, chugged the little rye that was left, and stumbled down the stairs and out to Reijo's music store. There he passed out with lumps on his head from the falls he had taken.

Reijo was playing his violin in his apartment above the music store, blissfully unaware of the noisy, passionate tryst being loudly articulated by Kerttu in a most definitive statement as to whom she belonged; Reijo had, coincidentally, been thinking quite fondly about her as he played his fiddle.

Although Kerttu didn't speak Finnish—Esa wasn't particularly proud of his origin and had adamantly refused to teach her the language—she was everything Reijo wanted: attractive, outgoing, smart, and sensual—and

Toivo's. Reijo still wanted revenge for what Tessa claimed she did with Toivo years earlier; he had never fully believed Toivo's version of the event in question.

Reijo didn't care that Tessa had married Pennanen, who was rich, Reijo's Home Guard Commander, and gentry; the latter gave him right to the first pick of anything.

But here in America it was different; here Reijo was on equal footing with every other man—the U.S. Constitution said so.

Reijo agreed with Esa that he was the better man for Kerttu and lamented that Kerttu was taking so long to see that for herself.

But Kerttu wasn't Reijo's only challenge: He wasn't a very good business man and it hadn't taken long before his music store's high overhead forced him to go to the bank for a sizable loan.

The loan didn't solve the problem—Reijo's business was still failing and he didn't know how he would pay the coming month's rent.

Reijo worried also about other events beyond his control: the newspapers and letters from home expressed the fear that Stalin—hungry for land with which to buffer the anticipated attack by Hitler on Leningrad—was massing the Red Army along Finland's border. On-going negotiations in Moscow between Finland's envoy Paasikivi and Stalin's Foreign Minister Molotov were known to be going badly.

Times were bad everywhere. The people of Finntown were worried.

. . .

Chapter Twelve

In mid-September 1939, a notice posted at the Finnish Lutheran Church somberly announced that Finland's Consul General in New York would be arriving with a grave, special message. As fate would have it, he would be arriving on Finntown's annual Artisan Day.

That Sunday Finntown teemed with people—children played among parked cars, trucks, and carts of all sorts; pedestrians strolled along the sidewalks in their Sunday best; and vendors cluttered the streets with stands offering everything from cracked dishes and second-hand clothes to homemade soup.

Here and there were American and Finnish flags; polka and tango music mixed with swing and could be heard coming from open windows.

"Extra! Extra!! Hitler in Poland! Read all about it!" On a street corner, a newspaper vendor behind on his rent hawked day-old newspapers—while at the nearby bus stop, a young U.S. Navy sailor with sea bag in hand tried in vain to console his weeping girlfriend.

All were oblivious of the drama unfolding down the street outside '*Reijo's Music America Store*'. Inside the store, prospective buyers bargained with the manager of the bank that held the loan on which Reijo had defaulted—but outside, outside was where the real action was taking place.

One minute Kerttu was happily helping Toivo hawk his paintings, which were propped on easels bearing signs '*Original Oils-Only $10 Each*'.

The next minute a drunken Esa, his ever-present bottle of rye in one hand, had grabbed Kerttu's hair with his free hand and was trying to drag her off. "Get away from my daughter!" he bellowed at the artist.

"Let go of her!" Toivo yelled as he tried to rescue his love from her father.

"Never!" Esa gripped Kerttu's hair even harder until she cried out in pain. Almost comically Reijo, not knowing what else to do, vigorously played discordant notes on the violin as if he was setting music to a silent movie.

"Esa, let her go, dammit!" Toivo wrapped Esa in a wrestling hold and the old man finally began to lose his grip on his daughter.

"Reijo, get him off me!" It was more of an order than a plea.

Reijo took the violin from his chin and with his free hand shoved Toivo against the music store's wall—right next to the '*Store For Sale*' sign.

"You heard Esa! Stay away from Kerttu! You don't deserve her," Reijo hissed from the depth of his scorned manhood.

"… but… you… do?" The pressure on his throat was severe; Toivo barely managed to gasp out the question.

Reijo clamped down harder yet on Toivo's throat.

"Be quiet! And take your damn paintings away from my store!" said Reijo who no longer owned anything more than his violin and the clothes he wore.

"It's… a… free… country…" gasped Toivo, refusing to yield to his foe but at the same time terrified to see Esa roughly pulling Kerttu away.

"Free country, my ass!" A coughing spasm overcame Reijo. "Nothing is free in America…"

He began to hyperventilate uncontrollably and had to release his nemesis. "Get lost. You're... bad... for... business..." He tried to suck air into his lungs; his face contorted from lack of breath and he pulled a brown paper bag from the pocket of his coat.

Toivo caught his own breath and backed up a few steps—deeply relieved to see Kerttu at last free herself from Esa, dash away from him and disappear from sight in the crowd.

"And you're so good for business that the bank took your store away!" The words slipped out of Toivo who, although fed up with his day, regretted his unkind remark.

"Can I do anything for you?" he asked his nemesis.

"Yeah, go...to...hell..." wheezed Reijo and leaned gasping for breath against the music store's wall.

"Reijo, you really ought to see a doctor—want me to get you one or some water or something?" Toivo was genuinely concerned and placed a consoling hand on his wheezing adversary's shoulder—only to have his arm shoved away.

"... I... said... get... lost..." gasped Reijo as he put the paper bag over his mouth and breathed deeply. "And take your crap away!" The paper bag did little to muffle the anger in his voice.

Toivo started to say something, but decided against it when he noticed a well-dressed, elderly man study his paintings. He apprehensively headed for the could-be buyer—he needed a sale; Kerttu had a birthday soon and he had bills to pay, including rent to Mr. Biederman.

"Who is the girl?" The elderly man pointed to a canvas with a young blonde angel riding the winged white horse.

"My sister."

"She's lovely."

"She's dead," said Toivo, his voice quivering a bit.

"Oh, I'm sorry to hear that. And who's the boy?" He pointed to the canvas with a young boy watching men with grappling poles pull a woman from a hole in the ice, near which a man lay with a stiff arm pointing to the sky.

"Me," said Toivo.

"And the dead people?" The elderly man hesitated to ask.

"My parents."

A moment passed.

"How old were you?"

Toivo hesitated. "Twelve, maybe. I'm not sure."

"Why did you paint flowers in the snow?"

"There were no flowers at the funeral," answered Toivo who well remembered the ceremony; it had been achingly cold.

"Would you like to buy one of my paintings?" Toivo disliked having to ask the question, but he had no choice; it was either that or scream with frustration.

"Let me think about it. Maybe later," the elderly man added when he saw the disappointment in Toivo's face; he then walked off.

Toivo wanted to yell after the man that he wouldn't have sold him a painting even if he had begged for one, but thought better of it and didn't.

He began to put away his paintings into his cart: it was a large wooden box on wheels, narrow enough to fit through doors but still wide and tall enough to keep a couple dozen large paintings protected from the elements.

Reijo's breathing had stabilized. He removed the paper bag from his mouth, put his violin away, snapped shut the case, faced Toivo and offered well-meant advice. "I heard what the old man said. You ought to paint blue dogs or children with big eyes. People buy that; they don't want your pain on their walls."

"Pain makes the artist," said he who hadn't sold anything for as long as he could remember and felt the abundance of pain in his soul.

"Art shouldn't hurt. I don't hurt when I play the violin," said he who erroneously believed he understood the subtleties of art and artistry.

Toivo started to say something about Reijo's violin playing—but didn't; neither of them realized that he had become Reijo's best friend and Toivo wasn't yet ready to accept Reijo's advice, well meant or otherwise.

"Why do you always make things so difficult for yourself?" Reijo took Toivo's silence as an invitation for more advice.

"Easy things aren't worth having," replied Toivo who never had experienced anything easy.

"Hey, Rembrandt!" Reijo wagged his hand with a hooked middle finger at Toivo. "Let's finger wrestle over her."

"Let's not."

"Come on! Show her you're a man."

"By finger wrestling with you? Yeah, she'd be real impressed by that." With that Toivo walked off with his cart full of bittersweet paintings, demonstratively reciting the order of American Presidents:

"George Washington, John Adams, Thomas Jefferson, James Madison..."

"You'll never pass the test!" Reijo's anger reignited.

"Why not? Because you didn't?" Toivo walked on.

Reijo, who had failed the U.S. citizenship exam six months earlier, picked up a large chunk of coal that had fallen off a truck and pitched it at Toivo, who instinctively ducked and watched the large chunk of coal land in the street and break apart.

Toivo turned and taunted Reijo with a laugh, continuing: "James Monroe, John Quincy Adams..."

Such was the relationship between Toivo and Reijo.

As Toivo passed the Finntown Art Gallery—which displayed high-priced paintings of big-eyed children in the window—he saw a '*Closed Due To Illness*' sign posted on the door.

He couldn't know that inside, on the floor, lay a letter addressed to him care of the gallery's owner. The letter was from a renowned art expert who had been shown Toivo's paintings some weeks earlier at Mr. Biederman's insistence; the art expert had been impressed; the letter invited Toivo to exhibit his paintings in Manhattan.

As Toivo walked on, pulling the cart filled with paintings he thought no one appreciated, a wheel on the cart began to squeak.

He stopped at Rosa di Vecchia's tiny flower stand, searched his pockets for money, but didn't find any.

Rosa was standing in the darkest corner of the flower stand, severely depressed. It was her seventieth birthday; yet no one knew but her. She had not had many customers that day, so she spent the time thinking too much about her eventual funeral and the clothes she wanted to be buried in—and that had made her feel especially old.

Then she saw the attractive artist who always made her heart flutter, although he was nearly fifty years younger; he was simply standing there—in deep thought it seemed, perhaps even lost in sadness.

"*Maestro*, what's the matter?" she asked, coming out from the stand, wiping her hands on the rag that once had been her wedding blouse.

He didn't say anything; he merely shook his head, reached out and touched Rosa di Vecchia's shoulder the way he always did when he liked someone and needed intimate, physical contact, then walked off with his squeaky cart.

"*Maestro*," she said, stopping him—she always called him *maestro*, which she knew embarrassed him and she found quite endearing; she had seen his paintings and was awed by the tragedies portrayed within them; she was a true Sicilian. "Here, take something home for *la bella bionda*".

She reached for some flowers; he started to protest.

"*Basta*", she said, holding up her hand as if she was stopping traffic and swiftly put together a nice, large bouquet.

"*Maestro*, today is *Santo di Palli*. It's a good day to be brave and ask important questions," she said, knowing that by inventing a new day of worship she had committed blasphemy, but she felt it was worth it. Nothing had gone her way so far that day, and Rosa di Vecchia liked the painter who, when he met her the first time, had told her with conviction "Life is wonderful". She wanted the best for him and his very nice girl who worked at the rude Romanian's butcher shop and always gave her extra meat, yet charged her less.

Rosa was concerned—there was talk in the neighborhood that the always-very-nice girl's always-very-angry father was going to end the young people's romance.

She could see that the painter didn't know what to say; she resolutely placed the bouquet on top of his cart and sent him off with a harsh gesture that was all show.

"*Maestro*, remember, life is wonderful," she yelled after him, surprised that she had to wipe away a tear. "*Caro*, don't lose her," she whispered, knowing full well how easily that could happen.

The times were changing.

. . .

Chapter Thirteen

As Toivo turned the corner to 'his' street, he saw too late that Mr. Biederman was sitting in one of his favorite chairs outside the entrance to his tenement, listening to Edward R. Murrow on the radio and eating a sandwich—which he put behind the radio when he saw Toivo; he didn't know when the young man last had eaten and wanted to avoid making his proud friend hungrier than he might already be.

"Keep right on walking this way, Mr. K., you and I need to have a conversation." There was little doubt that he meant it; he turned down the radio's volume.

"We do?" With dread Toivo approached the thin old man for whom he normally felt a genuine fondness.

"How was your day, Mr. K.?" Mr. Biederman asked; he had prepared for this confrontation for quite some time and wanted to begin it with conciliatory small talk.

"Fine, Mr. B. Real good. How was yours?" It was a nice thing to ask, but Toivo expected the worst.

"Not so good, Mr. K. You see, I have a dilemma; I have a renter who is a deadbeat and who I have to get rid of so the other renters will take me seriously. Do you have any thoughts on this matter?"

Toivo didn't know what to say. Biederman waited; he was not in a hurry and raised the volume on the radio.

"...Washington learned today that Stalin has ordered for conscription into the Red Army academicians, lawyers, artists, the unemployed, and other Soviet citizens of a certain group..."

"Jews, he means—the coward. Why don't they just come out and say it." Biederman turned down the volume again. He glared at Toivo and waited for his reply. When none was forthcoming, he hissed an exasperated "Well?"

"Yes, well… everyone takes you seriously, Mr. B., there's no doubt about that, so there's no need for you to do anything extreme."

Toivo hoped that Biederman would let him off the hook again; he was embarrassed and anxious; he didn't have any money, didn't want a confrontation with Mr. Biederman—whom he knew was his very good friend.

Over his loudly banging heart he heard the morose voice on the radio; he sensed that what was being said on the radio would also affect him and felt doubly anxious.

"It's the times, Mr. K. These are serious times and serious times require extreme measures."

… *extreme measures*… Toivo felt faintly nauseated.

"Are we friends, Mr. K., or do we have a problem because I can no longer let you pay the rent with your dreams or good intentions?"

Toivo heard Mr. Biederman, both what he was saying and what he wasn't—but the voice on the radio intruded:

"… Moscow claims the reports of Finland's planned 'refresher courses' for its military reservists would be tantamount to a disguised mobilization, an act of aggression…"

"You aren't listening to me, Mr. K."

"Sorry, Mr. B., it's just that… they are talking about…"

"Never mind what *they* are talking about! *I* am talking to you right here and now—so pay attention to *me*!"

Mr. Biederman was talking more to himself than Toivo, he was trying to blot out what had happened to Poland since it had been devoured by Stalin and Hitler some weeks earlier; the newspapers were filled with accounts of the atrocities being committed.

He feared greatly for his daughter, who along with her husband had decided to remain in Poland when he emigrated—in the part of Poland now under Nazi control.

"There's not a thing anyone can do about what is going on over there. Not a damn thing." Biederman almost never swore. "Make like it doesn't exist. Forget about it," he said, picturing the likeness of his daughter, her husband, and their adorable children—his only grandchildren. How he longed to hug them. Their photo hung next to the picture of his wife, Sayde, whom he thought of more often nowadays.

...Sayde...

He missed his wife. Lately she had begun to visit him when he slept. She smiled and held out her hand; he had not yet taken it, he wasn't yet ready—

A large stray dog with a well-practiced wagging tail sat down by Biederman. He absentmindedly scratched the dog's back, then glared at Toivo while Edward R. Murrow droned on:

"... large corporations in the countries lining the Baltic recently entered into international trade agreements..."

Biederman snapped off the radio.

"Mr. Muhonen rushed by here a while ago, angrier than usual," Biederman said. He had found that by immersing himself in others' affairs he was able to forget about his own pain—but he also enjoyed needling his young friend. "Why not marry his daughter?"

"I will, Mr. B."

"When, Mr. K?"

"When I have something to offer her other than love," Toivo said in a weary voice.

Mr. B. he had heard that reply from Toivo many times before.

"And when will that be?" Biederman always liked to hear the answer triggered by that question because it expressed his own needs as well.

"When I am Somebody," said Toivo, sad and self-conscious, deploring that he once more had to explain himself. He didn't know what to do with his hands, absentmindedly reached for the comfort of the bouquet of flowers Rosa di Vecchia had given him, and began to straighten the stems.

"When you are Somebody…" Biederman said slowly, tasting each word of Toivo's reply, leaning toward Toivo, stretching his neck as much as he could, carefully articulating his well-rehearsed thoughts and feelings so they would have maximum impact on the young man he loved: "Be Somebody with a job so you can pay me the rent, Mr. K."

Severe pain suddenly wracked Mr. Biederman's chest and shot through his left arm; the sensation frightened him —but the matter at hand wasn't yet concluded.

… not again… not now… not when my friend is here… there are things I must tell him… for his sake, not mine… oy… the pain again… my face… I must control my expression… can't let him see that I am in agony… breathe slowly now… say something… zeyn nisht a putz… say it now…

"Enough is enough Mr. K. One year is more than enough. Pay the rent in a week or out you go. Stop being a dreamer, be a *macher, Mr. K., a macher—a doer.*"

… the pain… why must there be so much pain… I can take the pain… but let me have it when I'm alone… veynt aleyn… will he understand that it's not the money… geld schmelt…that it's for him… his sake… oy, this pain…

The discomfort in Mr. Biederman's chest increased, nearly taking his breath. He didn't notice that the dog whose back he had scratched was eating his sandwich.

Toivo was oblivious of Mr. Biederman's condition; he was consumed by the cold feeling that spread from the pit of his stomach, affecting his breathing and causing a strange, vibrating, high-pitched noise in his head—a noise

77

that warned of danger; a noise he had not heard during the many years he had successfully avoided reality.

He felt disconnected from the world, as if he was in a trance; he gave Mr. Biederman a nod of understanding—there were no hard feelings.

Another wheel began to squeak as he walked off with his cart through the dark archway that lead to the tenement's inner courtyard. Wet laundry hung on clotheslines strung between the buildings; through the drying sheets and garments he could see that his window was open. He heard Benny Goodman's swinging "*Let's Dance*" being played full blast on a Victrola and knew that Kerttu was in his studio having a great time dancing the jitterbug by herself, wearing only his huge, white, collar-less shirt.

The gloom left him—he loved her so. He attached the cart to the block-and-tackle that he used hoist the cart up to his studio, grabbed the bouquet of flowers—then wild inspiration struck him.

In Toivo's studio, "*Let's Dance*" ended; the needle stuck in the record's end groove. Tiny beads of perspiration from hours of exertion dotted Kerttu's upper lip.

She reset the record, upbeat music again filled the room, and Kerttu relost herself in her vivid daydream of being a Broadway dancer—she was a good dancer, perhaps even great. By nature she had been blessed with wonderful rhythm and energy, a strong and fluid body, and the courage to execute creatively original, daring moves.

She was in the middle of a back flip—in the air and upside down—when through the window she caught a glimpse of Toivo silhouetted against the dimming sky.

Although the image was brief, it was so unexpected and bizarre that she lost her concentration; she landed badly, in a most ungraceful fashion. As she sat on the floor with the oak planks against her bare bottom, through the window she saw Toivo approaching—seemingly walking on air, his arms stretched out wide, a bouquet of flowers in one hand.

She jumped to her feet and rushed to the window—and found Toivo balancing on the clothesline she had used earlier that day; it was strung between the window where she stood to one on the courtyard's other side.

"Oh, hi, love. How was your day?" she said, feigning disinterest and hiding her fear that he might fall to his death.

But her composure wilted quickly when she noticed he wasn't maintaining good balance.

"Fine," he said, nervous now, trying his hardest to keep his stride smooth and even to prevent the clothesline from swaying. "Say," he continued, quite nicely, "Would you... uh... would you... uh... ma... ma... oh, no!"

He swayed in an ever-widening pendulum.

Unnoticed by them, the hook holding the clothesline pulley on the other side of the courtyard began to straighten.

Kerttu anxiously waited for Toivo's proposal.

"Yes, love, would I what?" she asked, purring demurely. "Would I what? Go on. Go on!"

The hook holding the clothesline pulley was now almost straight—the pulley began to slip free...

Toivo swayed with seemingly uncontrollable momentum. He reached deep inside himself, found a better connection between his sense of balance and his legs—and regained control of the clothesline and his courage.

"Okay... Kerttu, would you... would you... uh... would you... no, I can't do it—"

At that moment, as if by divine intervention, the hook straightened, the pulley released—and Toivo dropped like a rock.

Kerttu screamed and leaned out the window, grabbing for him.

Toivo hit the second-story clothesline, which stretched—and stretched—and then snapped! He continued to fall, still clutching the bouquet of flowers.

Leaning out the window, Kerttu saw Toivo hit the first-story clothesline that, like the second-story one, stretched—and stretched—and then flipped him over; he continued to fall—and watched in dread as the courtyard's cement rushed up to meet him.

She closed her eyes, heard a thud, opened them—and saw Toivo lying deathly still among fallen laundry and clotheslines.

Kerttu's screams brought Mr. Biederman and the other tenants running. Aghast, some stood back; others leaned with morbid delight over the fallen painter.

"He sure did it this time."

"He sure did."

"Mr. Biederman, can my son have his studio?" asked the mother of a thirty-nine-year-old son who sculpted marble in her kitchen and slept on her floor.

"Look—he moved!"

"Oh—he's alive," said the mother, the disappointment in her voice was unmistakable.

Toivo stirred and tried to get up; just then Kerttu arrived, out of breath, expecting the worst, and still dressed only in Toivo's white collar-less shirt—which she was reminded of as the cool evening breeze lifted the shirt and revealed her bare bottom.

Seeing the looks of delight on the faces of the men and prudish disgust on the women's faces, she pulled down the shirt to cover as much of her nakedness as possible, pushed away a shifty-eyed woman tenant who could have passed as a grave-robber, and leaned over her fallen man.

Toivo's eyes were just beginning to focus; he now more clearly saw the crowd around him—as well as Kerttu and the anticipation in her face.

He panicked; swallowed hard; tried desperately to think of something to say, but couldn't. His body hurt although nothing appeared to be broken. He was actually more concerned about his Kerttu, that she might be disappointed and have hurt feelings.

He wanted to comfort her and tried a smile, but his lips were too dry and stuck to his teeth; his fall had been somewhat... overwhelming.

"I'm fine—I think," he said, in a voice he didn't recognize as his, straightening the flowers still clutched in his hand.

"Are those flowers for me?" she said with an encouraging smile. "Would I what, Toivo? Would I what, my darling? What did you want to know?"

She had never called him darling before so he knew this was a very special—and dangerous—moment; he tried to answer her question, but he couldn't do it; he couldn't make the words fit his mouth.

Although she was both disappointed and angry, she nevertheless helped him up the stairs to his studio, mindful that on the stairs below them they were followed by one of the older tenants who was trying to catch an eyeful of her naked bottom, but she didn't care—she knew what she looked like, that her figure would pass anyone's inspection.

... oh, what the hell, it might even lengthen the old geezer's life and improve his disposition...

She was grateful that her father wasn't home. After letting go of her hair he had gone to her mother's grave to complain about Kerttu and his life of misery.

Toivo was in a great amount of pain, getting up the stairs was slow going; he had to lean on her shoulder—she was, as always, strong enough for both of them.

The "*Let's Dance*" record was stuck at the end of the groove when they finally reached the top of the stairs.

Kerttu led Toivo to the sofa, where he gratefully plopped down.

Kerttu heard a cough—and there in the open doorway stood the old geezer, with his hat in his hand, hoping for a miracle, the kind he had heard of from friends with vivid imaginations.

After bidding the disappointed geezer '*Good Night*' and closing, then locking the door, she reset the record and "*Let's Dance*" again filled the room.

She plugged a cord into an outlet. As their 'American Dream' mirror ball began to rotate, throwing thousands of sparkling fragments of light around the room, she beckoned for Toivo to stand.

"Come, my love, let's dance."

"Dance?! Now? I just fell three…"

"I know. I was there. That was then and this is now. Come. Dance with me."

"I'm in pain!"

"Of course you are after a fall like that. Come! Get up! Dancing will be good for you. It'll help you remember what you were going to ask me. Come. Dance with me."

"Do I have to?"

"You bet."

He got up, gamely tried a few steps, groaned and plopped back onto the couch, visibly in pain.

"Oh, my love, you *are* hurt! You could have been *killed*!"

She hugged him; clutched him; cupped his face in her hands; kissed him gently; unbuttoned his shirt; unbuttoned her own shirt, opened it and placed her bare body against his.

She cradled his head against her breast like a mother protecting a child and kissed him. While doing so she gently opened his pants; touched him, and he responded.

Their passion built and became so uncontrollable that they had to love; she opened herself for him—they merged; she gasped as she always did when he filled her with his being, and she eagerly engulfed him with hers.

They gave themselves over to their fervor; lost awareness of all but their own existence; they entered the level of euphoria so powerful that it enslaves those who are admitted——

Bang! The door was slammed open by Esa, who reeled as he discovered the two lovers' intimate moment—but he didn't leave; instead, he bellowed like a wounded animal:

"Stop! STOP!! STOP!!!"

Their abrupt plunge from the heights of euphoria to mundane reality was as jarring as Toivo's fall had been; the transition from safe bliss to angry confrontation was too abrupt and brutal. They disengaged—shamefully; Kerttu quickly buttoned her shirt and Toivo his pants, both felt cheapened while doing so——

"Dammit, Esa, you have no right to barge into my studio like this!" said Toivo, his chest still heaving.

"Don't talk to me about what is right, she is my daughter!" said the self-righteous father.

"Papa, I am a grown woman," said the daughter who a moment earlier truly had been.

"Stay out of this, dammit!"

"No, I will not stay out of this! You have no right to barge into Toivo's studio like this!"

"Studio?! It's not a studio, it's a... a... toilet! Look! Nothing but crap on these walls! And death! People want happy things on their walls!"

"I paint what I feel! And I'm not a happy painter, I hurt," yelled the wounded artist.

"And you should hurt, you son-of-a-bitch! If it wasn't for you she'd be having a career as a dancer!"

"Papa, stop! That's not true! I'm not good enough!"

83

"Yes you are, dammit! You're plenty good. You should be on Broadway! You should... you're... you're too good for him!"

Esa pointed an angry finger at Toivo, took a deep breath and glared at his daughter. "If your mother was here she would... she would..."

"She would what, Papa? She never got what she wanted either! You spend more time with her now at her grave than you did with her when she was alive!"

The truth echoed in the room.

Esa's face got beet-red. "Don't talk to me that way!"

"I learned that from you!" snapped his daughter.

"But... but... I don't want you with him!" Esa had tears in his eyes.

"That's too damn bad because he's the man I want!" yelled the daughter who had had enough of her father.

"But he's not a man!" Esa cried out, overwhelmed by the strange and unmanly sensation of tears flowing from his eyes—he had not wept even when his wife of nearly thirty years had died.

"He's more man than you ever were!"

There was sudden and deafening silence in the room. Esa opened and closed his mouth like a guppy.

Kerttu was angry, but not too angry to empathize with her egotistical and ignorant father's plight. "I'm sorry, Papa, I shouldn't have said that, but you have no right to do what you're doing."

"Yes, I do, dammit!" Esa roared with frustration—and hit himself in the face with a clenched fist.

Blood sprayed from a gash on his cheekbone and spattered his shirt. He touched his blood with satisfaction, then pulled his copy of Toivo's U.S. Immigration document from his pocket.

"As his sponsor to America I have any right I want!" Esa declared, having his own, unique perspective of U.S. Immigration Law. He the spat on the document for good measure and wagged it at Toivo. "I want you next to me at the meeting! Let's go, we're late!" He paused to catch his breath, and then added almost inaudibly: "All my friends are laughing at me,"

"You have no friends," Toivo said unkindly and with the authority of one who knows.

The male animal within Esa vibrated with primal, savage anger and he pointed an angry finger at Toivo. "I'm not going to let you win!" He then turned to Kerttu and wailed: "Why couldn't you have picked someone I understand? A real man! Someone like Reijo!"

"Sure you don't want to keep her for yourself? Like the little girl she once was?" Toivo asked sarcastically.

"You just wait! Let's see how smug you are after the meeting!" Esa stalked out the door, slamming it shut, leaving behind an ominous silence.

Kerttu sought refuge in Toivo's arms—and was startled by a crack of thunder.

Heavy raindrops began to fall on the skylight that for three years had been the portal through which their imagination had soared as they fantasized about their Better Tomorrow.

. . .

Chapter Fourteen

Under the tutelage of an intense amateur conductor, a choir was rendering the Finnish national anthem when the rain-soaked Toivo entered the packed Lutheran church.

The day before, Finntown's Lutheran pastor had informed the known rumormongers in the Finnish community that a dignitary from the Finnish Consulate in New York was arriving with an important message from Helsinki—a message so important that the sermon originally scheduled would be given some other day.

The rumor mill had worked as never before. The Lutheran church was so packed that even those people standing could hardly move. Chicago's hot humidity hung thickly over them, causing the people in the church to sweat miserably.

Toivo's heart was already beating hard with apprehension when Esa stood up in a front row pew and motioned for Toivo to take the empty seat Esa had reserved between himself and Reijo.

As Toivo reluctantly and apologetically made his way through the crowd, his whole being vibrated with an ominous premonition of what was to come.

Something bad is going to happen; I know it, I just know it...

Toivo thought of leaving and wondered why he didn't; it was as if a powerful force pulled him toward that space between Esa and Reijo—a space in which he sensed that his American Dream would be shattered and much of his future determined.

When Esa saw that Toivo was heading toward the space he had reserved for him, he grinned with satisfaction and finished what was left of the cheap vodka in the bottle he had hidden in a rolled-up newspaper.

Esa ignored the admonishing looks he received from those around him, wiped his mouth with the back of his hand, capped the bottle and gleefully rubbed his hands together, preparing for what was about to take place.

Toivo pushed his way into the pew and the seat between Esa and Reijo, still drawn by an invisible force, still not comprehending why he was there at all, yet knowing that whatever he was facing he had to face head on like a man.

As the choir finished the last verse of *Oh, Finlandia,* silence reined in the church—broken only now and then by the rustling of clothes, stifled coughs, and steel-capped soles scraping the floor.

Everyone stared at the large map that now hung from the pulpit. In accordance with well-established tradition the pulpit was high above the floor, making the not so subtle point to the ordinary mortals in the pews below that the pastor was closer to God than were any of them.

The map was of northern Europe. Finland's border with Russia was clearly delineated. Although the map ended just east of Moscow and clipped off the vast expanse of the USSR, Finland nevertheless seemed quite small.

The Lutheran pastor, a thin-lipped and unhealthy looking man, opened the rectory door and ushered in Consul Huhtamäki, a well-fed and well-dressed monocled bureaucrat.

The pastor looked his congregation over; satisfied that most were present, he then announced dramatically. "I am honored to introduce Consul Huhtamäki of the Finnish Consulate in Brooklyn."

Consul Huhtamäki began to deliver the speech he had given in the preceding weeks in many cities throughout America, always in the same flat tone.

"On behalf of the Government of Finland I thank you for attending this emergency meeting. The Government believes that a war with the Soviet Union is unavoidable and urges all able-bodied Finns abroad to return home and help with the defense of their homeland. Finland's Foreign Minister Tanner's meetings with his counterpart Molotov in Moscow have all met with an impasse. Discussions are ongoing, but the Soviet Union's position remains firm: Stalin is convinced that Leningrad's close proximity to the existing border makes the city precariously vulnerable should Germany decide to attack from the Baltic Sea, and Stalin wants Finland's border with the Soviet Union moved north and farther away from Leningrad."

He paused and reached for the glass of water on the podium.

Perspiration ran down Toivo's brow and back as if he were in a sauna as he sat crushed between Esa and Reijo, listening with only half an ear to the consul droning on and on. Toivo wasn't interested in the developments in Europe. He was in Chicago and in love.

He loved his Kerttu.

He loved his America.

He loved the air in the morning, the air that smelled of thousands of people and glorious things—things that mattered.

He loved life.

He loved to love.

He loved to feel.

But he didn't love the feeling growing in the pit of his stomach as the consul poked at the map with a pointer and explained the importance of the border.

Toivo knew about the border. He remembered the time when he was a child and had been picking mushrooms in the woods near the farm with his mother and father. They had not found chanterelles where they normally found them and had wandered farther in the woods.

They had walked and walked; the few mushrooms they did find were soggy, slug-infested, and inedible. His father stubbornly insisted they walk farther yet. They came to a wide clearing and noticed a tall black-and-white post standing halfway to the other side.

Toivo remembered how his parents had tried to hide their sudden discomfort, and how quickly they had turned back into the forest—so quickly that they didn't notice he had not only remained behind but had in fact walked out into the clearing to get an even better look.

Evenly spaced, tall, black-and-white posts stood in both directions as far as he could see——

Toivo had taken another step out into the clearing—despite a vague and ominous feeling, something so strange that his whole being vibrated.

He saw someone across the clearing on the other side, someone with some kind of a stick to his shoulder. Full of curiosity, he climbed up on a stump to get a better look.

The stick suddenly puffed smoke and something whizzed by his head.

His father had come running, grabbed him brusquely and hurried back with him into the forest.

It was the only time Toivo could remember his parents really being angry with him—although he sensed they had been more frightened than angry.

"…a Finnish freighter commissioned by the Government of Finland will arrive in Brooklyn in a few weeks to pick up volunteers for the Finnish Armed Forces. Volunteers will be provided free passage to Helsinki."

Consul Huhtamäki took another sip of water.

Toivo felt personally threatened by the consul's words, but he could see on Reijo's face that free passage home sounded good to him. Toivo had heard that Reijo had decided to return to Finland, but that he didn't have funds for the journey—he was completely broke, as were his parents.

As Toivo listened to Consul Huhtamäki he was overcome by an ominous feeling he knew so well—*something is going to happen, I don't know what, but something will happen; I just know it!*

"… and I thank you for coming. I must go. I have many other cities to visit."

And with that the consul left the church, ushered out the door by the pastor who needed to sneak his daily cigarette.

With the pastor gone, many of the assembled took the opportunity to escape the oppressive heat and headed for the front door.

Esa rose to his feet. "It's been twenty years since Finland got its independence from Russia. There's no doubt that Stalin wants Finland back—and we all know what it was like to be under Russia's thumb!"

He emphatically raised an angry fist. "I say every young Finn should go back and do their duty to serve the land we love."

He had carefully chosen his words with Reijo's help, and he had rehearsed his speech well.

People who knew Esa, for whom they had little respect, continued to leave, but there was a chorus of agreement from the remaining crowd, even some applause —especially from those who were a bit long in the tooth and had shared a bottle or two with Esa.

Esa put a hand on Reijo's shoulder and turned to the crowd. "Reijo has something to say. Stand up, son."

Reijo rose to his feet. "I'm going back," said he who had run out of resources and options in America.

Older Finns, and others with no particular place they had to be, murmured their approval of the young man's patriotic decision. Others continued to walk out the door.

Esa turned to Toivo. "What about you, Toivo?"

"I came here to be an American," said Toivo who in his heart truly believed he already was one.

"You are what you are," said Reijo who wanted company on what he perceived was his Road of Failure. "You can paint a zebra white and call it a white horse, but it's still a zebra."

"That's right!" said Esa. "Don't think you're so damn special, Toivo. You're shit like the rest of us! Why should Reijo go back and not you?"

"He doesn't have much of a choice since the bank repossessed his store," Toivo said in a low voice, not liking that he felt forced to expose Reijo's plight to the crowd, small as it was.

"We're not talking about Reijo! We're talking about *you*!" bellowed Esa at the top of his lungs, his outburst echoing between the plaster-clad walls. "I say Toivo has an *obligation* to go back! What do you others say?"

He glared at his drinking pals for their support, and they obliged with yet another round of murmured accord.

"Toivo, everyone agrees you should go back to your country, so off you go." Esa sat back down in the pew, his mission accomplished.

"You have an obligation to go back," Reijo added.

"The only obligation I have is to live my own life my own way!" Toivo responded emphatically and stood up.

"You can't have things your own way and expect the world at your feet," Reijo said, not knowing why.

"Who said I want the world at my feet? What about having the world at your feet and your self-respect in the toilet? You know all about that, don't you, Reijo?"

"Screw you, Toivo!"

Esa could see on the faces of the older Finns that they didn't like Reijo's choice of words in their house of worship. He stood up and pointed a crooked finger at Toivo and shook it vigorously with as much contempt as he could muster.

"I want you to go back to Finland and that's all there is to it!"

"Why, Esa, because you say so?"

"I want some damn respect from you!"

"It's always what you want, isn't it, Esa? What about what I want? It's old farts like you who start these wars because you know you don't have to fight them. You no longer have urges or dreams or goals that are important to you so all you do is eat and drink and talk a lot of crap and get others in trouble!"

Some older Finns in the pews didn't like how Toivo had described them; others didn't like to be present when truths were uncovered and began to leave.

Reijo faced Toivo. "You owe these men an apology!"

"For what? For speaking the truth? For being honest about how I feel? Unlike you and Esa, I don't hide my feelings behind fancy words like duty and country. Why don't you tell these men you claim to respect so much what this is really about?"

The question bewildered Reijo. He wasn't aware that the older Finns already knew about Esa's daughter, and that bets had been placed in advance on the outcome of this tug of war. "Are you going back with me or not?" he asked, grabbing Toivo's lapel.

"No, I'm not!" Toivo responded emphatically. He wrestled Reijo's hand from his jacket and headed for the exit.

"He is going back! I guarantee it!" bellowed Esa for all to hear—and he meant every word.

. . .

Chapter Fifteen

Some hours later, heavy raindrops hammered the skylight in Toivo's studio. Rainwater dripped from the studio's leaking ceiling into the pails and bowls Toivo and Kerttu had placed on the studio's floor.

Kerttu stood by the window watching a couple arguing in an apartment on the other side of the courtyard.

Toivo stood by an easel at the other end of the studio painting a self-portrait—his anxiety-ridden face.

The atmosphere was somber.

"How was the meeting?" she asked.

"Good," he responded. "Real good."

"That good, huh?"

"Yep." He paused for a moment, then asked hesitantly: "If you could have anything you wanted, what would that be?"

Across the courtyard the arguing couple began to throw dishes at each other.

"You forever," Kerttu said, and then added: "And a view of the ocean."

She turned away from the window and the arguing couple and looked at the painting closest to her, the one of Toivo's parents dead on the ice.

"How come you always paint things from the past? Painful things. Why don't you paint the future?"

A door slammed somewhere in the building—a crack of thunder followed.

"I don't know the future," he said. "I can't feel it."

"You could at least paint things you like." She peered at him from behind the canvas he was working on. "You could paint me, for example," she said.

He grinned and daubed the tip of her nose with paint. Undaunted, she took a paintbrush and painted a black mustache on him. "Now you look like a real artist," she teased with a big smile.

"Oh good, I was afraid I was going to have to cut off an ear."

There was sudden violent banging on the door.

"Toivo!" bellowed Esa and banged harder yet on the door; a piece of plaster fell from the ceiling. "Open the door! I know you're in there!"

Kerttu put her arms around Toivo.

"Why won't you marry me? It would make such a big difference to him. And don't tell me you won't marry me because you can't provide for me."

Esa banged some more on the door. "Toivo! I want to talk to you! Open the goddamn door!"

Kerttu hugged Toivo even harder. "Answer me please, Toivo, why won't you marry me?"

Toivo hesitated then sighed almost inaudibly, "I'm afraid to."

"Why?"

"Because God always takes those I love away from me."

She cupped his face in her hands, kissed him beaming with relief, and said with a grin: "Well, I'm not going anywhere—except to take a bath." She seductively opened her shirt, ignoring the banging on the door. "Don't you go anywhere; I've got plans for you and me."

"What kind of plans?"

"Our fourth anniversary kind of plans," she said, stuck her tongue out at him and sauntered off toward the bathroom—undressing as she went, leaving a trail of garments behind on the floor.

Toivo grinned like a Cheshire cat and began to scrape away his anxious face from the canvas with a palette knife —depositing the gooey mass in an already half-filled glass jar.

In the hallway, the emotionally ruined and physically drained Esa banged halfheartedly on Toivo's door a few more times. He slumped against the door, took a long pull from the cheap bottle of wine he clutched like a baby does its bottle, emptied it, and shuffled off with the heavy and uncertain steps of a drunken and defeated man.

In Toivo's bathroom, Kerttu settled into the freestanding cast iron and porcelain tub that was filling with water.

She gazed at the wavering flame of the candle she had placed next to a magazine on a wooden board across the tub.

Her thoughts were wandering freely: her breasts were full and she knew she was especially fertile this evening; earlier, while she stood by the window and looked at the arguing couple, she had decided to take charge of her future, to brave the times and allow that for which her whole being yearned to happen.

Content with her resolve, she began to wash herself when the hot water flowing from the faucet started to hiss and spit, and then trickled to nothing.

"Toivo, the hot water ran out again," she yelled into the studio.

Toivo put away the palette knife. He undressed on his way to the bathroom, his clothes fell as if by divine intervention right atop hers, got into the tub—raising the water level so that Kerttu could continue her bath—and watched her wash.

Their eyes met, and they kissed the way only those who love without fear, ego, or conditions can kiss; a kiss that is as much of an offering as it is a yearning.

The tub was small; their thighs pressed so tightly against each other's that they could feel their hearts beating in unison. They looked deeply into each other's eyes and soared into the nonjudgmental, overpowering realm of Love—a realm in which all is safe, soothing and healing, and filled with a yearning that it will last forever.

They breathed more deeply yet, leaned closer to each other, caught each other's scent and pheromones and became even more entranced; there were no thoughts, boundaries or restraints—only their unbridled longing for more of that moment and each other.

She touched him with both her hands, he stroked her, and their passion soared even higher—they were now One. The feeling grew and swelled within them—so much so they believed they might burst.

All sound came to an end; they were absorbed by moment, were completely free and unencumbered, yet even more captured by it. All else was erased; their only remaining urge was that all-encompassing need to remain One with the other—forever and more.

Esa came back to Toivo's door armed with a fresh bottle from which he took yet another long pull. He started to bang on Toivo's door again, but something held him back —it was as if he knew that he should not disturb the magic about to be conceived behind that wooden barrier.

He slumped to the hallway floor and sat with his back against the wall on the opposite side of Toivo's door and downed some more of his cheap wine.

On the other side of the door Toivo and Kerttu were in bed and in each other's arms. The mirror ball twirled in the ceiling and thousands of fragments of light danced upon the two lovers.

"Make me a baby, Toivo," she moaned ever so softly. "Make me a baby."

Near the bed stood the easel with the canvas of what had been Toivo's anxiety-ridden self-portrait; all that remained was the face-less outline of a human being.

The rain played on the roof and the skylight; water dripped into the containers.

In the hallway, Esa groaned awake after passing out on the floor. His head and body hurt and he glared at Toivo's door.

The two lovers were asleep in each other's arms when they were awakened by renewed pounding on the door.

"He's my father, but it's you he wants to talk to," Kerttu said, still far away in a world where all was good and their love was safe.

Toivo got out of bed, put on his pants, took a deep breath and opened the door.

Outside stood Esa, drunk and disheveled, filled with self-pity and hatred.

"Here's your passport. You can pack your crap because I have canceled your U.S. visa," he said and held open Toivo's passport to the page with the U.S. Immigration stamp where he had written in red '*Canceled by Sponsor*' and signed his name.

"And so you know, I wrote a letter to Immigration and put it in the mailbox on the corner. Your goose is cooked, so you might as well get packing. And here's something else for you."

Toivo was in shock over the matter of his U.S. visa; it took him a moment to realize that Esa was peeing on the floor by his door. He would have looked down had it not been for the look of satisfaction in Esa's eyes.

The trickling stopped; Esa buttoned his fly.

"Any questions?" Esa hissed and handed Toivo his passport.

The contempt in Toivo's voice and eyes was unmistakable. "Is this your idea of being a man?"

Esa's eyes wavered.

Toivo slammed the door in Esa's face.

"What did Papa want?" asked Kerttu, still lost in her own world of bliss and euphoria.

Esa had his ear to Toivo's door when Kerttu jerked it open. "How could you cancel his visa, Papa? What kind of man are you?!?"

Esa searched for the words, but he couldn't find them —the look of unrestrained loathing in his daughter's eyes was too overpowering.

When she slammed the door shut in his face Esa knew he had gone too far, but male pride took over—and it has neither rhyme nor reason. Esa bellowed like the beast he was: "What kind of man? I'll show you what kind of man! I'll show you!"

As he shuffled off toward his apartment, he broke into uncontrollable, self-pitying tears and had a difficult time navigating the stairs down to his apartment. His hands shook as he tried to unlock his door; he had to attempt it several times before he got it open.

As he closed the door behind him, there was silence— followed by an enormous, earth-shaking crack of thunder.

A few hours later, Kerttu jerked awake. She felt unaccountably anxious and looked at Toivo. He was still asleep; she knew that whatever had abruptly awakened her had not come from him. She dressed and tried to quietly ease open the studio door—but it was damaged from Esa's repeated poundings; its hinges squeaked and the sound pierced the night.

She paused and listened, hoping she hadn't awakened Toivo, stepped over the mysterious puddle outside the door, and tip-toed down the stairs to the apartment she shared with the man she no longer considered her father.

She opened the door—and screamed in utter horror.

Awakened by her screams Toivo raced out of his apartment and down the stairs.

He stopped abruptly when he saw the cause of her anguish, wrapped his arms around her and shielded her as best he could from the terrible sight.

She whimpered uncontrollably and couldn't take her eyes off her father's hanging body—Esa still swayed, if ever so slightly.

In his final desperate act, Esa had knotted the end of his only tie to an overhead gas pipe and the other end around his neck.

He now hung near the kitchen table; his face grotesquely discolored and contorted, a kicked-over chair at his feet.

. . .

Chapter Sixteen

The morning of Esa's funeral, Mr. Biederman was as usual sitting in one of his favorite chairs listening to the radio at the entrance to his building when a Government car stopped at the curb. Two men in suits and O'Rourke, the always-pleasant day-beat cop, got out of the car.

O'Rourke pointed discretely to Biederman and said something to the Government agent wearing a nicer, more expensive suit.

The nicer suit nodded as if he understood what O'Rourke had said, pulled out a paper from his inside coat pocket and approached Mr. Biederman who turned off the radio.

"Nice day," the nicer suit suggested.

"Nice suit," Mr. Biederman replied, he knew people; he knew the man was vain, only a vain man would spend four months' wages on a suit.

"Thank you. Got it from Siegel."

"How is he?" Biederman wanted to know. Siegel had forgotten to repay Biederman a loan, and Biederman had forgotten the amount of the loan, but he wasn't worried; it was almost like having money in the bank, Siegel was an honorable man—but Biederman wasn't sure that the bank remembered him.

"He knocked ten bucks off the price of the suit so he can't be doing that bad."

"Ask him to come and see Ben Biederman. My legs don't get me to that part of Chicago much any more."

He paused. That was enough of the niceties, now he wanted to take charge. He was certain he knew why they were there.

"So you know who I am and I know Mr. O'Rourke, but I don't know you two. What agency are you with and what can I do for you?"

The nicer suit flashed a badge. "Department of Justice. We want to talk to a tenant of yours, Kar-something. I can't pronounce the name."

He showed Biederman an arrest warrant.

"Oh, him." Biederman said. "He's gone. Moved out during the night. Didn't even pay his rent. What did you want with him?"

The nice suit wavered. "The department received a letter from a Muhonen-something, apparently another tenant of yours, claiming this Kar-something is an anti-American and U.S. Visa-less agitator."

"That tenant hung himself a few days ago." Biederman watched the impact the news had on the nicer suit and added: "He wasn't well."

O'Rourke cleared his throat. "I told you."

The nicer suit glared at O'Rourke and scribbled something on a note pad.

Biederman turned the radio back on. "I will let Mr. O'Rourke know if I hear anything about Kar-something. But I don't expect that I will."

And with that Mr. Biederman turned his attention to the radio, having concluded the U.S. Government's interview with him.

. . .

Esa was buried next to Kerttu's mother. Toivo held Kerttu for support as they stood at the grave and watched Esa's coffin lowered by four black cemetery workers and placed next to the wife he had so often abused.

"At least he can't hurt her now," she said, so softly that only Toivo could hear her.

The four men stepped back and waited for the signal to fill the grave with soil, but Finntown's regular pastor was nursing a cold and his substitute from the Swedish Seaman Church was both fresh out of the seminary and off the boat, spoke neither Finnish nor English, and had never before presided at a funeral.

Unsure of himself, the Swede looked to the workers for guidance; recent arrivals from the South, they felt the young man's hesitation, began to softly clap their hands in gospel rhythm, and crooned a hymn while the Swedish pastor read a eulogy in a language that none of the others understood.

Perhaps it didn't matter for other than Mr. Biederman, no one came to Esa's funeral, not even Reijo—even though Toivo had walked around Finntown and asked everyone who knew Esa to attend.

He had made sure to mention that it was for Kerttu's sake, but everyone was busy, or "had other things to do", even Reijo, who had left Finntown the day before the funeral.

Although Reijo felt beholden to Esa and would otherwise have attended, he had already bought a bus ticket for his journey to Brooklyn and to the Finnish freighter that left for Helsinki in a week.

Reijo knew he was never coming back to America and wanted to see some of the country in which he had become a failure.

Mr. Biederman had been very helpful to Toivo and Kerttu —but he had not been very happy; he knew he would miss them and their zest for life, the discussions with Toivo about matters both worldly and personal, the arguments which—when compared to his loneliness—were trivial.

He didn't want them to leave; he knew that with their departure some of his own self would leave as well.

He told Toivo to forget the back rent and that he would help him market his paintings.

Mr. Biederman greatly appreciated Toivo's talent, so much so that unknown to Toivo he had talked Finntown's Art Gallery owner into showing Toivo's paintings to an art expert from New York.

Several times he had reflected on his meeting with the gallery owner; he had watched the man's face as he studied Toivo's paintings and knew that he, too, had appreciated Toivo's work; thus he thought it odd that they had not heard from him.

The day before Esa's funeral Biederman had gone to Finntown's Art Gallery to inquire about the owner, only to learn that he had died the week before.

Mr. Biederman, an old man with an old person's concerns, was so bothered by yet another death of someone he knew that he forgot to ask the gallery's caretaker if there was anything for Toivo from a Mr. Rubin in New York City—there was, but it was lost in one of many other boxes in the office of the lawyer handling the art gallery owner's estate and probate.

"Stay, children, stay," Mr. Biederman had pleaded with the young couple he had come to adore. "Forget the rent, it isn't important. I'll keep an eye out for Immigration. I fooled them once and can do it again."

Although Mr. Biederman's offer to let them stay was tempting, Kerttu feared it was just a matter of time before a search by U.S. Immigration would lead to serious legal problems for Toivo.

Ever practical and eagerly looking forward to living on Toivo's farm in Finland, Kerttu convinced Toivo that leaving America was the best thing they could do; that way, should something happen and they changed their minds, they could always come back.

Mr. Biederman promised to keep Toivo's studio vacant for a year.

Kerttu paid Toivo's back rent with the money left over from Esa's simple funeral; there wasn't much—Esa had bought far too much on credit in the neighborhood.

Toivo and Kerttu sold as much of Esa's and their own belongings as they could find buyers for, but the times were still bad and the second-hand stores still overflowed with items and clothes from the Depression.

The young couple learned they didn't have enough money for the journey to New York as well as passage to Finland —and they were not about to part with the mirror ball. Nor would Toivo sell his paintings for the one dollar each he was offered by the Romanian butcher, who also held back Kerttu's final pay when he realized he would never have her as he had often fantasized he would.

Resigned to their departure, Mr. Biederman wanted to be as helpful as possible. He had connections to powerful men who controlled the trains that delivered goods from Chicago to merchants in New York; he called in a few favors and arranged for Toivo and Kerttu to travel by themselves, undisturbed by cops and railroad goons, on a particular day in a particular freight car carrying crates of Coca-Cola bound for the New York City Fair.

Toivo gave Mr. Biederman a painting to keep until his return.

It was Toivo's favorite; one that he had painted without Kerttu's knowledge and had kept well hidden.

The painting was of both of them; they were near the ocean; the sun kissed Kerttu's face; Toivo's face was in the shade.

Toivo asked Mr. Biederman not to show Kerttu the painting until they returned from Finland—it was to be his wedding present to her.

. . .

Two days after Esa's funeral Toivo and Kerttu sat in a freight car with the glistening mirror ball between them, their backs against Coca-Cola crates stacked from floor to ceiling, listening to the monotone clickety-clack of the train wheels hitting seams in the rails.

Toivo had his arm around Kerttu; their hands were joined and they were both deep in thought. She wore a black mourning ribbon on her arm, her eyes were moist: she was thinking about her father—how what he had done had been so selfish and hateful.

Toivo's face was set in stone. He dreaded going back to Finland—he had a premonition that things were not going to turn out the promising way Kerttu thought they would. He glanced at her, started to speak, but at that moment the diesel's piercing horn sounded, startling them.

The sun was setting when their New York Central freight train lumbered through Ohio and its near boundless fields of shoulder-height corn. Fading sunlight appeared intermittently through the maize, shone through the open doorway and lit on the mirror ball, causing thousands of tiny fragments of light to refract onto the ceiling, crates and floor.

Clickety-clack…clickety-clack… clickety-clack…

Toivo noticed the tears in Kerttu's eyes and squeezed her hand gently. He pried a Coca-Cola from between the broken slats of a crate, tried to open the bottle, cut himself and began to bleed.

He bandaged his hand with a handkerchief. Kerttu gave him her scarf to hold the bandage in place. They sat in silence with their thoughts; he with his dream of America, she with her dream of a peaceful life on a farm in Finland.

Night fell.

Clickety-clack…clickety-clack… clickety-clack…

. . .

Chapter Seventeen

Four days later, Toivo and Kerttu arrived in New York. When conditions allowed they had left the freight car's door open; no one ever bothered them, but they saw other travelers beaten and thrown off the train.

As the train pulled into Brooklyn they saw in the distance, silhouetted against the rising sun, the huge Ferris wheel at Coney Island.

In his coat pocket Toivo had an envelope that Mr. Biederman had given them at the rail yard in Chicago.

"Go to Coney Island," Mr. Biederman had said.

"Why?" Toivo had wondered. "That's an amusement park. I don't feel much like…"

"Go there," Mr. Biederman had said. "Go there for me. Open this when you stand at the entrance. Follow the instructions and enjoy yourselves; think of your old friend and…"

He had wanted to say more, but couldn't; he hugged them and walked off into Chicago's late summer's heat and humidity.

Toivo and Kerttu stood with their belongings at the entrance to Coney Island. They were awestruck by the colors, the noise, the joy and laughter.

Before leaving Chicago, Toivo had bought a large rucksack to which he had attached the mirror ball and into which he had stuffed his personal belongings and artist's equipment; he needed his hands free to pull the cart with his paintings and to help Kerttu carry her suitcase.

People noticed the mirror ball and the odd-looking cart; some thought Kerttu and Toivo worked there—she certainly was pretty enough and he, although attractive, seemed somewhat eccentric. Toivo and Kerttu were asked all kinds of questions about the rides inside, if there were any special shows that day and so on.

Kerttu was not amused by the attention given them. "The man on the phone said the ship leaves at six. That's in less than eight hours," Kerttu mentioned for the second time.

"Guess we should go in." Toivo wasn't very enthused. "I promised we would, but I don't feel like it. It doesn't seem…"

"You're right," Kerttu interrupted. "It would be a shame to go in and have fun like all those other people."

He burst out laughing. "You just will not let me have my doom and gloom, will you?"

She looked at him, smiling; she loved him for who he was: creative, idealistic, vulnerable, difficult, moody— and for having dreams, although she privately thought some were highly unrealistic and impractical.

Toivo was proud of the mirror ball—he liked what it represented for him and Kerttu and didn't mind that strangers asked him all kinds of questions about it, to which he would provide answers that he thought fitting and proper—but to keep the peace between him and Kerttu he covered it with his coat, reread Mr. Biederman's note, then approached V.I.P. entrance and showed Mr. Biederman's letter to the lady inside.

The lady didn't speak English well, but she fondly remembered Biederman, her sister's husband; she provided Toivo and Kerttu with passes to all the rides and coupons for anything they wanted to eat or drink.

With their belongings safely placed in a storage room, they joined the magic and excitement of Coney Island.

Toivo almost forgot that in a few hours his Dream of America would be coming to an end.

The rides went around and around, up and down, in and out; they ate hot dogs with ketchup and mustard and relish and onions, huge wads of spun sugar, candied apples, immensely large and salty pretzels—all topped off with a delicious, frosty ice cream cone.

For a few hours they lived and ate the American Dream; it was a glorious, grand experience—until a musical clock chimed and wrenched them back to reality.

Toivo was ever so quiet when they retrieved their belongings from the storage room.

The walk from Coney Island to Brooklyn Harbor was a long one; it was late afternoon before they reached the docked Finnish freighter.

Toivo refused to look at the vessel that would physically remove him from his Dream of America; he would look only at the distant Statue of Liberty—reliving the impact it had on him when he arrived in the land he had so fervently hoped would be his.

Without taking off his rucksack he sat down on a crate near the Finnish freighter and gazed at the statue that personified his dream; the mirror ball sparkled on his back.

"When I first saw her I thought she smiled at me," he said with some bitterness.

"I'm not surprised," she said. "They say the model who posed for the sculptor was a Paris prostitute."

"She was?" He wasn't sure if she was joking with him or not; for a moment he was annoyed since he thought she had merely made an attempt to chase away his gloom, but she nodded an affirmation that it had indeed been so.

"Oh—I didn't know that." He had lost yet another illusion and looked away from the Statue at the activity around them.

To the left of them lay the tidy, gray-hulled Finnish freighter, the S/S *SISU*; the Finnish flag, a blue cross on a white background, fluttered in the breeze on the freighter's fantail, under which large white letters revealed the freighter's name and her homeport, Helsinki.

The name *Sisu* was new; the freighter had been called t h e S / S *KIRSTI* after the owner's wife, until commissioned by the Finnish Government to pick up Finland's able-bodied men abroad.

The name-change had been part of the contract; the w o r d *sisu* denoted the Finnish personality—stubborn endurance and inner strength as well.

Tied to the dock nearby lay a dilapidated, black-hulled, rusting Soviet freighter, the S/S *KOMSOMOLSKAYA,* named after a term that was coined by Lenin to inspire Party unity.

The flag of the USSR, a hammer and sickle in gold against a blood-red background, hung limp on the freighter's fantail; it was so heavily soiled it took a stiff breeze to barely make it wave.

The name of the freighter's homeport, Leningrad, had been painted in gray on the ship's black hull years ago and was now barely legible; the name *Komsomolskaya*, however, glowed eerily bright in large golden letters against the rusting black hull.

The dilapidated freighter's hull leaked because of inferior welding; that it was named after the Communist Party's Youth Organization was an accidental metaphor and further evidence of the Soviet Union's preoccupation with form over substance.

The *Sisu*'s first mate and the ship's agent sat at a folding table at her gangway, issuing berths aboard the ship to a few young Finnish men with suitcases in their hands and patriotism in their hearts. Cleared to board the ship, the young men bounded up the *Sisu*'s rope and planking gangway that swayed alarmingly under their feet.

Reijo stood on the *Sisu*'s bow with a foot on the lower rung of the railing, playing along on his violin to the music coming from a group of Soviet seamen on the dock below.

From where he stood, Reijo could also see Toivo and Kerttu sitting on their own crate with their arms around each other.

Reijo suddenly felt lonely; he wanted to be noticed and appreciated. He bore down on the strings with his bow and played as loudly as he could. He tried to play beautifully too; he made sure that each note was correct, but no one seemed to hear him—the din around and below him canceled the effort he made.

He lifted his chin from his violin and heard the seagulls, the ships' engines, the lorries, and the shouting of the seamen getting the *Sisu*'s deck ready for departure.

He knew that no one had noticed him and loneliness overwhelmed him; he lowered the violin from his shoulder and his hand clutching the bow dropped to his side.

Last-minute cargo was being hoisted aboard the Soviet freighter. A couple of New York City policemen—there to ensure that none of the Soviets wandered off and became the Commie spies they had been warned about— impatiently looked at their watches and approached their wards.

Accustomed to official paranoia the Soviet seamen, who were simple men and good-naturedly drunk, spontaneously decided to serenade the gloomy policemen with a very special song.

The policemen knew the song was meant for them, but they weren't sure what it meant. So instead of enjoying it, they thought it best to be angry—it was in their unwritten manual that when in doubt, it's best to be aggressive.

Thus New York City's finest glowered at the Soviet seamen singing a harmonically complex, bittersweet folk song, for which *politruks* had written politically suitable verbiage—the old lyrics had been far too romantic.

Nicholas Habarov—named after Russia's Czar and, ironically, the son of Naumovich Habarov who had fired the decisive bullet that ended the Romanoff line, accompanied the sailors on an accordion. A few years older than Toivo, Nicholas had a steel-jacketed front tooth and a large, thick, dark reddish-brown birthmark that hideously disfigured his otherwise attractive face.

Nicholas shook his mane of blond hair and let his piercing blue eyes survey the world around him; a gifted musician, he glowed with enthusiasm and unrestrained love for life and his fellow man. He loved his Russia and knew her faults, yet soared with artistic inspiration and energy as he lovingly hammered out uniquely Russian chords on his anciently battered button accordion— unaware that a few days earlier his father, a staunch communist and rising local party leader, had been summarily executed in a gulag in western Siberia on Stalin's personal order.

He was likewise oblivious that Stalin, increasingly paranoid and suspicious of even his most loyal supporters, had ordered that all of Naumovich's relatives be located: the able-bodied of the group would be placed in a cannon-fodder regiment of the Red Army; the others eliminated as quickly and inexpensively as possible.

As Nicholas shared his Russian soul that humid evening in Brooklyn, he was blissfully unsuspecting of the fate that awaited him upon his freighter's return to Leningrad; he would be apprehended by the *NKVD* and sent north to a Red Army staging area in Soviet Karelia, not far from the USSR's border with Finland.

On their crate and lost in their own world, Toivo and Kerttu were startled when the Finnish freighter's horn suddenly sounded. A crane dropped a cable from the freighter's deck to the dock where the first mate and a seaman hooked it to the freighter's gangway.

The ship's agent put away his passenger manifesto.

Kerttu rose to her feet, but Toivo grabbed her arm and pointed to the distant Statue.

"Look at it—look how grand she is." His voice was cracking somewhat. "And she has so much that I want."

Kerttu cupped his face in her hands. "We need to go," she said, knowing that he didn't want to. Her heart ached as she saw his eyes begin to tear.

He rose to his feet and pointed to the statue. "At her feet it says: Give me your tired, your poor, your huddled masses yearning to breathe free—"

He sounded like a little boy—a boy with a dream that he feared would not become reality.

"That's me! I'm all of that! I'm tired and poor and a huddled mass yearning to breathe free!"

He walked off, stopped a distance away, paced a few times, and then turned to her. "You said yourself I belong here in America—and I *do*, Kerttu!"

The *Sisu*'s first mate and ship's agent heard his voice and looked in their direction.

"Let's go to Texas!" Toivo was energized with sudden enthusiastic, desperate inspiration. "Texas is huge! They'll never find me there! Or California! You can dance in the movies and I'll find a gallery to sell my paintings. We'll get a place and we'll put up the mirror ball and... and... and we'll get a place... and..."

His inspiration began to falter as she turned away from him. "And we'll put up the mirror ball... and... and..."

"And what? Live our lives looking over our shoulders?" she said, not unkindly, turning back to him and taking him in her arms. "I don't want to live like that, my love, and neither do you. Sooner or later Immigration will find you and you'll be deported and then you can never come back. Why can't we be happy on your farm?"

"Because it's not a farm, Kerttu... it's a ... a... a shack in the middle of nowhere! I owe money on it... and there's nothing there! Nothing but forest and fields and lakes and... and nothing!"

"But we'll be together, my love!" She treasured the image she had of his place far out in the Finnish countryside. "And we can work the land. Plant things!"

"But I don't *want* to plant things! I don't *want* to be a farmer!" He had eaten bark bread; he had gone hungry; he had been wet and cold.

"Okay—then we'll just lie around among the wildflowers and watch the clouds go by." All her life she had been surrounded by brick and mortar and asphalt and seen very little sky.

"But I don't want to be over there and lie around among the wildflowers and watch the clouds go by! I want to be here in America where things happen! Who's going to buy my paintings over there in the middle of nowhere?"

"I will," she said and smiled, knowing they had to leave and believing with all her heart that as long as they were together, things would work out.

But Toivo wasn't listening; he remembered so well his parents' anonymity—in life as well as in death. Tears welled in his eyes. "I don't want to waste my life on a farm. I want my life to mean something. I want to *be* Somebody!"

She hugged him; held him tightly. "You *are* Somebody, my love. You are my man."

There was another blast from the *S/S Sisu*.

"We need to go," she said—and saw his shoulders sag.

"Something bad is going to happen," he said. "I know it. I just know it."

Kerttu mustered up some forced enthusiasm. "You know—" She hesitated. She had never uttered a lie in her life, but now she proposed one: "You know, we can tell them we're married. That way we can stay in the same cabin—and then we can wake up together in the morning! We have never done that. Won't that be nice?"

Seeing that he remained disheartened and that her efforts were not working, she knew she had to be firm yet loving. "Let's make the best of this, my love. Give me a hug."

They embraced, picked up their belongings and headed for the Finnish freighter—he quite reluctantly and with heavy steps as if walking to his execution.

Toivo passed close by Nicholas Habarov who was headed for the Soviet freighter with his accordion on his shoulder.

Neither was consciously aware of the other; they were both leaving the exciting and returning to the mundane.

Neither could know that they would meet again—and that it would be a fateful encounter.

A pearl-gray Packard screeched to a halt at the Finnish freighter's gangway. A sign on the Packard's dash said 'Press' in large letters and 'The New York Times' in smaller type.

A man in his thirties got out of the car awkwardly, struggling with useless legs supported by crutches. He was unshaven and dressed in expensively shabby tweed; his intelligent, bloodshot eyes didn't waver as he gave the men at the gangway and the Finnish freighter the once-over.

A news photographer with a large fancy camera slid out from the front seat, found a composition that he liked, and took a flash picture of the crippled man and the Finnish freighter.

"Make sure you get the damn flag in the picture," growled Leo Arnold, the well-dressed, elderly man seated in the back seat of the Packard with a dying cigar in his hand.

The driver of the car opened the rear door.

"Close the damn door! It's my nephew who's leaving, not me," Leo snapped.

The photographer took another picture as the crippled man hobbled toward the freighter's gangway.

"And get him his bags," Leo growled, and then added, "Let him have his damn independence."

The driver yanked two heavy suitcases out of the trunk and hurried to the gangway where the ship's agent greeted the crippled man. "Good to see you again. Mr. Arnold, this is the ship's first mate. And this is Mr. Denny Arnold."

The crippled man narrowed his blood-shot eyes and scrutinized the ship's agent. "Do I know you?"

The ship's agent hesitated—their last meeting had not been a pleasant encounter; Denny Arnold had been far from sober and had exacted a promise from the ship's agent that he wasn't sure he could keep. "Well, we met last week when I delivered your ticket—"

The camera flashed again.

"I said take a couple of pictures! I didn't tell you to do a friggin lay-out!" Leo Arnold yelled to the photographer, annoyed that he couldn't breathe life into his expensive Cuban cigar.

Denny Arnold turned toward the car. "Thanks, Uncle Leo! See you."

"Not if I see you first! Lay off the booze—and try to honor your mother!" Leo reached for his lighter and motioned for the driver to leave—even though the photographer wasn't yet inside the car.

The driver hesitated; Leo impatiently kicked his foot into the back of the driver's seat.

The driver knew his job security was in serious jeopardy if he didn't comply with Leo's order and put the car in motion; the photographer grabbed the door and hung on for dear life as he ran alongside the car and finally gained enough momentum to throw himself in.

He landed on top of his camera and the flash went off.

"That's probably the best picture you took all day." Leo re-lit his cigar and looked back at the Finnish freighter.

At the gangway, Denny balanced awkwardly on his crutches. Reaching for the bags at his feet, he glared at the first mate when he offered him assistance—choosing instead to ascend with difficulty on his own, each hand gripping both a crutch and a suitcase with his useless legs mainly serving as counterweights.

Reijo came down the gangway to give Denny a hand, but Denny shot him a look similar to that he had given the first mate—a look that in no uncertain terms said he didn't want nor would he accept any form of assistance—and added for good measure a heartfelt "Fuck off! Get out of my face!"

Below, at the foot of the gangway, Toivo and Kerttu arrived with their pick and pack. The ship's agent demonstratively reached into his pocket and looked at his watch dangling from a fob. "You took your time. Only got single berths left," he said.

"But... we wanted to be together." Toivo spoke in English for Kerttu's sake; she didn't understand a word of Finnish.

"Should have been here sooner then!" the ship's agent growled.

The ship's first mate was made of kinder stuff. "I'll see what I can do once we are underway."

Toivo hesitated and then asked the question to which he feared he wouldn't like the answer. "How much are the tickets?"

The first mate looked at Toivo with some surprise. "Passage is free. Welcome aboard."

"Oh, thank you." Toivo began to drag his cart up the gangway with Kerttu right behind him.

"You two *are* going back to sign up, aren't you?" There was something about the young couple that caused the first mate to ask the question.

"Uh, no," Toivo responded; he couldn't tell a lie, regardless of the consequences.

"Come back here!" The ship's agent reached for a pad with ticket receipts. "Tickets are $180 each."

"Passage is free if you are going back to sign up," the first mate said, eager to please and help the young man. "You *are* signing up, are you not?"

...sign up... with the Army... I just want to paint and love my Kerttu...

Reality had hit him again: he who wanted only to paint and to dream, to love and to laugh; he who in his heart felt he was American and thought he had forever left his painful childhood in Finland.

"Are you going back to sign up or not?" The first mate was annoyed by the delay; he felt he had helped the young man as much as he could.

"Let's go. We don't have all day." The ship's agent was late for dinner and feared his Irish wife's wrath.

119

"We'll pay for the tickets," Toivo said. "We're just going back over there for a bit," he added, feeling more than a bit awkward.

The ship's agent held out his hand. "That'll be $360 dollars."

Kerttu carefully counted a stack of bills that she handed to Toivo who handed them to the ship's agent.

"And your passports." The ship's agent again held out his hand.

Toivo handed him his passport.

The ship's agent was clearly taken aback when he saw the page that Esa had marred. "Had your visa canceled by your sponsor, did you? And you're *not* going back to join your army. What are you, some kind of communist? A wise guy? Go aboard. Get out of here. Go on. Get." He made an entry in his logbook and gave Toivo back his passport.

Toivo wanted to explain how things had evolved to where they were, but decided against and bounded up the gangway with Kerttu and their belongings.

The ship's agent, who had thought Kerttu was one of the nicest looking young women he had ever seen, thought he had better make sure that she, too, wasn't a communist of sorts. "Hey, lady, come back here. Let's see your passport."

She turned and faced him square on. "I don't have one."

"What?" Toivo was struck with sudden fear. "You don't have a passport?!"

The ship's agent motioned for her. "Come back here, lady. You have to have a passport to get on this ship."

"Why should I need a passport to go back to where I was born? I have my birth certificate. Here!"

She handed her birth certificate to the ship's agent who glanced at it, saw that it was in Finnish and handed it to the ship's first mate. "What do you think?"

The ship's first mate studied the several-decades-old document. "It looks original, but one would think it would have been stamped with some kind of seal…"

Toivo felt faint. "Maybe they didn't have seals back then!"

The ship's agent felt a rumbling in his stomach and looked at his watch. "I've got to get going. A birth certificate doesn't hack it, lady."

"Why not? I was born over there! I was only a year old when we came to America! I don't see why I need a passport to go back to where I was born! Let's go aboard, Toivo, we already paid for our tickets! Let's go!"

She grabbed her belongings and pushed Toivo ahead of her and up the gangway.

"Lady, come back here! You're not going aboard without a passport!" The ship's agent counted out $180 dollars and gave them to Kerttu. "Here's your money back. Get yourself a passport."

"I'm not leaving without her!" said Toivo.

"You're leaving, with or without her. I already entered you in my logbook. Go. Get aboard. Get going!" He saw that Toivo wasn't budging and whistled at the cops standing by the *Komsomolskaya*.

Kerttu held up her birth certificate. "You don't understand—"

"But I do," said the ship's agent with the pride of one who does and the zeal of one who rarely gets to exercise authority of any kind. "I understand you don't have a passport, that his sponsor no longer wants him in this country, and that as this ship's agent and per my agreement with U.S. Immigration, I cannot let him stay in the U.S. of A. In short, he's going on this ship. So, if you want to go with him you'd better get yourself a passport."

"Where do I get one?" Kerttu winced when the *Sisu*'s horn sounded.

"The Finnish Consulate is up that street. Six blocks. You better get going. We cast off in an hour." The first mate signaled to a seaman on the freighter's deck to hoist down the cable for the gangway's retrieval.

Toivo and Kerttu stared at each other.

Kerttu dropped her suitcase. "I'll be right back."

"Wait! I'll go with you!" Toivo took the rucksack off his back.

"Oh, no! You're not going anywhere!" The ship's agent grabbed Toivo—just as the two cops arrived. "Grab him, boys! He doesn't have a visa!"

The two cops tackled Toivo, who struggled mightily to free himself from their grip.

Kerttu tried her best to get Toivo to stop resisting. "Don't fight them, Toivo! I'll be right back!"

"You'd better run!" urged the ship's first mate and pointed Kerttu in the right direction—she took off at a run with the tails of Toivo's overcoat flapping behind her, her shoes clattering against the cobblestones.

Toivo stopped struggling when he could no longer hear her; the cops released him and stood him up.

He caught a glimpse of her as she turned a corner and disappeared out of sight—and was filled with the ominous buzzing; the dreadful premonition of impending disaster he knew so well from previous events in his life was coming true again.

"Get aboard." The two cops demonstratively caressed the handles of their Billy clubs.

Toivo knew the intelligent choice was to comply; he hoisted his rucksack onto his back and dragged his cart up the gangway, leaving Kerttu's suitcase behind on the dock.

The *Komsomolskaya*'s horn sounded and two tugs began to pull the Soviet freighter away from the dock.

As Toivo reached the Finnish freighter's deck, the crewmembers were busy getting the *Sisu* ready for departure.

On the dock below, the ship's agent looked at his watch, and then folded his table.

Toivo felt as if he was going to vomit—until he saw Reijo look at him, grin a victor's grin, raise his hand with the middle finger extended and yell something that was drowned out by the *Sisu*'s horn.

Toivo's world was imploding; his entire being was in turmoil. He knew that what he had feared would happen, now *was* happening; he was reduced to an empty, aching shell so filled with pain and despair that his wildly banging heart was all that propelled his increasingly shallow breath—the rest of him had ceased to function.

He searched the dock for a sign of his Kerttu.

There was none.

. . .

Chapter Eighteen

Toivo stood on the freighter's deck and saw the first mate shove aside Kerttu's suitcase—it was in his way as he was readying the gangway to be hoisted aboard. He then checked his watch, gave a signal to the bridge—and another blast from the *Sisu*'s horn erupted; the signal for the awaiting tugs that the freighter was ready to leave.

Two tugs moved into position, one fore and one aft, to receive the *Sisu*'s towlines—Toivo was sure he was going to throw up; he could almost hear the silent scream that tore through his heart: *Stop! We can't leave without her! She'll be here! I know she will—*

The first mate checked the cable that he had secured to the gangway. He shook hands with the ship's agent, who put away his watch and said something to the two cops. Looking up at Toivo, one of them exaggeratedly patted his revolver while the other smacked his Billy club against his palm—letting the young Finn know what was in store for him on the dock below.

The ship's agent left with his table, chair and logbook. The first mate ascended the gangway that was winched aboard as soon as his foot hit the deck; again, the *Sisu*'s horn sounded.

Toivo wondered where his Kerttu was; his heart pounded so hard he feared it would burst through his chest.

The *Sisu*'s propeller began to churn.

Consul Huhtamäki was working late when he heard the frantic knocks on the consulate's door. He let Kerttu in, heard her plight, looked at her birth certificate, and was about to issue her a temporary passport when he noticed that her birth certificate lacked the official seal of authentication that the developing bureaucracy back home now required.

"A new birth certificate must be issued in the parish where you were born," he said, oblivious of the fury and anguish in the young woman's eyes. "A passport can then be issued in Helsinki and mailed to me here in Brooklyn."

Toivo stood on the *Sisu*'s deck looking for Kerttu, every fiber of his being screaming with the most dreadful apprehension.

Again the *Sisu*'s horn shrieked. Dockworkers released the cables that had kept Toivo in America—but now no longer could.

The gap between the *Sisu* and the dock widened—one meter... then two... then three...

The black water become an abyss that separated him from everything he ever wanted; he thought of jumping in and swimming back to where he belonged until he saw the two policemen still standing there, still ready for whatever might happen. This wasn't the first time they worked ships leaving Brooklyn Harbor with someone aboard who didn't want to leave their land of plenty.

Then Toivo saw her—Kerttu was running as fast as she could. She tripped on the tails of his overcoat and fell; he knew that she had hurt herself, but she got up and continued to run, a little slower now because of pain.

He saw the shock in her face when she realized that the ship had left her behind.

She paused by her suitcase standing forlornly on the dock and desperately searched for him on the departing ship.

He ran along the railing toward the stern—the ship was turning and heading out to sea.

Reaching the fantail, he stood next to the Finnish flag and flailed his arms wildly to get her attention.

She saw him and returned his wave. "Write me," she yelled.

"Where?" he responded, his being churning with the most awful feelings of despair.

"Finnish Consulate—Brooklyn!"

He acknowledged his understanding with yet another wave.

"I'll see you at the farm!" she added, knowing they both needed that reassurance to overcome their awful pain.

The sadness of their separation overwhelmed them—from the moment they met there had not been a day when they had not gazed into each other's eyes and hearts.

The distance between them increased: the tugs were efficient—the *Sisu* was quickly moved away from the dock and into the night.

When the *Sisu* was out of sight, Kerttu picked up her suitcase and walked off blindly, not knowing where to go.

He stayed on the fantail for what seemed like hours, looking back at his disappearing America—and his Kerttu.

Other Finnish-born passengers, including Reijo, stood nearby, filled with mixed emotions; some had more or less successfully dismissed America from their minds and now mumbled without great conviction to no one in particular that it was nice to be going back to Finland.

Reijo muttered that he didn't think America had been as great as everyone had said it was——

. . .

Chapter Nineteen

"No—I will not have him in my cabin!" Reijo slammed his cabin door shut in the face of the first mate who was standing in the passageway with Toivo and his belongings.

...bunk with Toivo... never in hell...

Reijo was not about to bunk with his archenemy. Since he was returning to Finland to rejoin his Home Guard unit, he could have had free passage and a hammock with the other thirty-eight men in the cargo hold returning to Finland to enlist; but he didn't want to spend twelve days that way—his pride wouldn't allow it. He had paid for his passage, even though that had left him with less than a dollar and he would have to walk home from Helsinki.

The first mate had a dilemma; there were only two cabins for paying passengers: the one with the tall angry Finn, and the one with the crippled angry American from *The New York Times*. He knocked on the journalist's cabin door and resolutely opened it, surprising Denny who was placing a dozen or more bottles of gin in the top drawer of the cabin's bureau. Denny glared at the intruders at his door.

"What the hell do you wa..." was all he got out before he was interrupted.

"Mr. Arnold, this passenger *will* be traveling with you." The first mate's voice left no room for discussion.

"I was promised a private cabin! The ship's agent said —"

"Ship's agents say a lot of things, Mr. Denny. This is not the Queen Mary, it's a freighter with very few passenger cabins and—"

"—and you can put him in somewhere else! I'm not sharing my cabin!" Denny started to shut his cabin door, but the first mate held it open.

"*The New York Times* does not own this ship, Mr. Arnold. You *will* share your cabin with this man! Take the top bunk," the first mate ordered Toivo and then stalked off, having had his fill of passengers for the day.

"Hey, come back here!" Denny hobbled on his crutches out from his cabin and into the passageway to stop the first mate—who slammed a hatch shut behind him, ending the discussion once and for all.

As Denny stood in the passageway and collected himself, Toivo placed his rucksack and mirror ball on the cabin's top bunk.

"Whoa, cowboy, I want that bunk!" Denny protested, feeling abused by life and having had enough for the day.

"Well, you can't have it," Toivo said, feeling abused by life and having had enough strife for the day as well. "He told me to take it."

They glared at each other, neither yielding.

The *Sisu* had now reached the rough seas of open water and the ship began to roll. Denny lost his balance and fell onto the small sofa beneath a porthole against which an occasional wave now splashed ever so softly.

Denny grimaced and reached for a bottle of gin in the bureau's top drawer, took a swig—but almost choked as Toivo pulled in his cart from the passageway. "What the hell is that?"

"My work. Paintings. You got a problem with that?"

"What are you so torn up about?" said Denny, who clearly was the more injured of the two.

"Why? Are you writing a book?" Toivo surprised himself with his caustic tone of voice.

Denny took another swig, and then offered Toivo the bottle. "Want some gin? Cures just about anything. Broken hearts. Shattered illusions. Name the problem, gin can handle it. Here, have some."

But Toivo didn't want anything cured just then.

"Tell you what—" Denny reached into his pocket and took out a coin that he expertly flipped in the air; it was a trick coin with heads on both sides. "Want to trust your luck? Heads I get the top bunk, tails you do."

"I don't believe in luck," said Toivo who seldom in life had had any—except when Kerttu was in his arms and then he knew that he had more of it than anyone else in the world.

"Well, let's put it this way then, I want that bunk and I intend to get it." Denny seldom gave up and made no beans about it.

"What about what I want? I hardly ever get what I want and now I want this bunk!" Toivo had the intensity of one who would do anything for a sign that he had some kind of control of his life—any kind of control.

"Why is that goddamn bunk so goddamn important to you?"

"It's no more important to me than it is to you!" yelled Toivo as loud as he could.

In the next cabin, Reijo banged on the bulkhead for quiet. Denny told him where to go—rapping back on the bulkhead with his bottle of gin. He then took another hefty swallow and watched as Toivo hung the mirror ball at the foot of the top bunk and began to unpack his rucksack.

Denny's bottles clinked against each other in the bureau's drawer as the freighter plowed through the angry sea.

. . .

Denny awoke from a drunken stupor, wiped gin and saliva from his chin and commented to no one in particular, "... great... wonderful... excellent... another fabulous day..."

Toivo, who with closed eyes was smelling Kerttu's scarf, blissfully remembering better times, so resented being returned into his sordid new Now that he nearly grabbed Denny, but restrained himself and exploded with: "Don't you 'great wonderful excellent another fabulous day' me! I didn't want to be with you either, but this is the way it is! Get over it! We're stuck with each other so let's make the best of it! An' I feel bad enough without your snide comments—so make a damn effort here, okay?!"

"Okay." Denny let the moment linger, and then again offered Toivo the bottle. "Sure you don't want a drink? No? Okay. You don't mind that I have one, do you? You're not a religious zealot, are you? Good, then life can go on in its customary fashion, which is me getting drunk whenever I can, for which I thank you and the horse you rode in on."

Denny knocked back another swig and sighed with satisfaction; he would soon be back where he knew he'd be safe—Oblivion.

He reached for another bottle, busied himself peeling off the bottle's label with his thumbnail while watching Toivo wipe the dust off mirror ball with the sleeve of his jacket; each totally preoccupied with that to which they were most beholden.

"So, d'you think there's going to be a war?" Denny slurred.

He liked to ask questions; it was the best way he knew to establish an upper hand and keep others at bay.

Toivo looked out the small porthole at the glittering ocean —from behind a cloud, the moon peered at him. "I don't know," he responded, although to some extent he did. He had avoided the details of the conflict between Finland and Russia ever since Esa first brought it up.

When Toivo walked away from his childhood home and the nearby village—seeing Finland disappear in the distance, he had with all his youthful might embraced the goal of becoming an American; he had given his whole being to America!

All his dreams were anchored in America—yet he had a peculiar and unexpected emotional attachment to the land he had left, Finland, the land where he had lost his childhood and so much of his innocence: the land in which he remembered little joy.

He now regretted the scant attention he had given the political details that others had studied and debated, details that might now put the coup de grâce on his Dream of America—a dream that was now but a memory.

"Wars are always about borders," Denny continued, feeling the gin: its comforting anesthesia rushing rampant through his veins, loosening his feelings. "It's always been that way. They move the borders here, there, everywhere. Since the beginning of time, the big boys have had their sandboxes in which their not-so-tin soldiers have fought and bled at their master's whim."

Denny sipped some more gin to further loosen his speech and thoughts. "Borders determine influence and influence determines power. Wars are at times about other things too, but always about borders and power."

In the silence that followed, Toivo could almost taste what Denny had said about power and war; a bitter feeling of helplessness spread from the pit of his stomach and consumed him with a premonition of even more dreadful things to come.

"Do *you* think there will be war?" Toivo could hardly ask the question.

"Oh, yeah." Denny knew he had the young Finn worried. "Too many have talked about it. Finland is a crumb for the big boys, a mere pawn in the game. It'll happen. It's in the cards; it's just a matter of time."

Denny saw anxiety in the face of the young Finn—it was time to move in for the kill.

"So, how do you feel about fighting and maybe dying?"

"Depends what I am fighting for."

"Them," said Denny.

"Them?"

"Yes, them—the people whose faces you see in the news."

Denny could see from the expression on Toivo's face that he now controlled the balance of power in the cabin.

Again he held out the trick coin he had used so many times to bring seemingly unmanageable situations under his control. "Okay, wanna flip the coin about the bunk?"

"I told you I don't believe in luck!" hissed Toivo, who was quite unnerved by what Denny had said about fighting and dying.

Denny lost his temper. "What the hell do you believe in then?"

"This." Toivo held up his middle finger.

"Same to you. You a proctologist or an asshole?"

"You wouldn't understand," said Toivo, who himself didn't; the separation from Kerttu was tearing him apart.

"Try me."

"I'm not feeling very happy and don't want to talk any more!" Toivo snapped off the light, climbed up into the top bunk and lay there cradling his mirror ball, listening to the blows dealt the *Sisu* by increasingly heavy seas as she plowed onward into the Atlantic.

He pulled Kerttu's scarf out from his pocket, held it to his nose and drifted in her scent.

. . .

In a Brooklyn boarding house, Kerttu lay sleepless on her bed in a very small room. The landlady had been unfriendly at first. Times were still bad and she knew well what young women could get up to: she had lost a daughter to the attraction of men, booze, reefer and heroin in the jazz clubs of Lower Manhattan.

But after Kerttu had shown the landlady a month's rent, she had become most helpful; there had not been anything she had not been willing to do for the miserable young woman.

After many hours of tossing and turning, exhausted from weeping and worrying, Kerttu fell into a restless sleep.

. . .

In Chicago, Mr. Biederman lay awake in his bed. It had not been a good day; it was Sayde's *jahrzeit*; sixteen years since his wife passed away and he had had no one to talk to all day. He thought of his Sayde and their years together; wondered if she missed him as he missed her; if she ever looked in on him—if she knew they would soon be together again.

    ... Sayde... shayna Sayde...

    And then he felt that stinging pain again; it began in his chest, went through his left shoulder and into his left arm where it lingered and throbbed until he took the deep breaths that made it go away.

    ... Sayde... meyn shayn royz... Sayde...

. . .

Chapter Twenty

The *Sisu* tossed about like a cork in a rushing creek; swells gripped the ship, raising and lowering it at will. Toivo and the life vest-clad Denny stood with Reijo and others at the *Sisu*'s leeward railing.

All pretended to admire the scenery and be unaffected by the force that shoved the *Sisu* up atop enormous waves as they clung to the rail, feeling as if they were floating in space and their stomachs no longer belonged to them. But before long waves slammed the ship down into the water's bowels, buckling their knees and sending signals of nauseating panic to their brains—even though there wasn't anything left in their stomachs to vomit.

The men simply stood there, spent and humiliated, united by their awe of Nature's might—though she had not even tried all that hard; the swells she delivered were relatively small compared to those that were yet to come.

. . .

At the boarding house in Brooklyn, Kerttu and the landlady were having tea. A needy person, the landlady felt she had regained the daughter she had lost, while Kerttu was grateful for the maternal fussing.

When she learned that Kerttu was awaiting a passport —which she knew could take weeks, if not months—and that the girl she had dreams of dancing on Broadway, she called her son, a stage manager in a cabaret on Manhattan's Lower Broadway.

He arranged an audition for Kerttu the following day.

The landlady had an ulterior motive: she thought Kerttu would make a fine daughter-in-law—much better than any of the floozies her son had brought home.

Aboard the *Sisu*, Denny hobbled away from the leeward railing in an effort to occupy his mind with something other than his nausea. He found the hatch that led from the deck into the engine room and motioned for Toivo; Reijo joined them, uninvited.

They stood on the top landing, looking down into the engine room, astounded by the cacophony of whirring, slamming, banging, and hissing—and the sinewy stoker shoveling coal from an enormous bin into the *Sisu*'s flaming boiler.

Denny took a swig from his ever-present bottle of gin and yelled, "It's like a goddamn inferno down here!"

"Now you've seen it. Let's leave!" Toivo jerked opened the hatch—but was knocked aside by Reijo, who slammed the hatch shut and grabbed Toivo by the shirt.

"Don't you try to ignore me, Rembrandt!" The bout with seasickness had debilitated Reijo; it had shaken his belief in his invincibility. He now wanted his manhood back—how he regained it wasn't important.

"Get your hands off me! Leave me alone!" Toivo wasn't in the mood for a confrontation with Reijo.

"Something bothering you? Can't accept that she deliberately missed the boat?! That she's too good for you?! That you don't deserve her?!" Hoarse from yelling, Reijo began to also wheeze.

"What are you talking about?" Denny's interest was piqued by Reijo's hostility.

"Stay out of this! It doesn't concern you!" Reijo wheezed to Denny and then leaned into Toivo. "Got you pissed off, do I? Want to erase me like you would a drawing, huh? Don't want to admit I was right, do you?"

Reijo held up his left hand with the middle finger extended and continued to taunt Toivo, wheezing: "Here! Let's see if you're a man or a mouse!" He wagged his extended middle finger like a hook in Toivo's face.

Toivo snapped—he, too, felt debilitated from seasickness and strife and needed to recapture what it was like to be Reijo's equal as a man; inflamed with rage, he locked his left middle finger with Reijo's.

The two antagonists began to pull and twist—trying with all their might to straighten or break the other's finger.

Their fingers remained firmly interlocked—neither was willing to relinquish his grip.

The standoff continued. They glared at each other; their fingers ached, each was completely absorbed in the other—nothing else mattered, neither noticing that the *Sisu* now rolled and pitched in increasingly heavier seas that made it difficult for Denny to maintain his balance.

Smug to be holding his own against the much bigger man, Toivo sneered at Reijo.

Frustrated by his failure to subdue his smaller opponent, Reijo slapped Toivo's face hard with his free hand.

Toivo reeled in pain and surprise before slapping Reijo back as hard as he could.

They glared at each other, clamping down even harder on the other's finger, savagely slapping each other's faces —harder and harder!

Entranced by the brutal confrontation, Denny nonetheless flinched at the *crack!* of the slaps.

Reijo groaned with frustration, clamped down on Toivo's finger with all his might—and broke it!

Toivo's breath whooshed out of him in pain and shock; he dropped to his knees, cradling his injured left hand and rocking back and forth as he suppressed a moan.

Reijo smiled, snatched the bottle of gin from Denny and contemptuously waggled it in front of Toivo.

"Want some, Rembrandt?"

Toivo ignored the bottle, rose to his feet—and challenged Reijo with his uninjured right middle finger.

Reijo grinned and handed the gin bottle back to Denny.

Again, the two men interlocked their fingers. They twisted; they strained, but to no avail, again it was a standoff, until——

Toivo erupted with pain and rage and unleashed the savage in him; he clamped down on Reijo's finger with all his might—and snapped it!

Reijo stifled his scream when he saw Toivo's satisfied grin.

Toivo grabbed Denny's bottle, took a swig, and offered it to Reijo.

"Want some, Shostakovich?"

Cupping his injured finger, Reijo refused the drink and spit at Toivo.

"No passengers allowed in here!" an angry voice yelled from below. The boiler stoker was looking up at them, bellowing: "Get out or I'll call the Chief Engineer!"

Reijo opened the hatch with his good hand—the wind-whipped sea roared; a gust of wind caught the hatch, ripped it from Reijo's hand, and slammed it hard against the bulkhead.

Heavy rain and foamy torrents of waves drenched them mercilessly as they stepped out on deck.

The sea was rising and falling—and the *Sisu* was no match for its power; the ship tossed and turned at nature's whim, barely making any headway; at times its single brass propeller whirled high above the sea.

An enormous wave gripped the ship and forced her as high as she had ever been.

Toivo, Reijo, and Denny could feel themselves grow ever heavier, their legs compress under Nature's force; they grabbed the railing and felt triumphantly safe—until Denny lost his balance and fell as a huge wave broke over the ship's bow.

The wave surged aft, engulfing all in its way—including Denny. Although antagonists, Toivo and Reijo were instantly united by concern for their shipmate; they hurled themselves into the foaming cascade and caught Denny with their broken hands as he was being sucked out into the Atlantic, desperately holding on to his crutches.

Both Toivo and Reijo cried out. Their broken fingers were shattered, their pain was enormous—they almost let go, but found the strength to endure, held on with all their might under the wave's enormous tow and somehow managed to pull Denny back on deck.

They propped Denny up, felt the bones in their broken fingers pierce their flesh—and didn't care that Denny shook them off and stalked away on his crutches.

Another wave broke over the *Sisu*'s bow; this time, Toivo and Reijo went their separate ways.

. . .

At the boardinghouse in Brooklyn, Kerttu sat by the open window and wrote the first of many letters to her Toivo.

A pigeon landed on the windowsill, tilted its head cunningly and cooed at her.

Kerttu managed a smile.

The pigeon abruptly flew off, a few downy feathers fluttered in its wake. Kerttu reached for one; it eluded her.

... Toivo...

She wept—as she had already done many times that day.

. . .

139

Chapter Twenty One

The *Sisu* forged ahead. The sea had calmed and night had fallen.

An empty bottle clinked back and forth on the floor of the cabin shared by Toivo and Denny. Toivo sat on the floor, rocking back and forth in pain, trying to fashion a splint on his finger.

"Sure you don't need help?" Denny asked and handed Toivo a half-empty bottle of gin.

Toivo took a swallow, but too much gushed forth; he wiped his chin with an unsteady hand. He was drunk, quite drunk at that, handed the bottle back to Denny and resumed his rocking.

Denny, who was equally drunk, sat on a chair by Toivo's cart, pulling out Toivo's paintings one by one, giving them the once-over. "Hot diggity, hot diggity, hot diggity dog..." he half sang, half said—more to himself than to Toivo.

"What does that mean?" Toivo wasn't really interested, just blearily trying to focus on something other than his aching finger.

"What? Hot diggity, hot diggity, hot diggity dog? Doesn't mean a thing, I just like saying it. Try it sometime, it's like chicken soup, can't hurt. Hot diggity, hot diggity—go on, try it."

Toivo couldn't push the words past his pain.

"Fine, don't try it then. How's your finger?"

"It hurts like hell."

"I bet it does. It looked like a twig to me. Here, have some more lady gin, it's good for you." Denny knew all about anesthesia; he was an expert at what one could find in Morpheus' arms.

He handed Toivo the bottle of gin and Toivo took a long pull; too long, thought Denny who snapped his fingers and motioned for Toivo to hand back the bottle— which Toivo reluctantly did.

Denny took another swig and held up Toivo's painting of a blond girl with halo and wings.

"How old were you when your sister died?"

"Why?" Toivo's finger, head and heart roared with pain.

"Never mind why. That's my job," said Denny. The word 'job' felt strange on the tongue of one who had only recently landed his first employment.

"What is?"

"What is what?"

"What is your job?"

"To ask questions."

"Why?"

"I'm a reporter with *The New York Times*."

"So why are you going to Finland?"

"I said there's going to be a war, didn't I? We went through this already, right here in this cabin. You were here. I saw you!" Denny was irritated. "So, how old were you?"

... how old was I... how old was I when my sister died...

"I don't remember," Toivo answered; he really didn't remember.

Denny studied the painting of the little boy with the priest and the men with poles and two drowned people on the frozen lake. "I can see why you don't believe in God," he said and put the painting back into the cart.

He reached under his bunk, located a bag and dumped its contents next to him.

"Would *you* believe" Toivo asked, sincerely curious. "I mean, if there is a God, why is there so much pain and suffering in this world… what's that?"

Denny was tossing pieces of a revolver back and forth between his hands. "A Smith & Wesson .38 caliber," he said. He peered into the revolver's bore and began to assemble the weapon. "Any idea why you started to paint?"

"No," Toivo answered, truthfully as always. "What's the gun for?"

"Self-protection, kind of like your paintings." Denny had studied man's mind and behavior, though his own mind had provided him with much food for thought as well. "When you paint, you control how things turn out, right? Right?"

"Right." Toivo answered, being both right and wrong.

"So, how are things turning out?" Denny snapped the revolver's cylinder in place.

"Is the gun real?" Once during a Home Guard exercise Toivo had seen one fourteen-year-old boy accidentally shoot another while cleaning a rifle.

"Very." Denny had a vested interest in the revolver he had ordained as the key to his eternal future. "You didn't answer my question. How are things turning out?"

"What things?" Toivo was numb from pain and gin but kept his eye on the revolver.

"Things! Things!!"

"Would you not point that thing at me!"

"Don't change the subject, we're talking here!" Denny was angry. "It matters! Every damn bit matters!!!"

"Why? How?" Toivo asked, keeping a wary eye on the revolver.

"Because we're all connected! We're all one!" Denny glared at Toivo, saw the look in Toivo's face and realized that he was aiming his revolver at him; he lowered the gun and took another swig of gin.

"Is the gun loaded?" Toivo felt more and more apprehensive.

"Not yet. It will be in a minute. Here—" Denny offered Toivo the bottle and began to load the revolver. "What happened to your lady friend back there at the dock?"

"I don't want to talk about it." Toivo remembered her scarf, pulled it out from his pocket and inhaled her scent.

"You don't want to talk about it!" Denny grabbed the bottle from Toivo. "You'd like that, wouldn't you? You'd really like to hide your feelings from me, wouldn't you? Well, let me tell you something. We're stuck with each other for the next nine days and I want to know who you are and what you are made of so we're going to talk about this whether you like it or not!" He took another pull of gin. "What are you so damn afraid of?"

A moment passed before Toivo answered—and then he was barely audible. "That I won't see her again…"

"*Now* we're getting somewhere!" Denny had finished loading the revolver and now spun the cylinder. "Okay, let's talk about God. What's your problem with God?"

"I don't think God likes me," Toivo said with his face buried in Kerttu's scarf, aware that he was both drunk and miserable.

"I know what you mean. Same here." Denny had never felt God's presence, nor had he wanted to.

Something in Denny's voice told Toivo that the balance of power had now shifted in his favor. "What happened to your legs," he asked, surprised by his forwardness.

"Why? Are you writing a book?" Denny had never been much for answering questions; he preferred asking them, but he answered nevertheless. "I jumped off a roof."

"Why?"

"I didn't have a gun." As he answered, Denny could taste the moment when he went off the roof.

"I don't understand," said Toivo, who truly didn't.

Denny paused; then let it flow. "I think I like men."

The admission lingered in the cabin; Denny had never admitted this before, yet his voice was as strong and vibrant as a cathedral organ and as mellow as a note from the finest violin.

He then added caustically: "You got a problem with that?" he asked.

"No, should I?" Toivo had knowingly never met a gay man. "What are you going to do with the gun?"

"I don't know yet," said Denny—and he really didn't. "Would you stop smelling her scarf! It's so... morbid." He absentmindedly spun the revolver's cylinder.

"Everyone wants to live a long life, but no one wants to be old." He repeatedly cocked and released the hammer of the .38; the metallic clicking was eerily loud in the small cabin. "I'm not much for guns, but they provide interesting options."

He turned off the light and studied Toivo silhouetted in the moon-rays that filtered through the cabin's porthole.

...was the artist honest with his response to my disclosure...

Over the engine's steady drone, they could hear the waves rhythmically lap the ship's sides.

"Night is my favorite time of day." Denny's voice had a bittersweet timbre. "I go on all kinds of journeys then... meet all kinds of people... make all kinds of things right... make 'em they way I'd like them to be—"

A ship's bell clanged in the distance.

"I'll let you know if I decide to do something with the gun," Denny said, sighed and added: "Then again, I'd probably screw that up too—".

In the silence that followed, Toivo climbed into his bunk and brought Kerttu's scarf to his face.

They lay in their bunks with their pains and thoughts, listening to the *Sisu* plowing onward.

Denny broke the silence. "I'm glad they put you in my cabin." He was startled that he meant it—then half-sang "Hot diggity, hot diggity, hot diggity dog…" as if to cover having exposed his Innermost Self. He then added: "Good night."

A moment passed; Toivo then responded: "Good night."

The *Sisu* forged onward.

The night became day.

. . .

Chapter Twenty Two

The Jolly Show Cabaret was once a Manhattan vaudeville house—and not a very nice one at that; neither was it a nice cabaret. Kerttu stood backstage in front of a lit mirror and nervously checked her pancake make-up, surrounded by other scantily clad showgirls hastily preparing for the evening's last number.

The letter Kerttu had written Toivo a few hours earlier leaned against the mirror in front of her; she had bubbled with exuberance as she told of auditioning for a dancing part in a show, that she got the job, and that the entrance for the patrons was on 14th Street—but the stage entrance was on Broadway. Broadway! She, who had been in New York only two days, was now dancing on Broadway!

She was going to mail the letter right after the show, but right now she was rushing to get ready for her first professional curtain call.

"Okay, girls, you're on in less than a minute!" Hank, the landlady's son and the cabaret's stage manager, stuck his head into the showgirls' dressing rooms. He lingered, hoping for an eyeful—though after six years of working with showgirls, one would think the novelty of working with nudity would have worn off. The veteran showgirls took their time; others, like Kerttu, dashed out the door toward the stage wings.

A juggler left the stage, cradling nearly a dozen balls, seemingly undisturbed by the catcalls, whistles and stomping feet that were commenting on his performance, urging him never to come back to the stage. The audience was filled with men who had paid for the right to express their opinions; they proceeded to stomp their feet in rhythm with the orchestra's rendition of *Beale Street Blues,* whistled and booed and yelled: "Bring in da goils!"

Standing in the wings, Kerttu was unnerved by the commotion on the other side of the curtain. Hank put a reassuring hand on her shoulder. "Don't sweat it, kid, they're gonna like you. I know they are. Just go out there and give 'em a smile like you would to your father and they'll love you from here to Greenwich Village."

He gave a signal. The orchestra segued into an even sultrier blues, the curtain rose, Kerttu and the other girls dashed out onto the stage—and the audience cheered and rose to their feet. All male, this was what they had come for; the juggler was an unwelcome distraction between the girls' costume changes.

The girls strutted their simple steps. Kerttu had learned the routine in twenty minutes; it had been so simple that she had thought she had misunderstood the instructions. She didn't have any stage fright to speak of, but when she saw the audience—and understood what the men really wanted—she knew she wasn't there because of her dancing skills.

The men motioned to her—she was young and new— they gestured for her to pull down the front of her already skimpy costume; some made lewd motions with their tongues and fingers.

Kerttu tried not to make contact with the men, but Hank grimaced and gestured for her to smile at the audience—and smile big, at that.

She feared for her job and smiled at the leering faces, losing her concentration in the process, getting grossly out of step with the others. She felt terrible and made a self-deprecating face, commenting on her mistake; the audience noticed—she was the freshest face on stage— and roared their approval of her honesty.

She beamed them an honest and good-natured smile, spread her arms in a grand and resplendent gesture, curtsied, and graciously acknowledged their approval.

A couple of the girls bumped Kerttu. One even pinched her. They didn't like to be upstaged; they were busy enticing men they had spotted earlier in the show and then entertained with sultry winks and bumps. These were men who might make their strutting about in ill-fitting costumes worthwhile: there were rents to be paid, things to buy, and families to be taken care of.

The music ended with the falling of the curtain and the cheers from the audience died. The entertainment and fleeting escape from reality were over. It was time to leave—and the journey home would be much drearier than the evening had been with the beer and the skimpily-clad girls; there were wives or girlfriends to be faced, loneliness and poverty to acknowledge.

Kerttu stood stage left in the wing; her first evening as a professional dancer had come to an end. The other girls had dashed off to the dressing rooms; they had more important things to prepare for.

Kerttu eased off her dancing shoes. Her feet hurt; the shoes were as worn as an old woman's skin and provided little support or comfort. She wiped her moist face with the back of her arm and wondered how she would get back to Brooklyn; she only vaguely remembered what Carol had told her about late evening transportation. She was startled when Hank put his arm around her shoulder.

"They loved you, kid," he said and squeezed her as arrogant men are apt to do.

"They did?" Her surprise was genuine.

"You bet. You're wonderful. Go on back out there. They're waiting for you. Go on out there and take another bow."

She doubted him at first, saw that he was serious, and then heard voices calling her name.

"How do they know my name?" she asked, both surprised and suddenly fearful.

"Oh, they're just loud and obnoxious," Hank said, skirting the issue, not about to tell her that he had provided her name to the patrons; he knew she wouldn't approve. "Listen, kid, they're not stupid out there, they know a good thing when they see it. Go back out there. Go on. Go back out there and take a personal bow."

Kerttu fumbled her way through the overlapping red velvet curtains and peered out through the opening —only to come face-to-face with her wildly enthusiastic newfound fans; some patrons who were leaving turned and applauded as well.

A red-faced man in his fifties was loudly summoning her, holding his bulging wallet high above his head, forcefully shoving his way through the crowd toward her, intent on only one thing—bedding the new girl before others did.

She ducked back through the curtain and found Hank there, waiting.

"So, what do you think of Lower Broadway, kid?"

"This is so wonderful," Kerttu beamed, but kept quiet her other opinions. "Thank you so much for hiring me."

"Well, yes, I took a big chance, I can tell you that. But you deserve it, kid; you're great—and beautiful. So, what about dinner tonight?"

The question hung uncomfortable between them for what seemed like an eternity.

"I don't think we should," she said, hoping not to offend him.

"Why not?" He was privately as well as professionally hurt by the rejection. "I'm worth it, kid."

"I'm sure you are."

"I'd love to prove it to you." He lit a Lucky Strike.

"I love someone else." Strength from her love for Toivo surged through her body.

"That's okay," he said. "I can wait. I've got lots of time—"

"I'm glad you understand." She smiled at him and walked away.

He smugly took a deep drag on his cigarette. He wasn't concerned; he knew dancers, had many tricks up his sleeve—and was owed many favors.

. . .

Chapter Twenty Three

Helsinki harbor was shrouded by fog as the *Sisu* docked. The journey had been far too long for the passengers and far too turbulent. The passengers filed off the ship on legs worn weary by the at times angry sea, gratefully stepping onto the granite pier—some demonstratively stomping their feet, happy to be back in their own land.

One young man knelt reverently and placed both his hands on the stone pier and was disappointed when he found it cold and unwelcoming.

Friendships had both flourished and died during the journey. Promises of phone calls, letters, and visits filled the air as the passengers departed; some stepped directly onto an awaiting Finnish Army bus.

Denny hailed a horse-drawn taxi; gasoline rationing was in effect. Toivo helped Denny with his luggage but knew better than to help him get into the taxi.

"Hot diggity—" Toivo said, but he didn't mean it.

They shook hands; the vehicle pulled away. As it turned the corner, Denny waved to Toivo. Reijo felt left out.

A foghorn *whooed* for attention in the distance; the foreboding sound lingered for a few moments.

"Guess you're going my way." Reijo said, hiding his mending hand behind his back.

"No, just heading to where I was born," Toivo said as he slung his rucksack with the attached mirror ball over his shoulders.

The cold, humid air enveloped the mirror ball, causing it to glaze over with a dull patina, suddenly making it seem empty and hollow, reflecting nothing.
Toivo grabbed the handle of his painting cart with his good hand and started walking. The wheels didn't squeak; he had greased the axles during the journey. The mirror ball bobbed on his back; nearby Finnish longshoremen who had never seen one thought it oddly out of place.

The foghorn *whooed* once more.

As they made their way north through Helsinki's residential areas, they passed the sports village built for the athletes of the 1940 Olympic Games—canceled because of the anticipated worldwide hostilities. Buildings made with pride and care stood welcoming and ready; their doors and windows unlocked for the visitors who would not be arriving.

Although Toivo and Reijo walked the same roads, caught rides on the same lorries, and sought shelter under the same buildings, they never talked—yet they knew they should; they knew they had much to talk about, much to say; they had sprung from common roots, and found much to appreciate about each other. Their differences were not deep, but male ego is a most peculiar phenomenon.

. . .

They negotiated an incline somewhere in the heart of their homeland, Toivo laboring with the cart that now seemed heavier than usual. As usual Reijo was walking some distance ahead. Toivo watched the big man's broad back, his powerful yet jaunty stride, the unassailable way he kept his hands on his rucksack's shoulder straps and his elbows tucked to his side; it was as if he made an effort to expose as little as possible of himself to the world—a great shame, thought Toivo, convinced that Reijo had more to offer than he realized.

Toivo was surprised by the sadness he felt when he watched Reijo walk; he remembered the anger he had heard in the endless conversations on the *Sisu* between Reijo and the other young men returning to Finland; they had talked about how mean-spirited and ignorant Russians were, how callous and dirty; how they beat their women.

Toivo wasn't convinced that the Russians were any or all of those things; he didn't personally know any Russians, but he knew Finns who were mean-spirited, ignorant, and callous; he even knew some who beat their women.

. . .

After a few days, when they came to a fork in the road, they took different paths. Reijo—who perhaps had sensed Toivo's thoughts even from a hundred meters ahead—had turned to Toivo, pointed to the northeast bound road, then walked onward onto the northwest one; Toivo sighed and took the road that lead northeast and would keep them apart, at least for the time being.

Despite its lubricant, a wheel on his cart began to squeak, and Toivo remembered Chicago—
    ...Kerttu...
    He tried not to think about her; he tried to ignore the pain in his heart, the throbbing of his broken finger, and the cart's squeaky wheel; he tried to occupy his mind with other matters, but Kerttu and Chicago overwhelmed everything else.

He entered farm country and came upon Finnish Army personnel placing man-sized granite boulders weighing many tons in a long row as far as he could see.

153

"That's a man-sized job," Toivo said to three soldiers his age as they finished putting in place a boulder taller than they. "What's all this for?"

"A tank barrier," hissed a profusely sweating soldier.

"Part of Finland's defense system," volunteered a third as he wiped his brow.

"It's called The Mannerheim Line," said a more talkative soldier, "after Field Marshall Mannerheim."

They thought it odd that Toivo didn't seem to know anything.

"Where are you from," one of them asked suspiciously.

"Chicago," Toivo answered, and then added in his very finest Finnish "Have a nice day."

As he walked on he recalled what he knew about the Field Marshall: he had been born in Finland more than seventy years ago, didn't speak Finnish very well because his family came from the country's minority Swedish-speaking population—but did speak fluent French and German.

He remembered that Mannerheim had been educated in Finland and Russia and had served in the Czar's Imperial Army for 30 years until he returned to his native Finland.

During the past year Esa had once or twice mentioned that Mannerheim was Supreme Commander of the Finnish Armed Forces, was known to be a genuinely good man whose every heartbeat resonated with Finland's needs—and that he deplored communism.

... Esa...

Toivo's heart grew heavy when he thought of Esa; the thought of the dead man led him right back to his despair about Kerttu.

... Kerttu...

He passed a gang of road workers having a break, smelled the aroma of their coffee and was flung back to one night in Chicago when Kerttu and he had been out walking and a street hawker drumming up business had offered them a free cup of coffee.

Surrounded by ugly tenement buildings, they had sat on a banister sipping the brew. Above the roofs in the distance they could see the top of Kaminsky Park and faintly heard the roar of the crowd.

The coffee had been delicious and made them feel quite special; it was a shining moment indeed.

In the midst of that poignant moment, Toivo had become aware of his worn-out shoes and pants, the paint under his nails, his scraggly and unshaven face. He had felt like a loser, terribly insignificant, worse yet—a Nobody.

Walking on that rutted country road in Finland, his recollection of Chicago tarnished further as he recalled that, gripped by insecurity, he had asked Kerttu the one question he always did when his emotional equilibrium was out of kilter: what would she wish for if she could have just about anything?

"Other than you, my love—a view of the ocean."

"From our farmhouse we could see a lake," he had mentioned, for no particular reason other than it happened to have been true.

"That will do," she had said with a smile and then wrapped her arms around him.

As he trekked northward toward rural Finland, the wheel on his cart began to squeak louder still—

Later that day, Toivo came upon an old couple in a meadow, dancing the tango to the music from a Victrola. He sat with his back against a birch and watched the contented couple dancing, swirling and twirling as if their age didn't matter. However, when they caught sight of him watching them, they stopped their cavorting; she stood dead still and he yanked the needle from the record.

Toivo felt bad—he had invaded their privacy and ruined their mood. He bowed apologetically in their direction and continued his journey.

That evening the sky was as clear as he had ever seen it. He was in a sparsely populated area; the road was seldom traveled and all the traffic he had seen was headed in only one direction, probably for the large community he had passed through many hours earlier. He knew it was Saturday night: the young men had water-combed their hair after their weekly sauna; the young women were wearing their carefully mended best clothes.

All the wheels on his cart now squeaked; the sound was eerily out of place in the pristine, moonlit landscape, marred only by the road that stretched like a faint scar as far as he could see. He knew his village lay at the end of the road. He didn't have any food or money; he had spent his last *markka* that morning and decided to walk all night until he arrived.

As if with a renewed sense of purpose, the mirror ball glistened in the moonlight; Toivo could see the slivers of refracted light on the pine trees and the ground around him. The electric motor that made the mirror ball turn grew heavier in his rucksack. Several times he considered taking it out and leaving it by the side of the road—it was that heavy. But he steadfastly walked on, enjoying the magic his mirror ball created wherever he tread.
    ... *Kerttu*...

He remembered how it felt when he was in her arms; remembered them watching the light reflecting off the mirror ball and onto the walls he had thought were theirs

156

forever; he knew now that nothing was forever—and wished for ignorance, not understanding.

He was startled when a bull moose suddenly stepped out onto the road and towered over him. They stared at each other—the beast at the man, resident at intruder.

The mirror ball shimmered. The moose was transfixed by it; he stared at it for a long moment, looked at Toivo as if he forgave him the intrusion and then stepped back into his forest.

As Toivo walked on through the night, he heard strange sounds from the woods and thought he was being watched by hundreds of pairs of eyes.

. . .

Chapter Twenty Four

Dawn was breaking when Toivo reached the crossroads outside his village. As he contemplated whether to take the long way around or the short cut through the village, two farm boys approached on a bicycle. Jussi, Toivo's overweight former classmate steered; on the luggage carrier behind him sat another former classmate, Timo, Jussi's best friend and companion, wearing a black fedora and using two long ski poles to help Jussi propel the bicycle forward.

The two friends pedaled and pushed as hard as they could; they were late for morning chores on their respective farms. The evening before they had been to a dance at the *nuorisoseurantalo*, the community center, where too much vodka and the beer-like brew *kilju* had flowed.

Their heads pounded and they had but one thought: to get home before their fathers woke.

Initially disinterested in the pedestrian with the odd-looking cart and the glittering globe tied to his rucksack, they didn't recognize Toivo until they were alongside him. Their mouths fell open. They lowered their heads, pretending not to be seen, went a way past him; then, having spontaneously decided that his return was too newsworthy an event to be reported by someone else, they turned around and headed back for the village.

As they sped past Toivo, they gave him only a slight, cursory nod.

Toivo knew it was just a matter of time before his and Reijo's return would be the talk of the parish.

The dreaded aching hum spread from the pit of his stomach until it flooded his whole being—he was back home, the place where his dream for a Better Tomorrow was born—and now crushed.

A few hours later, he crested the last hill and could see in the distance his weathered and dilapidated farm.

It was as if he had never left—he felt cold and empty.
    . . . Kerttu...

. . .

Chapter Twenty Five

The three graves were overgrown with weeds and his mother's marker had fallen apart.

By the time he had made a new marker, ripped out the weeds and placed a few pine branches on the graves, the sun was going down.

He rose to his feet, wiped the dirt off his knees and hands and looked at the graves.

... I should say something... what should I tell them... I'm back... I didn't do so well in America... the love of my life, the one who makes my life worthwhile and complete, is not with me but is far, far away...

In the sky, a hawk in full flight took a sparrow.

. . .

After a near-sleepless night, he sat in the kitchen, writing Kerttu a letter. Her scarf was wrapped around his mending hand. The wind whined. He smelled her scarf and immediately regretted it—tears filled his eyes.

A spider approached a fly trapped in a web at the dusty window.

. . .

At that very moment in Brooklyn, Kerttu was asking Consul Huhtamäki about her passport. She was told, just as she had been the day before, that pestering him wouldn't shorten the process—if anything it might lengthen it.

. . .

Being separated from Kerttu sapped Toivo's will; often he forgot what he was doing from one moment to the next. He had started the letter in front of him many times; each time he stopped after he had written *Dear Kerttu*: the word *Dear* had looked too… too trite.

What he felt for her wasn't trite, and he was afraid— afraid that she would never again hold him; afraid that she wouldn't receive a passport; afraid that she would grow tired of him—that she would grow weary of being poor.

As he stared at the mirror ball that he had placed on a chair in a corner of the room that held the echoes of a family that no longer was, he realized that what he had brought from America was an out-of-place memento of a Dream that would not become a reality.

The wind increased; the *whine* of the air being sucked through a crack in the wall became more higher pitched— it would be a cold day. He stuffed some peat in the crack, looked out the window at the whitecaps on the lake—then he heard a car.

It was a new, quiet car that had sneaked into the driveway; the door opened and Pennanen stepped out. He was now a captain in the Finnish Army reserve, as well fed as ever— and wearing a splendid uniform, a pistol in a well-polished holster on his equally well-polished belt.

Tessa sat in the car's backseat, wearing her nicest clothes and looking her very best. She well remembered the night with Toivo and how she had helped smooth his

161

transition from boy to young man—yet she had now decided to remain in the safety of the car.

As Toivo came out from his farmhouse, Pennanen stood stiffly erect.

"So, you're back—your loan is due within a year." He measured his words carefully. "If you can't pay it, I get the title to your farm."

"I know. I'm not an idiot." The matter of the loan had preoccupied Toivo ever since a return to his roots seemed inevitable.

"Ask him what he thought of America." Many times Tessa had wished she had just packed up and gone there and had forever left Pennanen and his damn wealth.

"Tell your wife it was big." Toivo still had the essence of America in his soul.

"Do you have any money for me?" Pennanen wanted to keep to the matter at hand and regretted he had not been more firm with his wife when she asked to accompany him on his visit to the debtor he knew could also be a threat to his marriage.

"No," Toivo said, "not even a single *markka*."

"Tell him I've been studying English," said Tessa. Against her better judgment she sought to be part of the conversation.

"You don't have *any* money for me?" Pennanen was incredulous; he couldn't believe the young man had returned from America, the Land of Plenty—yet not have the wherewithal to pay off the debt on his childhood home, a farm that had little if any value for Pennanen. "You must have brought *something* for me from America?"

"I didn't."

"I see." Pennanen decided to change the subject, but not without letting Toivo know, however obliquely, that he didn't appreciate Toivo responding to Tessa's comment.

162

"So America was big, was it?" He fingered the envelope in his hand, savoring the moment. "Well, you've come back at the right time. I have been advised by the Defense Department that we will be mobilized any day. Here's your notice." He held out the envelope.

Toivo froze: he felt as if an irresistible force had grabbed him and swept him into a tunnel. Pennanen's voice sounded hollow, his words threatening. Toivo was gripped by a dreadful, cold buzz that held him so tightly he had to force himself to breathe.

"I'm not joining. It's enough that I am here. If the Russians come, I will fight for what is mine. I will fight for what is right. I will fight for what I believe in. I will fight the Russians, or the Turks, or you, or whoever. I will fight with a pitchfork, if that is all I have. But I will not go off with you because you say so." He was surprised by his own fervor.

"Now, you listen to me, you—you piss-ant!" The words had slipped out; Pennanen regretted his momentary loss of control and took a deep breath. "You will be notified when the mobilization notice arrives. You will report to me as instructed. You will be ready, willing, and able to leave with us—or I will be back here with a firing squad to have your obstinate ass executed right here in your parents' barnyard, so help me God! Any questions?"

He waited, but none came forth. "Why don't you say something? Where's your sense of loyalty?"

"To what? To you?"

Pennanen wasn't accustomed to defiance; his hand inched toward his pistol.

Toivo was unrelenting. "Why should I be loyal to you? You only gave me the loan on this place so I would go off to America and be out of your way!"

Tessa bit her lip and looked away. She knew how sensitive her husband was about her relationship with Toivo. Over the years he had often asked her about its exact nature; she had always claimed total innocence. She now saw him grip his pistol's handle and heard him say:

"Serving your country is a noble cause!"

"If I knew my country and its cause, I might believe you!" Toivo responded, more than willing to debate the man he knew had only inherited his wealth, not earned it, and for whom he had little respect.

"Tell him about the dance at the community center," Tessa, as always, had her own priorities.

"Shut up, woman!" Pennanen immediately regretted having lost his temper, and added softly, "Be quiet and leave this to us men."

For a long moment no one spoke. The sun dipped below the horizon. The birds fell silent. It was uncomfortably quiet.

Pennanen cleared his throat.

"There's a special dance for our Home Guard unit at the community center since we are leaving."

"I don't feel like dancing," said Toivo who last had danced in his beloved Kerttu's arms.

"Go anyway, you idiot!" Pennanen immediately regretted his words.

"Don't call me an idiot, you idiot!" Toivo took a step closer to Pennanen and clenched his good fist.

"You listen to me, you—" Pennanen stepped back and realized that he was clenching his pistol handle so tightly it had gouged marks on his palm. He took a deep breath, closed the holster, and shook his forefinger at Toivo.

"Don't think you are somebody just because you've been to America!"

"What does that have to do with it? Your wife was born there!"

"Leave her out of this!" Pennanen got red in the face.

"Oh, Captain, the time!" Tessa knew how to end arguments. "I shouldn't interrupt you men, but I have a roast in the oven. It would be such a shame to have it overcook."

A moment passed as Pennanen pulled on his gloves and mulled over the confrontation.

"I can pretend this never happened." Pennanen liked both his roast and covering up unpleasant matters.

"But it *did* happen! It *did* happen!" Toivo's honesty knew no boundaries.

Pennanen stared at Toivo; he didn't understand what it was like to start anew in a land of opportunity where there were no real limitations as to who and what he could become—only to have been brusquely uprooted and replanted in the place where as a seedling he had been deprived of the nutrients needed for a harmonious core, and now be told how, where, and in what shape to grow.

No—Pennanen didn't understand that; he may have dimly sensed it, but he didn't understand it. He wanted to say something, something profound, but he couldn't find the words.

He huffed into his car and drove away.

Tessa surreptitiously mouthed Toivo a kiss from the rear window.

Toivo throbbed with anxiety. The resentment he felt for being yanked from his world of make-believe resurfaced; he loathed this reality, his pain, and his guilt—and hurled a rock at the departing car. "Piss-ant!"

The rock fell far short of its target.

In the sky, a noisy flock of migrating geese bid adieu to the land that soon be gripped by ice and snow.

. . .

Sometime during the night, the promised mobilization notice had been delivered. The weather had turned cold and frost coated the ground. The messenger's footprints were clearly visible. They led to the front door from the wooden gate that Toivo had latched closed across the road behind Pennanen's car.

Signed by Pennanen, the note tersely informed Toivo that their Home Guard unit would leave in six days—the morning after the dance at the community center.

Toivo crushed the notice into a ball and threw it across the room. Hunger prodded him outside and to the field where he foraged for old potatoes and some frost-blackened berries.

He found his father's old fishing pole, some fat earthworms, and quickly pulled a pike from the lake.

As he cooked the pike, he remembered a time when he had been a little boy and had gone fishing with his father. The father had caught all the fish; little Toivo had not even had a bite, even though he had spit on the worm and had put it on the hook so that its head freely wiggled. While his red-and-white bobbin floated undisturbed, his father's was pulled under as soon as he cast his line into the water—or so it seemed to young Toivo. He recalled how his father had let him sit where he had sat and let him use his pole. It didn't matter—he still didn't catch anything. Little Toivo had cried because he thought the fish didn't like him.

Big Toivo smiled bitterly—some things never change.

He realized he needed to bridge the abyss he had created between himself and the world in which he lived; to forego the world he had created with shear artistic will.

He accepted that it would take a few weeks before Kerttu would arrive—perhaps even longer—and when she did, he wanted everyone to see her for the wonderful woman she was.

He would make amends—he wasn't yet sure how, but he vowed that he would.

The old pastor came by later that day. He had walked; he was no longer able to ride a bicycle since he had lost much of his sense of balance.

He had aged far more than the number of years that had gone by; his lips moved even when he wasn't trying to speak; his fingers trembled as he wrote Toivo an almost illegible note on the pad he carried with him ever since he could no longer speak.

While sparse in words, the pastor's message was clear: he asked Toivo to look to the future, not the past; to search his soul for the good, not the bitter; to listen to the bass drum, not only the snare. The old pastor had spent years judging himself while Toivo was away; he knew he had not been a decent surrogate father and offered this message as an apology.

Toivo re-read the note several times. He looked at the pastor, who had nervously removed his hat and now awaited a sign that the best he had to offer had fallen on fertile soil.

"Thank you," Toivo whispered. He grasped the old man's good hand. A slight smile flitted across the pastor's face; he nodded, gently patted Toivo's cheek, and limped off down the driveway, settling his hat back on his head with quivering hands.

When he reached the wooden gate, he turned around. Toivo waved; the old pastor waved back.

"You can leave the gate open." Toivo had begun making amends with the community he had rejected.

He thought about what else he could do; it was then that he remembered the mirror ball—

. . .

Toivo sat at the kitchen table, dusting off the mirror ball. From his rucksack he had brought out the mirror ball's electric motor and made sure there was grease on its rotor. He finished by polishing the mirrors again for good measure—remembering Chicago.
... *Kerttu*...
He saw her radiant smile and the sparkle in her eye...

In anticipation of her arrival, he began to clean and scour the home that would be theirs; he couldn't have her see it the way it was. It took him several days—he was particular in matters concerning Kerttu.

As he cleaned his home, he noticed the care with which his grandfather had built the structure: how each log had been carefully fitted, how the doors had been made from thick planks that were held together with wooden dowels, not a nail or a screw could he find; he now understood why the slamming of doors had not been permitted.

He also marveled that after years of neglect, the home remained sound. He noticed things which he had not seen before: his parents' initials sewn into the linen, his father's carving tools with edges as sharp as ever; the kitchen tablecloth with which his mother had been so careful—for the first time, he really *looked* at it. It must have taken her months of crocheting—not a loop was out of place.

. . .

The day of the dance he woke up feeling uneasy and didn't know why. He polished the mirror ball one more time for extra measure and re-checked the grease on the rotor.

He took a sauna and ate the last of the pheasant he had snared; it was still early when he finished. He felt ever so anxious; to soothe himself he unpacked his paintings from the cart and began to hang them on the walls that had been decorated by his mother—but no matter how or where he placed his paintings, they didn't look right.

While moving a painting from one wall to another, he looked out the window and thought he saw Tessa on the crest of the road. But by the time he came to the window, the figure had disappeared.

He spent many hours arraigning and re-arraigning his paintings. But no matter how he tried and no matter where he hung them, the result was the same: they just didn't fit.

Darkness began to fall—it was time to leave. He wiped the mirror ball one more time, wrapped it in the black cloth that he had found in his mother's dresser, and then attached it to the rucksack—inside which he had already placed the electric motor.

His heart pounded as he started off for the community center.

It was a long walk—but his commitment was immense.

. . .

Chapter Twenty Six

Night had already fallen in Russia; the meeting at the Nearby Dacha, as Stalin's *dacha* near the Kremlin was called, was attended by Stalin, Foreign Minister Molotov, Defense Commissar Voroshilov, *Politbureau and Central Committee* member Khrushchev, and other high-ranking Party officials.

Khrushchev had returned that day from a hunting trip and had provided the wild game they were eating.

"Comrade Khrushchev, this bear you shot, is it Russian?" Stalin poked the meat with his fork.

"That, Comrade Stalin, is a Finnish bear. Not as large as the Russian." Khrushchev knew Stalin; he knew Stalin's whims had killed many men—men much more powerful than he.

"Wandered over our border, did it?" Stalin probed for a crack in Khrushchev's armor.

"Russian bears are too smart to get shot by someone as unskilled as me." Khrushchev understood that Stalin feared him as a political rival.

"And this grouse? Blown across by the wind?" Stalin poked the over-cooked bird on the large serving plate in front of him.

"I think so, Comrade Stalin. Russian grouse are too elusive."

"Let's eat." Stalin reached for the pieces he had selected.

The others at the table helped themselves to the food, but not Foreign Minister Molotov; he wasn't interested in

170

food—he was concerned with communiqués regarding the deteriorating relationship between the Soviet Union and Finland; the carefully worded briefings he had to compose for his political officers at diplomatic posts around the world. He was keenly aware that Stalin had a peculiar, naïve fondness for the Finns; he had to be gentle with him but decided to get the bothersome matter over with.

"Comrade Stalin, there is the matter of our non-aggression pact with Finland and world opinion—" Molotov didn't get any further.

"World opinion!" Stalin exploded. He stood up from the table, picked up the plate with the grouse and threw it through the closed window—the grouse flew once more and landed in the garden; the sound of shattering glass brought the NKVD guards running.

The primitive animal in Stalin had been unleashed—he feared world opinion more than anything. He knew its power and how it affected other world leaders in regards to the ability to compromise, to reach politically expedient agreements, and to look the other way. He clenched his jaw, breathed deeply through widened nostrils, and glared at Molotov, who silently berated himself for accepting the appointment as Foreign Minister of the USSR.

"World opinion is your responsibility, Comrade Molotov," Stalin said, strictly for the record; he knew the matter was ultimately his. "Times have changed, and we must change with them." He regretted losing his temper, revealing his peasant roots to those whose respect and support he sought, yet not needed.

"What will the world think of a bear that can be restrained by a flea?" Stalin added, resentful of Molotov's guarded demeanor.

Khrushchev thought he should mention that a flea could make life miserable for the largest of bears, but the look on Stalin's face didn't permit any poetic maneuvers.

"How long will your army need?" Stalin glared at Voroshilov.

A former bureaucrat who relished his position as Defense Commissar for which he was neither qualified nor suited, Voroshilov knew what Stalin wanted to hear.

"Ten days, Comrade Stalin. Twelve at the most."

Potemkin and Khrushchev were better informed; they studied the ceiling, leaving Voroshilov to fend for himself and his poor judgment. Stalin sensed dissention and slammed his hand on the table.

"Good," he said, circumventing a discussion. "I can see we agree."

He lit one of the extra-long cigarettes he had made especially for him, and began to pace, his hands at the small of his back.

"The Finns will not fight." In Soviet politics a chartered road had to be followed to its end. "They are proletarians. Kuusinen, who maintains excellent contacts in Finland, assures me that if we fire one bullet the Finns will lay down their arms."

Assurance from the expatriate Finn Kuusinen didn't sway the skeptics in the room. They didn't have any respect for the leftist Finn, although he was a member of the *Central Committee* and after Finland's fall would be appointed its president by Stalin. Kuusinen had not set foot in Finland for years and they knew that he, as well as Stalin—or any of them for that matter—more often than not were told only what others thought they wanted to hear.

Gazing at the window, Stalin felt the silence in the room. He whirled around, studied their faces, and saw in all— except for Voroshilov—poorly concealed skepticism. "Did we not twenty years ago extend them the independence they sought?" Stalin asked, expecting an answer.

No one spoke for the longest time; Molotov finally broke the silence. "We did. Lenin thought that keeping an eye on the Finns would be too consuming." Molotov didn't want Stalin to take the strange people to the northwest lightly.

"That was Lenin. Times have changed." Insulating himself from any future reproach, Stalin pointed his cigarette at Khrushchev—whom he knew to be ambitious —and added for the record: "The Finns have had their independence for twenty years. They should be grateful and not fight."

He took another puff on his cigarette, ground it out, and turned to Voroshilov. "You know what to do. Do it."

Thus Stalin concluded the matter of Finnish independence and the non-aggression treaty with Finland he had forced Molotov to sign seven years earlier.

. . .

Chapter Twenty Seven

A few bicycles and motorcycles leaned against the wooden sides of the community center at the village's edge. Plow-horses were tied to a fence. Tango music and smoke escaped through open windows into the cold night, mixing with condensing breaths of horses and young men gathered in small groups. They gossiped and swaggered and swigged vodka and *kilju,* a Finnish brandy that tasted awful but was easy and cheap to get.

A young couple with no other place to go had succumbed to their urgent craving behind a large elm; only they existed—they had blocked out everything else; they were now publicly enjoying each other's bodies.

The young men with their flasks paid the passionate couple scant attention; it would be impolite and besides, most wished they were in the same position.

The couple was approaching their desired destination; she was quite loud, unabashedly enjoying her journey and perhaps also showing off a little.

Aroused by the woman's passion, the young men put their flasks away in their hiding places and sauntered inside the community center in search of similarly passionate mates.

Inside the front door stood Reijo, proudly wearing a spanking new Home Guard uniform, but drunk beyond reason and rapidly losing his savoir-faire while ogling two women adjusting their clothes and makeup in front of a mirror next to the washroom.

Reijo was unaware that the two women were ignoring him; he was in that drunken realm of existence in which thoughts are too fleeting, too tenuous, too disjointed— beyond the point of self-censure and utterly unaware of his befuddlement.

In this haze Reijo tried his masculine magic on the women; he slowly paced back and forth with his hands at the small of his back, copying Humphrey Bogart whom he admired.

He had the air of someone important; someone who felt he deserved to be noticed—but most women weren't attracted to him, even though he was tall and handsome. Perhaps his hard and chiseled features told of his abrasive ways. His drunkenness didn't bother them. They knew about and had much experience with it: they lived boring lives, and there was no recreation available to them that provided a bliss comparable to that of the bottle. Daily life in the countryside was not an exciting existence.

Reijo made it clear that he was available, but the evening was still young for the women: hormonal desperation wouldn't set in until much nearer to closing time; with ample time still to look around for the optimum mate, there was no need yet to commit to a possible loser. Reijo got a smile or two, but no more—no warmth, no real interest, none of the feelings he craved so dearly.

Undaunted, he continued to beam his masculinity at the two women in front of the mirror, one of whom was perspiring profusely. The wood-fired heaters had been going all day and the community center was packed with people; it was too hot for comfort, and she had to refresh her lipstick—it was the cheap, wax-based type from Poland that turned liquid and ran after just a few minutes. Wiping her lips, she studied her face in the mirror and grinned lecherously.

"You know, he's back from America..."

Reijo heard her, straightened up and stood tall.

"I saw him come in through the back door with the custodian Juutilainen…"

"Who are you talking about?"

"Toivo, you know, the one who was with my brother in the Home Guard—the one with the really big you-know-what." She grinned and spread some more red food-colored wax on her lips. "Imagine doing the bump uglies with something like that."

"You got no shame." Her dark-haired friend grinned, sucked on a lump of sugar, carefully removed it from her mouth, wrapped a lock of her forehead hair around it, flicked away the excess sugar, and voila'—a perfect curl!

"I could use a real man," she said, pushing her hair into place. "Aren't too many around these days."

"Aren't too many around you haven't tried, you mean." Her sweaty friend laughed; she knew all the sordid details.

The two women giggled bawdily.

Reijo's face was dark with anger—hearing two women lusting after Toivo wasn't what he needed. He stalked over to Jussi who was picking his teeth while waiting for Timo to finish adjusting his fedora.

"Why are you always wearing that damn hat?" Reijo was more gruff than usual.

"Women like it. Want to borrow it?" Timo offered Reijo his beloved black fedora.

"I don't need a hat to get a woman!" At that point Reijo could have used the contents of an entire hat store.

"Evening, men." Pennanen had entered with Tessa.

"Evening, Captain." Reijo stood stiff.

"Evening, Reijo. You got your uniform. Good. That was quick. Well, you certainly look like a future corporal to me. How's your asthma? You used to have a problem with your breathing."

"I'm fine, captain, as long as I have my paper sack."

"You're sure? That asthma could get you excused from military service."

"I'm fine, Captain... just fine."

"Good." Pennanen helped Tessa take off the very expensive overcoat she had sent for from Stockman's in Helsinki.

"I hear Toivo is up to something," Pennanen said.

"Already?" Jussi always expected the worst from people.

"He was doing something with the caretaker a while ago." Reijo had been sharing a bottle of vodka with someone and had not paid Toivo much attention.

"Let's find out what he is up to." Pennanen took Tessa by the arm and escorted her into the packed main hall where an orchestra consisting of accordion, violin, and *kantele*, the octagon-shaped string instrument found only in Finland, played a tango.

The girls and women sat on benches along the windowed side of the room; the men and boys stood on the other side near the huge ceramic wood-burning stoves. It was still too early: few glanced across at the other sex and those dancing were mostly women dancing with each other.

Toivo and the custodian Juutilainen stood in the corner at the side of the stage. Toivo held the plug end of an electrical cord that led up the wall to the ceiling. An object covered by a black cloth hung from the ceiling and was the focal point for some makeshift spotlights. A string led from the black cloth to Juutilainen, who fingered it nervously.

"Are you sure it will work?" Juutilainen was a careful man.

"It did in America." Toivo knew well its magic.

"I don't know." Juutilainen wasn't comfortable; the item on the ceiling was too unusual. "I still need to think about this. Go get me a coffee."

177

Toivo dropped the electrical cord and headed for the concession stand. As he inched his way through the crowd Tessa appeared by his side.

"I thought of you all the time while you were gone," she whispered.

Toivo felt someone touch his crotch but wasn't sure if someone he was sliding by had done it accidentally or if Tessa had done it on purpose.

"Why? You're married to him." Toivo nodded toward Pennanen and Reijo who were talking with Juutilainen.

"But I don't love him. I love you. I always have. You know that, don't you?"

Someone touched him again—he now knew it was Tessa.

"Please don't do that," he said and then answered her question. "I know you always loved money and I never had any."

"I can make you happy, Toivo. I have learned things."

"I'm sure you have, but I have a girlfriend. She's in America right now, but she'll be here soon."

"But—why did you come back then?" Her lips quivered. "I don't understand... I thought—"

She saw that Pennanen had come in the room and was watching them like a hawk, gave him a smile and a wave, then walked off as if Toivo didn't exist.

"Juutilainen would like a cup of coffee," Toivo said to the woman at the concession counter.

"He has an assistant now, does he?" The woman smiled at Toivo. "Got a fresh pot for ya'."

Toivo got the cup of coffee and headed for Juutilainen who had switched on the spotlights and was nervously fingering the string tied to the object on the ceiling.

When Toivo arrived with his coffee, Juutilainen took a sip, then cleared his throat and announced: "I have something to say. Toivo Karjalainen has a gift for us from America... that's all I had to say." He yanked the string.

The black cloth fell away, revealing the glistening mirror ball; it swayed slightly; the light from the spotlights bounced off it and danced on the walls, ceiling, and upturned faces of the simple Karelian men and women.

They gasped—they had never seen anything like this.

Toivo picked up the electric cord and was about to plug it in when Reijo appeared with darkly flushed face.

"Why did you bring that damn thing here?"

"Why? Because..." He saw the unrestrained hate in Reijo's eyes. "Know what? No matter what I say, you wouldn't hear it anyhow—you just wouldn't understand."

He plugged in the electrical cord and was alarmed by the sparks that erupted from the outlet—but he was more affected by the gasp from the crowd as the mirror ball began turning, gaining momentum, its prismatic light twinkling throughout the room.

The crowd was awestruck.

"Oh, my God!" a woman let escape. "America must be beautiful."

Reijo glared at Toivo.

As the mirror ball spun faster and faster, the motor began to smolder.

Toivo was worried, but he smiled reassuringly.

The mirror ball stopped, the motor spewing sparks and smoke.

Toivo disconnected the cord.

The room was silent.

"You shouldn't have done that." Reijo took a step closer to Toivo.

"Done what?" Toivo was shocked by the electric motor's failure.

"Tried to buy these people—impress them with your Dream of America!" Reijo didn't want to be reminded that he no longer had one.

"I didn't try to buy these people! I just wanted them to feel what I have felt and see what I have seen!"

A smoking piece of the mirror ball's motor fell to the dance floor.

"I don't understand why the mo—" He then noticed that the electric cord in his hand was nearly too hot to hold and understood the reason for the motor's failure. "The electricity must be different!"

"A lot of things are different here," Reijo took another unsteady step closer to Toivo. "You shouldn't have done this. Just because you couldn't make your dream come true didn't give you the right to—to—do this to these people!"

"Do what? What did I do?" Toivo had merely wanted to share something that was meaningful to him with those whose approval he sought.

"What did you do? Look at them!" said Reijo.

Toivo saw the disappointment, the bewilderment, and the resentment in the faces of those around him.

Pennanen gave Reijo a surreptitious nod.

"You were warned about being different, weren't you?" Reijo jabbed his stiff fingers hard into Toivo's sternum. "Apologize to these people. Get on your knees, Rembrandt!" Reijo jabbed Toivo even harder, trying to force his knees to buckle.

"You know all about being on your knees, don't you, Reijo?" Toivo had seen the exchange between Reijo and Pennanen.

Enraged, Reijo punched Toivo in the face with his good hand. Toivo reeled back, his lip split open.

"That's enough!" Pennanen thought it was, but Toivo had other ideas—he leapt on Reijo and began to choke him; it took Jussi, Timo and Pennanen to pull him off.

"Go home, Toivo." Pennanen straightened his tunic, which was rumpled from the scuffle. He leaned close to Toivo and hissed under his breath: "And stay away from my wife."

Toivo glanced at the people whose acceptance he had sought and saw looks that were outright hateful.

As he headed toward the exit the wall of people parted as if he carried an infectious disease.

Once outside, the cold night air enveloped him. He soon began to shiver; he had forgotten his coat at the center. He walked off without it, his lip, hand and heart aching.

The walk home from the village was much longer than it had ever been—and he felt lonelier than ever.
... Kerttu...

He heard no sounds other than his own footsteps on the dirt road and the dreadful humming that permeated his being. The sky was partially overcast; the fleeting moonlight was bleak.
... Kerttu...

When he came to the crest in the road from where he could see his farm in the distance, he noticed how small and desolate it was; a cloud drifted across the moon, he lost sight of the farm.
... Kerttu...

He opened the wooden gate by the overgrown wheat field then closed it, latching it shut behind him. He entered the house, latching that door shut behind him as well. He stood with his back against the planks, the planks that could withstand the pressure of the worst storms, but not the weight of alienation from the community in which he had to live, the community to which he hoped his Kerttu soon would be arriving.
... Kerttu...

He lit the oil lamp, caught sight of his face in the mirror—and spit at his image.

He walked through the house, seeing his paintings on the walls.

... they don't fit here... they don't belong...

He ripped the paintings down and threw them out into the barnyard; shoved them into a pile, and set them on fire.

As the flames consumed the canvas that had held his self-portrait, he thought for an ever so brief moment that he saw an image of Kerttu's face.

... Kerttu... I'm sorry... I've failed you again...

He didn't see Pennanen's car quietly approach with its lights off and stop short of the closed wooden gate.

Pennanen stepped out, took the mirror ball out of the trunk and hurled it with a vengeance toward the fire in the barnyard.

The once glorious mirror ball rolled a ways before veering off into a muddy, weed-filled ditch. There it lay still, reflecting the flames of Toivo's burning paintings.

. . .

Toivo sat in his home, lonely, sad and in turmoil.

Kerttu... I hope you are well... in the morning I leave to become a soldier... please be here when I return...

. . .

Chapter Twenty Eight

The amber footlights at the Jolly Show Cabaret flattered the girls; they provided exactly the low and forgiving glow they needed. It was the last number for the evening; the girls were exhausted, miserable, and more than ready for the final curtain.

It had not been a good night: an out-of-towner with too much trouble in his heart and too much alcohol in his belly had pulled a gun on some customers who made uncomplimentary comments about the girl he thought looked like his daughter. A shot had been fired; miraculously, it injured only a wall. Enraged, the other patrons overpowered the shooter and beat him to death. While it had not been pretty, the crowd had certainly gotten their money's worth that evening.

Soon after the body had been carried away, the show continued, by the patrons' popular demand claimed the cabaret's owner. The girls were again kicking and strutting, shimmying their upper bodies, all the while trying to maintain the beaming smiles required of them, but many no longer had the energy to smile as naturally as they were supposed to. When their backsides were to the audience—which they were much of the time, the patrons knew that for legs one went to Radio City Music Hall. But for breasts and behinds the Jolly Show was the place. The girls would quickly wipe dry the inside of their lips with a finger then push their dry lips up onto their gums where they stuck in place, giving the patrons toothy smiles that from a distance were quite convincing.

Kerttu was exhausted—too exhausted to avoid looking at the awful man in the front row, the one with four missing upper teeth; all evening long he had tried to get her attention by flicking his tongue through the gap.

Six weeks had passed since she began at the Jolly Show; she was adamant that she wouldn't be there much longer. After six weeks on stage, the music was a distant drone; the dancing itself a blur of automatic activity, the lure of Broadway gone.

It was time for her to move on. She had met with Consul Huhtamäki earlier that day; he had as always been friendly and helpful, had told her a joke and she had laughed at all the right places. He had then become somewhat quiet and somber, regretting he lacked news about her passport; the consulate's teletype was reserved for diplomatic activity—and there had been a lot of that lately.

When the music ended, the curtain fell almost on top of Kerttu who was feeling nauseated again. She held onto the curtain with one hand gulping air, concerned that lately she occasionally felt this way. It wasn't like her to be ill. She took a few more deep breaths, watched the other girls run off stage—and suddenly felt a hand grab her ankle, pull her under the curtain, and out into the audience.

She landed on the floor, the awful man astride her, leering at her with his tongue flicking like a serpent's through the gap in his teeth.

"Got you," he said, reaching for her breasts.

"Got *you*," she said, bringing her knee up hard between his legs.

. . .

Chapter Twenty Nine

Pennanen's Home Guard unit had been marching for hours. At daybreak, the thirty-seven young men had proudly slung their newly issued rifles erect and high on their well-rested shoulders; now the rifles dangled every which way. Although some of them now found their rifle annoying—and privately no longer wanted to play soldier—they hoped they were important somehow to Finland's future as they marched toward the border with Pennanen pedaling alongside on a regulation army bicycle.

The men's attitude toward Captain Pennanen was respectful and disciplined but without any trace of inferiority. He was neither patronizing nor familiar; somewhat friendly, yet authoritative—no one did too much heel clicking; they had the air of men who knew they were of value to each other, their families—and their country.

Toivo and some others wore civilian clothes to which they had affixed the blue and white button denoting Finland's Military; others, like Reijo, were dressed in proper uniforms with the Home Guard *Suojeluskunta* 'S' prominent on their sleeves; still others wore civilian attire mixed with military.

They all carried rucksacks; they had been told to bring warm clothes and bedding, that there was no telling how long they would be gone or where they were going—but for certain there wouldn't be any beds to sleep in. Thus, although they all were dressed differently, the blanket rolls attached to their bulging rucksacks established a kind of uniformity. Reijo, who wheezed and gasped for breath, and often breathed into a paper sack, had strapped his violin case atop his rucksack.

Although no one called cadence, they marched toward their destiny in rhythm, their bodies moving as one, their soles making a steady crunching sound on the unpaved country road. Toivo found it somewhat amusing.

...thirty-seven pairs of feet... thirty-seven souls... moving as one giant body... a human centipede...of which I am a segment, a part of sorts...

He placed Kerttu's scarf to his nose; as he inhaled her scent, his mind drifted.

...Kerttu...

Next to Toivo marched Jussi, eating a huge, especially good homemade sandwich; he groaned with delight, smacking his lips between munches. He did this for some time—Jussi loved food, any kind of food—until others in the ranks began to feel hungry.

"Captain, when are we going to eat?" asked one hungry soul, unwilling to weather any more uncertainty.

"When we get there." Pennanen liked being back on active duty and away from the demands of domestic life.

"And when will that be?" asked a man who had blisters the size of eyeballs on his feet.

"Right before we eat." Pennanen liked being in charge, having all the answers, yet doling them out at his own chosen pace.

"I sure need to get something to eat." The hungry soul wasn't easily discouraged.

"It's not good for you to eat while on foot," offered a salivating smithy out loud while contemplating grabbing the remains of Jussi's sandwich.

They all knew that Jussi wasn't stupid, far from it, and that he was an unusual man. He liked to be called 'Big Fat Jussi', but no one would ever do so; he found that greatly annoying—it was his size he wanted to be known for, not his intellect or his deeply seated emotions.

They marched onward, each having an idea of what would be a good meal to have at this particular time. Many mothers must have felt their ears burning for these young men—all fully capable of defending their homeland—were intently daydreaming of home-cooked meals and Mother. For those who survived, it was as a phenomenon that would happen time and time again in the months to come.

"Jussi eats even in the outhouse." Timo offered; he had seen it with his own eyes.

There was good-natured laughter all around.

Jussi decided to get back at Timo.

"Did you see the girl Timo was with last night?" Jussi asked through a mouthful of food. "I've never seen one that ugly before!"

Timo adjusted his black fedora to a rakish angle over his left eyebrow.

"I have never in all my life held a woman who was ugly. I have walked away from some the next morning who didn't look like they did the night before, but the one last night— she was a beauty!"

"You'd bed a dog if it was wearing a skirt!" Jussi said, his mouth still full of food.

"So what's wrong with dedicating your life to making women happy?" Timo had long ago taken that vow.

Pennanen, who thought he had once seen Timo with Tessa in the shed behind the shoemaker's house, didn't like the direction the conversation was taking.

"One would think that one woman would be enough." Pennanen knew he wasn't likely to get another like Tessa.

"Captain, why should I make *one* woman unhappy when I can make so *many* women happy?" Timo had forgotten all about Tessa. "And the one last night, she wasn't only beautiful but happy. I don't think I ever got a woman down as fast as that one."

"Must have kicked the crutches out from under a grandmother!" said Reijo, who knew otherwise. He was still angry that Timo had seduced the pretty woman away from him during the last dance of the night.

There was laughter all around for the others knew, too. They had all been at the community center and had seen Reijo try his desperate best with the woman—yet they had seen him fail. Later, they had seen Timo leave with that same woman draped around him, his fedora firmly planted on her head.

"Speaking of kicked." Timo wanted to change the subject—he knew how sensitive Reijo could be; he had an old scar under his lower lip that attested to it. "Toivo sure must be some kind of an asshole to get kicked out of America!"

"Let's show Toivo how real Finns kick in gear." Pennanen began pedaling faster, forcing his men to a trot.

"Stay in formation!" he ordered and pedaled even faster.

"Jesus, Captain!" Jussi stuffed the rest of his sandwich in his mouth as he doddered along, failing to keep up with the others, farting with just about every other step and bumping into those around him—none of them knew, not even Timo, that Jussi's eyesight was failing.

"Hey Jussi lard-ass, stop that farting and move your big fat butt along." The men behind him were being impeded.

"Speaking of moving—Toivo, how come you emigrated to America in the first place? Weren't we good enough for you?" Jussi asked, hoping to divert attention from himself to the culprit who had brought on the change from march to trot.

"Seems you men aren't moving fast enough for him." Pennanen began pedaling faster yet; his men now had to run to keep up.

"I heard he didn't even want to do his military duty with us." Timo was angry. His fedora was slipping; he removed it and ended up running with it in his hand.

The men struggled to keep pace with Pennanen; their rifles and rucksacks bouncing wildly, making them feel highly undignified. They glared at Toivo, swearing at him under their breath.

The ranks spread out, the weaker falling behind, the stronger outrunning each other. They came around a bend in the road, and there was the rifle range—and the Finnish Army field kitchen. Some of the men sprinted toward it; two even beat Pennanen on his bike.

When the cooks let them know they weren't yet ready for them, Pennanen's men un-shouldered their rucksacks and rifles. Catching their breath and lighting their cigarettes, they lined up along the road to urinate together. When Toivo joined them, they turned their backs, some even demonstratively moved away from him—again he was shunned and stood alone as he emptied his bladder.

A few hours later, the young men watched with stuffed bellies as the field kitchen departed. In an atmosphere of camaraderie they then bedded down for the night; the campfires burned brightly, some men made coffee—it was truly a bonding moment.

Pennanen ordered Toivo to guard the rifle range's outhouse.

Toivo walked off to his post, not surprised by the selection; he knew Pennanen had much in store for him.

Reijo unpacked his violin.

Pennanen placed his blanket roll away from the others and sat in the shadows, sucking his pipe, studying Toivo, who was standing like a statue by the outhouse with a bayonet affixed to his rifle.

At a campfire, Jussi wrapped his blanket around himself.

"This has taken me away from what I do best."

"We just finished eating, Jussi. You ate like a horse."
Timo said, placing his fedora over his face.

Men laughed.

"Go ahead and laugh," said Jussi. "We'll just see how
well you do when it gets colder. Reubens painted people
like me."

"Reubens painted pleasingly plump women, Jussi, not
overweight Finnish farm boys."

More laughter—that subsided when Reijo began
playing a Gershwin tune.

Toivo stood at his post, remembering a time in his studio
when he was working on a painting and Kerttu, naked,
placed a Gershwin record on the Gramophone; the
exquisite music had filled the room, inspiring him at the
canvas. Kerttu gracefully danced in and out amongst the
easels, her movements reflecting the romantic melody.

"Ever wonder why there aren't any famous women
composers?" Kerttu had thought aloud, not expecting an
answer.

"Maybe women can't compose music," he had said,
without thinking.

"There's nothing women cannot do!" She had stopped
dancing, put on a shirt—her own—then turned off the
Gramophone.

"I didn't mean it the way it sounded." He understood
that he was in trouble; still he faced her.

"What did you mean then?"

"Nothing, really. It was a dumb thing to say—I wasn't
thinking."

"You need to watch out for that."

"Yes, you're right. Look, we both know that women
are more capable than men. You know how I feel about
you. You know I like everything you do."

"Even when I burn the beans?" She was quite serious.

"No, not when you burn the beans." He, too, had then
become serious. "I think the world of you."

They had just had their first confrontation—

"Things are not always what we think they are." She held out her clenched hands to him.

"Which hand? Concentrate. Which hand has the key to my heart?"

He pointed to her left hand. She opened it—it was empty. She then opened her right hand, revealing a gleaming golden key.

"Okay. There it is. Now you know there is one. Concentrate. Important things are at stake here."

She closed her right hand, then crossed her arms.

"Now," she asked. "Which hand?"

He pointed to her right hand. She opened it—it was empty! She then opened her left hand—and there was the key!

"How did you do that?" He had been completely bewildered.

"How would I know?" She had been quite sarcastic. "I'm just a woman and you know the limitations of that."

He stood by the outhouse with his memories, his feelings, and his thoughts, listening to his comrades snoring and grunting, thinking they were beasts, not men.

...Kerttu...

Several times she had claimed that men were beasts, noting that even Toivo was insensitive—that once past his initial lust and his inherent, primeval need, he could be less than endearing and more occupied with himself than with her. The fur would fly during those conversations.

They had finally agreed that sexuality was complicated; they had then slept for a while in each other's arms before she had to go home to Esa.

All of that had seemed to have happened to someone else; someone younger, someone with much less pain in his heart.

191

A star fell, streaking across the brilliantly clear sky; there wasn't a cloud to be seen, and no moon. It was so clear that the stars didn't merely shimmer—they sparkled.

... the mirror ball... the dance... what a fiasco...

His comrades' snoring and grunting reminded him of how joyless his life had become around them.

... is it them... or is it me... could I be that different...

Several times he had discussed his feelings and thoughts about life with Mr. Biederman. A kind and introspective man and clearly Toivo's friend, Biederman had voiced his concerns. He suggested that Toivo be more economical with his feelings and not let every matter affect him so deeply or let his emotions chart his course. His life would be much less stressful if he would think first, *then* act; feelings were wonderful, albeit best in smaller portions. Careful thoughts were of equal value.

Toivo had claimed that thoughts and feelings were the same. Mr. Biederman had shown him a hundred dollar bill, told him to study it hard and ask himself if he could use it. Toivo hadn't eaten for a day or two, Kerttu had a birthday the following day, and he owed his friend Biederman five month's rent. His friend then told him he could have the hundred dollars: all he had to do was not to think about a white polar bear—Toivo instantly thought about just that. It was his first real lesson about mind over matter.

Thus on a rainy day in Chicago, he learned from an elderly man for whom there was no longer a Tomorrow, that Man cannot control his mind; that it is influenced by all that it encounters. From that day, he knew that what Man *feels*—not what he *thinks*—is his unique personal treasure; from that day, he began to protect his feelings with all his might, aware that they were his truest Self.

Someone left the outhouse; the slamming of the door told him that his mind had wandered. He looked up at the sky, was awed by its immensity and felt his own relative insignificance.

... why am I here... what is my purpose...

There answers were not readily available.

While he listened to his comrades passing the night he reflected on his life, realizing that throughout much of it he had been fighting for the survival of a Self he didn't know.

. . .

Another heavenly body fell, a long shimmering tail marking its progress toward extinction.

... Kerttu... can we be together yet not lose our own Selves...

When they loved, she behaved as if he was the conqueror. But when his body and Self were absorbed by hers, he entered a realm in which he was the conquered party—totally vulnerable, though ever so safe. In that state, in that blissful, Heavenly Existence, neither one appeared to dominate—yet somehow they both did; for without the presence of each other, they would plummet to Earth like wingless birds.

That night, with the stars for company, he relived his life with Kerttu. It was a magnificent night—he relearned who he was and decided the others would learn as well.

. . .

Chapter Thirty

When Pennanen approached at dawn, Toivo was alert but understandably tired after his all-night vigil.

"See any Russian spies?" Pennanen asked, smugly superior.

"Can't say I have. Only a Finnish asshole," Toivo replied.

Pennanen stared at Toivo, whose eyes didn't waver.

A crow cawed in the distance.

Pennanen's stomach grumbled and groaned; he entered the outhouse and shut the door.

"Go away," he said, with less than his usual authority. "You're dismissed for now."

Toivo joined the others who were enjoying the food that mothers, wives, or girlfriends had placed in their rucksacks with loving concern—defending one's country was one thing; the uncertainty of what that would bring was another.

Toivo had not brought anything to eat for there was nothing at home *to* bring. The previous day, long before daybreak, he had closed up the farm and set off to join the others at the detached building on Pennanen's estate that served as the local Home Guard Headquarters. Before leaving he had licked clean the leftover pheasant bones and thrown them to the old badger he had seen peeking out from behind the barn.

The night had been dark when he closed the wooden gate. He didn't notice his precious mirror ball that lay tossed like unwanted trash in the ditch; the mirror facets he had polished with such care now dull and spattered with mud.

The mirror ball would remain unnoticed in the ditch for many months, taking on the patina that time's passage places on man-made objects left unprotected from nature.

Toivo watched the others eat. He wasn't hungry—he had eaten well the evening before. The meal served them by the Finnish Army had been tasty and filling; if that meal was an indication of what was to come, he might endure till Kerttu's arrival.

... Kerttu...

He smiled as he thought of her, reached for her scarf and brought it to his nose. While the others were eating, he reveled in his beloved's scent, rekindling feelings more nourishing than the finest of breakfasts—until Kerttu's mild scent was overpowered by the strong smell of freshly brewed coffee.

Men had stoked the campfires; they were now brewing coffee in personal pots that were licked by the flames. Some of the men were forest workers, some were miners—cooking over an open flame was second nature to them.

Toivo was alarmed that the smell of coffee could overpower her scent; his heart began to race when he remembered as if in a daze the cup of coffee they had shared another lifetime ago in Chicago.

... you, and a view of the ocean...

A crow landed in a nearby tree and cawed repeatedly as if it knew the soldiers below didn't have any ammunition.

Some of the men aimed their empty rifles at the crow, which cawed again, then quieted.

The sun broke above the horizon.

A lorry arrived; range personnel unloaded ammunition boxes and paper targets. The targets were the standard ones with circles that increased in value toward the bullseye in the center—but a creative soul at the printers had superimposed over the circles one of three caricatures: Stalin, Soviet Foreign Minister Molotov, or Soviet Defense Commissar Voroshilov.

Pennanen's men lined up for their ammunition; a grizzled sergeant looked them over.

"Two rounds per man. The Army is short of ammunition."

Reverently the men each took a pair of cartridges that shone in the morning sun, touching their smooth patina, feeling the tips; they held them to their noses, smelling the thin layer of grease that made them easier to load and—once fired—easier to eject.

They put the cartridges in their pockets, feeling their power, knowing their rights of passage were that much nearer.

The rifle practice was soon over—it does not take young men long to fire two bullets. The crow kept cawing in its tree; some men glared at it as if the annoyingly brazen bird personally challenged them. Pennanen borrowed Reijo's rifle and fired at the bird; it fell to the ground, feathers flew every which way.

As he gloated over his fine shot, Pennanen felt his stomach acting up again. Since his marriage to Tessa, it had become somewhat delicate, and he had not been feeling well since leaving Tessa at home yesterday morning—some vigorous men had been left behind at the village. One man in particular concerned him: his sergeant, Putki Pekka, whose physique was truly outstanding. A few days earlier, Tessa had innocently asked if Putki Pekka too was mobilized.

"Yes, my dear," he had replied. "But he has a bad knee."

"Too bad," his wife had said, with amazing concern. "I imagine you need every man you can get."

As Pennanen handed back the rifle to Reijo, his stomach knotted again; he could feel that there wasn't a moment to lose, and headed for the outhouse at a half run.

"Pack your gear and get ready to leave," he commanded as he ran, unbuttoning his tunic.

At the foot of the tree, the crow wasn't quite dead; it flopped around on the ground, struggling to get back up to a familiar spot.

Jussi stomped on it.

Then it was still.

. . .

Hours later, as Toivo and his unit sat in the freight car shoulder-to-shoulder with reservists from the city—which wasn't much of a city although larger than their village—he was still bothered by the death of the crow.

He was also bothered by the stranger from the city who slept on his shoulder and stank of beer and cigarettes.

. . .

Chapter Thirty One

Three hundred kilometers to the east, an armored train sped toward Soviet Karelia carrying Defense Commissar Voroshilov along with a cargo of Undesirables. After a rash of Soviet aircraft crashes, Stalin had forbidden commissars, *Central Committee*, *Politbureau*, or other high-ranking Soviet leaders from traveling by air.

Nicholas Habarov stood with one hundred and ninety-seven other men in a railcar that one week earlier had transported pigs stolen by the Red Army from farms in Poland. 'Undesirables' Stalin called them; history and the Red Army referred to them as 'conscripts'. Whatever their appellation, these men were packed so tightly that they could only lift an arm with the greatest of difficulty. While the night air outside was cool, the air inside was intolerably hot—and the stench from the bodies was unbearable.

In Leningrad, the day before when they had been loaded into the railcar, they had been shown a corner with buckets that would serve as latrines. For many hours after their departure, the men had shuffled around in the car in unison to allow everyone access to the buckets—it had been a nice show of camaraderie.

During the night, however, some of the Undesirables had begun to resist the communal shuffle—they were tired, depressed and hungry, and a seething anger seeped up from deep within. Many were Jewish lawyers, doctors, or intellectuals; others were known homosexuals or published poets or writers; there were artists, teachers, or actors; still more were convicts—some were combinations of these.

Although they were from different social strata, they shared a common denominator: they were perceived as threats to Stalin's power, to the social and political structure he was creating.

Unlike Lenin, who was cruel only to his enemies, Stalin was cruel to all and he lacked the emotional capacity of love for fellow man—an ingredient necessary to implement the communist utopia envisioned by Trotsky and other fathers of the Revolution. Stalin had a great appetite for warfare and terror. These men in the railcar were crumbs on his plate.

Although they couldn't control where they were going, they *could* control *what* they were doing. Tired of the shuffle, they simply stopped moving—impeding the communal access to the buckets. Those who tried to force their way through the wall of people were rudely rebuffed: their feet were stomped on; they were crudely pinched or had pencils or knives pressed into them.

Nicholas Habarov became aware that many around him relieved themselves where they stood—but he was a proud man and would resist the urge as long as he could; perhaps they would soon arrive at their destination.

Nicholas thought it best to keep his mind occupied, trying in vain to picture his wife and children happily gathered around him. His woolen Red Army shirt, jacket, and pants were strange to the touch; his knitted cap adorned with the red star and his boots made from a coarse felt composite were too small and distracted him.

... what did I do to deserve this...

Hours after his ship docked in Leningrad's harbor, he had disembarked with his belongings looking forward to getting home. As he walked away from the ship, a car had pulled up. Unknown men had leapt out and arrested him.

He was placed in the car's trunk, which was nearly full of new tires. Three times he had heard a whooshing sound—and after each whoosh the car had stopped while the driver changed tires. Although the car was new and had just arrived from the factory, Nicholas had heard the man complain that nothing worked properly, not even the windshield wipers.

The driver had also grumbled about the quality of the tires made by the Yaroslavl factory, the best tire manufacturing plant in the Soviet Union; the tire walls kept blowing out, even though the equipment that made them had been purchased from America.

What the driver didn't know was that in an effort to increase production and lower costs, the Yaroslavl manager had reduced by half the amount of wire cords that went into the tires—thereby weakening them. He also didn't know that similar shortsighted efforts were lessening the quality of nearly everything produced in the Soviet Union—ultimately weakening the giant nation. All he did know was that every so many miles, a brand new tire would blow.

At the *NKVD* station, *politruks* had torn apart his accordion and other belongings; looking for he didn't know what, smashing the gifts he was bringing his wife and children.

... my family... my fine wife and children...

He worried about them; he didn't know that they had been sent to a labor camp in Siberia.

The *politruks* had asked him many strange questions. They didn't believe him when he told them that his father had said nothing about being the Bolshevik who executed the Czar, or that he, Nicholas Habarov, had himself written the patriotic song that he sang for his appreciative shipmates while they drifted in the North Atlantic during the *Komsomolskaya*'s boiler repair—the song that praised the struggle of the masses against injustice and tyranny.

... I love Mother Russia... how can I be her enemy...

Finally, after seventeen hours of despair and dejection, Nicholas Habarov lost his self-esteem—joining the others who urinated and defecated where they stood.

. . .

Chapter Thirty Two

Denny thought the handsome Italian across the table from him smelled just right, but he knew the man was unapproachable.

"That's not a very nice thing to say about your wife, is it, Giancarlo?" Denny asked, looking past him for the attractive waiter he liked to look at but who he never could get to serve him.

They were having dinner in a restaurant near Helsinki's Hotel Kämp—all foreign journalists in Finland had been moved there by order of the Finnish Foreign Ministry. The political situation was alarming: the negotiations with the Soviets were over—Stalin had placed unacceptable ultimatums on the table.

"It's the truth and that's another difference between us Italians and you Americans," said Giancarlo Ferrando, the northern European correspondent for the Italian daily newspaper *Il Messagiero*. "We always tell the truth as we feel it at the moment." He grimaced and added an extravagant hand gesture. "However we can change our minds; that's Italian, you know."

"Yes, I know." Denny's nanny had been one—he remembered her well. When he was nine years old, she had kissed him on the mouth. When he responded by kissing her back, she had shrieked and ripped out chunks of her hair as she ran from his room.

"Must be difficult," Denny added—and meant it.

"It is incredible." Giancarlo's family name meant 'man of steel'; he, however, was more a man of pasta. "We Italians have this—how you say—emozione."

"Emotion", said Denny, who when he was sober was expert at controlling his.

"Bravo. Grazie. Emotion, I will remember. Sometime I stand next to my wife and love her; sometime I stand next to her and want to kill her. It is incredible what she do to me. You think maybe she is Serbian?"

"I don't know, Giancarlo." Denny was practicing his social skills. "Could be. But there's a song in what you told me that's for sure."

"You really think so?" Giancarlo hung on every word uttered by the crippled journalist from *The New York Times*.

"I do." Denny so far liked being the crippled journalist for *The New York Times* in Helsinki—everyone paid attention to him; everyone knew of the paper and that gave Denny great personal credibility. Everyone sought his advice, even accomplished politicians. It was as if he, personally, on any subject, could influence public opinion in America—for many, the center of the universe.

His crutches gave Denny additional power. When he stood, everyone else did; when he sat, so did they. Two days earlier he had interviewed an ambassador of the Soviet Union; there had not been anything the Russian diplomat wouldn't have done for him.

Denny enjoyed his life in Helsinki.

He also enjoyed his relationship with Giancarlo, who was very sweet, although not very bright. Giancarlo needed to have things explained, which gave Denny the opportunity to develop his non-existent journalistic skills —helping to shorten the time it took him to compose the articles he wired daily to his editor Uncle Leo. If Giancarlo understood him, so too would Uncle Leo.

"What did the Finns sing today when their minister returned from Moscow?" asked Giancarlo, for whom music was like Braille to the sighted. "It sounded serious."

"It was serious. It was a Lutheran psalm."

"Why were they singing a psalm?" Giancarlo had not been interested in the gathering of thousands at the Helsinki railroad station, but he clearly was interested in the salmon soup being served by the waiter.

"The Finns and Stalin have stopped negotiating." Earlier that day Denny had explained to Giancarlo the impossible situation the Finns were in. If they yielded to Stalin's demands, the Finns would lose their sovereignty; and once the Soviets were back on Finnish soil, they wouldn't readily leave. The alternative—asking for help from the Allies—would compromise the neutrality of their Scandinavian neighbors, placing them in the jeopardy they were seeking to avoid.

The Finns could only hope that Stalin wouldn't wage war against them that winter. They told themselves only a fool would attack them in the cold and snow—and that the war expected to break out any day between Germany and the Allies would sufficiently divert Stalin's attention.

"It's now a waiting game," said Denny, looking around for the attractive waiter.

"The soup is getting cold. Let's dig in," said Giancarlo, who liked American slang and whose priorities were always in order.

. . .

Chapter Thirty Three

"Did they ask me if I like to dig?" Jussi placed his foot on the shovel, bore down on it with all his might, hefted a load of fertile glacial soil, and threw it behind him. "Oh no, they didn't! But *children* like to dig! Did they ask *them* to come here and dig? Oh no, they didn't! They asked *me*, who gets dandruff from digging! I'm allergic to shovels! Look! I'm even perspiring!!"

"Women perspire," growled Reijo. "You sweat."

"Like a Turk," added Timo.

They were digging trenches outside the tree line of the wide swath that had been cut through the forest at the time Finland was granted her independence; the swath that now marked Finland's border with the USSR.

In the middle of the many hundred miles-long clearing, black-and-white border markers stood in a row like mute sentries from horizon to horizon. One of the border markers had tilted, standing at an almost jaunty angle.

Armed border guards on both sides studied each other through binoculars.

"Maybe it's from digging that my eyes are going bad." Jussi wasn't finished complaining.

"Your eyes are going bad because you have high sugar." Timo was concerned about his best friend. "Not because you have been digging for a couple of days."

"Look at the city boys behind us. Don't even know how to use a shovel." Jussi was unrelenting with his complaints.

They paused, wiped their brows on their sleeves, and looked at the reservists from the city digging trenches and fortifications farther into the forest.

"You're right, they can't dig. Maybe that's why they've got the rear." Timo was envious and slightly uneasy from a premonition he had.

"I don't think so." The postmistress' son attacked the ground even harder. "City boys get the rear, country boys the front. It's always been that way."

"How do you know?" Timo asked. He was always curious.

"I just know." The postmistress' son said no more; no one was supposed to know that his mother had intercepted —and he had read—some of Lenin's writings.

Toivo wasn't listening to the others; he was deep in thought, kneading some soil between his fingers, looking out over the border they had been told was mined.

"What if Stalin's boys don't come?" Jussi asked, as frustrated as ever. "Why then do all this damn digging?"

"It's good practice." Reijo liked that his muscles were bulging. "There might be a great future in trench-digging." He spit on his blistered palms and continued working.

Nearby, others felled perfectly good trees that were several hundred years old: the clanking of the axes mixed with the whooshing of the saws, the thuds of the shovels, and the grunts and groans of the men exerting themselves so that they might be safe.

Soil was moved from one place to another. Trees fell. The men dripped with sweat.

In this area of the border, there were no barb-wire entanglements or obstacles to impede an enemy; there were only mines—and they were on the Soviet side. The Red Army officers who had supervised the placement of the mines had recently been executed by order of Stalin, along with thousands of other officers, and their successors had not been able to locate maps of the minefields.

An assault into Finland from here would be hazardous, but one had been ordered nevertheless; contingency plans had been made with the help of *politruks*—political workers lacking any military experience.

A Finnish border guard stood at the edge of the forest with his binoculars, studying the wide barren slash of land that for most people was a mere line on a map. On the opposing side stood a group of armed Soviet border guards and *politruks*. A Red Army staff car pulled up some distance away; the driver waved a small red flag; the Russian border guards and *politruks* scurried off into the forest.

The Finnish border guard reported what he had seen to a runner, who dashed off to the nearby communications post from which a telephone line had been strung to Border Guard Headquarters. This report of unusual activity was soon placed on Mannerheim's desk with similar reports from all along the border.

. . .

In the Soviet forest within sight of the tilted border marker, nearly a thousand Undesirable conscripts reached the end of their journey. They shuffled to a halt, surrounded by well-armed *politruks*. Some were senior in rank; others were newly recruited from the Party.

The Undesirables were weary, hungry, and nervous. Some kilometers back they had passed several thousand regular Red Army troops and had been amazed by the number of tanks, field kitchens, supply tents, and the field hospital.

One of them, a teacher from a nearby village, raised his hand; he wanted to ask a question. He was ignored for some time before a senior *politruk* finally relented.

"What do you need, comrade conscript?"

"What about the minefields?"

"What minefields, comrade?"

"The minefields just past that tree-line." The teacher knew; he had helped install them.

"What is your name?" The senior *politruk* approached the teacher.

"Fyodor, Ivan—" The teacher got no further.

"Ivan Fyodorvich, let's take a walk and talk about this matter." The senior politruk placed his arm around the teacher's shoulder and steered him off into the forest.

They looked like the best of friends as they disappeared among the trees.

A moment passed.

A shot rang out.

The senior *politruk* reappeared, crimson spots dotting his otherwise impeccable ankle-length coat.

There was grumbling among the Undesirables. The senior *politruk* looked them over. Other *politruks* stepped closer, their weapons at the ready, causing a hush to fall over the men.

"Comrades, let me make this point clear. There are some mines beyond the trees, but you have little to fear. If your name or number is not on it, the mine cannot harm you. They were placed there by The Imperial Army a long time ago."

. . .

Chapter Thirty Four

Backstage at the Jolly Show Cabaret, the girls were rushing to get out of their costumes. It had been a long day and night—and it would be early morning before they got home. The girls unabashedly changed clothes in front of Hank as he paced with cigar in hand in front of a changing screen.

"… St. Louis… New Orleans… Los Angeles—Hollywood, kid! Three months on the road. With billing!" Hank had been an agent and knew how to sell.

Behind the screen was Kerttu, examining the profile of her stomach in a mirror. None of the other girls ever bothered with the screen—nudity served them well; their bodies earned them a comfortable living.

"I hope you understand what an opportunity this is, kid." Hank ignored the eye-rolling of the other show girls.

Out of Hank's view, Kerttu touched her stomach with both hands. "I'm so happy to have you," she whispered. "So very, very happy."

"This is your shot at stardom, kid!" Hank had been working on Kerttu for some weeks; that day he had decided it was time to move in for the kill. "Give me the word and the job is yours!"

Kerttu felt nauseated and reached for the pail she always had near. She retched.

"You feeling sick again? Maybe you should see that doctor I told you about." Hank dragged on his cigar.

There was a knock on the door and the assistant stage manager stuck in his head.

"Good night, everyone! And tell Kerttu I just heard on the radio that Russia attacked Finland an hour ago."

Kerttu vomited.

Hank puffed on his cigar, calmly eyeing the smoke rings he blew rising toward the ceiling.

. . .

Chapter Thirty Five

Toivo and the others in the half-finished trench recoiled from the barrage of artillery grenades exploding around them—battering them around mercilessly in a cyclone of unrelenting, powerful blasts. The shelling was beyond awe-inspiring, beyond imaginable hell—this was an Apocalypse with the Soviet Union unleashing all its might to eradicate an obstinate neighbor.

Pennanen's men winced as soil and shrapnel, splintered trees and boulders, body parts and unidentified matter showered down on them. They had no option but to lie there—there was no safe place to go. Some curled up in fetal positions, their memory of the womb instinctively reactivated in an attempt to regain pre-natal safety—some whimpered; others refused to, clamping their jaws shut even tighter.

A green rocket shot up into the air and glowed brightly against the morning sky. Although the Soviet Union had not formally declared war, The Finnish-Russian Winter War had begun. It was November 30, 1939.

More green rockets shot up into the sky that was darkening with grenades; more artillery and mortar grenades landed among Pennanen's Home Guard Unit, which along with two others had been positioned to provide support for the border guards in the trenches closest to the border.

Some of the men no longer winced—they were already hardened veterans after a few minutes of shelling. Survival instinct propelled some to look beyond the present moment; they reached deep inside and discovered qualities they didn't know they possessed.

"Look at those rockets!" Timo hung on with all his might to his black fedora that contorted from the blasts of explosions. "Must be Stalin's birthday!"

They recoiled from the shelling, braved the shrapnel and flying debris, peered over the bank of the trench—and saw hundreds of Red Army conscripts emerge from the Soviet forest.

Some of the conscripts carried pitchforks and shovels, others hammers and sickles. Some had paintings and photos of Stalin, others red flags with communist slogans in Cyrillic; still others had bouquets of flowers or loaves of bread in their hands.

Behind the conscripts was a uniformed brass band. A *politruk* gave the band a signal; the band struck up '*The Internationale*'—the communist party's unification song.

Another *politruk* gave the conscripts a signal; they joined hands and began to sing, continuing onward toward the border—just as they were about to enter the minefields, the *politruk* returned to the safety of the trees.

Pennanen's unit was provided momentary relief when Soviet artillery and mortar spotters inexplicably changed their aim; the shells began to fall farther from the border, some even landing among the reservists from the city.

Pennanen noted that the hoard of Red Army conscripts kept advancing and would soon be in the Soviet minefields. He pulled the slide back on his *Suomi* submachine gun and muttered: "Mines don't discriminate against their makers."

Pennanen was an amateur historian with knowledge of past military follies and he understood the situation. Stalin had virtually unlimited resources; Pennanen could easily imagine Stalin's resolve.

"This is it, men! Be ready to fire! And conserve your ammunition! Make sure every bullet counts!"

His men reached for their rifles.

"Maybe they are bluffing!" yelled the millwright, who always carried a rabbit's foot and a crucifix—even though he was Lutheran and at night rubbed garlic on his chest. "It could be just a test."

"This is not a test!" Pennanen had already counted seven dead around him, as well as many others who were seriously wounded.

His men peeked over the tops of their trenches; saw the horde approaching and quickly calculated that the five rounds of ammunition they had each been issued wouldn't be enough.

"This isn't Poland!" Reijo yelled at the advancing Russians. "You're going to have to fight to take Finland!"

Reijo's defiance despite the odds they faced gave others strength. They burst out in guttural agreement—a battle cry of sorts; the kind that instills strength in those who utter it more so than fear in those who hear it.

"But look at how many there are!" Jussi lamented. He was guessing: he was no longer able to see clearly past a few meters; his eyesight was rapidly fading—a fact he was concealing from his comrades at arms. "How will we bury them all?"

Stray grenades continued to explode around them. While some of the men remained in fetal positions, as if that would protect them, others no longer bothered to duck; they had noticed it made little difference—there was no hiding from what came from above. Men continued to be torn apart; they shrieked; they whimpered; they died.

The postmistress' son, who was a machinegun loader, turned to his gunner, the butcher's helper.

"Are you sure it won't happen to us?" He had to yell to be heard over the shelling.

"Yes, God is on my side!" The butcher's helper took the safety off his machinegun.

For Toivo it was surreal, reminding him of Salvador Dali's paintings where time and everything else was warped. He looked at the unsightly wide gash that had been slashed through the land that was called a border—and questioned whether it was worth fighting over or dying for.

He reached into his rucksack for his sketchpad and charcoal; he didn't want to be One with the carnage—he wanted to control what he saw.

He found a clean page and began to sketch his beloved Kerttu.

Hand-in-hand, the first wave of Red Army conscripts entered the minefields on the Soviet side of the border. Mines exploded; human shapes disintegrated into unrecognizable forms. As the first wave of Red Army conscripts blew apart, *politruks* ordered the second wave out from the forest.

The conscripts had heard the grenades hum as they passed overhead before exploding in the distance. When they had worried aloud, *politruks* had convinced them that the Finns were their friends and wouldn't fire. They were told to hand over the bread, the tools, the flowers, or whatever they were carrying to any Finn they encountered; to sing when ordered, and to continue walking until they reached the Baltic—which many conscripts knew was hundreds of kilometers away.

When the second wave of conscripts emerged from the forest and saw the piles of dead and heard the screams of the wounded, they hesitated and turned back to the *politruks* for guidance—only to find them safely ensconced among the trees, aiming Soviet-made machine guns at them.

The conscripts accepted their fate with resignation. They knew tyranny; they understood that resistance was futile but still held on to the hope that their name was not on a mine, grenade or bullet. They resolutely began to sing and forged on hand-in-hand toward the Baltic. It lay right there—just beyond their dying comrades, the minefields, the black-and-white border markers, and the Finns with their determination and guns.

A shell exploded near Toivo and showered him with earthen debris. He shook the dirt off his sketch pad, looked up, and saw the post mistress's son and the butcher's helper—the machine gunner who knew that God was on his side—lying smashed and torn, dead from a direct grenade hit. God was surely on their side now.

He peered over the top of the trench.

The conscripts kept advancing; their lips were moving, but all that could be heard was the thundering shelling.

As the few remaining conscripts from the first wave passed the border markers and entered Finland, the second wave entered the minefields. Mines exploded. More Soviet conscripts died on Soviet soil; many died grotesquely, their mouths agape in screams that were eternally frozen. Other conscripts kept advancing—some even kept on singing.

"They are coming closer!" Timo yanked his fedora tighter on his head.

"Really?! They are getting closer?! No shit they are getting closer!!! You're officer material!" Reijo wet his thumb with saliva and rubbed it on the front sight of his rifle.

As the first line of Soviets came into range, the other Finnish home guard units and the border guards on their flanks opened fire. Pennanen stood up and walked erect among his men, braving the flying shrapnel and debris.

"Hold your fire! Wait for my command!"

Now they could now hear the Soviet conscripts singing.

"But they are *singing*!" someone yelled.

"They are *Russian*!" Pennanen hollered. "Open fire!"

Most of his men fired their weapons on Pennanen's command; others, who had not overcome their reluctance to harm those who had yet not harmed them, didn't.

Scores of conscripts fell, torn apart by bullets; those who were not harmed were terrified. With their faces smudged from the smoke of exploded mines, shells, and gunpowder, they continued past the border markers toward the Finnish trenches; at their side, still in a formation, albeit ragged, were the remnants of the Red Army brass orchestra.

One of those first wave conscripts who had survived the minefield was Nicholas Habarov, his birthmark dark against his ashen skin. Tears streaked his cheeks.

... I don't want to die... my life should not yet be over...

Nicholas Habarov stumbled past a border marker, holding the rifle that he had been given—it wasn't fully assembled and lacked a bolt; thus it couldn't fire.

"It's merely for show," the *politruk* had said when the rifle was handed to him. "The Finns will not shoot you. They are our comrades, proletariat like us. The rifle is just so you will look military."

Nicholas shook his head, as if that would blank out the horror around him, as if that would raise the dead and heal the wounded. Enraged and embittered, he pointed his useless rifle at the distant Finns and yelled: "Bang!"

Another grenade landed close to Toivo and exploded. He flinched; the charcoal broke in his hand. He looked out over the top of the trench; hundreds of Russians were still advancing—they were no more than one hundred meters away.

"Shoot, goddammit! Shoot!" Reijo squeezed off another round.

All sound faded for Toivo as he dropped his sketchpad and reached for his rifle; the metal was cold, the wood cool and smooth.

"Shoot, god dammit! Shoot!" Reijo pounded Toivo on the shoulder with a hard fist.

Toivo reluctantly, dazedly, lifted his rifle to his cheek. He saw something in his sight—pulled the trigger—fired.

Nicholas didn't feel the bullet that hit him above the left eye. For an instant he heard a dreadful sound, then an explosion of white slammed him into——nothing.

His soul hesitated, then left; only his body hit the ground. Near it lay an impotent, not yet fully assembled, bolt-less Russian-made rifle.

"Don't just fire! Aim!" Reijo yelled at Toivo, who dazedly pulled the bolt back on his rifle, ejected the spent cartridge, and fed another into the chamber.

Toivo wasn't aware of killing anyone; the war was still young, as was his mind—its resilience wasn't yet diminished.

He nevertheless felt the loss of something sacred.

. . .

Chapter Thirty Six

Khrushchev stood by a window in Stalin's apartment and looked out over Moscow. The room was hot; he pressed his forehead to the cold windowpane for comfort. He thought he saw the U.S. ambassador on the street below, which reminded him of the recent speech by President Roosevelt in San Diego; the President had assured the American people that America would stay out of European affairs.

Murmuring voices sounded from the next room where Stalin and Molotov were poring over the initial reports from the front. The war was several hours old. Although Khrushchev was a full member of the *Politbureau,* he had not been invited to the briefing; Stalin, rightfully, regarded Khrushchev as a critic and a potential political rival. Khrushchev didn't care; he knew the reports from the war would reflect what the authors thought Stalin wanted to read—his own sources predicted a protracted struggle.

Khrushchev had openly—but not more loudly than was wise—questioned the nature and timing of the attack on Finland. Stalin had committed 780,000 Red Army soldiers against Finland's Army of 240,000—which Khrushchev knew could be increased within weeks to approximately 400,000. That would still leave the Red Army with a significant numerical advantage—more than 1,500 fighter and bomber aircraft against Finland's 120, and 2,000 tanks and armored vehicles against Finland's 18.

Khrushchev also knew that Stalin had given Voroshilov permission to fire 15,000 artillery grenades in one sector of the border alone—more shells than they had fired during all of the Great War.

The odds were on the side of the Soviet Union, but Khrushchev was concerned about the timing: winter loomed just around the corner and the Red Army was neither logistically prepared nor militarily equipped for protracted winter warfare—it would be best if the war could be ended in the ten days mandated by Stalin.

Khrushchev was also concerned with the morale of the Red Army troops in the field; he wondered if their determination was strong enough to carry them through. Resolve at the Kremlin, at factory meetings, at dinner, or at kitchen tables after a meal, was one thing; resolve on the battlefield—when one is hungry, cold, and uncertain why one is there—is another. It would be difficult for peasants and workers to remain devoted to Stalin when the bullets started flying; when men and dreams were shredded around them like cotton in a mechanical thrasher.

Khrushchev himself had served in the Red Army and had played a part in Russia's Civil War; he understood the difficulties of taking uneducated peasants and workers and making useful soldiers of them; he knew the Red Army's morale to be low.

Khrushchev knew much about many things; he had made it his goal to live to be sixty, perhaps even seventy. In the Kremlin, one would be allowed to grow old only if one possessed valuable and negotiable information—and Khrushchev had much knowledge: he received information whenever he needed it from those who wanted to be in his good graces. Thousands realized that someday he would be their leader.

Stalin had concentrated most of the Red Army on the Karelian Isthmus, the shortest route to Finland's capital Helsinki—a mistake, thought Khrushchev.

"It will only threaten the Finns and cause them to be that more vigilant," he had advised Voroshilov, who he thought was an idiot.

"The Finns will not fight," Voroshilov had replied—at best he was naïve.

"Comrade Voroshilov, if you are right, I will kiss your bare ass in the middle of the Red Square on Sunday at noon." Khrushchev knew how to brawl with bureaucrats; he had started his rise as a Party activist in a hardened Ukraine mining town where a man's life expectancy was no more than twenty-seven years.

While Voroshilov was an idiot, Stalin wasn't; the Soviet Union needed a quick and decisive victory in Finland—after which no effort would be spared to modernize the Red Army for the inevitable clash with Hitler's Wehrmacht. In most northern areas, the Finns had few regular soldiers—the rest were border guards, reserves from the cities, and home guard units—and Khrushchev knew that Stalin had ordered at least six divisions to attack those areas thought to be weak. The orders for the division commanders were clear: Cut Finland in half! The incentive was equally clear: You will do it—or be one head shorter!

Khrushchev, though, had not received information about the conscription of Undesirables. He didn't know that thousands of Soviet citizens were to be used solely to absorb what little ammunition the Finns had—that the last act of those comrades would be to pave the way for others who were deemed more valuable or useful. That crucial knowledge wouldn't be revealed until later when he interrogated Commissar Beria of the Soviet Secret Police, the *NKVD*. Czechs would later joke with their characteristically sarcastic and conflict–weary humor that the initials *NKVD* stood for "*Nevim kdy vrátim doma*" ("I don't know when I'll return home.").

. . .

Chapter Thirty Seven

Pennanen's Home Guard unit had suffered heavy losses, as had the other home guard units. The border guards, however, had suffered the most—it was their border, their mandate to defend it, and they had so done so to the last man. They now lay dead or mortally wounded; their lips twitched, their bodies spasmed, yet still they faced the enemy.

"Look!" Someone pointed to the Soviet forest, out of which roared heavy tanks followed by thousands of Red Army regulars yelling their battle cry "*Urra!*"

The Soviet Union's *real* attack on Finland had begun—

The Finns were out of ammunition; some ran among the dead and wounded conscripts in search of weapons and ammunition, but found only unusable relics from The Great War, loaves of inedible yeast-less bread, flowers— and leaflets which claimed the Soviet Union was of the common people and their friend. The Finns eagerly gathered the leaflets; they were in short supply of toilet paper.

The Red Army tanks drove through the minefields cleared by the Soviet Undesirables' bodies, crushing corpses, knocking down the now obsolete border markers, and clanking onward toward the Finns' first line of defense.

The tank drivers steered by their view through slits in the tanks' armor; slits wide enough to guide them, but narrow enough to spare them the full impact of the carnage. The tanks were the Soviet Union's latest; heavy enough not to register the bodies that were crushed under their treads.

The Finns were no longer worried about the Soviet conscripts—who they now realized were impotent: the conscripts had stopped singing, no longer held hands, and had dropped whatever they had been carrying. They now either sat on the ground or milled aimlessly about. The Finns' more immediate concern was the quickly approaching tanks. Those who still had ammunition fired past the conscripts at the tanks; their bullets flattened against the armor and bounced harmlessly to the ground.

It was time for the Finns to fall back.

At Hotel Kämp in Helsinki Denny leaned on the front desk. He was dressed in pajamas and shouted into the telephone he held pressed to his ear.

"Put Uncle Leo on, dammit, and do it fast!"

There was chaos around him as people frantically dashed about. In the distance, air raid sirens howled and church bells clanged.

"Uncle Leo, Russia has attacked Finland!" yelled Denny.

A bomb exploded and rocked the building; dust fell from the ceiling fixture onto Denny's face.

"How would I know you already knew? I've been trying for hours to get through to you! No, I haven't been drinking! Now listen, Leo, this call is costing *The Times* a fortune! Do you want to take down my story or not?" He could hear the drone of approaching planes—he could also hear Leo yelling on the phone.

Bombs exploded nearby. The building shook. More dust fell from the ceiling. The lobby was quiet; everyone listened with held breath to the planes' droning engines that grew louder and louder—then diminished.

The sirens kept shrieking—as did Uncle Leo. Denny put the receiver back to his ear.

"I'm back. Sorry to keep you waiting. We were being bombed."

Uncle Leo said something uncomplimentary; Denny blew up.

"Now you listen to me, you pompous ass! I may not have any experience at being a journalist and I may not be as good as you claim you were at one time, but I'm the only correspondent you got in Finland and being bombed at that–so take your damn prejudices and smoke them!"

With that, he slammed the phone down on its cradle.

The front desk clerk demonstratively lifted the receiver and tested the cradle with a stiff forefinger.

A British correspondent came in through the front door with a bunch of leaflets.

"The Russians are offering free vodka to those who surrender."

Denny thought at first that it seemed like an unusually kind and civilized gesture. On reflection, it was tacky: gin would have been much more sublime.

The phone next to him rang. He picked it up—it was Uncle Leo.

Several hundred kilometers to the north, machine gunners in Red Army tanks fired a hail of bullets at Toivo and his fellow comrades and the Soviet artillery shelling of the Finnish trenches increased in intensity as well.

"Fall back!" Pennanen's order was terse and unexpected; most of his men thought their trench would be the place where they would die for their country. They quickly retreated toward the relative safety of the forest and jumped into the city boys' trenches.

Toivo landed on a dead body, compressing its chest, from which an awful groan escaped.

With dust and smoke clouding his already poor eyesight, Jussi looked around and became frantic when he couldn't see Timo.

"Timo! Anyone see Timo?"

Timo was a hundred meters away; the fedora still clinging to his head as he tried to escape a speeding Red Army tank bearing down on him.

The tank lurched toward Timo, bumped him—and Timo fell.

The tank stopped for a moment, and then drove over Timo—crushing his leg.

Timo's scream couldn't be heard over the machine gun fire and the shelling. He waved feebly to his comrades but they were entrenched in the forest, flinching and ducking the bullets hitting around them.

"Fall back more!" Pennanen loathed having to give that order.

Many left the city boys' trenches and headed toward safer ones farther into the forest.

Jussi raised his head over the top of the trench and saw the figure waggling its arm in the distance. "Is that Timo out there? I can hardly see him! Is it?"

Others looked; the silence that followed gave Jussi his answer.

More bullets hit around them, tearing up men, trees and the ground.

The shelling increased; they were caught in a hellish inferno: the noise was deafening, the shock waves unrelenting—and there was no escaping any of it. They tried to protect their ears with their hands but the noise was merciless, found its way into them; many, even the strongest of men, whimpered from pain and helplessness.

More men left hurriedly for the safety of the forest— the smoky haze couldn't conceal the thousand or more Red Army troops now approaching.

Timo raised his arm again and tried vainly to raise himself from the ground.

More of his comrades left the trench in which Jussi fretted about his only friend.

"We can't just leave him there!" Toivo was aghast at Timo's plight.

They cringed as the approaching tanks fired their machine guns at them; they were in the last remaining Finnish forward position and now bore the full weight of the Red Army's fury.

More men abandoned the trench.

Toivo, too, crawled out from the trench, stood up, and was buffeted by the explosions of incoming artillery grenades. But instead of retreating to safety, he ran toward his fallen comrade through a blazing inferno of exploding shells— some of which hit dead men who stood once more before disintegrating.

Toivo reached Timo and grabbed him; as he struggled to lift the injured ladies man onto his back, Timo lost his lucky fedora.

From a trench farther into the forest, Reijo aimed his rifle at Toivo and had him in his sight as he rose from the ground with Timo slung across his back. Reijo kept his rifle with its one remaining bullet aimed at Toivo as the artist for whom he had such mixed feelings struggled toward them with Timo on his back, now and then hidden by smoke and cascading earth and debris from exploding grenades.

Pennanen stood next to Reijo, tapping his shoulder encouragingly and nodding ever so slightly, giving his blessing that Reijo squeeze his trigger and provide a final solution for their common nemesis.

Reijo wavered: he lowered his rifle.

Toivo stumbled through the hellish landscape with Timo on his back toward the relative safety of the trenches in the forest, where Jussi, Pennanen, Reijo, and the others followed his progress—each man having his own idea about how Toivo should proceed.

"Not that way, asshole!" yelled Jussi as he squinted to get a better view of Toivo and Timo. "To the right! To the right!! Now to the left! Left!!!"

Just then an explosion rocked Toivo; he fell to his knees and lost his grip on Timo, who whimpered as he fell to the ground.

A wounded conscript clawed at Toivo; he pushed the man away and once more hoisted Timo onto his shoulder.

As Pennanen and the others watched Toivo bring Timo toward safety, a Red Army tank crew spotted Toivo and headed for easy prey.

The tank was gaining on Toivo when several poorly-made Soviet artillery shells fell short of their intended targets; one landed on the tank, which exploded; the others landed between Toivo and his unit, momentarily obscuring him with smoke and cascading earthen debris.

When the smoke cleared, Toivo re-appeared and struggled the last fifty meters to the trench and his awaiting 'comrades.'

Pennanen and Jussi helped lower Timo to the ground —he was dead, his head and torso torn apart by an errant grenade.

Embittered, Jussi faced Toivo. "You son of a bitch! Why didn't you listen? I told you which way to go!" He jumped on Toivo. The others tried to pull him off, but it wasn't easy—Jussi was a big man.

The remaining Red Army tanks stopped at the edge of the forest; that was as far as the Soviet tank commanders were willing to go.

The soldiers behind the tanks were grateful. There wouldn't be any more fighting that day.

It began to snow.

. . .

Timo's black fedora, driven by the wind, skipped among the many hundreds of bodies and numerous burning tanks.

There was a near eerie silence, broken only by the whistling wind carrying the sounds of war: the moans of the wounded and dying, the crackling of burning tanks and armored cars.

In a Finnish trench close to the border, the wind flipped a page of an open sketchpad, turning it from a half-finished drawing of Kerttu to a page that was blank.

November 30, 1939.

. . .

Chapter Thirty Eight

Manhattan. Early morning. The cold Arctic wind that blew in from the Hudson River rustled the stacks of *The New York Times* that an ink-stained truck driver dumped at the 7th Avenue newsstand near the subway entrance that Kerttu was approaching.

After the news of Russia's attack on Finland she had been worried sick about Toivo. Too upset to go home, she had sat with friends from the show at an all-night diner, talking about men and life; they had not resolved anything, but time too precious to sleep away had been well spent.

At five in the morning some of the girls began yawning; it was time to go home.

When Kerttu saw the stacks of early edition *New York Times*, she immediately bought one and began scanning it intently. On the front page was a one-paragraph mention of the attack on Finland by the Soviet Union. Buried on an inside page was an article written by Denny Arnold, a *Times* correspondent in Helsinki. As the article had been written in haste, it lacked scope as well as details; it hinted that the ouster of the Soviet Union from the League of Nations was punishment for the dastardly invasion of a tiny, non-belligerent neighbor.

The article did little to reassure Kerttu—she had not heard from Toivo; Consul Huhtamäki had told her that mail could take as long as two months.

... Toivo...

In the all-night diner, she had reminisced about him; her love for her man had caused her body to contract. Then she had seen someone whose hands reminded her of him; she had blushed, remembering their first intimate encounter—she had been most immodest.

. . .

Chapter Thirty Nine

Field Marshall Mannerheim sat in his private office at Finnish Defense Headquarters in the inland city Mikkeli. His armed forces had done well that day, yet he cursed those in Helsinki who had not heeded his advice years earlier—when there still had been time. He cursed those, who for questionable reasons, had remained cautiously optimistic—it was their politically expedient short-sightedness that was now depriving his gallant troops of the arms and equipment they so desperately needed. He knew the morale of his troops was high, their commitment strong, their resolve deep—but he also knew they were short of ammunition and terribly deficient in numbers.

The sinew, *sisu*, of the Finnish citizens had saved the day; that and the astonishingly inept design and execution of the Soviet attack—Mannerheim thought Voroshilov was an idiot, that a child would have come up with a better plan.

Mannerheim looked through the reports on his desk; they clearly showed that politicians' follies would be paid for with soldiers' lives. He heard the din from the men and women outside his closed door and wondered how high a price his people would have to pay.

He knew about people's suffering, about military objectives, love and fear, and chilled vodka in the late afternoon and evening. He understood words and their shades of meanings; that home to the worker is not necessarily home to the factory director. He had fought in several wars and he had fought under many different masters.

This time he wouldn't have a master—he owed that to the Finnish People. He owed it to the man in the street, the woman in the home, the child in the womb, the men and women at the front—and he owed it to himself.

. . .

Chapter Forty

With the air reverberating with the sound of distant artillery, Pennanen's unit skied north along the border toward the far-off plumes of smoke—the Red Army had a seemingly unending supply of artillery shells: many of which fell far from their intended targets; others which didn't explode on impact but were a nuisance still.

That morning they had been in a firefight with a Red Army battalion. It had been their sixth battle in the four days since they were disbanded as a Home Guard unit. Mannerheim, who knew Red Army tactics firsthand, had largely reorganized his army into hit-and-run units after Stalin's initial attack on Finland. Pennanen's Home Guard unit had been merged with two others into a reinforced ski company and made a part of Finland's Army. Pennanen had been given the command; reports about his bravery under fire had reached his superiors.

Pennanen's company consisted of four *joukkue*, or platoons, of thirty five men each; Reijo was made sergeant, placed in charge of a platoon, and selected Toivo as one of his men. The platoons were largely self-contained: they pulled their mortars and machine guns in *pulkka* sleds with leather thongs attached to shoulder harnesses. Other novel equipment and clothing issued to them were the white, sheet-like garments that they wore over their clothes and which made them virtually indistinguishable from the snowy landscape. But they had not been provided a field kitchen; it had been sacrificed for the sake of their enhanced mobility.

Hungry and haggard, noses running, they headed for an Army field station where they would be fed, given a sauna, and issued fresh socks and mittens.

Two low-flying Russian SB-2 bombers appeared. Pennanen held up his hand; his men stopped. They had little to fear. The sky was overcast, and only when the sun was low could Soviet pilots see the ski-tracks of the dreaded enemy the Red Army called *bielov smiert*, 'white death'. They seldom saw the skiers themselves; when they did, it was often too late—the loss of Soviet planes from ground-fire had been high.

The SB-2 flight crew didn't see the Finns below; they flew onward toward their civilian targets farther inland. Pennanen motioned to his men. They skied onward; the going was easy—they were heading in the direction of their own country district.

Pennanen was preoccupied as he skied. Of the thirty-seven men who had left the village with him thirteen days earlier, only eighteen were left—two of whom were no longer fit for duty as they never lifted their eyes from the ground. Now he had other men under his command; men he didn't know, of whose abilities he was uncertain. He noted with concern that they skied in silence.

... I wonder how their morale is...

Pennanen remembered a saying expounded by an instructor he had had in officer school.

"Out of a sad asshole comes no happy fart!" The instructor had attached great importance to that expression.

Pennanen reflected on what the instructor had said.

... Toivo...

Of all his men, the one who mostly concerned him was Toivo; the artist was becoming more and more withdrawn from the others.

... if the Soviets don't get him... maybe I will...

Toivo disturbed Pennanen; it bothered him that some of his men respected the upstart who had been to America.

... upstart... Putki Pekka...

Three days earlier he had sent a runner to their village to inquire about his sergeant's knee. Pekka had sent word back that his knee was still stiff; Pennanen returned the runner with a note that suggested perhaps it was time for Pekka's leg to come off.

Putki Pekka arrived on skis the following morning. He had not looked Pennanen in the eye, but his knee had experienced a miraculously speedy recovery.

In his first battle, a stray bullet tore through the back of his head and killed Putki Pekka. His body remained where it fell.

... maybe Tessa will now have more time for her duties with the Women's Volunteer Corps and less time for clandestine romances...

Pennanen's stomach had cleared up by mid-morning.

Not far behind Pennanen skied Toivo, reflecting on that morning's clash with the enemy. Compared to others, in particular to his baptism into carnage at the border, this had been more like a skirmish than a full-fledged battle. Again Toivo had fired his newly issued *Lahti-Saloranta* light machine gun, and again he had killed men: men who had never harmed him, men he wasn't angry with—men who had dreams similar to his.

More of his spiritual essence had disappeared, leaving him increasingly dead inside.

As Toivo skied northward toward the country district where he had been born, his senses drained even further.

Oddly, he remembered one winter, another lifetime ago, when his father had taken him on a hunt for ermine—

They had waded through the snow some distance from the farm. His father found a spot he liked, then placed little Toivo underneath the skirt of a pine. The branches were snow-laden; from this vantage point they could see far, yet not be seen themselves.

His father walked to a nearby clearing. Little Toivo saw him take out his favorite knife: it was small and sharp. His father had then removed a mitten and nicked his palm with the tip of the blade.

Blood seeped onto the snow—his father made sure of that, then placed the knife tip-up in the snow and dripped some more blood on its blade.

His father sucked on his wound as he walked back through the snow to his young son who sat quiet and hidden under the skirt of the tree. His mitten concealing the nick in his palm, his father rejoined him.

They sat there for some time, gnawing on hardtack and sausage. His father wrapped his arm around Toivo, for whom it was a very special day.

The ermine appeared; it was in its winter coat and difficult to spot against the snow. The ermine had smelled the blood; it sniffed the air, ran a few steps, and again sniffed the air in effort to locate the source of the smell.

The ermine found the knife.

Toivo held his breath; he thought his father did as well—the ermine would bring much money in the village; it was said that kings and queens wore coats made from the skins.

The ermine sniffed the knife, and then licked the blade, cautiously at first, then eagerly. It licked and licked; Toivo was puzzled—he didn't think his father had placed that much blood on the blade.

The ermine slowed, but continued to lick; it slumped, yet continued to lick—very slowly now.

Then it stopped.

Slowly they approached the ermine. It didn't scurry away; its eyes were dull, its gaze distant. There was no visible blood; it was all inside the ermine's stomach—its tongue was cut to shreds.

Toivo, sickened, made his father promise never to hunt ermine again.

Toivo remembered that day too well—now he felt like that ermine must have: depleted of self, yet consumed almost to the point of self-destruction. He was drained; the good in him seeped out with every battle and skirmish.

He reached for Kerttu's scarf and greedily held it to his nose; her scent was faint, but perceptible. As if in a silent, translucently pastel haze he remembered Kerttu on the merry-go-round at Coney Island: smiling happily, she hung on to the mane of a white horse that moved up and down, while in the mirrors beside her the world went around and around—spinning faster and faster, becoming a blur——

"Get up!" Pennanen's voice was distant, yet near.

Toivo came to; he found himself face down in the snow. He looked up—the others were watching him. Pennanen leaned closer.

"Get up. Get your weapon out of the snow!"

Toivo struggled to his feet. The others skied away.

An artillery shell landed some distance away, exploding; a fountain of snow cascaded into the air. The men were undaunted; they now knew from experience that shells landing in snow a meter or more deep were more of a nuisance than harmful.

Reijo, who wheezed and hyperventilated as he skied, muttered:

"Damn Russians can't do anything right."

They skied on—and were startled when they heard *Teuvan Tiltu*, "Moscow Sally", over loudspeakers hidden in the not-so-distant Soviet forest.

"Finnish soldiers! Lay down your arms!"

"Guess she's talking to you, Toivo," said Jussi; he was still bitter about the loss of Timo, his friend and companion.

"If you come over here I will give you fresh-baked bread," continued *Teuvan Tiltu*.

"Guess she's talking to you now, Jussi," said Toivo good-naturedly.

No one laughed.

"Hey, Sally," yelled Reijo to the forest. "If you come over here we can put my Finnish sausage in your bread!"

The others laughed, but their laughter subsided; bawdy women beckoned them over the Soviet loudspeakers.

Reijo stifled a cough attack.

"Who would fall for that crap—" he muttered, oddly affected by the women's bold language.

"Yeah, their women are nothing compared to ours," piped someone from another district.

"And they got nothing but bad-tasting yogurt," chimed Jussi.

They skied on.

Teuvan Tiltu continued broadcasting behind them, but no one listened except for a hare.

They reached a burned-down village. Another ski unit tended their wounded and rested among the still-burning buildings. Frozen puddles of blood dotted the ground. The village populace was gone. They had taken their casualties with them; the ground was too hard to dig graves.

Many Russian corpses littered the area; one was buried in a snow bank so that only his uniformed arm stuck out.

As Pennanen's men passed by the corpse, some solemnly shook its hand.

A Finnish Ministry of Defense photographer filming the Soviet casualties panned to Pennanen's men as they skied by, their skis swooshing through the hard-frozen snow.

. . .

Chapter Forty One

The Jolly Show Cabaret's audience hissed as stagehands struggled to free a stuck backdrop. In the stage's right wing Hank had cornered Kerttu who with other showgirls waited to go onstage.

"I don't get it! A tour like that is what every dancer wants!" He was angry; he had called in some hard-earned favors to get Kerttu this offer. "It's the chance of a lifetime, kid!"

The backdrop was freed. It was hoisted with great efficiency and energy; the stagehands valued their jobs, and they knew from Harry the Greek—who worked the catwalk and saw and heard everything without being noticed himself—that Hank was likely to be bad tempered that night.

The audience applauded as the orchestra struck up a show number and the girls strutted out on stage.

Hank stopped Kerttu; his grip wasn't gentle.

"I can't keep this job open forever. What do you want to do?"

"I want to be with my man," she said emphatically. "And I will be as soon as I get my passport! Let go of my arm, please, the others are waiting!"

She rushed onstage to join her friends; they were already kicking and prancing.

The audience cheered.

Hank kicked a stanchion.

The stagehands exchanged bemused glances.

. . .

Chapter Forty Two

Mr. Biederman had received a letter from his daughter; she was someplace in Poland that he had not heard of and couldn't find on a map. Oddly, the envelope bore a New York postmark. She asked him for money—and that was quite unlike her, as was her choice of words; but it was her handwriting.

Biederman didn't know that she had exactly copied the typed letter given her by the Polish-speaking Gestapo officer, who had then stepped aside so that she could see her husband and children pinned against the wall on the other side of the internment camp's frigid yard.

Biederman went to his bank, withdrew the large sum of money his daughter requested, paid for a draft made out in her name, and wired it as instructed to a bank in Berlin.

He didn't know that his daughter was already dead, as were his son-in-law and grandson, or that his granddaughter would be allowed to work another two months in the internment camp's kitchen before she was discarded, receiving the ultimate dismissal; Biederman knew only that he had responded to the need of the daughter he loved. He wished she had sent a photo of her family.

... family...

On his way home from the bank, Biederman brooded about the nature of family; his brooding turned serious.

... Sayde...

He didn't consciously want to think about the wife he had loved so dearly, yet the thought of her abruptly surfaced more often recently; he didn't like to dwell on her, it worsened the stinging pain in his chest and the throbbing ache in his arm.

... Toivo and Kerttu...

Since their departure he had realized that his other tenants were old both in age and spirit—and he was weary of old age; he missed the passionate couple that had a zest for life and made his own life more interesting and vibrant.

... Toivo and Kerttu...

He missed them both; they had been like family.

... Toivo...

He missed the many philosophical talks he and Toivo had shared. The young artist believed each day should be a celebration of Life and he lived his life accordingly, each day fighting a battle for the integrity of his Self; an elusive task, since he kept changing as he matured. His young friend had found a way to use hunger as a measure of his happiness; he compared that empty, gnawing feeling with the exquisite contentment he experienced with his Kerttu.

... Toivo... what a fine young man...

If Toivo had a flaw, it was that he was so awed by life and all its complexities that he didn't feel he deserved happiness—much less did he deserve Kerttu, whom he felt was an angel on earth. When Biederman and Toivo went for walks and passed a church, Toivo had thought that each Madonna resembled Kerttu—that irritated Biederman; he held absolute beliefs about Catholicism and Divine Conception.

... conception... creation...

Biederman knew that when Toivo's artistic inspiration failed him he would go to the butcher shop where Kerttu worked, stand by the window and simply look at her—and that would annoy her. On more than one occasion she had gone outside with a bucket of water; if Toivo wouldn't leave, she would give him a kiss then douse him with its contents.

Sometimes, instead of going to the butcher shop to get drenched with water, Toivo would walk around and look at the different Madonna outside churches, although he would never set foot inside one; he would go no closer than to peek through an open door.

Biederman stood in his tenement courtyard and listened for laughter. There was none.

... *Sayde* ...

His wife would have liked the young couple; she had had a similar zest for life; she was a decent person, the nicest human being he had ever met. He missed his wife, her sparkling blue eyes that were clear as water; he missed Sayde——he liked to say her name aloud: *Sayde*—it made his heart beat steadier and stronger.

Lately he had been dreaming about her; the following morning it was especially difficult for him to wake up. He found that he was rising later nowadays and he didn't mind. There wasn't much for him to do: the rent was paid by those who could afford it; there were not many repairs needed—Toivo had done a good job painting both the interior and exterior: the building wouldn't need another coat of paint for many years to come.

As he walked to his second floor apartment, somehow the stairway seemed longer and the rise of the steps higher.

... *perhaps I should move down a floor*... *why bother*... *I won't be here that much longer*...

Sayde visited him more often recently; she smiled and held out her hand. Last night he came close to taking it.

He reached his door; paused before opening it. The building was quiet; there was no one for him to talk to.

... *Toivo had lived up just one more flight of stairs—*

He opened his door; the hinge creaked—*how fitting*, he thought.

He stood in his living room and looked at his life: the pictures of Sayde, their daughter, her husband, and the adorable grandchildren he had yet to hold in his arms; other people and moments long past; Toivo's painting that Kerttu wasn't supposed to know about—the one he had painted of the two of them, the one he had not signed, the one where his face is in shadow, she has a view of the ocean and the sun is kissing her face.

It was Biederman's favorite painting.

Mr. Biederman sat in his chair from which he could look out through the window at that which was his. He switched on the radio, listened absentmindedly, daydreaming about the *gefilte* Kerttu used to get for him; the *gefilte* the rude Rumanian butcher now kept forgetting to order, claiming it had been Kerttu's job to order delicatessen items and that it was Biederman's fault she was gone—

Biederman had never liked the man. He was a *schmuck*, but he was the only vendor within walking distance who had access to real *gefilte*. With food on his mind, it took Biederman a minute or so to register what the newscaster had just said: that the Soviet Union had attacked Finland. When he did, he became terribly upset—his friend Toivo might be in jeopardy. Biederman knew how much the young man—whom he considered a son—had dreaded returning to the roots he considered too shallow.

. . .

Chapter Forty Three

A fire raged under a large cast-iron soup pot. Many of Pennanen's men were huddled around the fire; some were eating; first aid personnel were tending to others.

Toivo and others were in line to be issued fresh socks and mittens—and there was Tessa, in the uniform of a *Lotta*, the Finnish Army Women Auxiliary Force.

"I think of you all the time," she whispered to Toivo. "Don't look, my husband is watching us."

And Pennanen was—like a hawk.

"I just need some socks and mittens." That truly was all Toivo wanted from her.

"You need more than that and I have what you need," she said, smiling at Pennanen standing out of hearing range. "For now, take these."

She handed Toivo socks and mittens, reached inside her coat and surreptitiously pulled out a pair of expensive kidskin gloves with a price tag still attached.

"Take these as well." She tore off the price tag and handed the gloves to Toivo. "I was going to give them to him, but his hands don't need them."

She paused and looked him in the eye.

"Yours do," she whispered—there was no question of her meaning.

"Get that damn line moving!" yelled Pennanen. His stomach was acting up again, for what reason he wasn't sure.

. . .

Chapter Forty Four

Hotel Kämp's lobby teemed with activity. Foreign correspondents stood in line impatiently shouting at their colleagues to finish dictating stories to their editors on the telephones reserved for the press.

Giancarlo was deeply engrossed in a conversation, not with his editor, but with his wife—which no one knew as Giancarlo spoke Italian and was the only one in the hotel who did. He gave a dirty look to the German who was next in line; a man everyone suspected was a Nazi spy—an assumption the man made easy for the gossip mongers because he kept to himself, was unpretentious, and wore a monocle that at times was less than sparkling.

"Cara," Giancarlo said to his wife and shot the German spy another dirty look, "I must go. Soon the Russians will begin to shoot at me again. Perhaps bomb me again. To get to this phone I have to walk across a sea of dead. It is a terrible war." He more than enjoyed being Italian—he thrived on it and nearly always took full advantage of the drama that his culture. allowed, encouraged, and provided for. *"Ciao, cara. Ciao."* He mouthed a kiss while hanging up, remembering too late to greet their children. *"Porca—"*

His wife had already hung up; she was crying for her poor husband who was in a terrible war in a country with a name she could neither pronounce nor find on their seven-year-old son's Atlas globe.

Giancarlo demonstratively held the receiver up for the German, handed it to him with the tips of his fingers—as if he was afraid the man would contaminate him with one of the evil poisons rumored to be in Germany's arsenal.

"Let's have lunch—and I feel like having salmon today."
Denny was standing there waiting for him. The reference
to salmon was their private joke; salmon was all there was
to eat—it was served even at breakfast. They had heard of
a Finnish law that stipulated hired hands on Finland's
farms couldn't be served salmon more than five times a
week; they had often considered invoking that law at
Hotel Kämp.

"Let's not eat, let's go and see the movies." Giancarlo
meant the footage from the front provided to foreign
journalists by the Finnish Foreign Ministry as part of
Finland's ongoing effort to invoke international sympathy
for its cause. To some extent the effort succeeded: both
the British Parliament and the League of Nations had
passed resolutions condemning the Soviet attack on the
tiny nation.

Denny wasn't interested in footage from the front; he
had rapidly become fed up with being stuck at Hotel
Kämp; he was bored with regurgitating the propaganda
provided by the Foreign Ministry's information officer
and was no longer enamored with being the admired
journalist for *The New York Times*. Most boring and
hurtful were his conversations with Uncle Leo, who
clamored for human-interest stories.

*... human interest... don't you know there's a war
going on...*

"No films. Let's get drunk."

"You are already drunk, my friend." Giancarlo could
smell the vodka on Denny's breath. He didn't mind,
really, because it made Denny so much more sociable.

"This is nothing," Denny said. "I'll show you drunk.
Let's have a really tall drink."

"Let's not. Let's see movies."

Giancarlo steered Denny toward the small room
where the Finnish Foreign Ministry showed its war
footage. "Did you hear from Madison Avenue?"

"Not yet, but I will," replied Denny. He hoped he was right; he wanted that advertising job—any job away from Uncle Leo. "I'm bored here. Aren't you bored?"

Giancarlo shook his head; he had met a gorgeous and interesting Finnish widow but had not yet told Denny about her.

They entered the screening room and sat down to watch the most recent film from the front. Martti, the always-dapper Finnish Foreign Ministry information officer, handed them a sheaf of papers that they knew had been heavily censored by the Finnish Ministry of Defense.

"I don't give a damn about numbers!" Denny crumpled the report he had just been given. "I need to know about people, not guns, tanks, and planes! I need some goddamn human interest stories!"

"You Americans want heroes." Giancarlo put his arm around Denny. "You want to put up statues." He had grown up in Rome, which had more than its share. "We Italians go out for dinner."

They watched the black-and-white footage; they had been to several previous screenings and were now more or less immune to the bloodshed that was on the screen.

"No one will remember this war," said Giancarlo. "No one."

At that moment Denny saw Toivo on the screen as he skied by a corpse whose arm stuck out from a snow bank.

Denny stood up excitedly.

"That was the Finn from the freighter!" Denny was so excited that he grabbed Giancarlo's hand. "The artist I told you about!"

He paused, struck by inspiration—and grinned broadly. "There it is! There's my goddamn human interest story."

He straightened out the crumpled sheaf of papers in his hand, grabbed the pencil from behind Giancarlo's ear, and began to write.

. . .

Chapter Forty Five

Kerttu stood on the corner of 44th Street and Broadway. It was late afternoon. She had been looking for work as a dancer all day, but had not found any: Hank had made sure of that before he fired her. He had made the necessary calls; the old boy network was still intact, the solidarity strong. All the stage managers gave the same answer: "Go back and talk to Hank."

Chorus dancers in their warm-ups streamed out from a rehearsal hall and rushed across the street for a quick meal at the deli. They dodged traffic and out-hustled each other; they had only a ten-minute break, the service was on a first-come, first-served basis. Anyone back late would be fired.

Times were hard.

Kerttu watched the dancers compete with each other to be first in line at the deli. She was still surprised that the girls from The Jolly Show Cabaret had been so supportive of her—some had openly wished they had her self-esteem; they remembered all too well the compromises they had made in order to get their jobs, as well as the ones they had made to keep them.

A ticket scalper pushed a beggar away from an iron grate that wafted warm air from the subway below; then the scalper straddled the turf he had made his own.

The wind was cold and warned of winter.

Kerttu pulled her coat tighter around her. Life on Broadway, or the 'Boulevard of Lights' as some liked to call it, wasn't all harmony, caviar, and champagne; it didn't matter at which end of it you were.

"Extra! Extra!" The newspaper vendor was more of a dramatic hawker than a paper vendor—perhaps because he was on Broadway.

"Extra! Extra! *Times*' correspondent reports direct from war in Finland!"

Kerttu bought a paper, opened it—and saw the article on an inside page with the caption "*From Artist To War Hero*". Written by Denny Arnold, it told of a young Finn who had been a tortured artist in Chicago and who now was a tortured soldier in Finland.

Although Denny spelled Toivo's first and last names correctly, and he described his paintings and his childhood, Kerttu couldn't believe the article was about her Toivo; the soldier described was so different from the man she knew and loved; she couldn't believe her man had changed that much.

She felt faint; her heart beat so loudly she could hear it thrumming in her ears; her stomach ached—her body worried about the baby.

She hurried to the subway; she had to catch a train to Brooklyn—there was still time, the Finnish Consulate was still open.

The train was slow; by the time it reached Brooklyn, Kerttu knew the article by heart. She waited impatiently for the train door to open, pushed people out of her way, rushed up the stairs to ground level.

She dashed across the street and into the Consulate, found the door open and Consul Huhtamäki putting on his coat—winter had arrived, even for a Finn.

She was out of breath. He patiently waited for her, brushing his coat as he did.

"I know I've been a nuisance, and I'm not now going to ask you to walk on water," she pleaded. "I just want you to give me a passport—any kind of passport; a one-way one, I don't care. I have to get to my man! Look what is happening to him! Look!"

She held up the newspaper.

Huhtamäki was close to retirement and longed for the small cottage he had bought in the countryside where people spoke in simple sentences—often in just a single word—which left little room for interpretation or disagreement. He scanned the article and pretended he had not seen it earlier, although he had—he had even discussed it on the phone with Finland's Embassy in Washington; the article had implications, public opinion and otherwise.

"Yes, well—" was all he said; he had been a political bureaucrat for many years. "I will telegraph Helsinki for you."

He walked to his desk, atop of which were stacks of papers that he rummaged through; he then found a bundle of letters that he handed to Kerttu.

"These letters arrived for you. I believe they are from him."

She hugged him elatedly. "Yes, they are" she said, hugging the stack of letters. "But look at his handwriting! It's so—shaky. Are you sure he's getting my mail? I've been sending it to his village like you said."

"I'm not sure of anything, I'm in the Foreign Service." He allowed himself some humanity now and then, but the experience was always so unfamiliar, so unsettling, that he had to balance it with well-practiced bureaucratic insensitivity.

"Are you sure you want to go to Finland? The country is at war and you don't speak the language. And it's cold over there. Fifty below zero."

"I don't care if it's a hundred and fifty below! I just want to be with my man."

. . .

Two days later Kerttu received her passport; that evening she boarded a Swedish freighter bound for Helsinki via Hamburg.

251

Sweden was neutral in the conflict between Finland and the Soviet Union. Swedish leaders had decided to continue a tradition begun decades earlier—and which had led to the Swedish Empire's loss of Finland, Norway, and Denmark; a tradition that had provided Sweden with political stability but deprived its people of much needed self-esteem.

The Swedish captain promised Kerttu a safe journey, yet she didn't sleep well that night.

The Soviet Union was expelled from the League of Nations the following day; that week, the Allied leaders didn't much care for Stalin.

. . .

Chapter Forty Six

It was the coldest day yet: Pennanen and his men were miserable; their noses ran; they shivered uncontrollably. Their orders were to remain positioned atop a hill from which they could see for miles. They had been there for several days, had not had anything warm to eat or drink, and their vigilant defense of Finland was taking its toll in more ways than one. That morning one more man failed to rise from the snow caves that served as their lairs—he had frozen to death. His name was Urho; he had been a miner, never saying much. Pennanen, after a short prayer, mentioned that Urho was a real Finn.

The red-haired Esko, an expert tree-faller who had been working in the forest since he left school at the age of thirteen, had spent many winters in the snow and knew how to stay warm—but that morning he removed three of his toes that had gone black from frostbite; he did it quietly—he didn't want to make a fuss.

Ice formed under their constantly runny noses; their breaths crystallized in the frigid air.

There wasn't anything to eat.

Dusk fell. The days were short; daylight lasted but a few hours.

Pennanen studied the frozen lake below through binoculars. A road lead from the woods to the lakeshore where a fisherman's shack stood; nets hung on pegs, as did a few crayfish traps.

The lake was large: it stretched across the border and into Russia. The ice was thick and would readily support men, horses, carts and wagons, but not yet tanks. The Red

Army preferred to cross into Finland on lakes; Finnish roads were narrow and bordered with woods from which well-hidden snipers could pick off invaders at will.

Pennanen thought he saw an indistinct mass approach in the extreme distance, but dusk was falling rapidly and he was tired; perhaps he was mistaken.

His men were spread out in defensive positions around him. Their weapons were at the ready, but they were not; they were tired, cold, and hungry.

Jussi crawled to Pennanen.

"Captain, is our food on the way?"

"My crystal ball is broken," said Pennanen, uncharacteristically sarcastic.

"There's fish in that lake," Jussi lamented.

"How do you know?"

"I've fished in it since I was four," Jussi said, and then added: "I need to eat, I'm cold."

"Do some exercises," Pennanen suggested well meaningly.

"I'm not that cold," said Jussi.

"Take the first watch. Being alert will warm you."

"I can't take a night watch, Captain. I don't see well enough anymore."

"You don't have to see Russians, you smell them."

"We don't smell all that good ourselves, Captain. Must have been weeks since we had a sauna." They missed saunas more than baths; baths cleansed bodies, saunas cleansed souls.

"Twelve days," corrected Pennanen. "Take the first watch."

"About my eyes, Captain——"

"To hell with your eyes! Get down to your post at the lake."

Pennanen had become alarmingly inflexible; his decisions were not always logical or well thought out—he was mentally exhausted; he had too much to think about.

Jussi slipped his *pieksu* boots with their upturned toes into his home-made ski bindings, put the rifle across his back, and schussed off down the hill to the lake.

Like the others Toivo was miserably cold; he couldn't get warm, no matter how he tried. He reached into his coat, withdrew Kerttu's scarf, and tried to smell it; he tried several times, he then gave up and put the scarf back inside his coat.

"What's the matter?" Reijo had noticed Toivo's dejected face.

"I can't smell her anymore—" Toivo stared at the scarf.

"Quiet, men!" Pennanen checked his logbook, then added: "And Merry Christmas!"

His men murmured "*Merry Christmas*".

The evening's first stars twinkled in the clear sky. The moon was nearly full.

It was Christmas Eve, 1939.

... Christmas...

They tried not to think about Christmases past as they shivered in the snow, but it was difficult not to—there wasn't anything else to do, nothing else to think about: the cold was that bitter, the snow that unfriendly, the crystal clear night sky with its twinkling stars not that alluring.

Toivo had just fallen asleep when Jussi awakened him. "Enemy approaching on the lake," Jussi whispered and moved off to awaken the others.

It didn't take them long to schuss down the hill toward the lake; they were like silent, armed white ghosts.

...bielov smiert...

White Death—the designation given them by their Russian foe was appropriate.

They quickly dropped into position along the frozen shore; some set up mortars.

In the distance a dark mass was approaching; a Red Army infantry battalion with horse-drawn sleighs, carts, and wagons.

Pennanen gave the go-ahead when his men with the mortars silently signaled they were poised and ready.

The first of many mortar shells exploded around the invaders, breaking the ice. Men and horses plunged into the icy water. Men screamed. Horses thrashed and neighed. More shells exploded. More ice shattered.

More screams, more neighing.

Men and horses floundered, then drowned.

Bielov smiert——

1939. Christmas Eve.

. . .

Chapter Forty Seven

Christmas Day, 1939. Kerttu had not been on Finnish soil since she was an infant. It felt strange to step off the Swedish freighter's gangway and onto the stone pier in Helsinki harbor; it was a homecoming of sorts, but an odd one.

As she waited for the taxi someone called to her from the freighter—it was the ship's limp-wristed cook, a nice man. She was sure he had a drinking problem and an abusive lover; scattered bruises often marked his body, but he made good food and had been quite friendly.

All the Swedes had been friendly. They all seemed to like America—but she had noticed several posters that reminded her of the leftist ones she had seen in working-class sections of Chicago. In the officer's mess there had also been a poster with a flattering picture of Hitler.

The Swedes had let her know they liked her, and when they learned that she had been born in Finland they let her know how much they liked Finland as well; she got the impression that Swedes worked at liking everyone indiscriminately—and that had made her uneasy.

In Hamburg the ship had taken on two German passengers; they were well-dressed, well-groomed, and well-behaved. She thought they were on a mission of sorts: they ate by themselves and stayed by themselves; she never saw them speak to anyone other than the Swedish captain—and then they punctuated the conversation with comical heel clicking.

The Swedish officers and crew were highly respectful of the Germans; Kerttu got the impression that although the freighter sailed under Swedish flag, it was under German influence.

When the freighter arrived in Helsinki, uniformed customs and immigration personnel met her and others aboard. The two Germans were met by serious men in somber suits and without any visible formalities were whisked off in a highly-polished German Embassy car.

Kerttu quickly hailed a taxi pulled by a high-spirited neighing horse. The driver opened the door for Kerttu, placed her suitcase in beside her, and asked her something in Finnish.

"Hotel," she said, for she knew not a word of Finnish.

The driver took her to Hotel Kämp—it was where foreigners stayed. He helped her with her luggage and looked suspiciously at the dollar bill she handed him. She noticed the German Embassy car parked around the corner; her fellow German passengers sat in its backseat, waiting.

The hotel staff was friendly and accommodating. A room would shortly be available; a guest was just leaving, a car awaited him around the corner. Ten days earlier the hotel's management had responded to the complaints voiced by uneasy correspondents; the manager had called the German Embassy about their suspected spy. The Embassy had cabled Berlin, the query prompting a quick investigation that resulted in a message to the German Embassy in Helsinki. That morning, as the Swedish freighter docked, the hotel had received a call from the German Embassy. Shortly thereafter, hotel management had asked the German correspondent to leave.

He had sadly packed his suitcase; he knew he was the only guest thus selected. After he packed he looked the room over carefully. He straightened the towels, the bedspread, and the carpet's fringes; he wanted to make the best possible impression: he was a proud man from a fine family and he regretted the ruse with the monocle—he had thought it would make him look less Jewish while he awaited the papers that would provide him passage to the

U.S.A. He knew there were two men waiting for him around the corner. He thought of escaping, but his family was still in Germany; he had to return—for their sake. He sighed; he had heard unsettling rumors.

As Kerttu signed the guest register she heard a heated argument in English.

"That is not the case, Mr. Arnold." Martti, the information officer from Finland's Foreign Ministry, was unusually adamant. "Absolutely not!"

"You're full of crap!" Denny had been drinking. "I know propaganda when I see it!"

"Mr. Arnold, please, there's a difference between fact and propaganda."

"What is called fact here is known as propaganda in Moscow!"

"Mr. Arnold—"

The information officer stopped himself—conversation was a wasted effort; Denny was that far gone.

Kerttu approached the two men. "Excuse me, are you Mr. Denny Arnold?" She trembled with apprehension when she asked the question.

"I'm Denny Arnold, the mister part is debatable." Denny had never been comfortable around women. He steadied himself on his crutches.

"Mister," he said, tasting the word. "Mister—am I a mister, Martti?"

Martti, the information officer, didn't reply—he wanted to leave; he had been through similar, nonsensical discussions before with Denny—more times than he cared to remember.

"I sure don't know." Denny could feel that last glass of vodka and knew now it had not been needed. But he was already on the spinning carousel and couldn't get off just because he wanted to.

"What do you think, Martti? Give me your honest opinion."

Martti wasn't a fool; he never divulged his opinion.

"I know how you feel. I don't know myself what I am half the time." Denny said, in spite of not wanting to say anything; he wanted to be quiet, to be somewhere else, by himself—he felt that despondent.

The young woman looked at him with eyes that were steady— and unnerved him.

"You're American, aren't you?" he asked, although he already knew the answer.

"Yes I am," Kerttu answered, biding the moment to ask the man on the crutches a question of supreme importance to her, feeling her heart beat alarmingly fast— but selecting instead to parry; she had a lot of skin on her nose. "Why do you ask? Aren't you rude to Americans?"

"I'm rude to everyone. Right, Martti?"

The answer was right there in Martti's eyes. Denny, who was a sensitive man under his façade, took several deep breaths—and then flashed Kerttu a broadly superficial smile.

"So, what can I do for you, madam?"

"Help me find Toivo Karjalainen." She said it very simply, yet her heart nearly burst.

"Toivo! Good ol' Toivo. Martti, that's the Finn I've been writing about! That's how this little war of yours gets newspaper coverage in America!"

The information officer still said nothing, knowing about Denny's liberties with reality. His country was at war and sometimes the end *does* justify the means.

"Good ol' Toivo. So how do you know Toivo, madam?" Denny had seen her blush and knew he was onto something.

"He's my boyfriend." Her pulse resonated throughout her body.

"No! You're "K" something?!"

"Kerttu."

"Right! Kerrrrttu! Got to get those rrrrs rrrrolling. So, Kerrrrttu, you got here after all. He was worried you wouldn't show. So, how the hell is my friend Toivo?"

"I thought you would know, Mr. Arnold."

"How? I haven't seen good ol' pissed-off-with-God Toivo for months." He paused. "Well, that's not exactly true. I did see him in some footage from the front—"

He saw pain in her eyes and ran out of words.

He needed a drink. He sucked the moisture from his mouth and swallowed hard—he desperately needed to get out of the room and away from everyone.

"Mr. Arnold, have you been drinking?" Kerttu asked, although she knew the answer; she had lifelong experience with drunks.

"You bet I have. Would you like some gin?"

She ignored his question; she had one of her own. "How can you not know where Toivo is when you've been writing about him?"

She held up *The New York Times* she had carried in her shoulder bag. Denny snatched the paper from her; his eye caught a front-page story about Mayor La Guardia being in trouble with the unions—again; he knew the mayor and had expected him to have troubles like those.

New York...

Denny felt a sudden longing for it.

"Mr. Arnold, where is Toivo?"

Her voice sounded as if it came from a tunnel.

... Toivo...

He wanted to go away, lie down; anything but be there in the lobby with them.

"Mr. Arnold, where is Toivo?" his friend's woman asked again.

... Toivo...

"I haven't got a clue," Denny answered truthfully, and with a great deal of discomfort. An idea struck him, inspired by the cable he had received earlier that day from a friend at a Madison Avenue advertising agency. The cable informed him that his series of articles on the hero Toivo Karjalainen were highly appreciated reading and the agency was seriously considering hiring him.

Denny studied Kerttu intently—and when Denny Arnold was focused, he had few equals.

"Martti, I have an idea. A damn good idea! I think even you might like it. Can you help this—I believe *pregnant* lady find her young man?"

Kerttu looked Denny straight in the eye. "Do you have a problem with me being pregnant, Mr. Arnold?"

"Not a bit. You being pregnant would make for an even better story, but that's not the story I want to write."

Denny turned to Martti. "Picture the caption: 'Lovers Reunited At The Front'! Now, there's a headline that will get your country the votes you need on Capitol Hill—and me closer to the Pulitzer!'

"Mr. Arnold, the front isn't safe enou—" Martti didn't get any further.

"I don't care! How does that grab you? You think I am worth more to you alive than dead, don't you? And you're right, I am! But if you don't take this lady and me to the front so she can see her man and I can write my Pulitzer Prize winning story, I will destroy every damn bit of goodwill I have gotten you in America—and that's the name of that tune! Don't mess with me, Martti; I'm on a mission! Get us a car—and get me a camera while you're at it!"

Martti knew that Denny's stories about the soldier-artist Karjalainen could further assist Finland to receive international support, political and otherwise: thousands of men and women from around the world had already volunteered to help Finland in its plight. But he also knew that permission to bring Denny and the pregnant lady to the front would have to come from the top of the Ministry. He would have to exercise all of his persuasive wiles—his career would be in jeopardy, but perhaps was it worth it.

Martti studied Denny's crutches as if they were the answer to his dilemma, as if they could prevent the excursion to the front, but Denny was in fine form. Like Hemingway, whom he had met and had drinks with, Denny did his best work when he wasn't sober and past caring; when all was spontaneous and non-judgmental; when instinct and talent ruled the moment; when courage was unleashed, caution squashed, and his internal editor— all creative individuals' worst nemesis—was silent.

"I'll need snowshoes on my crutches." And with that Denny sealed the matter. The look in his eyes demanded that he be taken seriously. He knew he had a great story in the making—it was his and his alone; it was his Pulitzer and he was not about to let it slip away.

Martti knew the Foreign Ministry and its needs; he also knew Denny. He sighed; he would have to find a driver with a car good enough to bring them to the northern front. He knew where Toivo Karjalainen was; with help from a friend at the Defense Ministry he had located the young Finn, on paper at least, a few hours after Denny's story broke several weeks earlier. That was then

———

... if Toivo Karjalainen is dead when we get there, Denny Arnold's story will sink Finland's standing in Washington...

. . .

Chapter Forty Eight

Pennanen anxiously watched the enemy reconnaissance plane as it circled high above the frozen lake then sped off toward the Soviet Union; he knew they would soon be paid another visit by the enemy in one form or another. He was concerned about the number of prisoners—they far outnumbered their captors. A few minutes earlier a runner from headquarters had delivered the message that Pennanen's company was needed elsewhere; a Red Army division would reportedly cross into Finland on a nearby road later that day.

Pennanen had too much to think about; he was exhausted, battle-weary. He gave Reijo an order to gather the prisoners. He then saw Toivo leaning against a fisherman's shack; it looked as if he was writing yet another letter.

Indeed Toivo was and it was an important letter—it was to Kerttu. He wrote how he deplored the war and his role in it, lamenting there wasn't anything he could do to end it—it wasn't like a work-in-progress painting over which he had total control; he was greatly troubled and questioned his will to live.

He wrote with a stubby pencil on the back of a Russian propaganda leaflet. The paper was moist, of poor quality, and kept tearing under the pencil's point. He tried to concentrate on what he was writing—but couldn't ignore the wet, miserable survivors from the Soviet battalion being herded together.

'So many died last night,' he wrote. *'I fired my rifle at those I saw were drowning, hoping to shorten their*

suffering. I've killed and loathe myself. What has become of me? What kind of person am I? What is my purpose on Earth now—do I even have one anymore? I loathe what I have become and fear that you will be ashamed of me—'

Gleeful shouts broke the stillness. Toivo looked out over the lake where Jussi and others were riding a carousel of dead horses frozen into grotesque shapes where they had succumbed. The men had found bottles of vodka in a Red Army wagon; they passed them among each other, taking long swigs; when the bottles were empty, they threw them at the corpses, cheering each time a bottle shattered into pieces.

Toivo tried to ignore the madness around him—even as he could feel his own creeping up on him.

'When I look at the dead I also see their children and wives... their mothers and fathers... if it wasn't for the uniforms I couldn't tell them from us—'

A bottle smashed into the shed above Toivo's head. He looked over to see Jussi glower at him—Jussi had meant for the bottle to hit Toivo; he fervently believed that Toivo had killed Timo.

"You killed my best friend, you son of a bitch!"

Toivo kept writing.

'I wonder if those who died really cared where the border was drawn... if it really mattered to them whether it was a hundred meters this way or that...

Another bottle smashed into the shed; he didn't even look up.

'I wonder if what really mattered to them was to have someone who loved them and children in whose image they saw themselves... I wonder if those who start these wars ever think about matters like these... when I look at the faces of the dead, I hope what they fought for somehow has gained in importance—'

265

The remaining prisoners were herded past Toivo toward the larger group of prisoners being guarded by Finns with machine guns. When a gaunt and shivering Russian stopped near Toivo to warm his bare hands with his breath, Toivo offered him the gloves Tessa had given him; as the man reached for them, shouts of protest broke out from the other prisoners—the Finns were placing machine guns in a threatening arc around them.

The Russian spit at Toivo, threw Tessa's gloves in the snow, and trudged off toward his worried comrades.

Toivo hurriedly slogged through the knee-high deep snow to Pennanen and Reijo.

"What are you doing?!"

"What has to be done! We're needed north of here and can't take them with us." Reijo looked away; he wasn't always as callous as he would have liked to be.

"But you can't just *shoot* them!"

"We have to, dammit! We can't just let them go! Get out of the way!"

Pennanen nodded to his machine gunners—who took aim.

"No!" Toivo waded through the snow toward the prisoners. He faced his comrades and their machine guns, spreading his arms wide as if to protect the Russians behind him. "You can't do this! They are human beings and soldiers just like us!"

"*Russian* soldiers! Sent here to kill Finns! Get out of the way!" Pennanen was furious.

A murmur rose from the prisoners; they were becoming agitated.

"No! This is *not* defending our country!" Toivo was just as furious as his captain. "This is *not* a noble cause! This is *murder*!"

"This is *war*! Step aside, dammit!" Pennanen unholstered his pistol and aimed at Toivo.

"Wait, Captain!" Reijo trudged closer to Toivo. "What do you want us to do? We can't take them with us!

And we don't have food for them—we don't even have enough people to guard them!"

"But you can't just shoot them! It isn't right!" Toivo was adamant.

"Out of the way, both of you! We have to do this!" Pennanen yelled at the top of his lungs.

"No!" Toivo remained in front of the prisoners, shielding them with his body and outstretched arms. "You can't do this! They are people just like us!"

One of the prisoners began to shout a Stalinist slogan; others joined in; still others began to head toward the nearby forest, some reaching for hidden bayonets, tree branches, rocks, and whatever else they could find in the snow.

It was impossible to determine who started it—perhaps the Finn who tried to stop one of the prisoners from escaping and got knocked down in the process.

The prisoners attacked—the Finns opened fire—utter chaos ensued——

When the haze from the gunfire lifted Toivo found himself in the snow surrounded by dead and dying Russian soldiers. A bullet had pierced the fleshy part of his thigh; several more had torn his loose-fitting white ski-suit but miraculously missed the rest of his body.

Toivo ignored his wound when he saw Reijo aim his rifle at a prisoner who was struggling to his feet despite being in his death throes "Don't shoot him, Reijo!" A primal wail that didn't sound anything like his own voice escaped him: "When will this end?"

"When there are fewer of them than there are of us!" Reijo lowered his rifle. The prisoner no longer tried to get to his feet; his life was ebbing.

Pennanen plunged through the snow toward them, his pistol aimed at Toivo.

"Damn you, Toivo Karjalainen!"

He pulled the trigger. The hammer clicked against an empty chamber. He removed the clip; stared at it; searched his pouches, couldn't find any ammunition; threw his pistol at Toivo—and missed.

"Reijo, shoot the son-of-a-bitch!"

Toivo faced Pennanen. "Shoot! Go ahead and shoot! I don't want to live like this! You lied! You said serving our country was a noble cause! Look at us! Look at what we have become!"

"Shoot the son-of-a-bitch, Reijo! Shoot him!"

"I can't just shoot him, Captain!"

"SHOOT HIM!"

"But, Captain—you need approval…"

"I'll get the approval. I'll have the son-of-a-bitch executed for treason. To hell with you, Toivo Karjalainen! To hell with you!"

Overhead passed a low-flying Russian fighter returning from inland engagements. The pilot banked the plane to get a better look at the carnage below.

A few prisoners waved their arms at the pilot; they were promptly shot by Finns.

The pilot, out of ammunition and low on fuel, shook a clenched fist at the Finns below, wagged his wings, and flew away.

Snow fell—softly, quietly, delicately coating the trees; each branch, each pine needle; each corpse; each hair.

. . .

Chapter Forty Nine

The snowfall had stopped; a cold white blanket shrouded the corpses. Near the fisherman's shack stood a somber firing squad: Reijo and eight others from Pennanen's ski company. They all had rifles; they all were looking at the shack with its door boarded shut.

Toivo looked out through the shack's glass-less window through which not even a small child could escape. He was at peace, even though he would soon die at the hands of his comrades. He tapped the mercury container of the thermometer outside the window; it was -48°.

He gently tapped the thermometer again—it shattered.

High in the sky, a Soviet artillery spotter plane appeared and began to circle.

Jussi arrived on skis and took his place in the firing squad.

"What did the battalion doctor say?" Reijo asked.

"That I'm going blind; something about sugar. Timo was right after all." Jussi's voice hardened. "I'm ready. Let's shoot the son-of-a-bitch! Let's get this over with!"

"Captain said to wait until he gets back with the official go-ahead." Reijo silently hoped Pennanen's request to have Toivo executed would be denied.

In the distance the whump of Soviet artillery started up; soon, shells landed and exploded not far away.

The Soviet artillery spotter plane descended somewhat; continued circling.

A misfiring Finnish Foreign Ministry staff car wheezed to a halt near the group; out stepped Martti, Kerttu, and Denny, who had a camera around his neck and ski-pole-baskets attached to the tips of his crutches.

Martti, the Foreign Ministry officer, studied the firing squad's somber faces.

"Any of you men know where we can find Toivo Karjalainen?"

No one replied.

The incoming artillery fire increased, but the explosions were still some distance away.

Denny spotted the face of someone who looked like Toivo peering out the window of the nearby shack.

He snapped a couple of pictures, but he didn't like the emptiness he saw in the haggard man's face; it sobered him.

If that was indeed the artist Toivo who experienced life with every fiber of his being; a tragedy had occurred.

If that was his friend Toivo, he was angered; if that was the soul who was angry with God, he had the right to be.

"Reijo!" Kerttu struggled through the snow to him; she was alarmed when he wouldn't directly look at her.

"What's wrong, Reijo? Has something happened to Toivo?"

As Reijo struggled to find a delicate way to answer her question, the artillery shells began exploding closer to them.

Kerttu repeated her question.

"Talk to me, Reijo, has something happened to Toivo?"

Reijo pointed; Kerttu saw Toivo and rushed to him.

Denny snapped pictures when the two lovers grasped each other's hands through the window.

The roar of many engines filled the air. A flight of Soviet bombers led by a single fighter dropped their loads; the bombs fell harmlessly in the woods. The bombers departed. The single fighter buzzed around like an angry bee—and then it too departed.

The Soviet artillery spotter plane re-appeared, circling.

Kerttu and Toivo held each other's hands and looked into each other's eyes; although each had changed, their love had not.

"My love, I was afraid I would never see you again," she said, gently touching his frozen, unshaven face.

He still didn't believe it was her—that she was standing there.

... she could be some kind of a ghost—

He touched her face with icy fingers that were numb, yet they told him that she was real—and right there in front of him.

"Kerttu... Kerttu..." was all he could say.

They stared at each other, uncomprehending—it was all so surreal; there seemed to be so much to say, but a jumble of emotion smothered the words.

All while the artillery shelling continued, increasing in intensity, and the explosions marched ever closer.

Pennanen arrived in a lorry, jumped down, and was immediately cornered by Martti; their conversation was lost in the rapidly increasing artillery shelling.

Denny turned to Reijo and asked him a question; he heard the answer, exploded with fury, and charged at Martti. "Martti, tell that dumb son-of-a-bitch of a captain that the man he wants to execute is a fucking hero in the American press! Tell him what that means! Tell him how little attention this war would get in the American press solely on its merits as a war! Zip, shit, nothing! The big goose

271

egg, Martti! No one cares! No one gives a shit if every fucking one of you dies, or whether Stalin runs your country, or Hitler, or Lady Godiva! No one gives a shit because they don't have to! They don't *know* you! They aren't related to you! What's the matter with you people? What fucking century are you living in? Tell that fucking moron how difficult it is for you to get your country favorable international publicity so your government can buy weapons and ammunition on credit! And then explain to me how numb-nuts over there can be allowed to execute the one and only hero you have in the American press—because he tried to stop captain dumb-ass fucking moron from executing prisoners of war! *He* is the one who should be shot!!!"

Incoming artillery shells exploded ever closer.

"Get the girl out of here!" Martti yelled, concerned about civilian casualties under his protection.

The driver vainly cranked the staff car's starter.

The explosions marched closer.

"Get the girl!" yelled Martti to the lorry driver.

Denny snapped pictures of the unfolding drama.

The driver ran toward Kerttu who was still clutching Toivo's hands.

"Are you ashamed of me?" Toivo worriedly asked Kerttu; he knew he wasn't like the others and had so many doubts about himself and who he was—*if he wasn't as bad a person as they said he was, why would they want to execute him?*

The shelling was loud: Kerttu couldn't hear what Toivo was saying—and she didn't get a chance to ask him to say it again; the driver grabbed her and carried her to his lorry. Ignoring her protests, he pushed her inside, leapt in, and shoved it into gear.

"Kerttu!" Toivo hammered at the shack's door that was boarded shut; his cry was lost among the explosions.

High above them, the enemy artillery spotter kept circling.

Kerttu freed herself from the lorry driver's grip, wrenched open the door, leapt out into the snow and headed back to Toivo. The driver slammed on the brakes.

Shells from heavier artillery began to land close by.

Martti caught up with Kerttu, swept her up and carried her back to the lorry. He shoved her back inside and held the door shut while he stood on the running board.

"Go!" Martti ordered the driver, restraining Kerttu still trying to escape as the lorry gathered speed.

From his perch on the running board of the lorry, Martti yelled to Pennanen:

"Get the artist out of that shed and back on duty! And get the American the hell out of here!"

As the driver tried to get his staff car running, Denny managed to take one last photo before Reijo shoved him inside the car.

Denny grabbed Reijo's sleeve, reached into his coat and pulled out his .38 that he handed to Reijo. "Give this to Toivo—remind him it's for self-protection!"

The engine caught; the driver headed off in the opposite direction from the lorry.

Artillery grenades were falling farther away in the forest.

Pennanen watched the staff car as it departed.

"I'll take that revolver," he ordered Reijo, then turned to the waiting firing squad. "Let the son-of-a-bitch out—"

The lorry careened down a narrow forest road with shells exploding all around it; Kerttu huddling next to the driver; Martti still hanging onto the running board.

An errant shell from a big gun exploded in the road in front of them; the lorry hit the crater and flipped over on its side, crushing Martti against the frozen road.

The lorry caught fire.

More shells landed nearby.

The driver pulled Kerttu out of the lorry's burning wreckage and dragged her to the relative safety of the forest.

More shells exploded among the trees.

Terrified, Kerttu protected her stomach with folded arms as she backed away from the explosions.

She stumbled over a fallen log and fell backwards with her legs in the air—just as another shell hit a nearby tree, splintering it and skewering Kerttu's legs with jagged wooden.

The lorry driver rushed to Kerttu and heard her moan:

"… the baby… save his baby…"

The driver didn't understand English, but he sensed her words were important.

High in the sky above them, the Soviet artillery spotter plane headed east, back to its base, done for the day

. . .

Chapter Fifty

A naked corpse stood upright in the snow at the side of the road; someone had hung a road repair sign on its outstretched arm.

The road was narrow and crater-filled, blocked by fallen trees and surrounded by dense pines. Human and horse remains were scattered here and there, along with shot-up, useless Red Army tanks, lorries, and wagons that had been abandoned—bleak reminders of a Red Army Division's recent attempt to gain control of the area.

As the Finns decimated the division, Soviet fighter planes and bombers had flown overhead, their pilots helplessly watching their comrades die on the narrow road below at the hands of the unseen enemy in the primeval forest.

Of the 18,000 Red Army soldiers, cooks, and nurses, few had survived—and of those, fewer than half had made it safely back across the border. Being back in the Soviet Union, however, was no guarantee of survival as many were located and executed by *politruks* for their failure to accomplish their military objective.

Hidden in the forest Pennanen and his men now watched another Red Army Division attempt to cross the border in order to tear Finland in half.

Another 18,000 men and women were crouched behind tanks, vehicles, and horse-drawn wagons that had been halted by impassable craters in the road. All suffered terribly in the bitter cold; the previous night the temperature had dipped to -56°. It was one of the coldest winters in Finland's recorded history.

Red Army soldiers who tried to fill the craters with rocks were promptly shot by Finnish snipers defending their country's sovereignty.

Pennanen and his men joined up with several other companies spread in a thin line in the forest near the road; they crouched behind trees and rocks, ensuring that none of the entrapped Russians escaped.

Toivo stared off into space, lost in thought, lamenting the endless death and suffering and his all-too brief meeting with Kerttu—fortunately unaware of her accident and the life-threatening injuries she suffered.

Red Army men and women warmed their hands on the exhausts of idling tanks and lorries; some were shot and fell to the ground, a few spasmed before quieting.

Toivo cringed as each shot rang out.

Soviet soldiers tried to dig burrows to shield themselves from the bullets thinning their ranks; their shovels and pick-axes clanged as they hit the solidly frozen ground—more shots rang out, more of them died with shovels and pickaxes in hand atop shallow would-be safe havens.

The Soviet invaders, rifles at the ready, frantically scanned the forest for a sign of the enemy—there was none.

One by one, the Red Army engines sputtered into silence as they ran out of gas.

One Soviet soldier hammered out a tune on his accordion. His comrades began to dance. More shots rang out; more invaders fell.

The music abruptly stopped; the accordionist had been shot.

The dancing stopped too.

There was a brief silence as though homage was being paid.

Shots were randomly fired; soldiers died at random.

A Red Army soldier began to sing a Russian lullaby in a lilting tenor.

Others joined in, then others; the volume swelled.

In the forest, prone in the snow and invisible in their snowsuits, Toivo, Reijo, and Jussi listened to the lullaby.

"Tell me what you see." Jussi wanted to know.

"They are singing." Reijo answered, unthinkingly.

"Really? You're officer material. I can hear they are singing, Reijo! I'm not deaf, I just don't see very well," Jussi said, frustrated and fearful of his advancing blindness.

Among stalled tanks enemy soldiers huddled over a fire, dropping a few frozen potatoes into a can of boiling water, impatiently watching the water bubble.

One man couldn't wait any longer; he stuck a fork into the can and skewered a potato; with his eyes closed, he savored its aroma, blew on it, and began to peel it with his bayonet.

A shot rang out——

Into the snow fell the steaming hot potato—still on its fork.

Behind an armored radio car, a nervous Red Army soldier crouched next to a wheel that was held to its hub with only one intact lug nut; the other lugs had been beaten sideways with a mallet to hold the rim in place.

He scanned the forest with his rifle in hand.

Inside the armored car, a radioman urgently whispered into his microphone: "Father Stalin, please help us."

A shot rang out from the forest—the radioman slumped over his radio.

Another shot rang out—the nervous soldier would be nervous no more as his comrades scanned the forest in vain for the enemy.

Perched high in a pine, a white-clad Finnish sharpshooter lowered his still-smoking rifle, grinned broadly and dropped a pine cone onto Toivo who was positioned at the base of the tree.

Toivo looked up and saw the sharpshooter grinning at him.

A bullet twanged—the sharpshooter tumbled and landed with a thud next to Toivo.

He looked up at Toivo, blood pouring from his head wound. He reached for him; there was so much he wanted to say—his life ebbed——

On the road, a Red Army invader tried to start his tank— the solenoid clicked a final few times and was silent. Red Army soldiers ducked into any place they could find that seemed to offer the remotest chance of safety. *Politruks* scurried among them, attempting to force them out, often shooting them. Examples had to be set.

Toivo couldn't watch any more. He shut his eyes—his entire being shrieked with battle fatigue. He was ashamed that he was still alive; he thought that Kerttu had rightfully abandoned him.

Men on both sides thought there was far too much fighting and dying over such a small forest road.

New Year's Day. 1940.

. . .

Chapter Fifty One

In a Finnish country hospital in northern Karelia, a nurse removed the chloroform mask from a young woman on an operating table. She then called for the overworked surgeon who was using bailing wire to sew up the chest of a young soldier who had died a few minutes earlier; a grenade splinter had pierced his heart. It was a strong heart, but all hearts have their limits, even those defending their country.

The young surgeon, who until the outbreak of the war had remembered each of his surgeries—every death as well as every success—now couldn't even remember the cause of death of the young man whose body he was making presentable for the undertaker. He was that tired, that emotionally drained; he hadn't slept for nearly fifty hours. The casualties kept coming.

He tied off the bailing wire and wearily shuffled over to look at the young woman: she was in an early stage of pregnancy and she was pretty; she looked a lot like his sister who had been killed when the school where she taught was flattened by Soviet bombers.

The note said the woman had been given morphine. He struggled to keep his mind clear while he looked over her mangled, splinter-filled legs, but he was distracted by more casualties: soldiers who urgently needed his attention—one was screaming in terrible pain.

The young surgeon had a dreadful dilemma; he solved it—

... her legs must go... there is a limit to what I can do...

He reached for an orthopedic saw.

"… his baby… save his baby, please…" The woman moaned softly.

With the limb remover in hand, he leaned closer to her.

"… save his baby…"

The young surgeon had spent six months at Boston College; hearing the English language again jolted him, made his heart race; a last vestige of adrenaline kicked in.

He put aside the orthopedic saw, reached for a scalpel, and began to cut into her legs.

… I can do it… I know I can… maybe she will walk again…

The soldier who had been in terrible pain no longer was; the nurse moved him into a closet; other wounded soldiers were arriving.

. . .

Chapter Fifty Two

Toivo and the others watched from among the trees as a *politruk* pulled Brigade Commander Vinogradov from an armored car and held a submachine gun to his chest.

The commanding general of the ill-fated division knew his life was finished. It had not been a particularly distinguished one, but he had been one of few in the Red Army to attain the rank of general before turning forty.

He braced himself against his onrushing death, refusing to whimper in front of his troops and the comrades suddenly turned foe.

"Comrades, Father Stalin is displeased with your efforts," the *politruk* called out loudly to the soldiers in hiding.

From their hideouts Soviet men and women watched their comrade general button and straighten his coat.

The *politruk* aimed a submachine gun at their leader's head and pulled the trigger.

The slide didn't move—it was frozen solid.

The *politruk* beat on his submachine gun with his fist.

Another *politruk* pulled a pistol from inside her coat and shot Vinogradov.

He stumbled and fell; his legs briefly kept moving—then were still.

"Father Stalin, why have you abandoned us?" A distraught soldier wailed.

The cry reverberated among the silent tanks and solidly frozen trees.

Others joined in.

Soon hundreds of Red Army men and women beseeched Father Stalin in a swelling crescendo; clearly they knew the cause they were there for wasn't worth their suffering and dying.

One man left his hole and began walking with his hands above his head toward the Finnish forest; others followed.

A *politruk* fired at the defectors with a submachine gun; some scurried back to their holes, others ran even faster toward the forest.

Reijo grabbed a Red Army soldier and dragged him to Pennanen.

"I have five children!" the soldier said, although he really had only two. "Let me live," he begged, dropping to his knees in the snow.

"Why should I?" Pennanen, like many Finns from Karelia, spoke some Russian. "What will you do for me?"

"I'll tell you where Marshall Voroshilov will be tonight!" said the Red Army soldier who treasured his life more than Soviet Union secrets.

Reijo turned to Toivo. "Amazing what people will do to live."

"Yes, amazing," said Toivo. "But why bother?"

The sky roared as four Soviet fighters swooped down on them with machine guns blazing; bullets tore up people, trees and the frozen ground.

Everyone except Toivo took cover—he faced the diving fighter planes with outstretched arms.

"Kill me!"

The Soviet fighters disappeared——

Toivo wandered off into the forest, wrenched by his inner pain and lost in the stupor of battle fatigue, dragging his semi-automatic rifle like an unwanted appendage attached to his hand.

He came upon an enemy soldier sitting on a log with a human head in his lap, intently carving a slice of flesh from its face with a knife.

When he saw Toivo, the Red Army soldier put the slice of human flesh in his mouth and proudly held up the head.

"*Ominya tavaritj* [my friend]," he stated, childlike, and then sliced off a piece of flesh that he offered Toivo.

Overcome by the depravity that he had been immersed in for weeks, Toivo let out a primal, protesting wail and fired his weapon wildly, killing the cannibal and spattering bullets into his surroundings.

Frantically he scampered further into the forest, blindly falling into a hole and landing next to two soldiers. One he thought was a Russian, the other a Finn; the two soldiers were embracing, frozen to death in sitting positions—their attempt to defeat the bitter cold by warming each other having failed so miserably.

Toivo was transfixed by the halo-like glow around the corpses' heads from the sunlight that filtered through the pines and lit upon them—a halo much like the one he saw around his sister's head.

He startled when Denny's Smith & Wesson suddenly landed beside him. He looked up and found Pennanen gazing at him with coldly encouraging eyes, sneering with contempt, as if he didn't believe Toivo had the courage to use the gun.

"Go ahead, use the yank's gun!" Pennanen spit in Toivo's direction and walked off.

Toivo reached for the revolver meant for self-protection. He placed its muzzle to his head. His heart fluttered, then settled into a strong steady beat. A peculiar kind of elation washed over him as he approached the freedom he was sure would momentarily be his.

He was squeezing the trigger when a hand from above reached down and wrested the revolver away.

"Killing yourself is not going to end this war!" Reijo said. Toivo stared at him, startled out of his suicidal reverie; Reijo was dressed in a Russian uniform. He gripped Toivo's shoulder firmly and continued with great conviction: "It will only end you and your dream—and then I will know that what you claimed was important to you, really wasn't. Here, put this on."

He dropped a Red Army uniform in Toivo's lap. "If you really want to do something to end this war, you will put that uniform on. We're going to kill Voroshilov. That'll put a kink in Stalin's armor."

. . .

Chapter Fifty Three

As Toivo joined the rest of the ski patrol for the mission, they heard a droning sound: a TB-3 bomber was approaching. At the time the largest airplane ever built, the TB-3 was a behemoth with a wingspan of 45 meters.

The TB-3's pilot and co-pilot were dismayed by what they saw below: another Soviet division seemingly annihilated. Tanks and armored cars were burning. Countless bodies of men, women, and horses littered the ground.

"Dead—all our comrades are dead," said the co-pilot, shocked and angry. "And not a single Finn to be seen."

"Must be down there somewhere." Just one week earlier the pilot had taken delivery of the plane at the factory in Novosibirsk. He was eager to get into battle; he had waited a long time for the opportunity to serve Mother Russia and Father Stalin.

The plane was a prototype, a rework of earlier models; this version had a retractable landing gear. After the pilot selected a crew, they had flown across five time zones, refueling at pre-designated airports where *politruks* greeted them with Party slogans and pamphlets that the crew was required to read before drifting off to sleep in a tent near their plane.

They had eagerly anticipated clashing with the neighbor that threatened the Soviet Union's stability. Now they were here, proud and eager to fight, ready to defend their country.

The pilot lowered the flaps, pushed the yoke forward and the rudder pedal to the right.

The glistening new bomber began a wide clearing turn. Bundled in a bearskin suit covered with waterproofed canvas, the nose gunner made several attempts to clear his frozen machine gun, but it wouldn't fire. He and his gun were exposed to the air; the wind-chill factor was -90°. The gun's newly applied grease, which had shone in the sun in Odessa, was frozen solid, less pliant than concrete.

The TB-3 flew low over the forest, skimming the tops of trees before it headed out over the snow-covered lake that Reijo's ski patrol was traversing.

The Finns saw the plane approach and quickly dropped into the snow, their white camouflage making them virtually indistinguishable from the Arctic landscape.

Too late, the pilot saw the Finns—who opened fire with their *Suomi* machine guns, hitting the TB-3 with hundreds of rounds; the co-pilot and nose gunner were instantly killed, the pilot badly wounded. The top and rear gunners frantically beat their fists bloody on their frozen weapons.

The pilot gave the engines full throttle and took the TB-3 out of the *Suomi* machine guns' range.

Furious with the Finns for destroying his fine plane and crew before he had been given the chance to do something heroic for his Motherland, the pilot put the TB-3 into a wide descending turn and then aimed the giant plane right at Reijo's men.

He brought the plane lower and lower—until the TB-3's propellers churned like giant egg-beaters through the powdered snow.

Reijo's men hunkered down deeper into the snow.

The pilot screamed with fury as he aimed his plane at the Finns who desperately tried to elude the scything propellers.

A propeller hit a Finn, shredding him, disintegrating the wooden blades. The engine raced and began to break apart; the pilot shut down the failing engine, gave the other three full power, and pulled on the yoke.

The TB-3 began to climb up from the snow on its remaining three engines, the pilot pulling on the yoke with dwindling strength.

Toivo lay flat on his back in the snow, compressed by the air pressure as the TB-3 thundered by just a few feet above him, splattering his face with hot engine oil. He tore off his mitten, wiped his face with his hand, and stared at the black oil on his fingers.

The pilot circled the lake and returned, descending until it again whipped the snow into a haze and tore another Finn to shreds.

The pilot shut down one more engine, gave the other two full power and pulled with all his remaining strength on the yoke.

The TB-3 ascended but with both engines on one side shut down, it started a wing roll.

The pilot, who had done everything he could for his Soviet Union, stoically shut down the two remaining engines and saluted his crewmates moments before crashing into the trees just beyond the shore.

Explosions rocked the forest, buffeting the air.

Reijo's men spread snow over the remains of their dead.

Toivo rubbed the enemy's black oil on his hand, feeling its abrasive patina.

Silently, the survivors of the ski patrol reloaded their weapons and skied toward the nearby border.

. . .

Chapter Fifty Four

Kerttu was dancing; the orchestra played a song she had never heard before, a style of music that was unfamiliar to her but was easy to dance to.

She had never danced better, never pirouetted so incredibly quickly—so quickly that she felt somewhat dizzy.

She was alone on a stage that was dark, so dark that she couldn't see her legs that suddenly throbbed with pain.

Neither could she see an audience; it was obscured by fog, but something was there—she could hear panting as if hundreds of beasts crouched in waiting.

Faster and faster she pirouetted—she had never before danced so well.

Ah, but her legs were tired and shrieked with pain.

The footlights were bright, different from The Jolly Show Cabaret; they were colder and spun along with her.

...my legs! What's wrong with my legs?...

The strange song continued, less pleasing now—

She spun endlessly, giddily, dizzily.

Her stomach lurched.

Her legs were screaming now, the pain filling the universe, blotting out everything except the droning sound that intensified her nausea.

The lights suddenly vanished.

She was alone—so terribly alone.

From far off she heard a weeping sound.

Someone gagged; she wondered who—
  She couldn't breathe—

She opened her eyes to find a stainless steel tray filled with bile resting coldly against her cheek.

She couldn't move her legs——they felt as if spikes had been driven through them, pinning them down——

—a stench filled her nostrils——

  ... oh, dear God, don't let anything happen to Toivo's baby...

. . .

Chapter Fifty Five

It was a clear night; a crescent moon hung in the sky. A transport plane with engines running sat on the road that served as airfield for the Soviet Union's 47th Army.

Nearby, a group of heavily armed Red Army soldiers a n d *politruks* guarded the biggest tent in the huge encampment.

Defense Commissar Voroshilov sat inside the tent listening to senior *politruks* and other civilians tell the military how to beat the Finns; they had brought Olympic skiers to train some of their elite soldiers, some had already strapped on their skis in their eagerness to please to Defense Commissar.

They waited for him outside in the cold; Voroshilov was a god of sorts, much like Stalin; rumors of his visit had spread among them days earlier, perhaps because it was so unprecedented.

No one noticed the seventeen skiers in Red Army coats and headgear who silently swooped in from the forest.

Toivo and Reijo schussed around the back of a tent and were instantly whipped by the transport plane's prop-wash. They shielded their eyes from the blowing snow— and ran right into Defense Commissar Voroshilov, whom Toivo knew well: only a few weeks earlier, he had fired two bullseyes into his caricature.

Voroshilov had decided to leave via the tent's smaller rear entrance; it was closer to the waiting plane, and he didn't want to mingle with the soldiers waiting for him at the front entrance.

The entourage of *politruks* obediently following him watched Voroshilov laugh out loud when he saw the amazed looks on the faces of the two Red Army soldiers who stood easily on their skis, a match for any Finn.

Voroshilov was encouraged, gave the shorter of the two a friendly pat on the shoulder, then continued toward the plane, completely surrounded and shielded by *politruks*.

One of them turned to Toivo, whose hand was on the *Suomi* machine pistol inside his jacket—he was ready; all he needed was a clear line of sight to his target.

"How do you know comrade Defense Commissar?" the *politruk* asked.

Toivo wheezed and coughed, pointing apologetically to his throat.

Near the camp's perimeter, surrounded by hundreds of elite Red Army soldiers, the rest of Reijo's patrol slipped out their concealed *Suomi* machine pistols and *Lahti-Saloranta* light machine guns.

At the plane's door Voroshilov turned to wave to his admiring troops when he saw the soldier, the one he had patted on the shoulder a few moments ago, take out a *Suomi* machine pistol from under his coat; at the same instant, Voroshilov noticed the soldier's uniquely Finnish *pieksu* boots and bindings.

Voroshilov bared his teeth and quickly scanned the other soldiers—more of them wore the Finnish boots and bindings; he shouted a warning to the *politruks*, pointing out the enemy among them.

The plane's pilot revved the engines to take-off setting.

Toivo and Reijo, directly in the transport's prop-wash, were forced to shield their eyes from blowing snow and debris and couldn't get a good aim at Voroshilov who disappeared into the plane that quickly commenced its take-off roll.

Toivo, Reijo and the other Finns opened fire on the departing plane.

Politruks and Red Army Soldiers fired at the Finns, instantly tearing most of them apart.

Bullets smashed Reijo's hands; he cried out and dropped his weapon.

Toivo wrapped his arm around Reijo and shoved him behind a tent that was then blasted by wildly fired shots.

The firefight was chaotic: the night was dark; there were few distinguishing differences between friend and foe.

Voroshilov's plane rose into the air and disappeared into the night.

Toivo grabbed Reijo, supporting him as they skied toward the forest.

Politruks and Red Army soldiers spotted them just as they entered the tree line. They fired in blind anger at the two fleeing Finns as well as into the bodies of the Finns already dead or dying in the snow around them.

Several of the Olympic skiers quickly strapped on their skis to pursue the two Finns, in such a frenzy to catch the intruders that they didn't stop to arm themselves.

The Olympic skiers' enthusiasm for the hunt quickly waned when Toivo fired a few bursts from his machine pistol; all but a few of them dropped to the ground; armed Soviet soldiers on skis and on foot then took up the chase.

Toivo and Reijo fled as fast as they could, bullets hitting everywhere around them—two of the Olympic skiers had grabbed weapons from the dead and were gaining on them.

Toivo and Reijo slowed, awkwardly shedding their bulky Red Army coats and headgear as they skied.

There was a burst of fire from the Olympic skiers; Reijo stumbled and fell, his back and legs riddled with bullets.

As Toivo bent down to pick up Reijo, a stray bullet ricocheted off a rock, twanged into his head and lodged in his skull, stunning him. He dropped to his knees, losing his hold on Reijo, turned around and fired his machine pistol, emptying it. The Olympic skiers went down.

Toivo grabbed a handful of snow and held it against his head to stop the bleeding. He pulled Reijo to his feet with the other hand, slung him over his shoulder and tried to ski. It didn't work. He dragged Reijo underneath the branches of a snow-laden pine.

Still pressing the snow against his head wound, he emerged, found a broken off branch, swept away their tracks, crawled back in under the pine's skirt, held his breath and listened—

—over the whine of the wind as it blew through the trees, he could faintly hear the sounds of their pursuers.

He bundled Reijo up as best he could, pressed fresh snow against the hole in his head and closed his eyes.

. . .

Toivo came to, heard shouts and realized he was numb with cold. His head throbbed. He touched his head wound and winced, looked for Reijo, but couldn't see him; it was too dark. He reached for him to check for his pulse, but couldn't feel a thing; his fingers were too numb.

He could hear their pursuers angrily complain as they searched the forest, their kerosene lamps blinding them more than helping them. Once they found the bodies of their Olympic comrades, they grew even angrier—firing bursts of bullets into suspicious-looking snowdrifts and other potential hiding places while they continued their search.

Toivo reached for Reijo and whispered: "How are you doing?"

Reijo's voice was faint. "...can't... feel...my legs... and my hands are all shot to shit—wish... I was...back in Chicago——"

Toivo's head throbbed. He touched the hole in his skull, thought he could feel the bullet move.

"... got you... in the... head, did they—guess... they didn't know it's empty— should... have... gone... for your... heart—you have something there——"

They shivered uncontrollably from the bitter cold; their teeth chattered like castanets.

Toivo bundled up Reijo as best he could. He gauged Reijo's condition by his faintly irregular breathing; his own heart pounded like a jackhammer, his head boomed with pain.

He closed his eyes and drifted.

. . .

Snow crunched under the feet of ambulance personnel carried as they Kerttu inside the Karjalainen farmhouse that the villagers had warmed and cleaned, preparing it for the injured visitor; the girlfriend of the man they had shunned, the soldier who was missing in action.

That night Kerttu lay with heavily bandaged legs in Toivo's bed, listening to the crackling fire in the kitchen's fireplace, picturing herself cooking meals for the two of them.

She touched the bedding, smelled the pillow—and smiled; his scent still lingered.

. . .

Chapter Fifty Six

Mr. Biederman sat in his favorite chair; he liked the way it hugged his backside; he liked the way its arms supported his.

When he sat in this chair, it was as if he sat on a cloud.

The chair was placed by a window. From his vantage point, Biederman could see a long way: not only the tenement courtyard bound by the walls and roof; not only the people who lived there or came to visit—he could also watch clouds that evolved into shapes which had never been seen before nor would ever be seen again.

He could see the sidewalk outside his childhood home in Krakow, the crack into which he had lost a *szloty* when he was 5 years old; the bench where Sayde and he had sat and talked about the future that had somehow come and gone so quickly; the hospital that wouldn't take her.

... *Sayde*...

He loved her smile; it lit up even the darkest of rooms. He loved her eyes; they sparkled and were as blue as the bluest sky, as clear as the clearest water.

... *Sayde*...

He thought of her and almost forgot the stinging pain in his chest.

He had almost taken her hand last night.

... *Sayde*...

She had smiled; everything had brightened, she was all he could see.

    ... this is a very nice chair...

A cold wind blew in through the open window.

    ... Sayde...

He closed the window.

. . .

Chapter Fifty Seven

Toivo woke; the enemy soldiers had resumed their search, apparently with renewed vigor. They were quickly approaching, now and then firing bursts of bullets; one hit the pine Toivo and Reijo were sheltered under. It cracked a snow-laden branch that fell and landed with a thud.

Toivo quietly reloaded his *Suomi* machine pistol. He was cold; his teeth still chattered uncontrollably.

Reijo was comatose; a trickle of saliva was frozen to the corner of his mouth.

On came the Red Army soldiers, still firing into likely hiding places.

Toivo shook the unconscious Reijo. "Don't you dare die on me," he whispered harshly.

No response. Toivo shook him again; slapped him hard—Reijo stirred.

"Stay with me, dammit," hissed Toivo, and shook him again. "Stay with me!"

He let go; held his aching head; closed his eyes.

After a while he could no longer hear the enemy.

. . .

Kerttu woke when the door banged open and Red Army soldiers burst in, quickly searched for other occupants, found none and approached her bed, staring at her; one yanked away her bedding and unbuttoned his pants.

Toivo woke up ridden with anxiety; he was panting, unable to suck in enough air. He listened for danger but the forest was silent except for the wind that blew through the trees; he listened to Reijo's breathing—it was shallow but steady.

Inexplicably panic-stricken, Toivo crawled out from under the pine, stood on unsteady legs and looked up at the sky.

It was a beautiful clear night; the constellations were starkly visible. Toward north he could see the dawning of the Aurora Borealis. More importantly, through the pines he could see a swath of land on which stood black-and-white sentries—border posts, beyond which he could see something burning.

His head pounded; he ached with cold. Abruptly reminding himself of Reijo's urgent need for a doctor, he turned to crawl back in to him when he saw—

—a perfect mirror ball spinning among the pines!

He was enchanted: the mirror ball cast thousands of tiny reflections—just like the nights he had spent with Kerttu.

Elated, he approached the mirror ball—some of its tiny mirrors fell like shimmering starry slivers to the snow.

He stopped and stared at it; it continued spinning—with stark black holes where tiny mirrors used to be.

He was utterly bewildered. He took a few more steps, reached out to touch the mirror ball—it vanished!

He stood there, distraught and befuddled.

Not far away, in Toivo's childhood home, a Red Army officer un-holstered his pistol and ordered his men away from the pregnant young woman with heavily bandaged legs who cowered as she lay nearly naked in her bed.

One soldier ignored the officer, turned his back to him, approached Kerttu and dropped his pants.

The officer raised his pistol and shot the would-be rapist in the head.

His other men reached for their weapons. The officer held them at bay with his pistol—but failed to notice the soldier behind him aiming an upraised meat cleaver at his head.

Above Toivo in the Russian forest, the Aurora Borealis fully erupted. The sky to the north danced with changing shapes and colors; it was a magnificent display of Nature's treasure chest. At a different time and place, under different circumstances, Toivo would have been awestruck.

Instead he tried to chase away the fear that inexplicably gripped him—a cold premonition that something dreadful was happening to Kerttu. He slogged back to the pine, crawled in under the branches and shook Reijo into consciousness.

"Let's go. We're leaving."

"Where… are we… going?"

"Home. The border isn't far away."

"You go," Reijo's voice was barely audible. "Let me die."

"Oh, no, we came here together and we're leaving together!" Toivo removed his white snowsuit, took off his jacket and wrapped it around Reijo. "I'll be back. I'll kill you if you die on me."

"You have to catch me first," said Reijo. He drifted off into an apathetic doze.

Toivo crawled out from under the pine. He wistfully looked around for the mirror ball, but it was nowhere to be seen.

His teeth banged against each other uncontrollably as he strapped on his bindings and skied off through the forest toward the border, now and then taking bearings with the compass hanging on a sash around his neck.

Above him the spectacular Aurora Borealis faded, then disappeared.

Toivo didn't notice.

He entered the wide swath of land that so many had killed each other over, passed a border marker and came upon smoking hulks of tanks and armored vehicles—along with thousands of corpses.

He warmed himself by a burning tank and caught sight of a dead Finn entangled in the harness of a *pulkka* sled on which he had pulled a heavy machine gun. Toivo dumped the machine gun, removed the harness from his dead comrade-at-arms, put it on, and skied off.

He passed a tank—and too late discovered a Red Army officer with a pistol aimed at him.

A meat cleaver protruded from the officer's skull; one arm hung limply by his side; he couldn't speak—his mouth moved, but no sound escaped. He tugged on his coat and strained to tell Toivo something—but only a garbled, frustrated moan escaped him. Again he feebly yanked on his coat. He gestured with his pistol toward the forest around them; another frustrated moan escaped him—and he raised his pistol.

Toivo suddenly understood what the Russian wanted. "You want to know where Russia is! Right there! Russia is there!"

Toivo pointed to the east.

The officer took a step toward his country, but his one good leg couldn't support him; he fell face down in the snow, struggled to stand, but couldn't.

Toivo put an arm under the wounded man, lifted him onto the *pulkka* sled, and dragged him toward a border marker.

A weather front was approaching; clouds drifted across the moon.

Toivo reached the square black-and-white marker, helped the wounded man out of the sled and propped him up against the Russian side of the marker.

Toivo's head ached worse than before from the physical exertion of helping the officer.

Suddenly dizzy, he pressed snow against his head wound. His legs gave out. He leaned against the Finnish side of the marker.

The Russian dropped his pistol, reached inside his coat and handed Toivo a silver icon; it shone with an image of the Madonna.

Toivo stared at it.

He was startled out of his daze by a shot.

The Russian officer slumped into the snow on his home side of the border, a single self-inflicted gunshot through his temple.

It was then that Toivo recognized the meat cleaver. A lifetime ago he had sanded and painted that very handle as a surprise for his mother whose hand had received far too many splinters from its unfinished wood.

Dark clouds obscured the moon.

Snow began to fall.

. . .

Chapter Fifty Eight

Kerttu gazed out the window at the whirling snow. She wanted to look anywhere but at the two uniformed men who stood at the foot of her bed. She feared them; she had seen the older one before on the horrible day she had last seen Toivo.

Denny Arnold had yelled at him.

... *did he have something to do with Toivo being locked in that shed*...

She felt a contraction twinge deep in her body.

It passed.

The men at the foot of her bed spoke in Finnish to each other and to a woman from the village. The woman had heard gunfire from the Karjalainen home when she arrived to check on Kerttu. She knew Pennanen that night was at home with a high-ranking guest from Mannerheim's staff; she had alerted him to Kerttu's plight.

Kerttu heard the man she had seen before say something to the younger.

... *he is too serious*...

Fear coursed through her. Her heart pounded. She tried to remain calm.

The younger man spoke to her in English: "Captain Pennanen who doesn't speak any English wants me to tell you that Toivo Karjalainen was a brave soldier—"

She vaguely heard him say that a patrol had not returned

—

A harsh rushing sound mercifully swept her away and spared her the pain of hearing them confirm her very worst fear.

. . .

Chapter Fifty Nine

Snow still fell. It was daybreak; Toivo could finally see his compass, which he consulted as he fought his way through the whirling snow, dragging the sled behind him.

His head throbbed.

His stomach heaved.

The snow-covered pines all looked alike.

He called for Reijo; didn't hear a reply.

He kept calling.

Finally—a distant, feeble reply.

Reijo was near death as Toivo dragged him out from under the tree.

"Leave me—" Reijo had lost a serious amount of blood. Every breath was agony.

Toivo leaned down over his nemesis. "I didn't come back here to leave you. You're going home with me and that's all there's to it."

"Let me die—"

"That's not up to me. I'm just not going to let you die in Russia."

And with that Toivo gently placed Reijo on the *pulkka* sled.

The load was heavier than he thought; hampered by his wounds, struggling through the deep snow, roots and fallen trees seemingly reaching out to trip him, the few hours of daylight had long since been replaced by darkness by the time he reached the border and entered Finland.

It was another clear night with a crescent moon. Eerie shadows were cast across the magnificent landscape as Toivo skied out onto a familiar frozen lake with Reijo on the sled behind him.

Instinct warned him of danger, but he had to keep moving—he could hear Reijo's breathing becoming shallower. He consulted his compass and skied on— unaware of the Russian soldiers on one shore, the Finnish on the other.

He was a mere speck in the vast landscape and had reached the middle of the lake when a sniper's rifle broke the stillness.

Momentum carried Toivo a few more meters before he fell face down into the snow.

There was dissent among the Finns as they studied the prone figure out on the lake.

"Who fired?"

"Not I."

"Looked like a Finn out there."

"Didn't ski well enough."

"I've seen you ski and wasn't impressed. Just how well do you think *you* would ski if you were pulling a *pulkka* with a heavy load? For sure not like you were on our Olympic ski team!"

"I suppose you want us to tunnel out there to find out who he is?"

"Well, we haven't done much good all day other than stare at the vermin across the lake."

. . .

305

Chapter Sixty

Giancarlo was practically salivating as he eyed the nearly full glass of gin and tonic that Denny was fingering.

"You may have it." Denny pushed the glass to the Italian and returned to his thoughts about Toivo.

He was greatly disturbed by the photos he had taken of Toivo and Kerttu at the border; by the emptiness in Toivo's eyes, his confusion over seeing Kerttu, her pain when she couldn't immediately recognize the man she loved. Over and over he studied the photos that had told a story very different from the one he had cabled New York. While he had not let the detail of execution for treason stand in the way of his personalized series of articles about the war, that day he drank less; the next day less still.

Giancarlo downed a mouthful of free gin and tonic. He and Denny were having dinner; neither spoke much.

The day before Denny had attended Martti's funeral, a somber, proper, efficient affair. He missed Martti but didn't think he bore responsibility for his death.

Martti's replacement wasn't as understanding or creative as Martti had been; he was much more cautious, like most Finns Denny encountered.

Denny fretted over Kerttu's fate until he learned that the hotel had received a request for her belongings from some village in northern Karelia.

Denny yearned for America; he had come to appreciate his country in a way he never had before. Other foreign correspondents had become bored; one had hung himself; Giancarlo had begun to drink.

The shyly attractive waiter had noticed that as Giancarlo's drinking increased and Denny's tapered off, the two men had less and less in common—and that they found each other less and less charming.

The waiter had little experience in worldly affairs; only once had he been outside Helsinki, and then only to a small, uninhabited island far out in the archipelago where for a day he and his friend frolicked in the nude. Yet he had come to believe that Italians were best when sober, Americans when drunk.

. . .

Chapter Sixty One

With a Laplander each on their backs, the two reindeer pulling *pulkka* sleds with Toivo and Reijo sped sure-footedly through a dense birch forest.

The Laplanders had been told their cargo was precious; they took pride in serving the country where they spent their winters, ignoring that, paradoxically, in summer they lived in the Soviet Union—they were nomads without boundaries other than those imposed on them by seasons and weather. They didn't have a country to call their own; the nature they could see and touch was theirs on loan, they used it, treasured it, but didn't claim it as their own.

The Laplanders' lives were simple, yet full; they never warred about land, only about women.

They found the field hospital despite having been given inaccurate directions.

It was nearly empty; most of the staff had left to tend to their many casualties elsewhere. Only two medics and a field surgeon remained. The surgeon had only a few instruments to work with; the rest had been sent to areas with higher casualty rates.

The reindeers' breath steamed in the bitterly cold air. The medics pulled the *pulkkas* inside the tent; it was easier than lifting the two wounded men, neither of whom should have been moved.

Wearily the field surgeon examined the man who had been shot in the head and torso. He washed the head wound with the last of his alcohol—something glinted; he reached for a pair of forceps and removed a bullet that clanged when he dropped it into a stainless steel receptor, then rolled noisily and heavily from its own momentum.

He bandaged the hole in the skull, then looked at the perforation through the torso and silently shook his head.

He examined the other soldier; again, he shook his head.

"Start my motorcycle. I'll take one of them with me."

"Which one?" asked a medic.

"Doesn't matter," answered the field surgeon, shaking his head silently at the two medics, who understood. "When I get to the hospital I'll have an ambulance come and pick up the other."

One of the medics went out to kick-start the field surgeon's motorcycle.

It took him a while to get it started: he had to pour red alcohol into the carburetor and encouragingly pat the gas-tank between kicks on the starter.

The *pulkka* sled with Reijo was closest to the tent flap; they pulled it outside and lifted Reijo into the sidecar; fate thus determined that Reijo was the one chosen to go the hospital.

The medics watched as the field surgeon drove off, his feet on the skids, the rear tire kicking up a plume of snow.

The Laplanders asked for their *pulkka* sleds back.

The medics moved Toivo to a stretcher and watched as the Laplanders rode off on their reindeer.

Toivo lay alone in the tent.

. . .

Kerttu was asleep in the Karjalainen home when she jolted awake from a nightmare and sat up in bed, distraught.

... Toivo...

The two medics could no longer tell if Toivo was breathing; they shook their heads; paced the deserted road.

"Where the hell is that damn ambulance?"

One leaned down and checked Toivo's pulse.

309

"Give me a hand. He's done."

They lifted the stretcher and carried it toward a snow-covered cadaver bunker. It was marked with a cross that was large enough to honor those inside, yet small enough not to distract those passing by on their way to the front.

A single kerosene lamp lighted the bunker. Corpses were stacked like cord wood to the ceiling.

The medics placed Toivo on top of other bodies.

It was freezing cold inside the bunker.

The medics stomped their feet and swung their arms about their chests. Their breath vaporized in the air.

They tried not to look at the bodies around them: Theirs was the business of life, they had not yet become immune to death; it bothered them, made them feel fallible.

They disliked being part of the burial detail—of which only they remained; the others had been called to the front where every man was needed. Unlike the Soviet Union, Finland had a limited numbers of people.

Finland was feeling her size, although there was no lack of commitment or resolve.

Countless bodies had been delivered over the last few days.

The medics lit a fire in the stove. When it had warmed, they melted snow in a coffee pot and threw in a small handful of coffee.

They watched the coffee brew; warmed their hands around the pot and leaned down over it, savoring the aroma.

Toivo didn't know what brought him back from the threshold of oblivion.

Dull pain gnawed his chest.

He was back in the Now, yet he didn't know from where he had returned or how he had gotten there.

He could feel his breath; it was shallow and labored, yet he didn't feel worried.

310

He had all the time in the world for each breath; he was not in a hurry.

The pain was what it was; it was just that—pain.

Then he smelled the coffee——

His awareness of life came rushing back; his first coherent thought was about Kerttu and he remembered her saying:

"... you, and a view of the ocean..."

Yes, he thought, *a view of the ocean would be nice—*

He opened his eyes and came face to face with the corpses around him—their faces that were frozen into masks of pain and fear; some seemed relieved; some were devoid of expression.

He saw bodies missing limbs; twisted bodies; bodies so mangled they little resembled humans.

Yet Toivo was unmoved by the horrific sights surrounding him—or by Death itself. His brief journey into nothingness had lightened his mind; what remained was calm and pure.

He felt his chest rise, knew he was breathing; his breath felt good, though feeble.

Again he smelled the coffee. "That coffee sure smells good," he said, to no one in particular; he was merely trying out his voice.

At the sound of Toivo's voice, the medics nearly jumped out of their skin—one accidentally knocked over the pot of steaming coffee, the other panicked and fled the bunker entirely.

. . .

Chapter Sixty Two

U.S. Congressman Dexter Quarry needed votes, ethnic ones; votes other than Irish—those he already had.

The more votes, the better; this time he couldn't fudge the ballots.

Votes cost money.

Quarry had been told that the old man sitting across his desk had that money, that he—was his name Biederman? —also had connections with the Brotherhood of Teamsters. One would have to live in a cave or be dead not to know that the Teamsters had clout; for example, when the union wanted to make a point, they had their drivers stop delivering bread to America's grocers.

Being neither dead nor a cave dweller, when Quarry had received a phone call from a friend who told him that someone high up in the Teamsters would appreciate a favor, he had been amenable; that was how the meeting with the elderly tenement owner had come about.

Again Quarry studied his visitor; A*mazing,* he thought, *the old guy doesn't look like much, wonder where he got his pull?*

"What can I do for you?" There was no need for niceties as they both knew the meeting had been arranged for a specific reason.

"I need a visa for a friend who deserves to live in America." Biederman got directly to the point; he didn't like congressmen who were for sale.

Congressman Quarry had a philosophical justification for the old man's visit—this was an opportunity to gain popularity with the people in his ward. Most were of

European descent and would appreciate attention paid to their needs, someone who would champion their causes in Washington.

"How much of a friend?" the Congressman asked. He had been in Washington and politics for years. Before that he had sold life insurance so he knew how to capitalize on people's needs and frailties—and how to cut a deal.

. . .

Chapter Sixty Three

In the short time she had been allowed to stand on her heavily bandaged legs, Kerttu had not yet mastered her canes. She sank down onto the first chair she found and stayed there—enjoying the sound of the wood that crackled in the kitchen fireplace, the smell of burning pine, the welcoming heat that spread through the house that was well-built and well-insulated.

Women from the village had scrubbed away the blood from the spot where the Russian had died; Kerttu had blotted out all else that had happened that day—the human mind can, at times, be merciful; all she knew was that the baby was alive, she could feel it moving now and then.

Although her heart and legs ached, Kerttu thrived in the home in which her man had grown up. She had grieved the loss of Toivo more than she knew she could— or should; she had not spoken or eaten until the thought of their child forced her to realize that she needed to be strong. She vowed to deal with her loss as best she knew how and had successfully stifled her tears for a few days. But now, immersed in his life and his childhood, she couldn't contain her emotions any longer; her tears burst forth like an overfilled dam under crushing pressure.

. . .

Meanwhile Toivo was fighting for his life; each breath tortured him as he was being unloaded from an ambulance at Helsinki Hospital. The ambulance driver had driven like a madman all night, regretful that he had misunderstood the directions to a more or less abandoned field hospital; fearful that his mistake would cost the brave soldier his life.

Two hospital attendants carried Toivo inside; the driver followed; he wanted to be certain the trip had not been in vain.

The young doctor who had been summoned by the emergency arrival bell examined the patient from the northern front and noticed that his breathing was alarmingly shallow and labored.

While the doctor examined Toivo, the driver impatiently related what he had been told: "One bullet was removed from his cranium; another pierced his left lung, nicked the descending aorta, and pierced the esophagus. Pneumonia followed re-inflation of his collapsed lung."

The ambulance driver knew Toivo's condition well; he had gone over it many times while he drove to the capitol.

"Why are his arms tied to the stretcher?" the young doctor demanded to know.

"He tries to get up and walk," replied the driver. "Says he has to get back to the front."

Toivo struggled to speak. "… to… live…" was all he could manage before drifting off.

The young doctor vowed that this patient would.

. . .

Chapter Sixty Four

Kerttu was adding logs to the fireplace when she saw a white-clad skier with a large rucksack approach.

She didn't recognize the skier; it wasn't the dark-haired, uniformed woman she had seen watching her from the road in a fancy yellow car, or one of the villagers who had carried in firewood or brought her food; none of them spoke English—she hoped this one did.

She was startled when he knocked on the door; she opened it, welcoming the human contact, yet also dreading what he might say.

He was young and high-strung. He withdrew a stack of letters from his rucksack and began to babble nonstop in Finnish:

"Captain Pennanen told me to find Lieutenant Lehtinen because he's been to the university but he had gone to visit his mother and I don't see why a university degree is needed to deliver a chicken and some food from the boys in the company and the postmistress was holding these letters for Toivo at the village post office and captain Pennanen said to inform you that he had been misinformed and that Toivo *did* make it back and that he brought Reijo with him and that the doctors think he will survive and I need to get back because I have to run some other errands and it will soon be dark."

He saluted and took off like a shot on his skis.

Kerttu yelled after him: "What did you say? I didn't understand what you said! What did you say? I heard you say Toivo's name! What did you say?"

He stopped and turned to her, but Kerttu was frightening in her anguish. He was already on edge and fled as fast as he could.

"What did you say about Toivo? I didn't understand what you said!" she yelled after him.

He never slowed; she had never seen anyone ski that fast —he was over the crest in the road and gone before she knew it.

. . .

Chapter Sixty Five

Helsinki Hospital, February 1940. Several weeks had passed since Toivo's arrival. His body was mending nicely; his spirit wasn't.

The bandage had been taken off his head, but not yet from his torso; he still needed several operations.

Propped up on pillows, his body was comfortable; still, he felt distraught when he looked out the tall windows and saw the snow falling.

Snow had been steadily falling for a week, the drifts creeping above the lowermost windowpanes.

He knew how difficult it was for both sides to fight in such conditions; he didn't want there to be any difficulty for anyone.

He worried about Kerttu; he didn't know anything about her, where she was, what she was doing, and feared she was ashamed of him for having been part of the carnage at the front, for having killed.

He wouldn't blame her for being ashamed of him. His being cringed from the memories of men now dead and gone, from the mode of their passing, their pain and suffering.

He knew somehow that all of that and more would be an indelible part of him—and he wasn't proud, even though he knew it had been for the sake of their country. He had failed other members of the human race whose dreams of a Better Tomorrow would never be realized.

He lay listening to the radio the young doctor had brought from his home and placed on the small table by Toivo's bed.

"... our mounting casualties, it is now a matter of days before Finland's resources will run out..."

He turned off the radio and pulled the sheet over his head so he could shed his tears in private—

"Hello, Toivo, how are you?"

Tessa, Pennanen's wife, stood by his bed, wearing a crisp, starched *Lotta* uniform and holding a valise and a bouquet of flowers.

"How do you think I am?" he asked. "We are losing the war; everything we did was for nothing."

"Not everything. I am here," she said and touched his hand. He pulled his hand away; she pretended not to notice.

"Why are you here?" He wanted to know.

"I heard about you and want to be near you so I asked for a transfer here. I brought you some flowers."

She placed them on his table, then touched his neck, gently, seductively. She let her hand linger, then sat down on his bed.

"I'm so proud of you. We all are. You are a hero; everyone knows how you brought Reijo back from Russia."

"I'm no hero, I'm just a..." He couldn't continue; couldn't explain himself, or how he felt. "How is Reijo?"

"I heard they had to amputate his legs and one of his hands," she replied, reluctantly.

"Where is he?"

"Up north somewhere."

"How is he doing?"

"Not well—they may bring him here." She didn't want to say more. "You don't know how happy I am that you are doing well. You don't know how worried I was when I heard that you—"

She paused and lowered her eyes; it was the first time he had ever seen her emotional.

"Of all the boys from the village, only you, Reijo, Jussi and my husband are still alive."

She raised her head and looked him squarely in the face. "I have left my husband."

"Why?"

"I have always wanted to be with you, to take care of you. It has been my dream."

It was an honest admission; she had never forgotten the night with Toivo. Although their intimate encounter had not been fully consummated, its emotional impact never left her; the bliss she had felt with him was never equaled by any other—and there had been many: Pennanen had unknowingly shared her with untold other men—whose faces she had substituted with Toivo's.

She touched Toivo's face gently.

He shrank back into his pillow; she pretended not to notice, opened her valise and held up the icon—light glinted off it.

"They found this in your rucksack. And this—she held up Kerttu's scarf—was in one of your pockets. Is it hers?"

"Yes," he answered. His voice quavered. He took the scarf from her and folded it around his hand.

Tessa placed her hand on top of his blanket—just on the inside of his knee. "Have you heard from her?" she asked, innocently.

He shook his head.

Tessa moved her hand toward his upper thigh, squeezed it almost imperceptibly, then took her hand away—she was practiced at this. "I heard she went back to America," she said of the woman she had studied from a distance only a few days earlier.

He turned away his face and pulled the sheet over his head.

"... *she left me... was ashamed of me... gave up on me...*"

She gave him the moment; she knew he needed it—it suited her strategy. "I'm sorry, Toivo," she said, touching him gently. "Women can be like that," she added, letting the weight of the statement sink in before continuing: "But I'm here and I will do anything for you."

She gave him another moment, and then changed tactics.

"They tell me that you keep seeing faces of people begging not to die."

She was quiet for a moment.

"I know how you feel." Her voice too quavered—she was quite an actress. "And I will not leave you like she did."

She moved her hand up inside his thigh until it should go no higher.

. . .

Chapter Sixty Six

Helsinki Hospital had been built during the Czar's reign. Over the years untold numbers of patients had looked up from their beds at the arched, cathedral-like ceilings that made the wards difficult to keep warm in winter but kept them cool in summer. The floral patterns were painted so precisely that one would think a machine had made them, instead of an artisan working for only room and board.

On March 13, 1940, none of the nurses, doctors, or recuperating veterans cared about the building's architecture or finish; they were listening to a somber voice on the hospital's public address system advising them that in a few moments Field Marshall Mannerheim's Order of the Day would be read on Finland's Radio. All held their breath—even though they all knew; many wept openly—the wait had worn them down.

Then they heard the words their military leader had written.

"We fought a good fight; we didn't lose, we came in a strong second. It is not your fault—"

That was as much as most of the listeners heard.

All over Finland, church bells clanged; flags were lowered to half-staff.

Finns who couldn't bear the outcome that they had fought so hard to avoid shot themselves.

In his bed Toivo closed his eyes, but he quickly opened them again. Distraught over having lost Kerttu and Finland losing the war, he could feel the madness

322

threatening like a dark cloud on the horizon. Somehow he summoned up the will to stay sane, to push away the cloud. When his strength waned he forced himself to count the petals of the flowers on the ceiling that arched high above him—anything to keep the troubling thoughts at bay.

Church bells clanged; grown men openly wept—he didn't want to, he bit down hard on his lip and stared at the ceiling.

... perhaps the flowers were daisies... perhaps marigolds...

The petals were pastel, with highlights of gold; he knew the artist had done his work with care—it was that exact.

He lost count—the lump in his throat distracted him; he had to start over from One.

The church bells kept ringing.

... perhaps a clang for each of the lives that had been lost or ruined...

At that moment one of the tall doors leading to the garden opened and an orderly led in Jussi. Wearing dark glasses, he had to be guided to Toivo's bedside and to the visitor's chair normally used only by Tessa.

"Will you be fine here?" the orderly asked Jussi.

Jussi didn't say anything; he merely nodded.

"I'll be back in a few minutes then," the orderly said and left.

Jussi remained quiet; he simply sat there.

Although Toivo didn't know what Jussi wanted, he knew he would have to begin the conversation.

"How are you doing, Jussi?"

Jussi didn't answer.

Helsinki Cathedral's bells began to peal, joining the others.

"Do you think the dead care that we lost the war but were a strong second?" Toivo asked, although he knew the answer.

Jussi still didn't respond.

"Do you think anyone will ever understand?" asked Toivo, who didn't.

"Understand what?" Jussi asked; his voice no longer sounded like his own. Since the onset of his total blindness his world had shrunk to not much more than admonishing voices in his head intertwined with the voice of the pastor. He spoke in archaic Finnish and used words like thee and thou. To Jussi, it sounded properly religious and important.

Another awkward silence followed.

Then Jussi withdrew Denny's .38 from his robe. "Toivo Karjalainen, I came here to ask thee, this gun that Reijo gave me to hold right before thee went off to kill Voroshilov, does thee want it back or can I have it?"

"You can have it."

"I thank thee."

Again, silence.

Toivo wondered why Jussi was using the formal 'thee' that sounded so awkward.

Jussi turned his head and listened for the orderly who wasn't yet back.

He was quiet for a long time before he next spoke.

"When thee is well again, will thee go home?"

"We are all headed that way." Toivo pulled the covers around him, suddenly chilled.

The church bells still rang, sounding sweetly mournful now.

"What does thee mean?" Jussi had always excelled at eating, not reasoning, and his mind was now filled with confusing voices and mysterious urges.

Toivo had been searching his soul and had given much thought to the matter of home and country.

"Perhaps home is where we are when we die." Toivo offered.

"What does thee mean?"

Toivo hesitated; although he had given the topic much thought, he had never before put his feelings into words. "It seems to me that between birth and death we're on this journey we call our *life*; the final destination in life is *death*—so death, then, is our real home."

"What about where we live in-between?" Jussi wanted to know.

"That's just where we rest during the journey, where we are nurtured for what lies ahead."

"There were times in the war when thee wanted to… to go home ahead of time. Does thee still want to?"

Toivo thought for a moment.

"No," he said, "As unhappy as I am with events in my life, I would like to believe that we are all important somehow; that what we do has a purpose; that we had to do what we did; that everything happens for a reason."

"If that is so, why can't I see?"

"Jussi, I don't know."

"Can thee see the orderly who brought me?"

"No."

"Guide me to the garden door."

"I'm not well enough to get out of bed."

"I said for thee to guide me, not to escort me!"

Toivo almost smiled—Jussi might have gotten religion of sorts but he still had that bad-tempered streak in him.

Jussi stood up from the chair and faced the light that came in through the tall garden windows.

"Walk straight now," Toivo said.

Jussi walked off; he trusted Toivo, finally.

"A little to the right—a little more—that's it—straight now—"

Jussi reached the door, opened it, and walked outside.

Toivo saw him as a silhouette against the sheer curtain; saw him face the sun, raise Denny's .38 to his head—and fire.

. . .

Chapter Sixty Seven

Denny anxiously paced the lobby while he waited for a cable that might not arrive for a few more days yet. He was expecting a job offer from a Madison Avenue advertising agency; the wait was painful, he felt as if his skin was crawling with stinging ants.

He noticed Martti's replacement post a notice on the bulletin board in the lobby; Denny waited until he left, then read it.

It was an invitation for foreign correspondents to attend a visit by Field Marshall Mannerheim to the veteran's wards at Helsinki Hospital. To Denny the invitation was a thinly veiled attempt by the Finnish Foreign Ministry to drum up support for a lost cause.

Too late, Denny thought, *the world's attention is already on other matters. No thank you*, he added regarding the invitation as he continued pacing the lobby.

He was bored. He had nothing to do, nothing to report, no one to talk to; Giancarlo had met a young Finnish war widow. After two nights with her, Giancarlo was deeply in love. He had checked out of the hotel, moved in with her, and had cabled his wife a final *ciao*.

He came by the hotel a few days later, asking for Denny. They met in the restaurant. Giancarlo was nervous; he needed advice.

"Denny, my friend, I am so very happy but also so very poor."

"How can I help you? I am possibly even more poor than you. At least you have the use of all your limbs."

"Ah, yes, what you say is so true. But this woman has me so confused. She is like a mad tiger in bed; I never thought I would experience anything like this. It is fantastic! But I also need to make money. What can I do?"

"You could sell your memoirs. I can see it on bookstands everywhere, 'My Life With A Finnish Tigress' by the expatriate Italian war correspondent Giancarlo Ferrando."

"Please be serious, I am in much pain."

"Open an Italian restaurant. You'd make a fortune."

"Restau…Yes! Bravo! A wonderful idea! Fantastic! I will ask my wife for recipes and you will be guest of honor at the opening."

With that Giancarlo stood up, hugged Denny—and was gone.

As Denny paced the lobby he knew too well—every mark, every stain, he had seen them all far too many times before. He enviously watched another correspondent leave the hotel, his bags packed; the war that had brought them together was over.

The end of the war had not been what Denny wanted. He would have liked for the Finns to have won so he had paid scant attention to the terms of the settlement. Vaguely he knew a border had been moved farther west, that Finland had ceded thousands, perhaps millions, of hectares.

Denny paced, slower now, it was late in the day. He stopped by the window to watch a contingent of departing Norwegians, the last of several thousand who had come to help a neighbor in need.

Denny thought of the more than 11,000 volunteers from all over the world who had arrived in Finland too late to make a difference. They were now leaving or were already gone; richer in experience; most of them none the worse for wear.

Military supplies and equipment were still arriving from abroad, from countries where politicians had been tardy and efforts made too late.

He knew from the papers that world sympathy for the Finns had waned. Editorials that used to express satisfaction that a David had stood up to a Goliath now expressed concern: a much bigger war was now in the making; much more was at stake much closer to home, much more of a threat to their readers and their readers' ways of life, their dreams and needs.

He also mulled over his latest discovery: that when politicians and leaders fail their people and bring them closer to war or despair, they gain in popularity since they are then needed more than ever. He couldn't recall a single example of a war that was started by the People; the igniting events had always been dictated by the Power in charge.

He checked for a cable—no, he didn't have one; yes, they would call him when it arrived.

He paced the lobby, passed the bulletin board, and reread the invitation.

...well, I suppose meeting the Field Marshall, who seems to be an interesting man, will be a far better pastime than waiting for a cable in this damned lobby...

The patients at Helsinki Hospital learned of Mannerheim's visit when wards that were already clean were scrubbed and dusted, when sheets and dressings were changed before turning yellow, when teeth and hair were brushed more than they needed to be, and bodies were bathed although it wasn't yet Friday.

They endured the preparations without much complaint; the visit was a welcome break from the routine of death and dying.

. . .

Chapter Sixty Eight

As Mannerheim strode in—tall, erect, impeccably dressed; his boots newly polished and his hair freshly watered; the vodka he needed right under his belt—the men grew quiet, as did he.

He stopped by the door and looked the room over. These were men he had hurled into battle to slaughter strangers for reasons about which they had not been consulted—yet they had to obey.

He saw bodies and souls that were broken; still he knew in his heart that the choice he had made was the right one: a knee that was bent under an aggressor's might could never straighten and carry the weight of the Finland they treasured.

He looked at men whose gazes didn't waver; the heartfelt salute he gave them surprised even him. The men in their beds responded in kind—the moment that followed would forever remain in their minds; the silence was so deep and engrossing that the sparrow pecking the windowsill sounded louder than a cannon.

He approached the bed of a man from the north who had lost his arms, ears, toes and nose.

"I am Mannerheim, your leader of sorts, responsible for thy pain, yet ignorant of thy name—"

The Finnish language was still strange on his tongue, although he practiced it daily.

"Aimo Korvonen," Aimo responded, and added with pride: "From east of Oikarainen where the Kemijoki flows wild."

"Been on her once and was awed by her might." Mannerheim gripped Aimo's shoulder and said with regret: "For thy sacrifice, we are deeply in thy debt."

An aide standing next to Mannerheim opened a birch and steel box; the Finnish seal adorned its lid; its contents were sacred—mementos of honor.

Mannerheim placed on Aimo's pillow a medal fresh from the mint, moved to the next bed, and repeated the greeting.

As he moved away from the door and farther into the ward, the space behind him filled up with aides, politicians, doctors and nurses, *Lottas*, and many more.

Toivo saw them approach and shrank in his bed—the crowd was too large, the event was too big. Tessa sensed his plight and came to his rescue; she stood by his bed, proud of her knowledge.

At the rear of the large crowd were two foreign correspondents, Denny and a German man—this one *was* a spy. With them were several Finnish journalists; some of whom knew about the failed attempt to assassinate Voroshilov and that there had been two survivors. The matter would never be mentioned in the Finnish press; it had been purged from the archives, the assassination attempt had not been successful; positive matters were the order of the day.

Denny was bored. All he could see was the backs of those in front of him and the veterans already honored; a newly minted medal was pinned to each of their pillows. He couldn't see Mannerheim—there were that many people.

The young doctor—who, to his colleagues' amazement, had managed to save Toivo when he was brought in—stood next to Tessa as Mannerheim leaned down over Toivo.

"This is Karjalainen," the young doctor said, proud of his achievement with Toivo—of whom he had also become quite fond.

"I hear thee is stubborn and refuses to die." Mannerheim had been briefed about Toivo.

"I hear you are stubborn yourself," Toivo replied in standard Finnish; he had never mastered the formal.

Mannerheim smiled, relieved that for a moment he didn't have to strain with the formal language.

"Are they treating you well?"

"They beat me three times a day and feed me once," Toivo replied with a refreshing sense of humor.

Mannerheim laughed and sat down on Toivo's bed.

"Careful, Marshall, I am still bleeding a bit."

"I would be proud to have your blood on me." Mannerheim meant what he said.

"But we lost—" Toivo still carried that burden in his soul, all that effort, all that suffering and dying—all for naught.

"No, son, we didn't." Mannerheim whispered conspiratorially. "We only agreed to stop fighting."

An aide coughed conspicuously. "Marshall, the schedule..."

"The schedule—there is always a schedule." Mannerheim sighed, rose to his feet and took a light-blue envelope from the aide.

"Karjalainen, this arrived for you from Washington." Mannerheim handed Toivo the envelope. "And here is something from the Government of Finland."

He placed Finland's Medal of Freedom on Toivo's pillow, leaned down, and whispered: "I know about you, son. I know what you did and what you didn't do. I also know about Voroshilov. With a thousand men like you I could win any war."

He rose and saluted the admirable young hero then continued to the next bed; the group around him followed.

At the rear of the group, Denny briefly spotted Toivo but Toivo's experience with Mannerheim had so overwhelmed him that he didn't notice Denny—he couldn't notice anyone or anything.

He craved privacy, but there was none; the room was filled with people; he pulled his sheet right up over his head.

Denny approached Toivo, elated to see his Finnish friend alive, but Tessa stopped him.

"It's okay, he knows me," whispered Denny; he had noticed Toivo's need for solitude—Denny wasn't totally insensitive.

As soon as Tessa heard Denny's English she was jolted by fear.

"But *I* don't know you," she hissed as she pulled Denny away from Toivo's bed.

"What do you want with him?" she asked awkwardly —it had been a while since she last spoke English.

"To say hello. I was surprised to see him alive. A week ago I received a letter from his girlfriend—"

Tessa interrupted with a finger to her lips. "Ssssh, he doesn't want to hear about her!"

"Why not?" Denny asked, quite perplexed.

"Because—because I am his nurse and I know what is best for him!"

"Really? Maybe you should get yourself a turban and have a booth at county fairs." He saw the angry look on her face. "Maybe not. Okay, so you know, she wrote that she is living on his farm. I got the impression she believes he is dead. Maybe she should be told that he isn't."

"I will take care of it. I know her. Her name is Kerttu. She is blond, like common Finnish girls."

"She *is* blond, I give you that, but I don't know that she is common. Okay. Good. Well, tell him that I will come back some other time. My name is Denny. Denny Arnold."

"Always ask for me. My name is Tessa. Lotta Tessa."

"OK, Lotta Tessa, I will do that."

He was strangely surprised and pleased to see Toivo alive. He looked at the horde of people still in the room, decided to leave, and headed for the door.

Tessa made sure he had left, that the door closed behind him, before she walked back to Toivo's bed.

"Can I do anything for you?" She sat down on his bed.

He remained under his sheet.

"Who did you speak English with?" he asked.

"Oh, just some man."

"What did he want?"

"Oh, nothing. He just talked and talked, like Americans do. Aren't you going to open the letter from Washington?"

Toivo hesitated, then opened the light-blue envelope and read its contents.

"What does it say? What is it?" she asked, tingling with excitement.

"A visa for America—a permanent visa for America ____"

"Oh, Toivo, that's wonderful! Where should we go first? Oh, I know—New York—and then Arizona! I've heard it never rains in Arizona! This is *so* wonderful!" She spontaneously hugged him, but was taken aback by the serious look on his face. "What's the matter, my love? You always wanted to be an American."

"I don't know if I can be one anymore." That dream belonged to his different Self; the Self that no longer existed, the Self that along with those of untold other men and women was lost forever.

Having fought for Finnish soil had enhanced its importance; changed their relationship.

... maybe I belong here after all...

He had lost the dream of one country and gained a bond to another.

. . .

Chapter Sixty Nine

After having mulled things over for several days during which he had been uncommunicative, when next Toivo saw Tessa he was ready for her. "I need to paint," he told her. "I have to get out of this bed. Talk to the doctors, Tessa. I know they listen to you."

She watched his face like a hawk does its prey, leaning closer to him with her hand on his thigh. "I'll talk to the doctors. And I'll get you brushes, paint, anything you want."

Something flickered in his eyes.

"What is it?" she asked with a sudden flash of concern.

"You're so nice to me," he said and didn't resist as much as he had when she leaned down and hugged him.

. . .

An icicle fell from the eave as Kerttu closed the Karjalainen door and hobbled across the barnyard.

The melting snow had uncovered the remnants of a pyre. As Kerttu bent down and picked up the charred remains of Toivo's self-portrait, she felt the loss of her man and her advanced pregnancy suddenly weighed heavily on her.

. . .

Chapter Seventy

With brushes and tubes of paint in his hand and wearing a robe that concealed the bandages around his chest and stomach, Toivo sat on a bench in the hospital's entry, staring at the huge, white wall.

He unsteadily stood, approached the wall, and touched it hesitantly; reluctantly, thought Tessa, who was watching him from around the corner, deeply shaken by some news she had just received.

Toivo's first brush strokes created the eye of a crow; Tessa didn't understand its significance.

She stood there for a moment, watching Toivo, dreading what she had to do; then she approached him, hesitated, and said:

"Reijo was just brought in—"

. . .

Tessa buttoned her sweater and pulled the blanket tighter around Toivo. She had him in a wheelchair; his legs were still shaky.

The part of the hospital they were in was cold and eerily quiet: the personnel were ghost-like; they were dressed in all white, subdued and silent on their crepe soles.

Down the corridor they went, Tessa's footfalls echoing hollowly; the late afternoon light seeping through the white curtains was lifeless, the shadows foreboding.

Tessa consulted the slip of paper she held with trembling fingers, then pushed the wheelchair ahead while she looked for the door with the correct number; she found it—noting that it was marked with a cross.

She touched Toivo's shoulder; he unwrapped his blanket and rose to his feet.

Sadness engulfed him when he saw the cross on the door; it wasn't that he was unprepared—it was that the cross made matters so... final.

Tessa stepped back and sought refuge in a shadow.

"I'll wait outside," she said and left.

Toivo opened the door; its hinges were eerily noiseless.

Reijo lay pallid and alone in a room that was intensely quiet and starkly Spartan: the curtains were sheer; the light sparse from a northern exposure, the ceiling light that shone was a definite necessity.

Toivo closed the door behind him and approached the bed.

Reijo sensed someone's presence; he opened his eyes, saw who it was and managed to be brave—momentarily.

"Guess I should have stayed in Chicago." He tried a smile, but it failed. "They took my legs, Toivo—and my hand..."

They looked at each other in silence, much more than words flashed between them.

"Tell me about the Other Side..." Reijo's voice was barely audible.

"It's...peaceful." Toivo knew; he had briefly been there.

"... peaceful..." Reijo reached with his only hand for Toivo. "Will you stay with me tonight?"

"Yes, I will stay with you."

Tessa stood in the garden, looking through the window at Toivo by Reijo's bed.

She was smoking a cigarette, a habit she had just started. It was an urbane mannerism; she had seen it in the movies—all the stars did it, why shouldn't she? After all, if she had lived over there, she, too, could have been in the movies. But as much as Tessa wanted to belong to that glamorous world, she didn't want her taste for it to be noticed; she would cover the smell of the smoke with eau de cologne.

She took a deep drag, felt the nicotine rush through her veins and watched Toivo pull the sheet over Reijo's face and turn off the light.

. . .

Chapter Seventy One

Atop a hill far from Helsinki, Tessa and the young doctor who had saved Toivo stood discretely by an ambulance.

Some distance away Toivo sat in a wheelchair, a blanket wrapped around him, a black mourning band on his arm, gazing out over the valley below. Reverently he kneaded moist Finnish soil between his fingers, offering a brief, silent prayer for all those who had suffered and died for it.

The look in Reijo's eyes still haunted Toivo. It had been the look of a man who knew he had not yet fully lived, of one who had lacked the courage to reveal his most vulnerable self; the look of a man who knew he had robbed himself of the only thing that truly was his: his genuine Self; his own true feelings.

Toivo had been taught by Mr. Biederman that feelings cannot be transferred, that no one can feel for you; they might die for you, think for you, but they cannot feel for you—other than 'sorry', and that, he knew, was usually brought on by arrogance more than compassion.

He smelled the soil in his hand; its scent reminded him of his childhood—for a fleeting moment he no longer felt the terrible burden of his worn-out adult Self.

He was surprised and grateful that the child's lightness was still in him: there still was hope for a Better Tomorrow—he was certain of it.

. . .

Chapter Seventy Two

Helsinki Hospital. A clock struck midnight. A hard, cold rain drummed on the copper roof.

Toivo stood on a high ladder in the entry, intently painting a section of the mural: men silhouetted against a setting sun, marching off to war with rifles on their shoulders; their backs straight, their heads held high.

A hospital orderly walked by. He ignored Toivo and the mural; the staff was used to seeing the artist who was that hussy *Lotta*'s patient, some sort of dependent of hers; used to seeing him spend all his waking hours on recapturing the past, a eulogy of sorts—*morbid*, thought some, *let's keep life going*.

Toivo suddenly felt very tired; he had lost his creative inspiration. He climbed down the ladder, sat down in a chair.

He thought about the next operation he would soon need; the surgeon had told him about it earlier that day; he had said it would make him feel better.

Rain fell.

Rain also fell in Chicago, where it was still day. Ben Biederman sat in his chair by the window. It was Friday and time for him to receive the rent.

He was tired: tired of doing nothing; tired of collecting the rent from men and women he knew couldn't afford it; tired of receiving *geld* he didn't need.

... what am I, a bank or a mensch; a croupier or a giver... enough already...

He was tired: tired of pain; tired of thinking; tired of living as the soul that he had become.

...toyt nakher... zayn oys...

He was tired of the body that no longer held together; tired of hips and knees and hands that ached; tired of walks in the nights to the potty by the sink, the fumbling in the dark—the fear of missing.

He was tired: tired of the stinging pains in his chest, the stitch in his shoulder, the distress in his arm.

Most of all, he was tired of being tired.

... oy vey es mir...

Then it hit him—he didn't even have time to close his eyes—it hit him like the dense mass of an oncoming locomotive; a painful, tumultuous swirling sensation that gripped him, ground him, and brought him to tears. It held him, shook him, and engulfed him completely.

His breath escaped him with a grating gasp, the pain torrential, the rain on the window—

Darkness.

Then light—blinding light.

He saw his wife—not clearly, but he saw her; she stood by the door—

... Sayde...

He couldn't move, not even a finger.

... Sayde... mit mir...

His wife held out her hand.

... the chair...

He knew he had to abandon his chair.

His heart let go; the last of his breath escaped him.

The light grew stronger, whiter.
    ... Sayde... my Sayde...

The light blinded him; it swirled around him, wrapping him in a soft caress.
    ...Sayde... and then—

—there she was, directly in front of him.

... Sayde...

Again, she held out her hand——

—this time, he took it.

. . .

Chapter Seventy Three

Mr. Biederman's door had been open a crack; it always was on Friday evenings when salaries had been paid and the rent was due.

The shifty-eyed tenant stood in the room, staring at her landlord. She had come to tell him she wouldn't be able to pay the rent; she had done this before and each time it got surprisingly easier.

She held out her hand to him, showing him that it was empty—that she had nothing to give.

She stared at him.

He sat in his worn-out chair at the window, staring unblinkingly back at her.

She realized his eyes saw nothing.

It didn't take her long to go through his belongings. She knew she had to hurry; others might soon arrive.

... eight cents and a dirty hankie... not much of a landlord...

Then she noticed the painting. It was large—too large, really—but the young man in the shadow reminded her of her sons, long gone; surely no one would mind that she took it—after all, it was just something hanging on an old man's wall.

She lifted it down and quickly left.

On the wall where it had hung, the paint was darker, richer.

Ben Biederman's body was in his chair, but his soul was with Sayde.

The rain continued to fall.

. . .

Chapter Seventy Four

Spring had come to the Karjalainen farm. The snow had melted, even in the ditches and on the north-facing hillsides.

Yellow butterflies fluttered around Kerttu as she tilled the soil on her hands and knees, creating the vegetable garden of which she had always dreamed. She was at the end of her term and immensely pregnant; the canes on which she still depended leaned against the building.

Warm from the work, she blew the hair from her eyes with a puff of breath, watching a swallow searching the eaves for a nesting site. Near her, sleeping on her favorite sweater, lay the puppy she had found tied to the door a few days earlier; it yelped in its sleep, and she smiled contentedly.

She had resolved her loss of Toivo; while she still grieved him, she had found a measure of peace.

She still thought of him, but in her mind's eye she had buried him and bid him farewell; she was getting on with her life; she was going to make the best with the resources she had—she didn't have much, but the country district and the village supported her; somehow everyone seemed to know of her connection to Toivo; it was implied that she had a right to that which had been his.

The language was a barrier—there was no one she could talk to—and she often damned Esa for willfully cutting her off from her roots by not teaching her Finnish.

In the compost heap on the other side of the barn an old badger competed with two hedgehogs for insects and worms.

The animals abruptly scattered when they heard the car.

Pennanen drove into the barnyard. He noticed Kerttu but remained in the car; his stomach was acting up more than usual.

The attack was soon over and he got out, feeling awkward in a civilian suit with a bouquet of spring flowers in his hand.

Kerttu rose, supported by her canes. She recognized the man; he awakened painful feelings in her. She didn't like her tranquility to be disturbed.

The puppy woke up and defended Kerttu against the intruder, with a wagging tail and an infantile bark.

Pennanen handed Kerttu the flowers and cleared his throat

"You me go visit Toivo in hospital," he said in English. He had rehearsed the speech for several days. It was all the English he knew.

"I'm sorry, what did you say?" She didn't believe she had heard right; her heart began to pound alarmingly quickly.

He didn't understand what she had said, but he saw that she was bewildered. "You me go visit Toivo in hospital," he repeated.

... Toivo... in hospital... could it be true...

Pennanen saw that she was baffled and nodded encouragingly.

"Toivo is alive? He is alive? My Toivo is alive!?!"

Pennanen heard the joy in her voice and knew he was that much closer to getting back his Tessa.

. . .

Chapter Seventy Five

Toivo stood atop a gardener's pruning ladder in the hospital's entry. He was painting a gruesome scene on the wall, which was already filled with depressing scenes—including one of Reijo in repose.

Hospital personnel walked by—few looked at the painting; their lives were gloomy enough.

Tessa entered, took a seat on a bench, and coughed discretely.

Toivo climbed down, wiped his hands with a rag, and studied his mural from a distance.

"Sit down and rest, my love," she said.

He reluctantly complied, critically examining his work.

"It's wonderful," she said of the painting.

"No, it isn't. It isn't right," he said, aware that for him the old reality was safer than the new; that he felt guilty for being alive, responsible for the comrades who no longer shared his existence.

"It just isn't right."

"I like it," she said and put her arms around him. "What does it mean?"

Her question annoyed him. "Mean? What do you mean, what does it mean?"

His question bewildered her—she thought artists equitably and fully resolved all matters of Life. "It must mean *something*," she said, feeling awkward and left out, even though she had her arms around him.

"I wouldn't know what," he said, feeling awkward, lonely, and misunderstood.

There they sat, together yet apart; he immersed in his quest to depict how he felt about the war, give it justice and pay tribute to all; she bent on keeping the man who would unlock the door to the future she sought in her fantasy land of unrealistic dreams.

Tessa heard a door open. Someone took an implosive breath. She turned and saw Kerttu standing in shock outside the entrance's glass-paneled door, staring at them; she didn't see Pennanen, he was standing behind Kerttu and away from the door.

Tessa arrogantly raised a mocking eyebrow at Kerttu and possessively hugged her Toivo.

Kerttu dropped the bouquet of flowers she was holding, closed the door and walked away from the hospital with Pennanen, their faces masks of pain.

"It doesn't feel right. It isn't right," said Toivo of the mural. Oblivious of what had happened, he dislodged himself from Tessa and rose to his feet. "It doesn't look right."

He climbed back up the ladder and resumed painting.

. . .

Chapter Seventy Six

Several hours had passed. Toivo was still working on the mural. Tessa tiptoed into the entry and placed the Russian officer's silver icon on a table.

Moments thereafter the entrance door swung open. In came Denny, full of energy and clearly in a hurry. He glanced at the mural and boomed: "You sure can't carry that one around on a cart! Listen, buddy, I don't have much time, I've got to catch a ship and have got to go!"

"Hey, Denny, how *are* you?" Toivo was thrilled to see his friend.

"I got a great job on Madison Avenue so I'm a lot better than last time I saw you, and so are you, I gather." He picked up the silver icon from the table. "So this is it? Hell, it's solid silver. Okay, I'll buy it—but I've got to go!"

He took out his wallet and began to count out a stack of *markkaa*.

"Denny, what are you doing?" Toivo wanted to know.

"I'm buying this... *thing* here." Denny said and turned to Tessa. "How much is it he owes on the farm? Was it 13,000? Okay, here it is. Hell, I might even be getting a bargain."

He handed the money to Tessa and looked up at Toivo, who—flabbergasted—stood on the ladder as if frozen.

"Okay, stay up there for all I care. I love you, but I've got to go. And when you're through making like Michelangelo, take a look at these clippings here."

He placed a stack of newspaper clippings on the ladder. "I made you a celebrity, buddy, and the world loves those; celebrity is the thing of the future. And don't worry about it, it's got nothing to do with you, or who you are, it's just business."

He looked at his watch. "Oops, I've got to run. Listen, it's been good to see you. Don't come down, stay up there on the ladder, it sort of suits you; another guy, long before you, spent most of his life facing ceilings and walls and he went on to major fame. Okay, I'm off to sell soap on Madison Avenue—and this time it's upper bunk all the way!"

He started for the door, turned and pointed at Toivo with one of his crutches. "Remember I love you," he said, and again headed for the door. "And don't worry, those are just words, and you know words can't harm you."

"Denny, you mean more to me than I have words for." Toivo paused, started down the ladder. "Hot diggity, hot diggity, hot—"

"—diggity dog." Denny interrupted, completing the sentence, wheeled around and grinned at Toivo, but tears brimmed in his eyes. "Got to go."

Denny pivoted to hide his face and re-started toward the door. "If you'd called an hour later I would have been gone," he growled over his shoulder at Tessa.

"Thank you for doing this, Mr. Arnold. I'll make sure Captain Pennanen gets the money."

"Fine. Guess I can give this thing to my mother. Who knows, she might even like it... now, that would be a first —"

He stopped by the door and faced her. "You're a woman, let me ask you something. Pink soap. D'you think women might like pink hand soap? Don't know? Okay, I've got to go! Got to go!"

He wheeled around on his crutches and was heading out the door when a veteran in neat shirt and tie—with a black patch over one eye—walked past him.

"Wow, what a great look!" Denny was delighted. "Hey, *Lotta* Tessa, where can I get one of those? "

"One of what?" she asked.

"One of those eye-patches that guy was wearing. Never mind, I'll get one in the Big Apple."

Tessa opened the door for him and he headed toward the street where a taxi waited, talking to himself and anyone who might be listening—he overflowed with creative enthusiasm.

"Now, *that* was a great look! Put that look with the right product and—and that's it! That's it! It's in the *presentation!* Substance has nothing to do with it! With the right presentation any moron can sell anything." He had arrived at the taxi and whirled around.

"Hot diggity, hot diggity, hot diggity dog!" He said it loudly enough that Toivo could hear him.

Tessa closed the door just as a hospital orderly handed Toivo a letter and left.

Toivo glanced at the envelope, tore it open, and began to read.

Our baby is due in a few weeks...

Tessa ran after the departing orderly, grabbed his arm and hissed: "Damn you! You know all his mail goes through me! Damn you! You don't know what you have ruined!"

Toivo heard Tessa and turned to her. "It's from her! Kerttu is here in Finland! She never left. She's been here all this time. I can't believe it! And I am going to be a father!"

He tasted the word, the notion, the idea.

"I am going to be somebody's father... "

The letter amazed him; it sent his emotions soaring. "She is here—she never left me—I am going to be somebody's father."

He was genuinely stunned.

As was Tessa—she was aghast; her world crumbling around her.

"I am... so... so happy for you," she said, her ears ringing with her lie, distress and anger coursing through her veins.

Toivo devoured Kerttu's letter. Some parts he had to read over and over; she had been angry and hurt when she wrote it, so much so that her handwriting slashed across the page and was difficult to decipher.

"For a while she thought I was dead, then she was here at the hospital… and she is angry with me—"

He put the letter down and turned to Tessa. "Can you imagine? She has been on the farm all this time. I thought she was in America! And she hopes that I still care for her —*care* for her? Doesn't she *know* that? I *love* her!"

He was overjoyed; started to pace, thinking out loud: "I have to write her, talk to her. Help me get out of here, Tessa! Talk to the doctor, he listens to you; I think he might be afraid of you. Ask him if I can have that operation now instead of later. Will you do that for me?"

In a daze, she nodded.

Toivo realized he had the brush and the palette still in his hand; he looked up at his somber mural.

"That is all wrong—so terribly, terribly wrong!"

That night, he wrote Kerttu a letter.
She answered.
They wrote each other daily.
They rediscovered their magic.

. . .

Chapter Seventy Seven

Toivo's operation was a success, but his recovery was slow. He spent his waking hours working on his mural and writing his Kerttu, whose advanced pregnancy had kept her from undertaking the long and arduous journey to see him.

The mural was in transition; hospital personnel watched the transformation with great interest. Somehow they knew that the change would be important.

The days passed.

The morning Toivo finished the mural the staff found him asleep against the wall opposite his painting, a paintbrush in his hand, contentment on his face.

People from all walks of life stood in silent awe admiring his work.

It was a masterpiece — a huge mirror ball that in its facets portrayed vignettes with visions of a Peaceful, Better Tomorrow.

. . .

Chapter Seventy Eight

On a beautiful day in late spring 1940, Toivo was allowed to go home.

The Helsinki railroad station teemed with people. A passenger train was due to leave; its doors closed; those departing bid adieu to the friends and relatives gathered on the platform to see them off.

A subdued Tessa likewise stood on the platform next to Toivo's doctor. He was admonishing Toivo, who leaned out one of the train's open windows, wearing a Finnish Army uniform with the Medal of Freedom above the left breast pocket.

"——you should not be leaving. I don't like this! You need to recuperate another six months!" The doctor was terribly concerned—his good work was being threatened.

"I want to live, doc, not recuperate! I appreciate all you've done for me, no one could have done better, but I have someone I love, a child to raise, land to plow, and a field of wildflowers to lie around in!" Toivo leaned further out the window and offered the young doctor his hand. "Thank you, doctor. Thank you for everything."

The doctor left, passing by Pennanen waiting some distance away; he knew Tessa had things she wanted to say in private.

"Toivo, the train will make a special stop for you," she said, dreading the confession she had to make.

"Why?" Toivo wanted to know.

A one-legged soldier hobbled by on crutches. He saw Toivo in the window, stopped, and saluted.

"I was looking for you. I heard you were going home. I was with the boys from the city in the trenches behind you the day the Russians attacked. You were some kind of soldier, Karjalainen. I saw what you did. I'm honored to have been there with you."

Again he saluted; then he hobbled off.

The train began to pull away.

Desperation flickered in Tessa's eyes. She quickly handed Toivo a piece of paper.

"Here. The loan is all paid for."

The train gathered momentum; she walked rapidly alongside it, stifling tears. "My husband and I are leaving for America."

The train gathered more momentum. Tessa nearly had to run.

"They say it never rains in Arizona." Her tears now flowed unchecked. "I'm sorry, Toivo—please forgive me."

"Why? Forgive you for what?" Toivo was blissfully unaware of her subterfuge.

The train drew away.

Tessa could no longer keep up. She stopped, then stood there on the platform, waving.

Toivo waved back.

The train rounded a bend and was then out of sight, with only quickly disappearing smoke and steam marking its departure.

Tessa sobbed as Pennanen led her away.

Toivo closed the window, sank into his seat. The compartment seated eight, but the conductor had told him he would have it for himself—orders from Finland's Railways.

He pulled out Kerttu's scarf and smelled it as he watched the buildings of Helsinki grow smaller and smaller. Soon the train wound through the countryside.

He was happy, gloriously happy—he was going home! His love and his child and a Better Tomorrow would be there.

The train's whistle hooted—seemingly cheerfully.

. . .

Chapter Seventy Nine

In a darkly serene pine forest near the fiercely fought-over border in Northern Karelia, a lily of the valley struggled for light in the shadow of a rusting, broken-down Soviet tank.

A Red Star was still faintly visible on its turret; its bent, impotent cannon pointed to the sky. The skeletal remains of a few soldiers lay scattered nearby.

A train whistle and a cacophony of slamming, banging, and clanging broke the stillness.

The locomotive, trailing steam and pulling passenger cars, thrust forward at great speed; the ties below it and the trees next to it swept by in a blur.

In a passenger car corridor, a group of passengers stood on their toes, trying to see past the sweaty conductor who blocked a compartment with drawn curtains.

"They say he is somebody," a thrilled passenger said; like the others, he had never seen anyone famous before. "We just want to look at him!"

Inside the compartment Toivo sat by himself at the window, looking out at the passing scenery. He had grown less and less comfortable in the army tunic with the medal above the breast pocket. He unbuttoned the top buttons and eased his fingers under the collar, massaging his skin where the material had chafed. Closing his eyes, he leaned back in his seat and tried to ignore the conversation that filtered in through the closed door.

"It is him, the hero Karjalainen in there, isn't it?" someone asked.

Toivo was reminded of the medal; he unpinned it and sat fingering it, rubbing his fingers over its surface. He placed it on the table by the window; stared at it; pushed it away from him.

"They say before the war he was a famous artist in America."

... America...

The train's whistle shrilled again as the locomotive slowed.

At the Karjalainen farm the puppy tugged at Kerttu's apron while she, in the last days of her pregnancy, her stomach enormous, pulled weeds from the garden, created from her longing.

She thought she heard a train whistle in the distance; her heart began to pound.

... maybe it's him... maybe it's my Toivo...

Several miles away a train stood still on the track, far from any station. Passengers and train personnel watched as the old young man in shirtsleeves bounded down the stairs and walked quickly off toward the east, a rucksack on his shoulders.

On the seat of an empty compartment lay a neatly folded Finnish Army jacket; atop it lay Finland's Medal of Freedom along with a light-blue U.S. State Department envelope with a permanent U.S. Visa.

On a road that he had walked less than a year earlier upon his return from America, Toivo inhaled the air of early summer.

... home... to my Kerttu... we're going to have a baby... what a life... what an incredible life... what an incredibly wonderful life...

It was a beautiful day. Crickets and birds serenaded life, butterflies danced; fluffy clouds billowed in the azure sky. A balmy wind buffeted the countryside, promising an even warmer summer.

As he approached the crest in the road from where he could see the farm in the distance, he stopped and removed his boots, placed them neatly side-by-side at the edge of the road, and continued walking on bare feet.

Kerttu shielded her eyes from the sun. She thought she saw someone at the crest of the road—and it was him!

He was waving his arms wildly; he began to run toward her on the road he had believed he would never again feel under his feet.

Kerttu was overcome with happiness. Her tears flowed unchecked. She opened her arms and hobbled toward him as best as she could—her man was home, at last.

They ran into each other's arms at the wooden gate, the one she had made sure was always open, where since spring she often had stood and wistfully looked out over the wheat field, hoping that Toivo would be home to lie in it with her among the wildflowers that had blossomed.

They clung to each other, savoring the moment for all eternity; at last, the world was whole again.

He gently led her into the wheat field his grandfather had sown forty years earlier. Although it had not been cultivated for many years, this year the wheat had returned on its own, abundant and waist-high—as were the wildflowers.

He picked a bouquet for his lady.

As the warm summer gusts played with the wheat stalks and the birds and the crickets made witness by their presence, Toivo knelt and asked Kerttu to marry him. She accepted.

They lay until sunset amongst the flowers and the wheat, watching the clouds drift by. Her head was on his chest; he held her securely.

Unbeknownst to them, their mirror ball lay nearby, partially hidden by weeds in a ditch. The spring rains had washed it clean. It once again shone brightly—and in its shadow, a lily of the valley triumphantly reached for the sunlight.

. . .

Kerttu gave birth to a girl—a healthy, bright, beautiful girl. They named her Dawn; she was the beginning of their Better Tomorrow.

. . .

The war had changed Toivo: he was more thoughtful; he felt an attachment to the land that prior to the war he had ignored. Now and then he stuck his hand into the soil that was his, kneading it between his fingers, appreciating its richness and significance.

They bought a horse. Toivo tilled the land and planted crops. Kerttu gave him some canvases; he unpacked the paints and brushes from his rucksack. He worked the land and he painted. His creativity soared; his paintings were more serious, more profound, and more universal in subject and theme. She took them to the village, where they became highly sought after. He charged less than he could have and he never signed his work, but the buyers didn't mind. They knew that something important, created by a person with a tranquil connection to life's mysteries, hung on their walls.

In the evenings, Toivo and Kerttu would sit with their daughter and look out over the lake in which bass and pike were plentiful; in late summer, the setting sun was so perfectly aligned that its last rays reflected off the water and onto their faces.

Their days and nights, their every moment, were filled, so saturated with love and understanding that those who knew them thought it a wonder. There were moments so powerful that they would close their eyes and whisper their gratitude; Dawn would gurgle, smile, and reach for them—instinctively drawn to her parents and the tranquility that shone from them.

Their Better Tomorrow had finally arrived.

. . . . .

Epilogue

On June 25, 1941, less than one year after Dawn's birth, a decision was made in Helsinki to wage war against the Soviet Union in order to recapture the land lost during The Winter War.

When Toivo received his mobilization notice, he led Kerttu down to their field. As they lay together in the summer sun amongst the half-grown wheat, her head on his shoulder, Dawn in their arms, he gently broke the news of his departure.

He wiped away her tears and said he would return.

A few days later, while crossing a meadow in Soviet Karelia, Toivo stepped on a mine. His body was interred in the Soviet Union; his name was added to a Finnish archive.

When Kerttu was informed that Toivo would never return, she walked down to their wheat field and stood at its edge for the longest time, cradling their child to her chest. She bowed her head and kissed Dawn's silken hair that was wet with the tears she couldn't hold back.

After a moment, she lifted her face to the sun for its kiss, took a deep shaky breath, and pledged her life to their daughter.

. . .

Kerttu never again set foot in the wheat field. She found other places to pick the flowers for her home. Their blossoms reminded her of the times when she and Toivo had lain in each other's arms and watched the clouds go by. She remembered how content he had been, how grateful; how strong had been their love, how clear had been their enjoyment of the Better Tomorrow that they believed would be theirs forever more.

In 1946, when it was again safe to cross the Atlantic, Kerttu returned to America with Dawn.

Kerttu never held another man in her arms; she didn't want to—her memories were too precious.

She raised Dawn by herself. She took odd jobs. They lived in odd places. They were always together.

They often talked of Toivo.

Dawn keenly appreciated that her father had been kind, thoughtful, and loving; that he had been a man of action and commitment as well as a dreamer; that he had enjoyed resting with her mother among the wildflowers and had taken time to watch the clouds go by.

From her mother's memories of her father, Dawn learned about dignity and about respect for one's life and self. At the schools she attended, she was the one her classmates sought out. She became a teacher. She married a kind man, a man much like her father had been. They have three children: two boys and a girl.

Kerttu wasn't proud—rather, she was grateful.

Tessa and Pennanen settled in Arizona. They bought a small trailer park in the desert outside Tucson. Tessa never changed. She never did develop a *sense morale,* and Pennanen often had problems with his stomach, but it was Tessa who became ill and died at the age of 44 from cancer. Pennanen faithfully stayed by her side. He was with her when she died and mourned her loss far more than she deserved.

Not long after he buried Tessa, Pennanen drove as far as he could into the mountains near Sedona.

His car was found; he never was.

Denny became a very successful advertising executive. He was innovative, his advertising copy was legendary, his larks extraordinary—perhaps because they were born of his profoundly authentic self. He dated someone for a few years. One weekend he invited a few friends to his wedding on Fire Island. The bride, Steve, was an accomplished oral surgeon with a practice near Lincoln Center. All the guests thought the wedding was a grand affair, that it was fabulously well arranged, and that it was just another of Denny's larks.

At the end of the ceremony—which was conducted by a gallant Episcopalian—Denny faced his friends, leaned on his crutches, raised his arms high and wide, grinned broadly, and said:

"Hot diggity, hot diggity, hot diggity dog!"

Denny and Steve recently celebrated their golden anniversary. They live in New Hampshire on a small farm; they have a myriad of pets; it's an animal sanctuary of sorts. The courage that brought and kept them together has served others as well.

. . .

Kerttu lives by herself in Carmel, California.

She has a view of the ocean...

... Toivo...

. . . .

The Winter War

Although it changed the course of history, the Winter War was a forbidden topic of conversation in the Soviet Union until 1989 when *Perestroika* a n d *Glasnost* opened memories, hearts—and archives.

The war broke out on November 30, 1939. It ended on March 13, 1940, having lasted a mere 105 days; as many as 1.3 million men and women lost their lives— victims of Josef Stalin's contempt for fellow man.

Without a declaration of war, smugly relying on Russia's manpower base of 180 million inhabitants, Stalin had the Red Army attack Finland with its population of 3.7 million, initially sending nearly 1 million Red Army soldiers and conscripts—many of whom were unarmed Jewish doctors, lawyers and academicians—against Finland's 340,000 defenders; approximately 2,000 tanks and armored vehicles against Finland's 25, and more than 1,000 bomber and fighter aircraft against Finland's 118.

The Soviet Union's attack on tiny Finland ignited empathetic responses around the world. In addition to nearly 1,000 North Americans, many of Finnish origin, more than 11,000 other men and women from 27 other countries—including my father, a Jamaican pilot and a Samurai-descendant—flocked to Finland to assist that country in its plight. Most, though, arrived far too late to make a difference to the war's outcome.

Although the Finns were outnumbered and outgunned, the Soviet Union's losses were staggering: The Red Army reportedly lost nearly 1,000 aircraft, 2,000 tanks and armored cars; and out of the total of 1.5 million troops sent to Finland, the Red Army officially admitted losing 200,000. However, in his memoirs *Khrushchev Remembers*, former Soviet Premier Nikita Khrushchev claimed that as many as 1 million Russians may have lost their lives during The Winter War.

The names of 25,243 Finnish men and women—who lost their lives for something they believed in are known. But the names of perhaps as many as 1 million Russian men and women—who lost their lives for a cause they didn't understand, and to which they were not emotionally attached—never will be.

Stalin never occupied Finland; he wisely let the Finns be.

Although Stalin never officially commented on the lessons learned from the Finns, documents from his secret personal archives published in 1997 in a book by Professor Hannu Soikkanen reveal that immediately after the Winter War, Stalin summoned his top military and political leaders to a review of the Red Army's failure.

Lasting a week, the unprecedented meeting led to the execution of half of the Red Army's Officer Corps, most of the Generals, and a number of Soviet military and political leaders. This resulted in a restructuring of the Red Army—which changed the course of history, because, when Hitler a year later attacked the Soviet Union, Stalin used the tactics learned from the Finns and successfully defended the Soviet Union against Hitler's vastly superior military machine.

Other large nations later in history unfortunately failed to learn from The Winter War: notably, the engagements by the United States in Vietnam and Iraq. Curiously, even the Soviet Union must have forgotten, as its wars in Afghanistan and Chechnya illustrate.

Historians and military experts everywhere have long known that Finland's disproportionately low losses during The Winter War were attributed to the unique psyche of the Finnish men and women who, vastly outnumbered and outgunned in one of the coldest winters in recorded history, managed with amazing resolve to safeguard the sovereignty of their homeland—for some, at a heavy price.

Although from many races, cultures and countries, the men and women of the Winter War shared in death one common denominator: their dreams and hopes for a Better Tomorrow were never realized.

Bo Svenson
Pacific Palisades
November 28, 2015

* * * * * * * *

www.ingramcontent.com/pod-product-compliance
Lightning Source LLC
Chambersburg PA
CBHW021432240626
47153CB00001B/117